For the Love
of
Annie Dupree
A Novel by - TJ Ginn

The Oedipus Animal

Oedipus Greek: Οἰδίπους *Oidípous* meaning ("swollen foot") was a mythical Greek king of Thebes. He fulfilled a prophecy that said he would kill his father and marry his mother, and thus brought disaster on his city and family. This legend has been retold in many versions and was used by Sigmund Freud to name the Oedipus complex.

Human sexuality as proved is an amorphous existential observation of a true differential that plots on a hysteretic bell curve that plots to the natural logarithm of what is normal.

There is no possibility that you understood what I just said. So continue on.

Edit release December, 2022

Other Works - Available on Amazon.com

The Ecstasy of my Dream
"A look inside the esoteric world that resides within you, how to reach it and what to do when you get there."

Children of the Seven Hills
Is it fiction or is it reality? This is a mind-blowing walk through how we got to where we are today. It is a fiction drawn from reality with so many, many things from our history that you will remember and can relate to. It explains philosophy and ideology and how it is we got to the zeitgeist of the day. This could be the unexpected awakening you were looking for.

Dilation - A science fiction that brings out the 'Buck Rogers' in all of us. It poses your most personal questions about space and time.

Poetry and Prose, Aphorisms and Thoughts
Collected over the years it is now finally assembled; TJ Ginn's writings extraordinaire. From love to philosophy and even humorous quips; It is centered as always on Christian theology and at all times draws on kindness as the only true necessity.

The Praus Probability
He was living in infamy. A worldwide bounty was on his head. He had been made wealthy by his invention and now lived to destroy it. Stealth is now necessary for his survival because the bounty is "Wanted Dead or Alive." His network of comrade's aide him in his underground endeavors. So dedicated are his friends they commit all of their wealth to his success.

His name is Jarrod Praus. His invention is the 'Praus Probability Machine.' Everyone loves it and cannot see it is doomsday approaching. He must, at all cost, destroy it.

Perihelion Engineering, 'The Universe Not in a Nutshell'
TJ Ginn breaks the bonds of traditional physics to redefine long accepted norms. Causality and the Big Bang theory are refuted. The velocity of light is proved to not be fundamental. Combustion and thermodynamics is taken to new horizons and the magic of magnetism is revealed to be push and not pull as well as gravity being shown to be pressure and not a magic unsolvable mystery attractive force. For the first time in science history, dark matter is defined, as well as the red shift observation refuted, to support Albert Einstein's original proposal that the universe is infinite. The unified theory is here…

Table of Contents

The Dupree Home in Sailor Park

The Louisville Queen

Introduction

Hermaphrodite
In biology, a **hermaphrodite** is an organism that has reproductive organs normally associated with both male and female sexes.

Homosexuality is romantic or sexual attraction or behavior between members of the same sex or gender. As a sexual orientation, homosexuality refers to "an enduring pattern of or disposition to experience sexual, affectionate, or romantic attractions" primarily or exclusively to people of the same sex.

Heterosexuality is romantic or sexual attraction or behavior between persons of opposite sex or gender in the gender binary. As a sexual orientation, heterosexuality refers to "an enduring pattern of or disposition to experience sexual, affectionate, physical or romantic attractions to persons of the opposite sex."

The Absurdity of the mechanism of the Orgasm.

Shrouded in the framework of the Human Psyche is a physiological point of ecstasy. Mysteriously planted in our realm and perhaps in the realm of all other species is a psychological / physiological juxtaposition called the orgasm? What does this mean?

Certain physical actions and stimulations and certain thoughts or mental excitations in the metaphysical (thought world) cognition (thinking) causes the orgasm. It requires mental arousal in image and imagination in conjunction with physical stimulation to produce the orgasm. Image though visual includes tactile imagination in the vision impaired.

Children hide their Sexuality.

Instinctually children hide. How is it that they know no shame, but express discernment at disclosing their titillation, their excitation and their naked exposure? They feel no quilt but yet they hide their self-exploration of their genitalia.

Brutalization by association.

If you are not like me, you are not acceptable.

Psychosexual infantilism - Psycho-logic defense – Dénouement by **Sigmund Freud** can be countered by mere simplicity of thought.

Children are effervescent and quiescently blind. They bloom from the darkness of a void of knowledge and become. They respond to their new body that responds to the differentials of hard and soft, light and dark, warm and cold and delight and pain. They cry when discontent and coo when happy.

Instinctually they respond to a physical compulsion of genital stimulation with no rationality and with no emotional connection except self-adulation and these are considered natural. It is no different than nursing on the breast. It involves no learned behavior or permission. It is pre-cognitive.

Again the Existential Absurdity of the Orgasm.

Proved is the biochemical hormonal function of testosterone on the sexual libido of both male and female. Don't argue this if you have doubt; look it up.

And the King would allow only Eunuchs (castrated males) to serve the Queen.

You cannot describe color to the colorblind; nor sight to the unsighted, or even sound to the deaf, and no mortal can describe the compulsion for the orgasm, and children hide their most secret discernment.

The only animal that wears clothes is the human animal. Prolific are the religious scriptures pertaining to nakedness and the insinuation of the shame of your nakedness.

Children as toddlers have no inclination of shame. Quickly, by their parent's instruction, they are taught to cover and thus we hide our most secret discernment.

And thus we harbor our most critical judgment. Are you chaste (pure, innocent, uncorrupted, virtuous, honorable, and unsullied?)

One might consider that the circumcision of the male is the religious and furthermost extension of naked shame. It calls you to rise above your animal instinct, reconcile the compulsion of the orgasm with responsibility and think about the consequences of your actions. One might consider the Jewish law of circumcision on the eighth day. A child is given no choice, but it is done to them. You will know your shame and we have cut you a priori.

In Judaic Law <u>only</u> is the continuation of the circumcision by law, requiring chastity, condemning infidelity and extramarital fornication.

The Unbridled Libido

Hedonism suggests animal disregard. Fornicating without regard to the connection between the orgasm and procreation is pure animal ignorance. Humans without limits breed without limits and without limits in a finite resource such as the earth; the only control is the natural collapse of the system.

There is no defense against the all-powerful orgasm without law and education. You will have to watch the suffering on scales you cannot imagine.

The Oedipus Animal

Well known is the fact that the male animals sire, such as that in cats and dogs, wolves and lions they will kill the young males and eat them. It is assumed that they are eliminating their possible sexual competition. It would stand to reason that if a male animal survived, thanks to its mother's protection, that he would be endeared to his mother and come into competition with his father, perhaps not over the mother alone, but for all the females. Existential scientific observation bears out this truth.

The Nurturing Father

Not uncommon in all species is the male that assumes the female role in nurturing the young, both the male

8

and female offspring; this is especially true in the human animal since there is no record of fathers killing sons for fear of competition. Placing the human male as a villain by generalization has no statistical foundation. It cannot even be placed on the bell curve because factual documentation can find no incident of the _Oedipus Complex_ in reality. It only exists in mythology. After adolescence the male is nurtured by the father's adoration to guard and protect and instruct the male child as to the nature, strength and toughness that is extraordinarily required of him. These are isolation, suppression of weak emotions, endurance and competition. This is done by a nurturing father to build strength in his son for protection and confidence building.

Thus the Oedipus Complex as to the male child in competition for the mother's affection should be laid to rest as a fallacy so rare that it cannot fit into any statistical model. However male competition for the female is the source of wars and the ego of men manipulated by the female cunning and the all-powerful want or rather need for the orgasm across the void of understanding confuses us all with a compulsion whether held in secret and singular or shared and known.

And where is love in all of this?

Annie Dupree has the answer.

Eiffel Tower 1889

The Cancan in Paris 1890's

Cincinnati on the Ohio 1835

Cincinnati on the Ohio 1890

SS. La Bourgogne 1885

11

On the River Ohio

James Marcus Dupree and his wife, the lovely maiden Mary Ann Buffet, were the proud parents of four children. First born; a girl then two boys and then another girl. Their first girl, the protagonist of this account they named Antoinette Marie and of course she was a pampered and proud Dupree for James was a steamboat captain and major shareholder of the "Louisville Queen." This stern wheeled steam riverboat was one hundred and seventy feet of luxury with staterooms and cabins and parlors and a dining room served by cooks and waiters.

Now you know what the parlors were for, mostly gambling and I must say that the cabins and staterooms were the private retreats after hours for drinking and frivolity.

As it was called the "Louie Queen" had its home port of call a little west of Cincinnati but sailed to Pittsburgh Pennsylvania at the east of the Ohio and also all the way west and north to St. Louis, Illinois and as far south as Memphis Tennessee. Captain Dupree would not sail down any farther on the Mississippi because it would take him too far from his wife who was nestled comfortably in her three storied Victorian home in Sailor Park, a burg just west of Cincinnati on the river. Their home had a fourth story which was a widow's walk. This was a watchtower where the wife of the captain could watch up and down river for the return of her love; for sadly at times river men were consumed by the mighty Ohio and never returned. The bereaved widow would morn and sit in the tower watching and hoping for her husband's return.

13

It was a stately mansion well furnished with woodwork and furniture from all over the Midwest. Mary Ann Buffet-Dupree was the instigator of the large family, for that was her entertainment for the many months that her Captain Dupree was away. Most of the warm months she never saw her captain accept in his passing for a day or two at home in summer. Winters were a joy for her and the time when they made all those babies. She had her Captain from late November to the first of April. During the long spring, summer and fall she made her children and home her joy.

Now she knew what the "Louie Queen" was. It may have been a means of transportation but this was not a cargo boat. It was a floating hotel. On the long trips the Louie Queen made for hours of time to fill and thus people entertained. Down river runs were fast with the current, but upriver runs took days and days as the Louie Queen struggled against the current, stopping at many towns to take on wood to burn in the fire box of the boiler and food for the travelers. The Louie Queen always had a full roster and made lots of money that pleased the shareholders as well as Captain Dupree. Mary liked it too, for she lived lavishly albeit lonely. She turned her mind away from the frivolity she knew sailed with the Louie Queen and never questioned whether her husband was faithful for he always came home for the winter and he treated her like a Queen.

Now Antoinette Marie, who they just called Annie, had a four-year separation from her first brother. Annie did not know she was spoiled and protected, that is just the way it was. Having a baby brother for her was delightful. She so looked forward

14

to a family playmate even thought she was learning from experience that boys at first don't play with little girls. Besides, she never wanted for anything; she had dolls and toys and lots of friends. As time went on there was another brother and then to her delight a sister, but Annie was seven years old when her sister Leah Anna was born. Annie was outside the bedroom door when the doctor and midwife delivered Leah Anna. Annie screamed when her mother screamed. Her brother's births she had not witnessed for she was sent to her aunts. Leah Anna came early without warning and with no time to shuffle Annie off to her aunt. This experience, even though her mother laughed after Leah Anna's arrival and was filled with joy, horrified this young girl of seven years. Annie knew then that she would never have children. Like a wedge driven down and through to split a log, her young psyche had formed.

Annie naturally emulated her sophisticated and refined mother. She was taught to carry herself well. As she grew through her teen years and primary school what was emerging gave her mother concern for Annie was becoming a woman of uncanny beauty. What troubled her mother was that she knew Annie knew she was striking. Her dark nearly black large eyes contrasted with her milky skin and with her straight, long, dark brown hair that flowed down her back to her derrière, she was a picture of loveliness.

Her mother kept her in tow constantly reminding her of her expectations. No fraternizing with boys, no promiscuity. She was to go to finishing school and continue her education in literature. Her mother told her that with her looks and a good head she could be an actress in the theater if she so desired, and that you cannot achieve anything if you destroy your reputation.

Annie is now twenty-one and home for vacation from Colette Rousseau's school for girls. It is an arts school that her mother insisted on. They teach history, language, music, ballet and theater arts. Annie absorbed French because she heard it spoken between her mother and her aunt. She loved music but played no instrument. She only studied the classic masters and their history. She of course, because of her mother's insistence took theater arts. Along with all of this was refinement instruction that was given to all the girls at the school.

This is the "Gay Nineties," Eighteen Ninety-one to be exact in the middle of June. Annie is an impetuous twenty-one-year-old and was smart as well as good looking. She and her dubious classmates mocked their instructors when they would sneak out, find some wine and have fun. You cannot stop impetuous youth. Annie is polished and one hell of an actress.

Annie unpacks her travel trunk delivered by courier to her bedroom at home. She enjoys a cool bath prepared for her by her mother, a cool wash off of the summer heat. She then joins her mother on the veranda.

Mary calls to her through the screen door, "Annie si vous plait" (if you please). She continues in English with her sweet French accent that Annie emulates, "Please join me on the veranda." Annie responds, "Oui Ma, ma." As she mocks her mother's accent lovingly.

Annie adores her mother, almost idolizes her with great respect. Now at home she is dressed in a light down to the ankle, floral print gown and she is bare foot. She comes through the screen door exclaiming, "Off with the corsets' and the button-down shoes and the layers of petticoats that make me sweat." Her mother quickly says sternly and abruptly, "Annie! Take my shawl and cover you breasts, your nipples are showing and your young brothers will be home soon. I'll not have them ogling their sister." Annie obliges with a smirk, takes the shawl, casts it around her shoulders then flaps it like a bird over her breasts to create a breeze and exclaims, "It's too damn hot." And then with sarcasm she says, "My prankster brothers used to peak at me through the keyhole of the bathroom, it is nothing they have not seen; hellish devils."

Mary sighs, "Is that what you are learning from Madam Rousseau's school, to curse like a sailor. Annie, if you frequent foul language then a time will come when a slip of the tongue will embarrass you. If you just don't use those words, you have no fear of slipping. Annie responds, "Mother, dear mother, I want to be all that you want me to be and I will carry myself to your liking because I love you, but I'm not a child anymore. I know the hypocrisy the world is made of and I won't live in ignorance or shy away from the truth"

Mary smiles and says, "What is the truth dear?" Annie scowls, grabs the end of her hair and places a wisp across her upper lip as if to simulate a mustache, "Women are to be chaste and refined pent-up in the home while men perform whatever debauchery they please. In France, mother they are called courtesans and here they are just whores."

Now Mary scowls and looks sternly in her daughters eyes, "You're not learning this from Madam Rousseau, what, are you prowling the streets of the city, learning this from your girlfriends? Antoinette Marie Dupree, your father and I put you in a very expensive dormitory for girls and expect you to honor us with your good behavior." Annie trying to relieve her mother's angst, "Mother I am good, no man will ever enter my vestibule. I am as chaste as a woman can be. I decided long ago that I will never have a child and destroy my body, and thus marriage for me 'Cela ne se produira jamais' (will never happen)."

Her mother sighs again, "What has happened to you that you are so, so callous?" "I'm not callous, I'm just decided." Mary says, "You sound cold, Annie." "I'm not cold mother, I saw you through the door when you gave birth to Leah Anna, I screamed when you screamed, I saw the blood and that is not going to happen to me, period."

"You are so young, you will change and you will want children," Mary advised. Annie quickly returns, "I will adopt; mother enough of this, I'm so happy to be home. Mary says, "Sure darling, I just worry about you."

Annie says, "I worry about you too mom with daddy always gone on that floating casino." "Annie, that floating casino is paying for all of us and your father sacrifices every day he is away. He so much looks forward to winter so he can just stay home with us. He's a dedicated man."

18

Annie mumbles barely audible, "Dedicated to gambling and fast women." Mary snarls, "Don't you dare think of your father in that way." Annie recoils, "Is he faithful?" "To a fault young lady and here is how; our bank account is always well set, he returns on schedule and treats me like a queen. He houses and guards his wife and family like a white knight and he will never let you go cold or hungry. You have me steaming young woman and I have had about enough of your misgiving." Mary starts to cry. Annie starts to cry and through her supping speech, "But is he faithful?"

Mary, "oh mon dieu fille (Oh my god girl,) it does not matter; he cares for me very well and I will not question his generosity." "Oh mama, that floating hotel is full of trouble." Mary says sternly as her tears subside, for she knows her daughters innocence and naïveté, "Your father will be home the first of July, he is going to take us all on that 'floating casino' for a month-long trip up the Ohio to Pittsburgh so you can go to an Italian Opera and the boys and Leah Anna can have a fun summer. So, I'll have no more wild imaginations about your father. He loves you."

Annie leaps up with great excitement, "Pittsburgh; Opera?" Mary relaxes, "Yes, Pittsburgh, yes opera." Annie rushes to hug her mother around her neck almost choking her and Mary says, "And you and I are going to take the train to Cincinnati and buy you some new clothes, so how about your faithful father now?" Annie exclaims, "I love him so much mom, it is just the idea of marriage and children and trusting men. I don't trust them, and I don't ever want to be pregnant." Mary calms down; "Okay dear, the boys will be home soon and we should help Miss

19

Helen in the kitchen. Helen was a live-in nanny that had been with the family for years.

Just then the boys showed up on their bicycles. They had been to a summer tennis school. James Junior was now seventeen and his brother Marcus was sixteen. They were strong and tall and typical with their boyish energy. They both ran to the veranda with excitement to see their sister home from boarding school. They hugged her and told her how good she looked, and James said, "Girl, if you were not my sister, I'd have you on the rug in a minute." To which Annie said laughing, "Over my dead body you would." Marcus who was not to be out done said as he punched his brothers' arm, "She would rather have a good-looking gentleman like me than a scruffy ruffian like you. With that they showed their boyishness and started play boxing. To which Mary says in her beautiful French, "Arrêtez vos bêtises (stop your foolishness,) now go wash up for dinner, Helen has worked very hard in a hot kitchen. We will have dinner in the gazebo out back; it's too hot in the house. Maintenant allez, allez (now go, go). Antoinette, tie up your hair darling you will be cooler; come let us help Helen." Just then Leah Anna comes running across the yard yelling, "Annie, Annie." She flies up the steps to the veranda and swings her arms around her sister. Annie, a bit taller than Leah Anna lifts her off her feet in a big hug. Leah Anna is two years younger than Marcus, but at fourteen she is full stature, developed and slender. Annie says to her, "I love you kiddo, I missed you. You are looking more like a woman every day, so stay away from the boys. Leah Anna laughs and they all proceed to the kitchen to help Helen.

Dinner was ready and Helen joined them as always, she was part of the family. The conversation was easy and Annie was happy to be home. The boys teased her as always. She told them all about the school of Madam Colette Rousseau. Annie admitted it was uppity and stuffy and rigid, but that she liked the studies in history and music. She mused about a two act play they performed that was written by some professor at Pennsylvania University for an all-female cast; it was called 'A Woman's Place.' Annie laughs, "In the end of all I really liked it because it broke the bonds with social stigma and made a statement that women are equal too." She tosses two pieces of bread and bops her brothers on the forehead and says, "You bastards get all the opportunity."

Mary says, "Antoinette, Compte tenu de votre langue maternelle (mind your tongue). You have been given as much as them if not more. Annie rears, "I get boarding school while they will get college." Mary blurts out, "If they don't change their ways, they will be stoking the boiler on the Louie Queen. Helen laughs and almost chokes. They all laugh. Mary shakes her finger at her sons and says, "Aucun alcool (no more alcohol), I heard from Mrs. Groesbeck the German lady that lives near the church. She said that you were behind the General Store making too much noise and acting silly. She said you looked drunk. Vous pensez que je suis stupide (you think I am stupid?) I could smell it on your clothes; stale beer stinks."

The boys cover their mouths as if to hide their smirk as you can hear their pallet blocking their nose with a snort. Annie says, "And next, with your shenanigans, you'll get some poor girl pregnant, have

21

to marry her and be miserable all your life." James retorts getting a little too serious, "That will never happen to you Antoinette, am I right?" Annie gets defensive, "What do you mean by that?" James again, "Do you remember two years ago when you and Ben Hamilton, the guy that lives on the east side of Sailor Park, were kind of friendly?" Annie with her piercing eyes stars at James and says, "Yeah what of it?" Well he said he thought you really liked him and when he tried to kiss you, you shoved him away and ran, and from that day on you never talked to him again. Have you got something against men?" Annie relaxes and throws another piece of bread at James and laughs, "Not at all you twit, I love men, I'm just not ready for one of them to have their way with me; I'm a Lady."

Mary says, "Bien fait ma darling (well done my darling.) James says, "Ben said that maybe you are," he pauses to think and then says in French, "lesbienne, femme homosexuelle (Lesbian, female homosexual).

Annie smacks James' hand and hard, "Arrêter votre sale bouche (hush your filthy mouth,) I'm as normal as can be, besides it is none of your prying business and you best, my brother, not be swayed by rumor and innuendo; it can cause horrible misconceptions." Leah Anna who had been sitting quietly watching all, gets up and comes around and hugs Annie from behind while she sits, "Don't listen to these brutes, they tease me all the time; men are such fools, chasing us all the time and when they don't get their way, they are mean, just awful mean." James not to give-up on goading his sister, "Ben says he still loves you and just does not understand what happened. You should hang on to that guy, his father's carriage business is doing very well. His dad is sending him to Harvard Law School and rumor has it they are negotiating with Henry Ford to make seats for Automobiles. Ben is going to be very rich."

Annie ruffles, "Nobody is going to want those smelly, noisy stupid machines, I saw one in Cincinnati, they are awful and they scare all the horses, besides why is it that a woman is supposed to set her life on nothing more than children and the graces of a man to lock her at home with the children while he gallivants in frivolity. Pas pour moi (not for me), and I'm sure you know nothing about the Women's Suffrage Movement. Look it up my brother James and you will see a hoard of women that want the power of the vote." James is stunned; his sister is learning more than finishing at that school. He starts to stutter and … Mary says, "Assez de cette, (enough of this) boys carry the dishes to the house, give the scraps to the cats and wash the pots too. Helen has had enough for this day. Leah Anna go with your sister to bed and don't giggle all night, you can go with us to the city tomorrow; you need new clothes too for our trip to Pittsburgh. James and Marcus, your father is bringing you clothes from St. Louis. I hope I don't have to alter them; he's bringing you shoes too; at least that's what the telegram said. I expect you to stay around the house tomorrow and not cause trouble." "Yes mother," they say in unison.

The sunset cooled things off a bit and a nice breeze came up off the big Ohio. Crickets were chirping and frogs were crooning and night fell on the house Dupree. Mary alone in her bed thanked God for her children, "Merci seigneur pour mes enfants" (Thank you Lord for my Children.)

23

The Excursion to the City

Mary rousts the children early, she pops her head in on the boys each with their own room and says the same to each, "Avec vous (up with you). I want you to clean out the shed; you have made a mess of it. The gardener could not find the rake or shovel and after that is done there is lots of wood to be cut. We will be back just before dark and you do whatever Helen tells you, comprendre (understand?) They in turn both jump out of bed and acknowledge their mother for Mary is a force to be reckoned with. She then went to each of the girls rooms and again says the same to each, "Avec vous (up with you), wash and dress and don't pull your corsets too tight, it is going to be hot today. Wear your large, feathered hat to block the sun and bring your parasol. Helen, put fresh pantalettes and stockings in you dresser. Button your shoes all the way up; we will be walking quite a bit. Now hurry up the train is at eight. We will have tea and toast on the train. Presse-toi; presse-toi (hurry up; hurry up.)"

Mary had arranged a carriage to pick them up at seven thirty. They were just minutes from the whistle stop station in Saylor Park. What a picture they were as they emerged from the house to the carriage. There had been a light rain in the early morning and the coachman put down a rug so they would not muddy their shoes when they stepped from the veranda to the taxi. Mary says to him, "Will there be more rain?" He replied, "No madam, it was just a sprinkle. It's too hot for rain. The almanac says maybe next month but we sure could use it for the farmers." Mary says, "Get up now girls, no time to lose; Leah Anna pull you dress away from the mud."

In the carriage Leah Anna holds tight to Annie's arm and giggles, "We're going to the city, aren't you excited? I haven't been there for ages. There are so many people and godawful smells." The train station is near the slaughterhouse and it stinks. "Mama, where are we going first?" Mary says, "Tea and toast is not much of a breakfast; we will go to Grumman's Café for brunch before we go to Shillito's department store." Leah Anna screeches with delight, "Shillito's, they have the latest styles from New York." Annie says, "Mother, may I get an ankle high dress? All the girls are wearing them at school and I feel so old fashion and my dresses are always dragging on the ground."

Mary says, "Oh mon Dieu! (Oh my God), next they will be back to bosom lift corsets and exposed cleavage. Well, I suppose if that is what the other girls are wearing, just keep your legs covered never show your stockings in public." Annie astonishes her mother, "Heavens mother, why is everyone so Victorian." Mary returns, "Because we are now civilized and don't want to fall to decadence."

Annie thinks to herself, *'Yeah, they just do their decadence behind closed doors and don't talk about it. Syphilis is rampant because men are dogs just looking for the next bitch. Oh God if my mother really knew my thoughts.'* Leah Anna squeezes Annie's arm as if to say, don't egg her on. It is like she could hear Annie's thoughts. She and her sister were very close and of course Annie told her almost

26

everything on her mind. Annie was a vibrantly alive thinker and questioned everything.

They arrive at the station and board the train. Mary says, "I know the coachman said it would not rain, I sure hope he is right." They move to the dining car as the train starts off for Cincinnati. It is only an hour ride to Cincinnati station. Cincinnati is the main hub for all trains heading from east to west and it is a very busy place. Mary orders tea and toast for all and they enjoy the view as the train tracks follow the Ohio River all the way. The river is full of barges mostly and occasionally there is a steam paddle boat. When Mary sees a steamer, she always mentions, "I wonder how your father is doing." The girls comfort her and Annie says, "Daddy's a strong and smart man mama, remember he's the captain." Mary says as she gazes at the mighty current and speed of the boats going down river, "I know dear but this river can be treacherous." Annie says, "But, he's the best mama, he can beat anything." Mary thinks to herself, "Telle est la confiance de la jeunesse (Such is the confidence of youth.)"

They arrive at Cincinnati station and find a taxi. It is a twenty-minute ride to the café and they can walk to Shillito's Department store from there. They have brunch and then shopping. Annie, a true debutant sees and wants everything. Leah Anna is a little more conservative. Mary says, "Girls, we have to carry everything on the train, there is only so much we can handle so I'm going to limit each of you to four dresses, four pantalets and petticoats: four stockings, two purses, two hats and two pairs of shoes. The corsets you have are just fine and with all of that we will have to hire a porter to carry everything. You can have a couple of scarves and two pairs of earrings and you can each have one perfume and that is it. Your father will have a fit but we are going to an opera in Pittsburgh and I want you to look nice."

Annie and Leah Anna were astonished, it was more than they expected. When they arrived at Shillito's it was like heaven on earth to them. Such styles, such elegance and the time just flew by. Mary was pushing them, "Girls we have to catch the five o'clock so make your final decisions; it is almost four. They both know they have seen everything and choose. They had already sniffed every perfume too. It was a lot of packages and like Mary said they had to have a porter and a cart to get it to the street. The taxi driver wasn't happy but he loaded everything. He hoped at the station he could find help to transport it to the train. The porter at the station helped them and they put everything in the baggage car.

On the ride home they had tea and a sandwich; they were starving form the many hours of shopping and it was hot on this June afternoon. They opened the window of the train and a cool breeze flowed in off the river as the sun was lowering in the sky when Mary exclaims, "Oh no," for she sees black clouds rolling in from the northwest. It is going to rain, I knew it. We will have to leave the packages at the station and have them delivered. I hope we can find a carriage at the station."

The train pulls into the Sailor Park station and it is pouring. They disembark with other dismayed passengers; arrange for the storage of their packages till morning and they look for a carriage but there is none. They talk to the Station Master and he said over

28

the noise of the rain as he stood behind the ticket window, "There will be one; you'll just have to wait. They are stuck in the mud, I'm sure. All these folks need one too. You all will have to decide who goes first.

It's been a long day. There are four others who needed a carriage. They all talked and decided that two, a man and his wife should go first, because they were going another direction. Then they would ride with the other couple going the same direction. They would drop them off and then they could finally be home. It would be after dark and they hoped the rain would stop, but it did not.

They finally arrive home. The coachman who is drenched pulls back the rain flap that hangs from the canvas top and shouts, "Best I could do with the rain and mud Mrs. Dupree." Mary and the girls see that there is yet another twenty feet to run through the rain till they reach the veranda. Mary shouts, "Up with your dresses girls and run." They all hike their dresses and with parasols in hand dash to the porch dodging puddles and mud holes. The boys are standing on the veranda watching the whole scene and shouting and laughing, "Come on, hurry up!" and laughing again. James says as they reach the veranda, "It's not often we get to see pantalets with legs in them. And such fine legs they are."

They are drenched. Their wide brim feathered hats were sagging. Annie and Leah Anna were laughing along with the boys but Mary, seeing the girls shoes all covered with mud was not too happy; she shouts, "Boys get some rags and wipe off your sisters shoes and get us towels for our hair. Rapidement maintenant, Rapidement Rapidement!

29

(Quickly now, quickly, quickly). Annie and Leah Anna flop in the porch swing, pull off their hats and waited with mud on their high button shoes for the boys to return with rags and towels. The boys return and Helen too. James proceeds to clean Annie's shoes; Marcus does Leah Anna's and Helen cleans Mary's. As James kneels, he says, "You all got to have a fun trip while Marcus and I got to work, right, well we went to cut the huge pile of wood and the axe was dull so we went to town to the Holston's Smithy to get it sharpened, and guess who we ran in to? Ben Allan Hamilton. He was picking up a load of iron works for his Father." Annie said, "Oh my." James continues, "Anyway, he heard you were back from boarding school and wondered if he could drop by to see you. I said, "Sure, she'd love to see you." With that Annie smacks James on the head and says, "Why did you say that? You don't speak for me." James snickers and says, "Hey, ouch, what's wrong with a little visit?" Annie lays back and rolls her eyes, "There are things you don't know." She pauses, "you should just stay out of other people's business." She wipes her hair with a towel and says, "Are you done with my shoes. I should boot you with one of them." James says, "Tout mon cher (Quite my dear.)'

Annie gets up and heads for the house. Mary says as Annie leaves, "Put all your wet clothes in the bath, all the whites will have to be bleached and blued in the morning. James says, "I'm sorry Annie, but Ben will probably be here in the afternoon." Annie says, "Damn," and stomps through the door. Leah Anna laughs: she likes Ben and secretly wishes she was old enough for him. Mary says to Leah Anna, "Rendez-

30

vous avec votre soeur (go with you sister) help her undress and you likewise, you both can bathe in the morning and we have lots of laundry to do and I don't want Helen to do it all. Boys have you had enough fun? Kiss votre mere (Kiss your mother.) They adore her and kiss her cheek in turn. And Mary says, "Maintenant avec vous (now off with you,) I have a list of things you can get from the store in the morning and you can have the rest of the day to do whatever you want." James and Marcus say, "Oui mere, bonne nuit (yes mother, good night.)

Mary says to Helen, "I have such good children; I just worry over them so."

The day is done, the rain is subsiding, the house is cool and the frogs are croaking loudly. They are all exhausted and sleep comes fast, such a quiet wonderful sleep.

1890's Train Car

Annie's Secret

Morning is filled with busyness. There is laundry and cleaning and the polishing of shoes. The white undergarments are boiled with bluing to make them white and then hung on lines in the sun. James and Marcus walked to the general store with a wagon to pick up their mothers list. Mary had a garden of herbs and flowers and this day was cool and fresh for the rain had brought with it a northern breeze and it was pleasing for her to prune and cultivate.

Annie and Leah Anna were helping with all the chores and hanging laundry on the line. Leah Anna had to listen to Annie grumble about Ben Hamilton's assumed visit as she went on about the things she had learned at school; things such as the women's suffrage movement and the ideas of Karl Marx and the oppressed proletariat. She made no distinction between them; oppression and entrapment and suffrage were all the same.

Annie releases with a litany, "Why does one abuse the rights of others regardless of their station and our constitution, "where all men," and she emphasized the word men, "are equal but not women equal to men. Men want to put a woman in a nested cage to have their way, while they do whatever they please." Leah Anna, responds, "Annie, I maybe only fourteen but I like boys, they are so nice to me and it's fun to watch them trip all over themselves trying to get my attention, they give me flowers and Jason McClure gave me this necklace, see." Leah Anna pulls the gold chain out from under her high collar blouse and shows it to Annie. Annie says, "And, what did he expect in return?" Leah Anna says, "I told him this does not mean I will kiss you and it does not mean I won't see other boys." Annie responds, "Good girl, does mama know you are wearing jewelry given to you by a boy." "Of course and she gave me warnings about kissing and stuff." Annie takes Leah Anna by the shoulders and looks her straight into her eyes, "Men don't know what they are doing and they are fickle. They try to catch you with sweetness and bobbles just to have their way. They do it because they are compelled, not because they think about it. They are dogs in heat and stupid women are the same way, driven by their compulsion and in that moment of stupidity they are stuck with the burden."

Leah Anna, "I'm too young to know for sure. You sound cold and mean." Annie lowers her voice gets close to Leah Anna and whispers to be sure her mother does not hear, "I'm not cold or mean, I have a strong compulsion and I love men; that's why I have to keep my distance, I don't trust myself. Ben Allan Hamilton is so good looking I want to have him right there on the grass. Have you seen his muscles, he is so strong he could throw me like a twig but he's a man and wants me all his own and I don't want that." Leah Anna giggles. Mary sees them and just gives them a quizzical look. Leah Anna whispers, "I knew it, I wish I was old enough to fall in his arms." Annie says in French because she had heard this phrase so many times from her mother, "Compte tenu de votre langue maternelle (Mind your tongue), and I swear you to secrecy, I'll have nothing to do with Ben Hamilton, he's going to college and I'm going to school and perhaps even to Paris to an acting academy and all that would be ruined if I married him and got pregnant. Now do you understand? If you want to be

34

something, like and actress and do things besides being a baby factory, then fight your compulsion my sweet sister, be smart."

Annie thought she had given her young sister good advice but Leah Anna turns her back to her mother who is across the yard and toward Annie. She clutches her groin through her long dress, looks at Annie and says, "Sometimes when I'm alone I can't help myself, I touch myself and dream about it Annie, am I bad? Is it wrong to touch yourself and dream? And I worry that I'm weak. I kissed Jason when he gave me the necklace, I kiss him a lot and he touched me and I got scared. I wanted to have him so much and I made him stop."

Mary is getting curious about the girls long conversation and wants to know, but she keeps her distance. Annie whispers again, "Now he has touched you and the bastard is going to brag about it. Leah Anna, you have to go to school like me and do something with your life." Leah Anna gets a little sharp, "I may be only fourteen but I'm not like you. I dream about marriage and children." Annie responds, "And, I worry about honesty and fidelity. I don't trust men because I have seen how they are, they may be with you but will turn their head to look at a pretty girl even while they are walking with you arm-in-arm. They want them all."

Leah Anna inquires, "Is it wrong to touch myself." Annie laughs and her mother can see but not hear, "No it's not wrong, it's a good way to satisfy your compulsion and to avoid the real thing. I use a candle sometimes. Leah Anna giggles and says, "Me too."

It has the best of Mary and she has to know what her girls are talking about; she walks over, "What are you two giggling about. Annie dodges the question of course, "We are just laughing about boys tripping over themselves to get our attention." To which Mary retorts, "Profitez de votre jeunesse (Enjoy your youth) Vous ne serez pas assez pour toujours (you will not be pretty forever.) Finish hanging and then go help Helen with lunch, quickly now before it gets too hot to breathe. Annie, if Ben is coming this evening, you can have a cool bath this afternoon and splash on a little perfume." Annie says, "I'd rather stink so he will go away." Leah Anna says, "Annie, I know your secret." To which Mary responds, "What secret?" Annie quickly returns, "It's no secret mother, I don't want to have children, and Leah Anna, you shut your mouth or I'll not talk to you ever again." As they enter the house Annie whispers in Leah Anna's ear with earnest, "keep your mouth shut sister!" Leah Anna speaks in a loud whisper that her mother could hear, "I will, I will, I promise."

They have lunch and lounge under the big Oak tree in the back where there is an old rope swing with two ropes and a wooden seat and a hammock and white wooden lounge chairs. The rest of the day could be lazy and for Helen too. All that was yet to do was take down the laundry when it is dry. They talk about the excitement of their trip to Pittsburgh and the Opera. Their father would be there in less than a week. They will sail in all the luxury of the Louisville Queen for a week while they meander up the Ohio taking on passengers and dropping off passengers at towns along the way; what an adventure. Captain

36

James Dupree gave them a wonderful life and they all respected it.

At about two in the afternoon when the heat was well set at about eighty-five degrees Mary suggests, "Annie, why don't you go now and have a cool bath. Trim your under-arm hair; that is where most of the odor comes from. Use some talc to keep you dry and you can use some of my perfume, save yours for the trip. Annie says, "Can I borrow your tortoise shell combs for my hair?" Mary says, "May I dear, it is May I, and yes you may." Annie kisses her mother on the cheek, "Thanks Mama." Mary says softly "Tu es le bienvenue mon cher (You are welcome, dear.)"

Annie heads to the bathroom on the second floor. The bathroom had a pump that was fed by a spring water cistern that her father engineered when they built this massive house. The water was so cool. It had a wooden stove and large pots for heating the water in the winter. It was so wonderful to live in this modern age, such convenience. There would be no heating of the water today; the chilly water would be so refreshing. They had soft soap and this spring water was like rainwater, with a little sloshing it made mounds of bubbles. Annie added a little fragrant oil for more delight.

Annie is pondering all, the trip, the opera and Ben, as she thinks of his name loudly in her mind. She did not tell Leah Anna all of her secrets. She really enjoyed Ben's attention but would not sway from her plans for her life. She is a serious woman and would not be taken for granted. She locks the bathroom door and everyone knew she took long baths of luxury but they did not know all.

She goes through her ritual. She fills the large copper bathtub, adds the oil and lathers some soap. She places a towel on the floor beside the tub. She digs down deep in the cedar chest that is full of towels, boxes of soap and bottles of oil. At the very bottom she retrieves a candle that is rough with drippings. She ties up her hair in a twist and then gazes at her naked body in the long mirror on the wall. She fondles her voluptuous breasts and gently rubs her groin. She is standing over the towel because she knows what will happen. She uses the candle while her imagination of Ben and his prowess is only fantasy, but a good fantasy. In short order she gushes all over the towel. She cannot subdue her tiny screech and hopes no one heard. She stands with her legs spread and quivering. She drops her head to see the wet towel. She pauses in ecstasy and holds on to the tub for balance. It takes a minute or two and then she steps into the cool bath. She sits and then lies down in the water while she regains her senses.

No one will know, she thinks, no one should ever know, this is my secret and I refuse to become a whore, or a kept woman because of my compulsion. She thinks, '*My God that felt good and that will suffice. Perhaps mother is right, maybe I will change as I get older, but I think not.*'

Twenty minutes or so pass and her fingers are wrinkling. She gets out and towels off while standing on the towel the received her gush. Once she is dry, she dips the floor towel in the bath and wrings it out. Her mother always wondered about the drenched towel but never asked. Annie was prepared if she ever did. Her answer would be, I splashed water on the floor. I can't help it getting in and out of that slippery tub. I have to clean it up and the towel gets dirty so I dunk in the tub to rinse it. This sounds like a good answer if her mother ever asks, but Mary is not stupid and she is loving enough to never ask. She knows and she knows Leah Anna is on the way. What she is proud of is Annie's self-determination and self-protection and hopes Leah Anna will pick up some of Annie's traits.

Annie trims her arm hair and powders. She puts on her robe and returns to her bedroom. She selects a white cotton dress and dreads putting on her corset which she really does not need with her outstanding figure, but her mother insists. She puts on her pantalets first, then the under blouse which helps hide the definition of her nipples which with her endowment is hard to do. Then she steps into the corset which is laced loosely. The stockings are white cotton to hide the ankle. Leah Anna buttons the high-top shoes and helps with the dress thrown over her head and buttoned from the back. The dress has a high collar with lace. There is lace down the back, around the waste and on the bottom fringe. Leah Anna helps to wrap her long dark hair on top of her head and install the tortoise shell combs to keep it. With a little rouge and a tamping of powder on her face, there is only one more thing; it is a drop of her mother's very expensive floral perfume from France applied behind her ear and on her wrists.

She is a picture of loveliness and she knows it. She knows the power she has over men. They will bust their shins looking at her not seeing where they are going. Her mother worries at every encounter with boys who are now men. How will she deal with it?

Can she be strong, sensible and kind at the same time and not abuse this beauty.

It is five thirty in the evening and Ben arrives in one of his father's carriages. It is pulled by a single dark red mare and has only two seats. It has a collapsible canopy and is beautifully upholstered in leather. Ben pulls up, steps down and lashes the horse to the fence. Ben is six feet tall, strong but not overly muscular. He has dark hair and short sideburns. He is dressed impeccably with polished boots, pressed fine cotton pants, a white shirt and starched collar. He has on a black ribbon tie, western style and black felt hat with a three-inch brim that is trimmed in suede. He has dark brown eyes and a strong chin. He is a picture of masculinity.

Annie is standing on the veranda and Ben shouts hello as he walks up to the landing. Annie reaches out her hand cordially to prevent him from attempting to hug her. She says, "Hello Ben, how are you." Ben responds, "Doing quite well, thank you very much." Ben says, "And you Annie how are you? You've gotten even prettier after your year in school." They continue in idle conversation and Annie escorts Ben to the gazebo in the back where Helen had prepared some lemonade, tea and cookies. They sat in the gazebo alone. Mary had to shoo Leah Anna away from the window, "Leave them in peace, I'm sure your sister will tell you all about it."

Mary liked Ben but knew her daughters determination. Mary was the one that wanted her to be an actress; you see Mary was in a theater company when she met her Captain Dupree. James was in Paris with some French investors that were going to help him build the Louisville Queen. Mary wanted out of

40

Europe. There were protests and unrest and she feared another war was brewing. James Dupree fell head over heels for her when he saw her in a play. Dupree was not shy. He was tall, good-looking and confident. At his young age of twenty-five you could tell he was captain material. In short order Mary, in a rash decision and with a leap of faith married Dupree and sailed to America. She had always hoped to act on the stage again, but Antoinette was in her belly and she set aside her ambition, perhaps she could live it through her daughter. She never forced her desire on Annie; she only pointed the way if she wanted to go.

After a while of sipping tea and munching on cookies, Annie suggests they go to the swing that they both played on as children. Annie sits in the swing and sways while Ben stands with his hat in his hand. He can feel the formality coming from Annie; she was really holding him at a distance. Of course he did not like it and being a strong sort he finally and mistakenly decides to press her, "Annie, I love you and we would make the most wonderful couple and make beautiful children and have a happy life." Annie knew this was coming, "Ben you are going to Harvard law school, and I am going back to Madam Rousseau's finishing school, mother wants me to try acting and Madam Rousseau has told me of acting companies in Paris that she can get me in. So I should just give up my ambition and make babies? The inflection in her voice raised like it was a rhetorical question rather than a statement. She is trying to be kind but put all the cards on the table, "I think not." Her temper wells up, "Men always do this, I know you love me and I have feelings for you, but I'm not going to give up my opportunities so you can have

41

your dream that places me at home. Don't you understand that seems like prison to me? You really don't know much about me or my wants and desires, you only have this image or dream and that dream shuts me out and puts me into your fantasy."

Annie starts to cry, "I will never have children; can't you understand that. You want a family and I am horrified of pregnancy. I'm not going to do it Ben. Ben is overcome by Annie's tears. He fights back the emotion that is welling up inside him. Real men don't cry and their logic turns his confusion to anger. Ben puts his hat on as a gesture that he was leaving. He stands ridged, pulls his shoulders back, reaches out his hand for a formal handshake and as Annie reciprocates, he leans down and kisses her petite hand, "Annie my dear, you will change, I only pray my love will wait for that day. Go to school, go acting in Paris," he says with sarcasm, and when you fail, I will be waiting for you."

This turned Annie's tears to contempt, "Don't wait too long Ben, I don't plan to return." Ben turns and walks away not saying a word. He goes to the house to say goodbye to Mary and thank her for her kindness, "Misses Dupree I don't know why your daughter is so callous and downright mean. I sure tried to love her and I hope someday she will change." Mary consoles him, "Ben sometimes you have to let people be who they are, time can change the heart, don't be dismayed." Ben is crushed and in his controlling male ego all he knows is he wants Annie with a powerful lust, and the beast is sent away weeping secretly.

Annie runs to her bedroom not saying a word. She falls on her bed and weeps, she cared about him and lusted after him but would not succumb; she was angered and broken and confused. Her mother did not bother her; Leah Anna knocked on her door lightly and when she did not answer she left her alone. Thankfully the boys were not around. Mary feared they were drinking beer behind the general store. Annie subdued her crying and fell to sleep. She didn't even undress and slept the whole night through.

In the morning Mary knocks on Annie's door and she answers. Her mother pokes her head in and says, "I've prepared a basket of food for Mrs. Groesbeck by the church. I want you girls to use the boys bicycles and take the basket to her. You can wear your summer pantsuits and straw hats. Don't get them dirty. Mary see's that Annie slept in her clothes, "Wash up now, your sister is waiting. Annie rouses and says, "Yes mother." She mumbles, "You treat me like a child." Mary says calmly, "You will always be my baby, I can't help that."

Annie quietly, "I hope I don't disappoint you." Mary comes to sit next to her as Annie slumps over sitting on her bed. Mary holds her hand, "You are doing just fine, stay strong; I understand the mind of a woman more than you know. You have to keep your feelings in check and follow your dreams. I came all the way from France to a new strange land. I barely spoke English but your father gave me all his attention and care. He knew it would be hard for me. Finally we arrange for your Aunt Lisa to come here too, which made me feel I had family close by. Lisa was with your grandmother in France when she died. I was so broken when I could not be there for my mother, but we make our choices and if you have love in your heart, you do what you feel you need to do for

43

your happiness, whatever that is. So stand strong, no one loves you more than me, always know that." Annie grabs her mother with a long hug. Mary says now, "Get dressed and go have some fun. I want you to ask Mrs. Groesbeck if she saw my boys again behind the general store."

Annie laughs, "Those boys, certains ennuis (certain trouble.) Mary instructs, "After Mrs. Groesbeck go to Tanner's Pond, the troublemakers are trying to catch some catfish for dinner. We'll have catfish, sweet potatoes, fresh green beans from the garden and corn bread." Annie says, "Yum." Mary adds, "I got a telegram this morning, your father is in Louisville and will be here in two days. He will have a rest and then it's off to Pittsburgh. Annie screeches with joy.

Journey on the Ohio

Captain Dupree arrives on schedule. He runs a tight ship and knows that passengers are waiting on schedule and unless there are circumstances beyond his control he is always on time, just like the trains. He knows that people ride his steamer because it is fun and spacious and luxurious as opposed to riding on a rough stuffy train. His successful business is in delighting his customers.

You can imagine the details of loading on supplies for meals that are all cooked exquisitely in the boats galley. The laundry for towels and clean sheets for the beds are done by laundry services up and down the river from Pittsburgh to St. Louis and Memphis. They are loaded on by the hundreds. They on load firewood for the boiler at every major stop. He maintains a staff of porters and waiters and maids who all share bunk rooms onboard the Louie Queen. She is spit and polished and nothing but comfort. It is a lot of work and James coordinates it all. Mary is always impressed at his sharpness and ability. Of course that's why she married him.

The family will be staying in two staterooms just next to the captain's stateroom, which is just behind the wheelhouse in the front and uppermost deck of the boat. The boys are in one room and the girls in the other. James forewarned all the crewmen and women alike from the master steward to the boiler-men that his family would be onboard and they were to be at their best with no swearing or drunkenness or they would be dismissed at the next port up the river, wherever that may be.

James hired a coach to take him from the dock to his home. The entire family was sitting on the veranda watching for his arrival. When they saw the carriage coming up the drive, they all leaped to their feet. Mary's heart was pounding; they were all rushing with joy. They loved their father. He was such a fun and confident man. He always teased each of them in turn with fun and goading and he was finally here.

This strapping man in the uniform of a steamboat captain was waving all the way up the drive. He steps out of the carriage only to be swamped with bodies. Mary first latches on to his neck. She is only five feet and four inches and against James six feet she looks so petite. He lifts her off the ground with such ease while all the children smother him too. James just laughs with a roar, "It's so good to be home; how is my lovely family. The kids back away because they know what is coming, a kiss, a powerful long kiss. Mary's feet never touch the ground as she pulls off his hat and strokes his hair. Finally to let her breath he sets her on her feet then sweeps her up and carries her up the steps to the veranda. James says, "I missed you so. My absence not only made my heart grow fonder, it made me weep for my Mary Ann." He had a way with words and how to love a woman, he adored her and she knew it. Then there was another kiss as she sat on his lap in the porch swing. They did not hide their passion from the children but they did not display it foolishly. This was a special time.

Helen brought tea and sweet breads and cakes to the front veranda because it was cooler there in the morning. They all munched and drank and listened to their father talk about the last few months away. This

46

spanned from the last week of March till now the last week in June. He had stopped once passing by for two days in May which was far too short a visit. Now they were going to have a long family vacation to Pittsburgh and the Opera. James shared Mary's love for the performing arts and felt it added elegance and purpose to and otherwise laborious life. Their children were being exposed to culture and that please them both.

James looked out and said, "Boys the delivery wagon is coming, go help them unload, I have things for everyone. Mary starts to get up and James said, "Mary just relax they will get it." Mary relaxes, "What all did you bring this time?" James ran down the list in his mind, "Well, I got the boys wool blend tailored suits with tales for the Opera; they are gray pinstriped trousers and black coats. I got them linen shirts with cuffs and cuff links and black silk bow ties and felt top hats. It is about time they learned to dress. I got two steamer trunks, one for the girls and one for the boys. I found that French vanity you saw in that catalog. I found it in St Louis." Mary screeches and squeezes his neck as she was still sitting in his lap kissing him. "I got a cameo broach for each of the girls and some other necklaces and earrings."

With that Annie and Leah Anna jump up and say in unison, "Daddy where is it?" He said, "Look for a red box with ribbon," and before he could finish, they ran, so he had to shout, "Inside you'll find boxes with your names on it." He laughed, "They are too spoiled." Mary agrees, "And you love spoiling them." James said, "True, but none to compare to you." Now alone, James buries his face in Mary's bosom. Mary helps him press against her and then pulls him back

47

to kiss him again. James merely says, "I love you." Mary, likewise, "And I love you, my darling." They are both in their mid-forties and after twenty-two years together they were comfortable.

James Jr and Marcus come with the vanity less the mirror. The captain said, "Carry it carefully to our bedroom." It was on the third floor, which was almost exclusively reserved for them. Mary had a sewing room and there was a separate parlor overlooking the river where Mary and James would spend many hours in the winter listening to phonograph records and reading by the fireplace.

The girls are looking for the red box and cannot find it. They shout from the wagon, "Papa where is it." James told Mary, "I hid it; I just wanted them to root for a while. James calls out, "It is in the second trunk in the bottom drawer." He then says, "And I brought you something else my sweet. He lifts Mary easily off his lap and places her by him on the swing. He reaches into his inner coat pocket and pulls out a long narrow jewelry box, and places it in her hands. Of course she says, "Oh James," as she slowly opens the velvet covered hinged box. It makes the creaking sound they all do. Inside was a gold necklace with a dangling cluster of large diamonds each on a swirled flatten chain. They were flattened so they would all face forward. Mary said, "James we are well off but this must have cost a fortune."

James said, "I'm not unscrupulous but the woman I bought it from was going to sell it no matter what. She needed to get to Memphis and she needed sustenance for the trip. I provided her passage and gave her another thousand dollars. If you don't want it, we can sell it for five times what I paid for it. Mary laughs, "No I'll keep it. It will look wonderful at the Opera." James laughs, "And I will have to carry my pistol to keep you from being robbed when you wear it." Mary puts it on, pecks him on the cheek and goes to the mirror in the foyer. James relaxes in the swing feeling good and delight at all the joy his family brings him.

The boys return and he says, "Take the mirror up and don't break it. Just set it against the wall, I will attach it later. Then you can carry in the trunks. The girls know which one is theirs. Put it in Annie's room and you boys share the other one, it has your new clothes in it. Try your clothes on to see if they fit and put them back on the hanger. Keep them neat." Mary returns: she is so pleased. She sits beside James and leans her head over to his shoulder. James sighs with contentment. Helen puts her head out the front door and inquires, "Lunch in the Gazebo?" Mary says, "I'll come help you." To which Helen replies, "I'll not have that, you sit with your husband. The girls will help me." James and Mary rock in the swing and take turns chuckling about the events of their children. Mary tells on the boys about the suspected but not proved incident with beer behind the general store. James says, "I'll deal with that. I'll get them good and drunk till their guts come up." Mary smacks James leg, "I don't think that is the way." James said, "It worked for me when my dad did it. I can't stand the smell of the stuff. I much prefer a fine brandy with my love." And of course that invokes more kisses from Mary.

The boys return in their suits; the fit was good except Marcus' pants were too long, Mary says she would hem them later in the afternoon. There was not much time to waste. They would leave in two days.

The girls found the jewelry and wearing it they ran to hug and kiss their father. Mary said, "Mon, vous regardez charmant (My, you look lovely.) Put it away now and help Helen with lunch." Annie could not help feel like a little girl around her father. She could not wait to have him alone to tell him all about school and how much she had learned. She wanted him to see her as a woman and not a little girl.

They had lunch and James headed to their bedroom for a nap. Mary hemmed Marcus' pants and they fit well. She showed the boys how to tie a silk bowtie. Annie and Leah Anna laid out their clothes and decided what all to take. They had to share a trunk so they grappled over what to take and what to leave behind. Mary had her own trunk and told the girls they could each put some things in hers. Captain James had all his ware onboard the Louie Queen and had nothing to pack. So the busy day is done and Captain James Marcus Dupree and his maiden Mary Ann Buffet-Dupree retired to the privacy of their parlor and boudoir.

Shortly after dark when all the noise of their children subsided, they climbed up to the widows tower. Mary was in a shear evening gown and shawl and James was in pajamas and a smoking jacket. A near full moon was rising to the east and reflecting on the river. A cool breeze was blowing from the northwest and it felt so good. They had a comfortable double rocking chair with cushions where they relaxed to talk and fondle each other and kiss and caress.

Mary told James of Annie's encounter with Ben Hamilton and how she would support her in whatever she decides to do. How she hoped she would continue toward an acting career but if she decided not to, that was okay. Mary sighs, "She is so adamant about not having children. She says that children are the whole point of a marriage and since she does not want children, what is the point of a marriage. She says no man will settle for that. She is so afraid of pregnancy and I can understand that. It is hard for a woman to see her body go through that change and then the fear of giving birth."

James acknowledges and agrees though he was only there for Annie's birth. He tried to be there for the other births but the schedule was impossible to predict. He said, "We should have tried in the summer so they could be born in the winter when I was home." Mary said, "If you remember we did try on some occasions when you would port in Sailor Park for a day or two in the summer. It just did not happen. Mary laughs, "Amour rapide (fast love,) you pleasure me and then leave me all alone to roll in my bed." She tickles him and jumps on top of him spread legged and breathes heavy in his ear, "So pleasure me now my Captain and don't be in a hurry." The separation of being an additional floor above the children and on the widows walk, the center of which could not be seen from the ground, gave them privacy. So they let go their passion and Mary said, "Pull it out in time James, we don't want another child." And so he did because he loved her.

As they lounge in ecstasy James says, "I wonder if Annie is attracted to women and is hiding it." Mary responds, "I don't think so, she says she

51

adores men, but you never know. I will love her no matter what." "And me likewise," James agrees.

They are so comfortable but don't want to be found on the widows walk in the morning, so they drag their tired bodies down and go to bed for a good sleep.

Morning comes and the day is filled with more planning. Captain James walks to town to visit with some of the locals and to check up on the rumor of the boys and beer. Nothing much to do except wait for the departure the following day. They would be up early for a carriage and wagon that was due at eight o'clock.

In the afternoon Annie finally gets to talk to her father alone. She saw her dad resting in the gazebo and joins him. Leah Anna was passing through the kitchen and headed out back when Mary stopped her and said, "Let Annie and your father talk, she needs to tell him about school and I'm sure there will be conversation about Ben, so leave them alone." Leah Anna grumbles but goes to the front parlor and plays on the piano.

James puts his arm around his little girl as Annie begins to tell him her learning. She tells of her history learning and music appreciation. She talks about acting, but she was most interested in hearing her father's opinion on women's rights, as well as communism versus capitalism. "Papa, I went to a women's march in Cincinnati. I just watched; I did not join in because I'm just learning about it. I think I really agree. Why don't women get to vote? I think our opinion matters and I think we are just as smart as men." James laughs, "No question you're just as smart. I think men don't trust women when it comes to hard decisions. I know that seems wrong. Men see themselves as tough and women as soft if not weak. Lord knows girl you're not weak. It's a man's mind that needs to change. I trust your mother. She helps me in almost every decision but say for instance if I asked her to run the Louie Queen. No man would trust or respect her. She may be smart enough but could not tell those ruffians on the boat what to do. So that's kind of how other men feel about the vote, if women start making the decisions our country will be weak or other countries will see us as weak."

"Papa, England has a Queen and they seem to do fine." James responds, "She does not rule anymore; the elected prime minister and parliament govern the country; they sort of followed the United States with a democratically elected body that governs. The opponents of a women's right to vote here in the states say that next women will want to run for office and I don't think that a woman could put up with the bullies, they will not allow that. But you keep on my darling girl; you're strong enough to help make things change, Lord knows you've got the beans for a fight and Lord knows I trust your mother's smarts sometimes more than trusting my own. You sure got it from her. Just trust your woman's sense and don't take on a fight that ain't worth winnin'."

Annie feels that her father is on her side. "I guess mama told you about Ben Hamilton?" James nods, "Yep, nice young man, I think he has a good head on his shoulders." Annie responds, "It's not that I don't think he is smart and good looking and a good man papa, I don't want to have children and stay at home all the time and I know that all he wants is a good wife and babies. He doesn't even know anything about me, he just has his dream." James says, "You may change in time." Annie ruffles a bit, "Everybody keeps saying that. I'm not going to change, don't you understand." Her father sees her dander up and comforts her, "Don't get mad dear, I love you so much, besides you can do all kinds of things after you are a famous actress." Annie laughs and gives him a big hug.

James Jr and Marcus race speeding around the house on their bicycles and skid to a halt at the gazebo. They say in unison, "Hi papa." Their dad now sounds like the captain he is, "Come up her boys and have a seat, we need to talk. Annie kisses his cheek and heads for the kitchen she knows the boys are going to get a lecture.

The boys know what is coming. James starts in, "You know that liquor has ruined many a good man. What kind of life would you have if I was a drunkard? If I drank, I would have wrecked the Louie Queen long ago and you would have no life at all. I've got pretty good evidence that you boys were drinking beer behind the Harper's store. You are too young to drink and I'll have no more of it. Besides you're making a bad reputation for yourself in town. I don't want people talking bad about my boys. Do you understand? You are not too old for a whippin', so if I hear of it again, I'll have you behind the shed. Do you understand me boys." They in unison say, "Yes father." James directs them, "Now go wash up and help your mother; dinner is soon." The boys with their heads down and tale between their legs head for the kitchen.

Captain James had brought a prime cut of beef; some fresh vegetables and potatoes and Helen and Mary made them a fine feast. He also brought fresh eggs and a slab of pork for breakfast. Tomorrow was the big day and it would start early.

At the dawn of the day, the journey begins with hustle and bustle and for the boys and the girls it is almost panic to not forget anything. For the Captain it was not stressful, he sat in the swing watching and waiting calmly as mayhem ensued in the house. Mary came and sat with him finally, "I think they are finally ready." She knew the carriage and wagon were due at eight. It is quarter till and James directs the boys to bring the three trunks down and place them near the driveway and they obediently did just that. Right on time the wagon and carriage arrive. They are loaded and this lovely well-dressed family with their Captain in uniform, with jest and joy in their hearts they are off. Helen waves and says, "All will be well here, have a nice trip." They all wave to her and say again and again, "Bye Helen, we'll miss you." Helen was pleased to be home alone for some peace and quiet.

They arrive at the dock and immediately the first officer William Tarkle runs up to the captain still sitting in the carriage. Dagnabit Capin' in his vernacular, Jimmy was guiden' the barrel crane when the strap broke and it fell on his leg; broke it clean. We just hauled him off in the wagon to Doc's house. It hurt him bad. Captain James said, "Damn, did it look like it could be fixed?" William said, "I think so but he's going to be on crutches for a long while." James replies, "We're going to be short a good man, can you find someone to take his place." "Yep, already thought of that, his younger brother volunteered. He's learned a lot from Jimmy." Captain Dupree agrees, "Yeah, his name is Mark, right? He's a good man, a little young but if he wants to learn, tell him to get his gear, we'll shove off within the hour. William, have these trunks loaded to the rooms. Boys go along and show them where they go. Put your mother's trunk in the corner near my bed and you know where the rest go. The boys had been all over the Louie Queen and knew every inch, from the boiler room to the wheelhouse. They were in love with this boat and fashioned themselves as being a captain someday. Captain Dupree had other plans for them; he wanted them to have something other than a difficult life on the river.

Mary, Annie and Leah Anna exited the carriage in all their regalia looking spectacular. They felt so special as they crossed the gangway, then up the stairs to the third deck and into their lovely spacious staterooms. All the eyes of the crew, porters, stewards and waitresses were on them just to get a glance at the children and how they have grown. They had been coming aboard once in a while as they were growing up but James kept them isolated for short visits because the Louie Queen was a gambling establishment and sometimes there was risqué entertainment, not for the eyes or ears of children. There were drunks and loud mouths and ruffians sometimes. It was not uncommon for the boat to slow near the shore and a passenger to be escorted off at gun point. Captain Dupree would not tolerate disturbances on his boat. Any guns had to be locked in the pursers safe. Any cheating at cards if accused and witnessed by another could get you tossed ashore anywhere that happened to be. The captain was the law.

Mary and the children get settled in and unpack for the four-day journey to Pittsburgh. They would stop at Summit, Kentucky then Parkersburg, West Virginia and then finally Pittsburgh. They would be picking up and dropping off passengers along the way.

Captain Dupree got the boat readied for steam. The whole family went to the wheelhouse which was just up the passageway passed the captains stateroom. James orders the sounding of the horn signal which indicates departure. The gangway is hauled aboard, lines are cast off. Three blasts of the steam whistle and the Louie Queen pulls away from the dock against the current of the mighty Ohio and upriver she goes: dead ahead and steady this massive boat steams into the bright morning sun on the beautiful glistening water. Captain Dupree only directs the first officer and the helmsman. He sits behind the helm in his raised captain's chair and directs. Mary stands on one side and Annie clutches his arm on the other. The boys and Leah Anna are at the windows watching in awe. James orders, "Right of the river." This tells the helmsman to steer across the river to the right side and clear of down river traffic. Once they reach that point and are clear of all other boats, James orders, "First officer has the command. He says, "William, eyes front and steer her well." William says, "Aye, aye capin." James turns to Mary, "Come my love, let's have breakfast, I'm starved. Mary takes his arm and the children follow them to the main dining room. Everyone greets them along the way, it is a wonderful day.

They all sit at the captain's table looking so fine. Captain Dupree is waited on hand and foot. They have coffee and each order their hearts desire. Mary is on James' left and Annie is on his right. Leah Anna sits next to Annie and James Jr is next to his mother and Marcus is by his side. Annie quizzes her father about the operation of the Louie Queen, "Papa how does all the gambling work, I mean, are you afraid you will lose money?" Her father explains, "We run three games, roulette, blackjack and dice, on those games the odds are greatly in our favor, sometimes there is a big winner, but mostly people lose. On the poker tables we provide a dealer and the house gets twenty percent of the pot regardless. So we always do well." James quips, "The hard part is heavy drinkers. When they start to lose, they get mean. That's why we have a brig. We don't allow guns, they have to put them in the purser's safe when they come on board, but if someone hides a derringer we don't know. Ladies don't usually play poker but one time this ole' gal sat in, got drunk and was losing. She accused a man of cheating and shot him in the shoulder." Mary interrupts sternly, "James, that's not decent conversation over breakfast." Marcus says, "Wow dad, did you lock her in the brig?" Mary says more firmly, "That's enough. Leah Anna, sit up and stop clinging to you sister." She then says to the waiter who was standing over the shoulder of Mary and James, "We will have eggs, bacon and toast for everyone." Captain Dupree adds, "I'll have a small steak too if you please. Anyone else want steak?" All the children say, "Oh, yes please papa." Mary says, "None for me thank-you."

58

Annie continues to quiz her father, "Is the revenue from all the rest good. I mean, the rooms, the liquor and the passage tickets, how does that compare to the revenue of the gambling." Her father leans toward Mary, "What are you raising here a businesswoman?" Mary chuckles, "It is none of my doing but it is good for her to understand finances." James says, "All in all the services are about sixty percent and the games bring in forty. Maybe I should have you to be my purser since you are so interested in money." Annie, "No thanks, I don't want to always be on the river like you." Mary says, "When you are all grown, I'm not going to stay in that big house alone, I'm going to join your father on the Louie Queen." James says, "That will be a great day my dear."

Annie can see the adoring relationship her mother and father have and, in her mind, she thinks, 'I will never have that. My father is such a rare man. But is he faithful on all the long summers away from mama? I'd like to think he is but men are men.' She is beginning to understand the movement, the one of suffrage. She has a passion and desire for men and she knows it but what is developing in her before she even knows the 'term' is feminism.

Breakfast is almost finished and the boys are chomping at the bit to be excused so they can go on deck and see the sights of the river. James Jr says, "May we be excused." Mary responds, "Yes and don't fall overboard being silly." Leah Anna asks if she can go too. Mary says, "Oui vous pouvez (Yes you may,) take care not to soil your dress. Annie, go with her and keep an eye on your brothers." Annie says, "Oui mere (Yes mother.)"

They hustle off while Mary and her Captain are left alone. James starts in, "Oh my, my boys are wild, my oldest daughter is guarded and callous for such a young age and Leah Anna is the only one who seems normal. Mary chuckles, "Everyone is unique, the one quality they all have is they are good of heart and kind and that comes from our loving them. They are adventurous and unafraid and that is a good thing." They leisurely sip their coffee and then decide to take a stroll on the deck. They wander toward the bow of the Louie Queen and join their children.

Captain Dupree upon greeting his sons reaches into his pocket for his money clip, "Boys, I'm going to give you each twenty dollars to play the games, but that is it. If you lose, don't expect more. Girls it is not lady like for you to gamble unescorted, so if you would like to play, I will go with you." Leah Anna says, "Oh papa , I do not want to gamble." Annie retorts, "I don't care for gambling papa but I'll take the money to buy things in Pittsburgh." James laughs, "You are frugal are you not Annie?" Annie takes her father by the arm and pulls up close, "I just think wasting money is sinful when so many are poor and wanting." Her father returns, "You can't save the world Annie." She replies, "Maybe not papa but I cannot do what I feel is wrong." James hugs his daughter, "You're a fine lady Annie with good scruples." Annie says with zeal, "Papa, you called me a lady, do you finally see me as a woman and not a child?' Her father laughs with a hearty zest, "Oh my word yes, yes indeed. Mary says, "Young lady, you're a young lady." Annie with a bit of sarcasm, "Of course mother, of course."

Well as you would expect the boys made a beeline to the games. The money would not last long. Leah Anna clung to her mother and Annie sat on a bench at the bow just enjoying the view and the Louie Queen steamed steadily up the river churning against the current. At full steam she would do only eight knots as measured against the land. In fact she was doing fifteen, losing seven knots to the current. They steamed all afternoon and into the evening to reach Summit Kentucky which is very near West Virginia. A fog was coming up when they reached the dock and tied up. Passengers were waiting to board as well as a few disembarked at Summit. The steamer was quiet now with no churning of the big engine and all would get a good night's rest. The partying and gambling went on till late but Captain Dupree and all his family were stowed away by ten o'clock. James Jr had lost his twenty dollars and to his peril because of Marcus' goading, Marcus had won fifty dollars.

Captain Dupree rises early; he washes up and orders hot water for the copper tub that is in his state room. Mary would bathe and then Annie and Leah Anna. The boys were instructed to wash with the basin that was in their stateroom. This all had to be done before they again went under steam. The Louie Queen was the most stable of boats but the current causes the boat to pitch a bit which would slosh the water out of the tub and make a big mess. All the bathing is done and the captain heads to the wheelhouse and directs the maneuvers away from the dock. The next stop would be Parkersburg, West Virginia.

All is well and by midafternoon James Jr had talked his brother Marcus into loaning him twenty dollars. His father admonished his son that borrowing money for gambling was a dangerous thing that could turn into a bad habit, "Son you should live within your means; now give the money back to your brother." James Jr reluctantly followed his father's instructions, so he sat beside his brother at the roulette game and watched Marcus lose the entire fifty dollars. James laughed and goaded him with every loss. This turned into a contentious dispute that was seen by Mary who was lounging near a window. She motioned to her husband who was nearby and just pointed at her sons. Captain Dupree walked up to them and just stood there looking, saying not a word. Marcus started to whine to his father about his brothers goading to which Captain Dupree under his breath and through his teeth, "I will have none of this. Respect your family and don't make a scene, now off with the both of you. Settle your differences, you are brothers." The boys knew it was over and quietly left the gaming parlor. Leah Anna and Annie who were sitting at another table in the parlor just giggled. To which Mary shushed. All the waiters, the barkeep and the hostess were delighted to see that their family was just like any other family.

They made Parkersburg by four in the afternoon and tied up at the dock. The captain took them all to a restaurant he frequented that was near the waterfront. The crew was busy loading on wood for the boiler and other supplies while the maids cleaned and more passengers embarked and disembarked. Evening came and a full moon was rising and glistening on the river, this wonderful, mighty river. Again it was a restful night and on the early morning they would steam for Pittsburgh. This was a long stretch of river. They would not make it all the way and would have to anchor forty miles from their destination because there were no towns or docks to tie up to. It all depends on the current of the Ohio.

Now you must know, they had to anchor in an uninhabited part of the river. There were many tributary streams and Caption Dupree took the helm and guided the Louisville Queen up a stream he knew well. There they would anchor for the night because the flow was light compared to the mighty Ohio and the boat would be calm and stable.

James loves this particular spot. It was at the edge of the Smoky Mountains. It was quiet and serene in this deep valley. The mountain rose steeply and the cool breeze that flowed down the water shed was delightful on this hot July night. All the passengers came on deck to feel the breeze and to watch the light fade over these beautiful mountains. The frogs and crickets were beginning their nightly noise and the lightning bugs were sparkling everywhere. As night fell the only light besides the fireflies were the lamps of the Louie Queen. The darkness of the deep forest was ominous. People remarked how good it is to be a dweller in a municipality instead of this dark dangerous forest.

Captain James and Mary were on the forward deck and Annie and Leah Anna were with them. The boys were on the aft deck with a lantern. They were hanging it low to see what fish they might see in the dark water. James remarks to Mary, "There are many a hungry bear in those forests and a lot of backwoods

63

hill folk. I've given some a ride to Pittsburgh on occasion. They are poor ignorant people, how on earth they get by is a wonder. Some are still carrying muskets that were handed down to them from the war. Some still harbor hatred and sing rebel songs. I make them give up their guns of course. If they won't give up their gun then they don't get onboard. They have no money so I make them help the stokers with pitching wood, poor ignorant bastards." Mary slaps James hand, "Compte tenu de votre langue maternelle (Mind your tongue.)" Annie says, "My, how do they ever survive in the winter?" James answers, "They have shacks in the woods next to their moonshine still. They stay drunk all winter. They live off of deer and rabbit. Most have bear skin coats and they stink." Annie shrugs, "Eee-ue, I can't imagine living like that." Mary says, "Viva la civilization (Viva the civilization.)"

They are anchored some distance from shore so any would-be perpetrator of mal intent would have to swim. Captain Dupree has an armed guard to stand watch during the night. As the last glimmer of light fades and the stars come out it gets quite chilly in the river valley under the cover of the West Virginia Mountains. They all retire to the main parlor for warm tea and a late snack of pastry. The night passes with the wonderful sounds of the forest and in the middle of the night at about three o'clock there is complete silence.

At daybreak you can hear the boiler coming to full steam as the steam vents release from time to time indicating the Louie Queen was ready to steam away. The children head for breakfast as Captain Dupree takes command in the wheelhouse. He orders

64

weigh anchor and then all-about to port. The Louie Queen comes about to steam out of the calm of the tributary and to again enter the mighty Ohio. It is on to Pittsburgh.

If the current was steady, they would reach Pittsburgh by noon and have Lunch at 'The Franklin,' Mary's favorite hotel. It was where they stayed as newlyweds. This is where they stayed while James laid plans for the building of the Louisville Queen in 1870. This is where Annie was conceived. They of course then moved to Louisville, Kentucky and rented a home for the two years it took to build the boat. On occasion James took Mary to Cincinnati the largest metropolis between Pittsburgh and St. Louis. James loved the hills of Cincinnati and wanted to settle somewhere outside the hustle and bustle of a big city. They of course chose Sailor Park and at that time only dreamt of building their dream house.

Mary had told Annie that Pittsburgh is where she had her beginning and that Louisville was where she was born. All the other children were born in Sailor Park. Mary remarked to Annie, "Perhaps that is why you have such a rousing spirit, because you were moved around too much when you were young." Annie returns, "I don't remember much mother; besides I don't have a rousing spirit just because I question things." Mary says, "No dear, I'm just teasing you, you are a lot like me in many ways. tu es comme ta mere; courageux (you are like your mother; courageous.)"

They were all standing on the upper deck as Captain Dupree commands the boat and docks in Pittsburgh and on the south side of the Alleghany River just beyond the junction of the Alleghany and

65

Monongahela rivers that form the Great Ohio. Once secure he gives instructions to First Officer William Tarkle. James and his family would not be back onboard for a week, so all responsibility for the Louis Queen lay with William. William remarks to Captain Dupree, "Ya know them coal salesmen will be harpin' on me to buy that damn coal." Dupree says adamantly, "You just stand your ground; coal just soot's up the smokestacks and blackens the sky. I don't like the smelly stuff. Just load on burly Oak and Poplar as always William."

All the trunks of clothing were off-loaded and a wagon and carriage were procured to carry them to the hotel. Mary had made sure that all the children were dressed and looking their best. Annie was giddy with excitement. She had never seen Pittsburgh or an opera. She wore a royal blue dress that was trimmed in white lace. Her hair was up as her mother had woven it in a swirl and pinned it with her tortoise shell combs. Leah Anna complained and explained that she gets to wear them next. Mary vowed to buy each of them a set of combs if she could find them and thus, she could have hers again for herself.

With a broad brim blue feathered hat and parasol to match this picture of loveliness disembarked the Louis Queen with poise and grace in Pittsburgh, to languish in a fine hotel; to dine and entertain. Annie and Leah Anna giggled all the way in the carriage to the hotel. It was just a half a mile from the dock to the hotel. Annie wanted to appear as a mature woman but could not help feeling giddy and childish with excitement.

The ride went past the shanty town that was near the river where most of the dock workers and poor lived. Annie was always dismayed and felt uncomfortable being well off and seeing poverty. She knew her good fortune and felt the protection afforded her by her parents. Captain Dupree was in his uniform and carried a pistol inside his coat. Robbery was not uncommon and self-protection was still the best way. Pittsburgh had a substantial police force but going from the docks to the downtown area where most of the police are, is a reason for caution.

They arrive at the Franklin. It is just two blocks from the Opera House. Mary especially enjoyed this hotel because it had a touch of Paris and was lavish in elegance. She knew it would cost them a lot but this was a once in a lifetime experience with her family. The children were all so grown and it would not be long till they were all gone. She harbored a quiet lament for she loved her children so. James likewise cherished his family and on this occasion no expense was too great. Their accommodations were ready and they were greeted in the carriageway by porters and the concierge.

They would be staying on the top floor of this six-story ornate building. The boys were fascinated to see an elevator. They had heard of them and were excited to ride all the way up. Annie and Leah Anna clutched their mother's arms with trepidation as this new-fangled contraption started up. Mary remarked that they did not have this thing when she and James stayed there so many years ago. Mary exclaimed, "Oh mon, attente sur les filles (Oh my, hold on girls,) as they went up. The boys said, "Wow!" James laughed and said, "It is better than walking up all those steps."

They arrived at the top and the door was opened by the operator. The girls, including Mary dashed off to the security of the floor, fearing this contraption might fall. Again James laughed while the boys thought it was great. James said, "Boys, you are going to see another marvel, the opera house has Edison's electric lights for the stage. That will be something to see." Annie said to her father, "Papa, I saw one in Cincinnati, it was amazing how it burned inside the glass with no smoke or anything. They said it was because the air can't get in and that it takes air to burn things but I still don't understand this electric stuff. James said, "It takes a dynamo to make the electricity and wires to carry it. A man showed me a dynamo and I felt the shock from the electric wires. It is like a machine that makes lightning and the wires carry the lightning into the glass bulb. It is really amazing. They tried to tell me I should put a dynamo on the Louie Queen but it costs too much money." Annie responded, "I like lamps and candles, I don't like all this new stuff." James said, "Well my dear, it is the way of the times, new things are happening everywhere."

They were shown to their rooms, the boys and the girls each had their own and of course Captain Dupree and Mary had the large suite. Each room had a separate room with a bathtub and vanity and mirrors everywhere. They all had lavish French furniture and beds; it was a dream. The boys were bouncing on the beds when their father came in, "Boys, tomorrow in the afternoon I'm going to take you to a baseball game. I heard the Pittsburgh Allegany's are playing against our home boys the Cincinnati Red Stockings. You boys play baseball but now you can see some real pros play. It is quite a site. They throw the ball so fast you can't even see it. James Jr said, "Wow papa, can we maybe get a new glove or maybe a bat or ball?" James senior replied while ribbing both Marcus and James in the side, "I'll get both of you a glove, a new bat and a ball, how's that?" They both jumped to grab their father with joy and James Jr responded, "This is a real bang of a vacation, the best dad." Captain Dupree did not spoil his boys but at times he let them know how much he appreciated them.

The girls opened their trunk and unpacked their clothes and then knocked on the door of their parent's suite. Mary answered, "Oui mes chéris (Yes my darlings)." Leah Anna and Annie asked if they could come see the view from their balcony. They were dressed in cool summer white. Mary said, "Yes, but don't hang over the railing or make a spectacle of yourselves." Annie thought to herself, *'they were six floors up, who could even see them. Mother is such a prude protecting us so.'* The boys came too; it was such a sight with all the busyness in the street, what a thrill.

Captain Dupree and Mary relaxed with a glass of sherry compliments of the hotel. Annie joined them while Leah Anna pouted being considered too young to indulge. So Leah Anna taunted the boys, "Let's go ride the elevator to the lobby and get some candy." Mary gave them a dollar and off they went, leaving Annie with the adults. She wanted to go but fought her girlish nature to stay and enjoy her maturity and the glass of sherry in the midafternoon. Annie says to her mother, "What will we do while the men are at the baseball game mother? Surely, we do not have to go watch a bunch of sweaty men throw a ball around all afternoon." Mary laughs, "Aucun mon cher (No my dear.) I will take you and Leah Anna shopping. There

69

are some most amazing shops just down the street. You will love it." Annie sighs with relief, "Oh, thank you mother. No offence papa, baseball is for men." James smiles, "No offence taken, I just want to burn some of the boy's energy."

The rest of the first day was spent about the hotel. They had dinner in the beautiful dining room and took a stroll in the park just opposite the hotel in the evening as the sun went down. It was uncommonly cool for this July evening and they all enjoyed the breeze and the sound of locusts fading, and the rise of the crickets chirping, and still the occasional firefly appeared. The gas streetlamps were being lit and the sound of busy Pittsburgh quieted for the night.

The sleep was wonderful in the plush beds and they all rose early. Breakfast was brought to the balcony where they all dined while overlooking the view. The Alleghany could be seen as fog lifted off the river by the warm summer sun rising which produced a pink, orange and red color in the fog. They chatted about the plans of the day. The opera would be the following day in the evening. James had received a program of the opera delivered by courier and Mary was perusing through the pages. The opera will be an adaptation for Giuseppe Verdi's 'Rigoletto'. Mary remarks that she knows one of the singers in a supporting role. James says that Mary should visit the opera house which is just two blocks away and visit her acquaintance while they are out shopping. Mary agrees and then begins to tell Annie the story of Rigoletto since she is aspiring to be an actress. All the children listen as Mary tells the story, "Rigoletto is a hunchback jester in the court of the licentious Duke of Mantua. Rigoletto keeps his beautiful daughter Gilda in hiding only allowing her to stay at home and go to church in an attempt to protect her virtue from the duke who seduces every woman that catches his eye." Annie laughs, "It sounds like men to me." Mary shushes her and says, "Just listen to the story." Mary continues, "Rigoletto openly jests and mocks the women the duke seduces and the nobleman of Mantua do not appreciate either the Duke or Rigoletto. They gossip that Rigoletto has a lover, to which no one can believe that this ugly man could possibly have a lover. It is mistakenly Rigolettos' daughter. Count Monterones' daughter was one of the dukes conquests and vows to take vengeance on both the Duke and Rigoletto. Upon hearing of Monterones' vow of vengeance, the duke has Count Monterone arrested. Monterone places a curse on both the Duke and Rigoletto and Rigoletto takes this curse very seriously. Gilda had been so secluded by her father that she did not even know what her father did for a living or even the name that he goes by.

An unscrupulous man named Sparafucile, who is secretly an assassin for hire, offers his services to Rigoletto knowing of the curse. Rigoletto refuses him so Sparafucile admonishes him that they are the same and thus chides Rigoletto and says 'I Sparafucile kill with the sword but Rigoletto kills with his words.'

The duke now knows of Rigoletto's beautiful daughter which he thinks is Rigoletto's lover and he pretends to be a student at the church so he can woo her with his cunning. Thus Gilda falls in love with the duke.

71

The Noblemen fool Rigoletto into assisting them with the abduction of the countess Ceprano, one of the dukes courtesans, when in fact they are going to abduct who they think is Rigoletto's lover but is really Gilda." Anne interrupts, "These men are so wicked mother, is this then the opera?" Mary says, "Calme maintenant, écouter (Quiet now, listen.) They blindfold Rigoletto who thinks he is bait in order to lure the countess to come to his aid to free him. It is rather Gilda who comes in and the noblemen abduct her. Rigoletto over time comes to know the truth, that it was his daughter who was abducted. He collapses in anguish and remembers the curse placed on him by Count Monterone."

"The duke discovers that Gilda was stolen away and the noblemen present her to the duke as Rigoletto's' lover; they are still unknowing she is Rigoletto's daughter. The duke seduces Gilda and has his way with her." Annie says, "Stupid girl." Mary raises her hand as if to say just wait and she continues, "Rigoletto tries to get to his daughter to save her from the wiles of the duke and the noblemen beat Rigoletto as he pleads, 'It is my daughter not my lover.' Rigoletto reaches Gilda too late and Gilda tells him of her love for the duke. He now swears vengeance against the duke and in a beautiful duet between Rigoletto and his daughter, he sings of vengeance while she sings pleading for her lover the duke." Annie laughs, "Truly she is a fool."

Mary smacks Annie's hand, "Il vous suffit d'écouter, (Just listen.) The best is yet to come and the music and singing is wonderful. Now this horrible Duke seduces Maddalena the sister of Sparafucile the assassin and the duke sings an aria about the fickle

72

nature of women while Rigoletto tries to convince Gilda that the duke is vile. Rigoletto then bargains with Sparafucile to kill the duke. He orders Gilda to dress in men's clothes and to sneak away to Verona during the night and he would follow later. Gilda still loves the duke in spite of his unfaithfulness. Maddalena pleads with her brother Sparafucile to spare the duke. Sparafucile sings that he must provide Rigoletto with a corpse and that if he can find another victim any corpse will do. Gilda learns of the plot of her father to kill the duke and decides to try to intervene before he is killed. Dressed as a man she enters Sparafuciles' chamber Maddalena is pleading with him to spare the duke. Sparafucile seeing a strange man entering his chamber mortally wounds Gilda. Sparafucile wraps the corpse in a sack. Then Rigoletto comes to pay Sparafucile and nothing is said. Rigoletto sings and rejoices that he has the body of the duke which he is going to sink in the river with rocks. Rigoletto, about to complete the dastardly deed hears the duke singing a reprise of 'La donna è mobile' in the distance and is confused. He opens the sack to discover his daughter mortally wounded but still alive and he weeps as she dies in his arms.

Annie just says, "Stupid girl to love such a horrible man." The boys are astonished at their mothers' knowledge of the opera and Marcus asks, "How do you know all of this mother?" Mary replies, "It is not a new opera. They were doing it all over Europe twenty-five years ago. I saw it in Paris just before I met your father." Leah Anna says, "It is so sad." Mary says, "Yes, but the music is fabulous and that is what opera is all about, the singing and the passion." Annie says, "It is always the women who

73

suffer." Mary says, "Antoinette, ne soyez pas si grave (don't be so serious,) you will enjoy seeing the production." Annie says, "Yes of course mother."

The girls get ready for their shopping as James and the boys head off for the ball game. They would have lunch at the playfield and the ladies would lunch near the theater.

It worked out so well, Mary found her friend Louisa Palmonti. She was an Italian woman that she had worked with in Paris. This was a great opportunity because they all got to go backstage to see the production firsthand. Annie was enthralled and delighted to see all the makings of a real production. Leah Anna was also inspired though she had no interest in acting. They visited the dressing rooms and saw the scenery and the many costumes and props. It was fascinating seeing such a big production. Annie knew that acting was what she wanted to do and she was so encouraged. Louisa told them of her travels and she and Mary reminisced. Annie was glued to the conversation and was amazed to know of her mothers' worldliness. She saw her mother as a professional woman and was so proud. Now, Annie could not wait to see the opera in its entirety even if she did not like the plot of the play.

That evening at dinner in the hotel the conversation was fun. The boys told of the game and showed off their gifts. They each received a ball cap with the emblem of the Cincinnati Red Stockings. Mary had found the tortoise shell combs for the girls which they were wearing. They talked about the backstage visit to the opera house. Captain Dupree was pleased that Mary had found her friend and that they got to go behind the scene. Mary was also delighted. It made their visit to Pittsburgh just that much more.

They retired for the day after a stroll in the park for tomorrow was the opera. They would spend the day lounging and bathing and preparing for the event. It would be completely formal for this evening affair. All the men would be in top hat and tales of which the captain instructed his sons as to how they should carry themselves. The ladies would dress in black also with trims in white lace and they would wear knit shawls and carry a small bouquet of fresh flowers. They were hoping for a cool evening because corsets were a must. They only had a light snack for dinner because they would attend the reception for the players after the opera and there they would dine.

At precisely seven o'clock their carriage arrived to take them to the theater. What a lovely picture this was. The entire family looked superb. The evening was indeed cool because clouds had come in that threatened rain. The ladies with their hair done up so exquisitely were concerned. James calmed them saying, "The carriage men have umbrellas so don't worry." It was only two blocks to the opera house but it would not be fitting to walk on such an evening as this and Captain Dupree wanted to arrive with all the pomp that was due these beautiful women and young men.

They were lighting the gas street lights early; because of the cloud cover it was already dark as they arrived at the Pittsburgh opera house. It was a sold-out performance and quite crowded. Annie was enjoying the scene as they entered. James had reserved a box seat just to the right of the stage. They had time to gaze at all the audience and of course the girls were commenting on the many beautiful gowns the ladies were dressed in. Shortly the ushers dimmed the house gas lamps and the orchestra began to play the prelude. Annie could feel goose bumps on her arms. She was enthralled.

Then the electric lights came on and shone on the curtain. Everyone let out an ooh because the lights were colored with filters of red and blue and green. The boys were fascinated and quizzed their father more about the dynamo and how it worked. Mary shushed everyone as the curtain rose. The opera began.

Annie clutched her mother's arm at times during this fabulous production. She was so amazed at her mothers' account of the play and how well she knew it. Though it was in Italian Mary would whisper and explain each aria and its meaning. When the intermission came the porters brought Champaign for the adults and sweet soda water for the children. Annie again to Leah Anna's dismay got to sip Champaign. When Mary wasn't looking Annie poured some into Leah Anna's glass which made Leah Anna happy. Of course Mary saw but said nothing, it was a special night.

The opera resumed and everything was as Mary had said. With Rigoletto's final solo and the death of Gilda, the girls wept, what else could they do. The curtain fell and the applause was deafening. The performers made their curtain call and flowers were presented to Gilda and then more flowers were thrown to the stage. It was wonderful.

They lingered a while in the booth remarking about different points in the performance. The boys were fidgety after having sat for so long and were anxious to go to the reception because they were hungry. James had them wait a while so the crowd could clear and then they headed for the main entrance, out the mezzanine to the carriageway. It was no surprise; it was raining but not heavily. They stood in line with the patrons of the opera each waiting for the next carriage. When it was their turn, they moved to the curb for boarding. As they were about to enter the carriage, a woman poorly dressed and with a shawl over her head came from out of the darkness with her hand covered with a glove outstretched as if to beg for money. A constable came up behind her and with his night stick, tapped her on the shoulder and said, "Move on miss, no trouble here." She was startled and she lurched backward. She tripped on the curb and fell catching herself with her gloved hand. Her shawl fell from her face while her hand began to bleed through the glove. It could be seen that she had sores around her mouth. Annie gasped and reached to help her. Mary grabbed Annie and James yelled, "Don't touch her!" James himself reached down to lift her by the arm and said quietly, "She has syphilis. She's contagious." Mary helps James lift her up, being careful to only touch her clothing. The police officer says to the woman, "You shouldn't be begging on the street, go now and leave these folks alone." Annie ruffles and shows her true color. She takes her father by the arm and with an insistence that would not be refused, "Father, take her to the hospital." James hesitates for a moment and Annie looks him in the eye and says only, "Papa." She gave him a look that no father could refuse. Captain Dupree commands, "Boys, take Leah Anna and get the next carriage. Go to the hotel and wait for us there." James takes the woman and helps her into the carriage. Mary and Annie follow. James instructs the driver to take them to the infirmary. Annie weeps and reaches into her purse and grabs a handful of her few dollar bills and gives it to the woman who takes it with her other gloved hand. She cups the money in her lap and says through her blistered mouth, "Thank-you."

James says to her, "The hospital will cost money and I'm sure you don't... Annie interrupts her father, "Papa, this is not the time to talk about money, she is bleeding." Captain Dupree just shuts up. He knows he will pay for it or his 'Florence Nightingale' daughter would never forgive him. Annie occasionally quoted Miss Nightingale from her studies at school. Annie just sat in silence and looked pitifully at the woman who is sobbing also. They arrived at the infirmary and took the woman inside. They were received by a nurse who sent an attendant for a doctor. Shortly the doctor came and looked over the woman. The doctor said they could patch her up and let her rest for the night but that there was not much they could do because her disease was advanced. James asked how much it would cost and he was obliged to pay. They placed her in a wheelchair and while against her mothers' wishes, Annie touches the woman on the shoulder, she takes more money she had pilfered from her father and places it in the woman's hand with the other money she was still cradling. Annie then smiles at her saying, "I pray you will be well; I hope this will help a little."

They departed the hospital to return to the hotel. They sat in the carriage in silence. They will not attend the reception. Annie only said, "Thank-you father," as she wept. Mary held Annie's hand and patted it lightly. She knew the depth to which Annie hurt and her feminine anger against promiscuity knowing that poor woman was a prostitute. She knew her daughter was all bottled up with emotion and passion and confusion. Mary knew that her husband would have taken the woman to the hospital because he was a generous man but Annie had responded by instinct and spoke so fast that others could only follow her lead. Her nature and spark was tenacious and Mary feared that this could lead to a troubled life and that Annie would always be wrestling with things beyond her control.

The next day was somber. There were no plans. Leah Anna and the boys went to the park. Annie sat with her parents on the balcony. Mary wrote a thank-you card to Louisa explaining why they did not attend the reception. James was reading about electric lights and dynamos and Annie chatted with her mother. They had not talked yet about the incident the night before but Mary was waiting and knew Annie would start in. Finally Annie could not resist, "Women don't have much else if they don't get married except working in a garment factory for low wages or changing bed pans as a nurse." Mary just listens. "I mean, maybe she can be a baker or cleaning woman but be a doctor or engineer or boat captain," she looks at her father, "I think not. Women aren't allowed. It troubles me as we read in school, Florence Nightingale does not think women want anything other than common jobs. We read her paper; she said 'men were better suited than women to lead in complex jobs; She says women want a soft life and that she cannot find enough women to train for all the need there is for nurses. Well, excuse me, I do not want blood and guts all my life, but I sure do not expect a soft life. Not that I would trust a woman to be a boat captain," this time smiling at her father who looks up from his reading, "I realize that there are some things that woman cannot do but there are a lot of things that women are prevented from doing." Mary says rhetorically, "Do you think that poor woman had syphilis because she lacked opportunity Annie? I'm sure you are not that naive." Annie responds, "Given the right situation, if you have no education and you are alone and hungry what would you do mother?" Mary answers, "Not that dear, I would find some other way." Annie says, "That is because you are educated and intelligent, not everyone has that ability. I'm sure if, -God forbid- we took the time to hear that woman's story you would find that she was not very smart or privileged and that is when unscrupulous men take advantage." Mary returns, "Men get syphilis too dear; they get their punishment just the same. It is promiscuity dear. In Paris they do the Cancan. The girls hike their dresses and the men flock to spend their money to see it." Annie gasps, "Mother I know, please don't talk about this in front of my father." Annie blushes: James laughs and adds, "Annie the difference is staying faithful to your beloved and not acting like a dog in heat with every bitch on the street." Annie again gasps and blushes and retorts, "Papa, please don't call them bitches, that is foul, but I will agree on the term dogs." James scowls and returns to this reading.

Annie continues, "Syphilis is such a horrible disease, as bad as leprosy and people die such a horrible death. There is no cure and more and more people are getting that terrible thing." Mary says,

80

"Just live a good life and you have nothing to fear, that is all people have to do." Annie returns, "But, don't you think something should be done to change people?" James interjects as he stands and kisses Mary on the cheek, "You cannot save the world Annie, you just need to take care that you live right. I'm going to leave you ladies to talk. I'll find the kids in the park if you don't mind?" Annie apologizes, "Papa, I did not mean to run you off." "Not at all dear, talk to your mother." James pats Annie on the shoulder and leaves them alone. Mary had picked-up on James' intent to say, "Straighten her out."

Annie continues, "That poor woman was only in her thirties and she is sure to soon die a horrible death." Mary sighs, "Oh mon cher Coeur (Oh my dear heart,) I got to this country in eighteen seventy, just five years after the civil war. It was horrible, the devastation with wounded men missing limbs and graveyards spanning the outskirts of every town along the Ohio. The wounds of that war are still here and the people are still fighting it over and over again. It seems it will never end. We do the best we can and live what we believe is right and we cope with the rest. I fear you take too much upon yourself." Annie leans forward in her chair, "Oh mother, I'm no worse for wear. I just think sometimes I should be a nurse or a teacher or something to help instead of just being an actress, playing my life away and never facing the many problems."

Mary consoles her, "You have more than enough time to do many things. Youth is for playing and so you will never say I wish I would have done this or that." Mary laughs, "And then you can be a nurse later after your beauty is gone." Annie laughs,

"Who me, I will always be beautiful like you." Mary swoons with a stroke of her hair and a sheepish look, "Moi, Oh au contraire (Me, oh to the contrary.)" Annie moves over to sit beside her mother in the love seat she was in and hugs her, "I'm going to be a political writer and convince everyone they should listen to me." Mary laughs, "Now you are really asking for trouble." Annie retorts, "Well, at least until women get to vote so we can help tell these brutish men what for." Mary hugs Annie back, "All men are not brutes." Annie agrees, "They should all be like papa."

Mary and Annie decide to join the others in the park. Just one more day and they would board the Louie Queen and head back to Cincinnati.

More than an Education

The journey home to Cincinnati was pleasurable and did not take as long because it was down river with the current moving them along quickly. James stayed only one other day and put the Louisville Queen back on schedule to Mary's dismay. It had been such a wonderful time on their vacation. The rest of the summer Annie, Leah Anna and the boys played like they were kids with tennis and fishing and bike riding. The girls helped their mother with cooking and sewing and the boys were given painting jobs around the house. August was hot and uncomfortable and on occasion they would all sleep in the upper floor of the mansion because the breeze was better. By September the nights on the Ohio cooled down considerably and it was a welcome relief. On September the fifteenth Annie would return to school in Cincinnati. Leah Anna and the boys were already attending the local High School which started on September fifteen.

Mary was decorating the house with dried flowers and ribbons of brown and orange for the joy of the fall and harvest time and Halloween coming up in October. She so loved the fall because it meant James would be home by late November and all that winter. Annie would be home for Thanksgiving and stay through Christmas but for now she was anxious to get back to school and studies. Mary saw her to the train and she was off. Annie looked more like a woman every day and Mary knew that soon she would lose her little girl to the world.

Like a true debutant Annie arrived in the city greeted by carriage men and porters to haul her trunks and escort her to the boarding school. Madam Rousseau greeted her personally, "Bien Mlle Dupree, comment était votre été? (Well Miss Dupree, how was your summer?) Annie rolls her eyes and smiles, "Bonjour Madame Rousseau, C'était merveilleux. (It was wonderful.) We went to see Giuseppe Verdi's Rigoletto in Pittsburgh." Madam Rousseau gasps, "Oh mon Coeur, (Oh my heart,) it is so sad in the end. The poor man lost his only love, his daughter." Annie chides, "I loved the production but the portrayal of a stupid girl falling in love with a pig of a man made me ill." Madam Rousseau laughs, "Aucun stupide filles ici. (No stupid girls here.) Here we learn the best ways to protect your virtue so the world will know the finest and most intelligent women Miss Antoinette." Madam Rousseau always called Annie by her proper name. She was a stately woman and always a model of formality which she considered her purpose. Annie went along with all the pomp and learned all the formality and grace expected of her at her mother's behest but always under her breath and not spoken was her rebelliousness and sarcasm. This was her way of maintaining a sense of truth that lies beneath all the circumstance and pretentiousness. Annie was a pragmatic realist and though she teased herself with humor she really was not laughing inside. Like her mother said, 'she was too serious,' but her observations were unavoidable.

Annie got settled in and reunited with her fellow schoolmates. One friend in particular, she was delighted to see. From down the hall in the dormitory Annie yells, "Shannon Aileen Brennan yar lookin' like a shamrock wid dem green eyes you are." Annie was trying to mimic Shannon's Irish accent. Shannon yells back, "None the likes of your French ass all dark and sexy aye?" Shannon had a mouth on her and her parents hoped the finishing school would put some polish on this flaming Irish girl. She was from a wealthy family and spoiled. She had reddish blond hair, blue eyes and with a thin frame she was tall and striking. She came running at Annie and grabbed her with a big hug. Annie likewise squeezed her and said, "You'll stop that cursing or we'll beat it out of you girl." Shannon laughs, "They'll soap my bitch's mouth but that won't get dirt out of my brain." They ducked into Annie's room and fell on the bed laughing and shushing each other for fear that someone would hear.

Annie and Shannon were a team, a 'tour de force' of feminine ideas. Shannon perhaps was a bad influence on Annie because by herself Annie was reserved, but with Shannon she was more outspoken and she liked the way Shannon was so bold. She wanted to be like her, sassy and unafraid. Shannon pushed things to the edge and at the same age as Annie of twenty-one she was already a drinker from an Irish family where whisky was just part of life.

They shared their stories of the summer and Annie told her about Ben Hamilton. Shannon says, "He sounds like my kind of man, so if you're not going to use him, you could push him my way." Annie laughs, "You had better want babies and be prepared to stay home because that is what he wants." Shannon replies, "You sure ain't doin' that are ya' lass?" Shannon knows Annie well and her position on marriage and pregnancy; she continues, "You just swell up like a balloon and pop the little ones out, it's no big deal, your hips are made for it. My mama had us three and says it's easy after the first one. Anyway, I can see myself as a mother after I've sewn my wild oats. Not now but later and you can't wait too long or you'll end up an old maid. No man will want." Annie ruffles, "Then fine, no man will want me. I'm not going to swell up like a balloon and pop anything out of my belly; my belly is going to stay where it is." Annie hits Shannon with a pillow and likewise Shannon does the same saying, "You will change, I only hope it is not too late." Annie screams, "Argh, everyone keeps saying that you-will-change, all of you are making me crazy."

Annie grabs Shannon by the hand and pulls her to the window overlooking the busy street, "See all those people milling around and doing what they do? In the back of their mind, especially men, are their secret thoughts of sex. You can tell, when a man is talking to you, he is really thinking, 'I'd like to have her in the grass out back behind the shed.'" Annie had lowered her voice acting as a man. Shannon smacks Annie's butt, "Now tell me you're not thinking the same thing you sexy girl. I know you; you've got that look that drives men wild and you just play coy. Tell me you do it to yourself." Annie says, "What?" Shannon repeats, "Do it to yourself; masturbate you silly. Awe, you don't have to tell me. You do it, everybody does it." Annie smiles and with another attempt to sound Irish says, "None that I'll be tellin' the likes of you girl." Annie pushes Shannon away while with a blush in her cheeks and smirking grin Shannon could see her confession. Shannon seizes the moment and, in a whisper, "How do you do it?" Not waiting for an answer, "I use a rough candle. I hide it in my dresser." Annie, with and uncontrollable laugh covers her mouth with both hands to silence her outburst. Her squelched laugh backed up into her nose and with a nasal wrenching she blurts out with a gushing whisper, "Shannon Aileen Brennan, I don't need to hear this. Now I have this image in my head of you doing it." Shannon cannot stop herself, she giggles and chides, "And, where do you hide your candle Miss Antoinette Marie Dupree?" Annie says, "Stop; that is enough out of you."

With that they hear Madam Rousseau coming up the stairs. Madam Rousseau always announced herself as she came up knowing that all the girls, ten in all, would scramble to hide their secrets. Some had liquor; some had hidden sweets and most had secret letters for boys. She could hear the scampering as she arrived on the second floor of the boarding school. All the girls sensibly appear at the door of their individual rooms that enter on to the main hallway. Madam Rousseau begins, "Ladies, and from now on that is what you will be, ladies; the rest of the day you have to yourselves. Get settled and prepared for tomorrow and at seven o'clock sharp you are to be at breakfast already bathed and ready for a good day. At eight o'clock we will meet in the theater parlor where I will give you your curriculum for the fall semester. Madam Rousseau was walking down the hall in the most poised manner with her hands folded and arms bent at the elbow. You could see as she walked a marked grace to her pace. She was in her mid-forties. She had dark brown hair done up in a braid and always dressed impeccably. She was attractive and anything but demure. The girls all wondered, since she was not married, if perhaps she preferred the company of women. She turned at the end of the hall and then strolled back to the stairs, "So, good evening, ladies and be sharp and all together early tomorrow." With that she departed down the stairs.

The young ladies went about their business. Annie elbows Shannon lightly, "I wonder where she hides her candle." Shannon snickers, elbows Annie in return, "Now you've got it girl."

All the girls have dinner in the large kitchen rather than the dining room. Madam Rousseau felt it gave them a more home-like feel. She did not attend the dinner but rather went out with a friend. It was intentional to allow the young ladies to be unencumbered and to get to know each other again after the long summer. It was warm and cozy in the kitchen with the late September evenings turning quite cool. They were to have soup and roasted chicken with baked potatoes and fresh bread. They were cared for very well by Madam Rousseau's staff. Their life was one of comfort and Annie knew it. On the other hand Shannon had always been well-to-do and while Annie lived comfortably, she knew Shannon was just a rich girl with expectations. Annie would help the staff set the table and cut the bread and so forth and so did most of the girls but Shannon would not. She would rather sit and stroke her long hair while others did the work. She didn't even notice this as uncommon. That was the way it was at her home; she was waited on.

Annie says, "Shannon, if you're not going to help then sit out of the way so we can get the table set." Shannon smiles, "Don't go on with me Annie, you will never get anywhere serving if you intend to be served. It is the upper crust you know dear." Shannon was teasing, "At least that is what my

88

mother says; you must have expectations or be left behind." With that Annie sits down to the table which was now set and says, "There, I did my part, and I expect you will now do yours and that is to be served. Sit my dear and let's eat."

All the girls laughed and sat down. All of them were debutantes from substantially well-off homes and they were served. Miss Ellery, Madam Rousseau's assistant joined them at the head of the table. She was in her late twenties and she fit in well with the girls. She enjoyed listening in on all the gossip while always being a liaison for Madam Rousseau. Miss Ellery, reaching out with both hands says, "Now ladies, hold hands and let us say grace." They all join hands and Miss Ellery gives thanks, "Dear father in heaven, watch over us and bless this house, bring to each of us your divine will and help us to be our best in all our endeavors. Thank-you for the meal we are about to receive in your Holy name, Amen" The girls all say Amen and Shannon lightly kicks Annie who is sitting beside her and says, "I wonder where she hides her candle." Annie snickers and the girl next to Shannon on the other side says, "What candle?" Shannon says, "You would not understand, never mind."

Dinner is finished and all the girls retired to the dorm rooms and take turns in the two bathrooms at the end of the hall. They were served fresh hot water for each in turn. The evening was a bustle with each lady showing off their clothes and accruements of jewelry. Then exhaustion set in and the lights dimmed. Tomorrow came early.

The theater parlor was for many purposes. It had a stage with a curtain for small plays. There was a ballet wall with support rails and mirrors. The main floor was waxed hardwood which was for training in formal ballroom dancing. They had folding chairs that were racked to the side for when guests and parents would come for visits.

The girls arrive sharply at eight o'clock after breakfast and Madam Rousseau begins, "Ladies, each of you take a chair and place it near the stage in a straight row." Shannon whispers to Annie as she drags her chair, "This thing is too heavy." Indeed they were heavy oak chairs that were cumbersome to move because of the way they folded. Annie whispers back, "You are such a sissy Shannon." They get arranged and sit down. Shannon and Annie are always together. Shannon whispers again, "I'm not going to do any exercises this year. Last year, that stupid medicine ball she made us throw made my arms have muscles. I don't want muscle bulges in my arms." Annie whispers, "They say it firms the breasts." Shannon who was pleased with her endowment looks at her chest and says, "Nope, not me, their just fine the way they are. I don't need them any firmer, but you could use a little help." Annie shushes Shannon, "Mine are just fine, now be quiet."

Madam Rousseau goes up on the stage, "Quiet down now ladies. Miss Ellery, will you please pass out the curriculum?" Miss Ellery gives each of the girls a leather-bound tablet. In it was the curriculum and pages for note taking. She continues, "This semester we will focus on the romance languages, their origins and how they relate to each other. I don't expect you to become fluent in all but only to learn some phrases. We will cover Spanish, French, and Italian and of course English. We will do translations of each. We will start each morning with exercises to get your blood moving. With this Shannon lightly kicks Annie who whispers, "Stop kicking me, you're going to cause a bruise. I know you don't want to exercise." Madam Rousseau who is as smart as a fox says, "Shannon you can bring the girls water since I know exercising is beneath you." Shannon blushes and all the girls laugh. They think Shannon is a tart and most of the girls won't deal with her. Shannon does not care. She is going to do what she wants and nothing more and Annie likes that.

Madam Rousseau continues, "Exercise, then language and then mathematics before lunch. After lunch there will be practice in public speaking and then we will study art history till three in the afternoon. Then we will work on our seasonal play to be presented before Thanksgiving." She looks again at Shannon and says, "After dinner, those of you who don't mind exercise can join Miss Ellery in ballet lessons. I of course will teach ballroom dancing until eight in the evening. This should make you exquisitely tired for a good night's rest."

Shannon whispers, "Slave driver. I can't believe my parents pay to have me tortured. All this just so I can catch a rich man." Annie whispers, "Not me girl, I want this so I can get into the theater and travel." Shannon is getting Madam Rousseau's attention again because she keeps talking. Shannon goes on, "My parents asked me if I wanted to go to Europe. I don't need the theater to go travel. I could ask them if they would send both of us together. I'm sure they would. Then we could go have some fun."

Madam Rousseau announces, "Alright ladies, return your chairs to the rack and go to the library. Shannon, you carry Antoinette's chair too since that is the only exercise you will get today." Shannon says, "Awe, now she is picking on me," but she grabs both chairs and drags them across the floor notably showing her disgust. Annie follows her and helps her put the chairs on the rack. They head to the library and begin their language studies. The day progresses nicely with Annie waiting patiently for the theater practice. Madam Rousseau announced that they would be doing a short play based on Louisa May Alcott's 'Little Women,' as you remember, last year we performed 'A Woman's Place' by Professor William Horton. This year I thought it would be good to honor a female author and since you read the novel last year the story should be fresh in your mind. We have four main characters you can all read for; I will pick who gets what part. There is Margaret the oldest, Josephine the second eldest; Elizabeth is next and of course you know she dies and then there is Amy who is the youngest." Madam Rousseau turns to Shannon, "Shannon, I would like you to read first for the part of Elizabeth, because she is demure and this will require you to really act, because you are anything but demure."

Shannon whispers to Annie just before taking the stage, "She is picking on me again." She takes the stage and Madam Rousseau instructs her to sit in a rocking chair that was placed center stage, "Now Shannon, turn to page two hundred and ten and begin with the passage where Beth (Elizabeth) is adoring her room and all her favorite things as she is getting weaker from her illness and how even her sewing needle has become too heavy to lift. Shannon turns to the page and skims it over. She knew the story very well and she gets in character and begins to read, "Jo, (Josephine) I have so been pleased that you have tended over me these many years. Thank you for collecting all my favorite things here in my room. I still read fathers books and I love Amy's sketches and I so enjoy watching all the children from my window. My dear, take my embroider hoop for me, my needle even feels heavy these days." Shannon mimes handing away the sewing things and leans her head back in the rocking chair and rolls her eyes in a weak gesture and rather than read for the play she recites a quote from Shakespeare's Hamlet, "I'm dying Horacio, I'm dying." All the girls laugh at Shannon's mockery and blatant over acting.

Madam Rousseau chuckles a bit herself and then quickly regains her composure, "Shannon, you were quite good up to the point you turned into a comic. Beth is the most passionate and loving character in the entire story. It is by her that the other girls so cherish and respect their on lives. I think this will be a good part for you, I want you to get inside Beth's character." Shannon accedes and agrees. She does not really want to be an actress but she enjoys pretending and being in the play. All the girls take their turn reading for the various parts. Annie wanted so much to play the part of Josephine (Jo) who is the most instrumental and outstanding character. Though Annie was not the tomboy that Jo was supposed to be, her acting ability really showed when she got into character. She especially like the feminist stance the character portrayed in that Josephine chose a male companion in Professor Bhaer who was strong yet tender and intimate while respecting a woman's individually. Madam Rousseau agreed. Annie would play Josephine.

The evening came and Annie did some ballet exercises with Miss Ellery. Annie believed the exercises helped strengthen her legs and benefited her with her poise on stage. Shannon did the ballroom dancing with Madam Rousseau. Shannon kept an eye on Annie as she went through the many stretches and bends of ballet as if looking at Annie's body was a more prurient interest. Annie was aware of Shannon's gaze and likewise was Madam Rousseau. Annie also saw that Madam Rousseau saw what she saw and thus all three knew as Shannon had revealed her fascination with Annie. Shannon had enjoyed seeing Annie play the tomboy in her reading earlier that afternoon. Though Annie was the picture of femininity, Shannon saw Annie's ability at role playing and somehow Shannon found that enticing. Shannon's personality was like a sharp edge cutting through the quick to the bone. She had it all figured out. Her striking beauty was a gift she did not take lightly and she knew that she could bend the rules of society and with cunning she could rule her realm, both with men and with women. Madam Rousseau adored these girls and though her wisdom harbored her very own secrets unrevealed, her mission was to protect and guide them.

The evening is at a close and the ladies return to the dorm for bathing and relaxing and they knew that the morning would come early and that Madam Rousseau would not tolerate tardiness. Exhausted they fall fast to sleep. Shannon roused in the middle of the night and at about three o'clock she tip toed to

Annie's room. Quietly entering she moved to the chair by the window and sat. In the moonlight she could see Annie sleeping and she watched. It was about a half hour when Annie turned in her bed and saw the silhouette of Shannon in the moonlight. Annie startled but quickly saw the blue-white glow on Shannon's hair and knew it was her, "What are you doing here?" Annie inquires. Shannon replies, "I couldn't sleep." "Aren't you exhausted?" Shannon breathes a deep sigh and whispers, "No, I didn't exercise like you. You see, exercise just makes you tired and old too fast."

Annie wakes and sits up a bit, "Shannon, what am I going to do with you?" Shannon sarcastically says, "I'm dying Horatio, I'm dying." Annie yawns, "What do you mean dear?" Shannon says, "Don't you just think that life will pass you by so quickly and you won't get to know and do all the things you want to do, and how you have to give up one thing to get another when you really want both, and if you wait or make a hasty decision you will have to live with it forever, how you can't decide what you want to do and if you don't hurry up you will be too old too fast." Annie now fully awake and caught by Shannon's epiphany, "Shannon, my word, I could have never guessed that you were so troubled. You seem so Laissez-faire about everything. What is bothering you girl?" Shannon whispers, "Life is happening too fast and I don't know what I want." Annie responds quickly, "None of us do, we just live day by day." Shannon leans in a bit, "I can feel my parents want me to get married and get out of the house, it is like they are hurrying me and I don't know if I want that. Your parents know you don't want to be married but mine will never accept that. They talk all the time about grandchildren and how wonderful it will be." Annie consoles her, "Can't you just talk to them." Shannon places her elbows on her knees and places her head in her hands shaking no, "My parents are strict Catholics and that is that. You get married, have children and christen them in the church. What is worse is that I think I am like Madam Rousseau." Annie says, "What do you mean?"

Shannon leans back in the moon light, "Oh come on Annie; Madam Rousseau likes women. She has no husband and never will have." Annie with understanding, "Oh, and you think you want that too, do you like girls more than boys." Shannon ruffles in a whisper, "Oh, don't be patronizing. Isn't it obvious to you that I like both and that I feel awkward and out of place?" Annie said, "No, but now that you mention it, it makes sense as to why you are so rebellious. I know the feeling that if society can't accept you the way you are then there is something wrong with society. We are on a crusade to change what people think and I fear we will be martyred for our lost cause." Annie is showing her exhaustion slipping back down in her pillow. Shannon cannot help herself, "Do you like the company of women Annie?" Annie smiles at Shannon, "I've thought about it. I think I like men most but I don't think I can do what is expected of me and I wonder if that will leave me alone for all my life and perhaps that leaves me with only one choice, to find a woman who shares my concern. I don't know Shannon; I'm too tired to talk."

Shannon says, "You are in my head exactly, you do know what I am feeling." Annie says, "Bon, maintenant passer en mode de veille (good, now go to

96

sleep.) Shannon sees that as an invitation, "May I lie down beside you to sleep? Otherwise I'll talk all night?" Annie about to fall off says, "Yes, yes, come on, sleep." Shannon slips into bed with Annie and feeling the comfort of her body she falls fast asleep. Morning came and before anyone awoke Shannon quietly goes back to her room leaving Annie with a kiss on her cheek. Annie adored Shannon and with all her mixed feelings she had no fear of her and knew that whatever the future brought, they would always, always be entwined.

The schedule at the school was rhythmic and consistent Monday through Friday with weekends off to do whatever they pleased, the girls were all from prominent families and on Friday they would receive an allowance from home. With frugal advice from Madam Rousseau about their expenditures, these spoiled young women would embark to the city for shopping and dining. Visits to the Cincinnati Art Museum were an incline ride up to Mt. Adams in the beautiful Eden Park where on this chilly October day there would be the last playing of the band at the Parks large gazebo. This was just above the beautiful water reservoir. Families would picnic and couples arm in arm stroll the walkways. There were vendors of all sorts selling hotdogs, popcorn and candy. Everyone dressed quite nicely these days and the girls saw it as an opportunity to be seen in their best. Madam Rousseau insisted they travel at least two by two and never alone. Of course you can tell that it was Annie and Shannon that were always paired. The girls generally went to places as a group with Miss Ellery as chaperone. Miss Ellery felt more like she was one of the girls rather than a chaperone. The girls were comfortable with her because she respected their maturity and good sense and did not lord over them. If they wanted to go off some where she only said, "mind the rules girls and stay two by two and be back at the dorm by dark or Madam Rousseau will call out the guard, if you know what I mean."

Annie and Shannon were slowly wandering about when they noticed a few women holding signs that said, "Voting is a birth right like Lucy Stones Name." Annie knew what that meant and Shannon asked her, "What does that mean?" Annie responds, "It is probably one of the lessons in our history class that you ignored. Lucy Stone some forty years ago refused to change her name when she married Henry Blackwell or she would not be married. For me I will keep my name thank you very much and I'll keep my bed to myself." Shannon said, "liar, you will do it, I know you will, you may not be married and it may not be in bed, hell you might just be standing up, but you'll do it, you lusty girl." Annie responds, "Hush your dirty mind Shannon, let's go talk to them," pointing to the women holding the signs.

Shannon tags along and listens as Annie starts right in. Annie says to the one who looks like the leader of the group, "Don't you know Florence Nightingale says men are better suited for law making?" She was being sarcastic and the woman in charge knew it. The woman said turning to the others in the group, "What do you think ladies are men better suited for law making?" They all heard the sarcasm in Annie's voice and knew she was one of them. One lady blurted out, "Laws to keep a woman pregnant and in the kitchen." They all laugh. Annie goes on about Susan B Anthony and Elisabeth Stanton and

98

how South Dakota just voted us women out again just one year ago in 1890. Shannon is dumb founded. She had no idea how much Annie knew about all of this. Shannon was sheltered in her luxury life and was just becoming aware. She sees Annie in a new light and sees herself aweing at her very existence. Annie was so vibrant and articulate, knowledgeable and strong.

Annie bids farewell to the demonstrators and asks Shannon if she wants to head home ahead of the others so they can sneak to a restaurant and have some wine. Shannon says with a gleam in her eye, "Irish whisky for me girl, let's go." They find Miss Ellery to tell her of their plan. Miss Ellery said they should be mindful of the time and if it got dark to take a taxi to the school and not to walk. Annie and Shannon take the incline down to the city as Shannon leads the way to a Pub she knows where the young men from Xavier University would go on Saturday night. Xavier was a Catholic school. Annie agrees but with the reservation, "If they start getting drunk and if you don't leave, I'm leaving without you and you can find your own way home.

So here are two single young ladies, well dressed, going into Malone's Deli and Pub. Annie knows her father would never approve but Shannon is the instigator almost dragging Annie each step of the way. Shannon is saying, "It's the nineties girl, we're not babies, and I'll knock any bloke who tries to have 'is way with ya' straight on 'is ass." They enter together arm in arm and Annie is relieved to see couples together in the darkly lit pub. They sit in a booth and a barmaid comes over. Shannon says, "I'll have a double Jamison's and I think this lass wants some wine." Annie says, "No, I'll have the same as her as she winks at Shannon." Shannon grins, "You don't have sea legs like me; you better go light." Shannon was from a family of Irish drinkers and was sipping the brew early on. Annie's father hated drunks and raised his family the same but Annie was going to taste life for herself and was up for anything to try.

Shannon raises her glass for a toast, "Here is to our fathers who have sent us to the best 'good little girls' finishing school." Annie laughs, "Your brother is in Xavier, right?" Shannon winks, "You bet your bottom dollar, he's going to be a banker like my father, guardin' the vault and seeing who gets what at interest rates. I don't mind, I don't want to do that stuff anyway." Annie responds, "My younger brothers will go to Oxford but my father will have to beat them to go, they are just ruffians. Maybe they will change when they get older, and my sweet sister Leah Anna will get the same as me."

Annie sips her whisky and leans in, "The only reason I don't go mad is my mother knows Madam Collette Rousseau who knows the theater arts of Paris so well, that with a letter of introduction I will be in acting school in Paris as soon as I finish Rousseau's classes next year. If I didn't have that hope of excitement, I don't know what I would do, kill myself probably." Shannon smacks Annie's hand, "Don't you ever say that, never again, I would die if you died." With that Shannon shoots her glass of whisky and signals the bar maid for another. People look and Annie notices, "Shannon, don't let these people think we are wild, everyone is looking."

Shannon says as she receives another whisky, "My brother knows the owner and the owner owes my father's bank for a loan on this place; no one will say anything." The bar maid grins and says to Annie, "Want another Lass?" Annie says, "Why not."

The sun is going down and they forget the time till it is too late and they are too drunk to care. Annie tells Shannon, "That's enough, we are going home." Annie leads and Shannon, as composed as she can be follows. A kind gentleman at the door hails them a taxi. It is about a fifteen-minute ride back to the dorm and Shannon is leaning against Annie with her head on her shoulder. She is lamenting about how Annie knows where she is going and what she is going to do next. Shannon in a mildly alcohol slurred voice, "Annie, I don't know what I will do when we graduate in spring, I'm totally confused. I'm not a fighter like you, all I know is what my mother is, a good mother." She sighs, "I guess that's good enough." And then out of nowhere and showing her drunkenness Shannon jumps up, "I know, I will go with you to Paris and be your lesbian lover." Shannon grabs Annie and kisses her with a real and passionate kiss to which Annie responds with surprise. Annie lets it happen and knows Shannon is drunk but Annie does not respond with passion in kind. Shannon relaxes and sits back, "I'm sorry." Annie knows Shannon is not really sorry, she also knows Shannon is inclined to be extremely feminine and maybe in time will actually evolve to be completely lesbian, that perhaps her only issue is how difficult it would be for her family. Shannon may be just pretending all the time to show of herself what she thinks people need to see.

Annie ponders that her best friend is living a lie for the benefit of others. Amazing how drunkenness exposes things that perhaps should not be seen. Annie loves Shannon but does not have any hidden agenda about her sexuality. She is a woman of extraordinary understanding and grace. She is not afraid of being lesbian, she is not afraid of men. She sees her mother and fathers passion; she can see it in herself. It is like Lucy Stone keeping her maiden name. She is afraid of losing her identity in marriage and losing her life for a husband.

Annie jumps up just before the taxi arrives at the dorm, grabs Shannon by her breast and kisses her with the same passion, Shannon responds in kind. Then Annie pulls back and looks her in the eye. "If you go to Paris with me, which my father will probably approve so I will have a chaperone, none of this is to be known, besides Shannon I know for fact you like men."

They help each other from the taxi to the entry of the dorm where of course Madam Rousseau and Miss Ellery were at the door. They heard the taxi coming. It was after ten. Collette Rousseau did not say a word, she could smell the whisky. Miss Ellery started in, "You are making me look bad as a chaperone. I told you girls to be mindful of the time. I suppose ten o'clock is not late for you, but it is late for me. Here I am worried sick and... Collette interrupts, "Ladies, I'll expect you to spend your Sunday getting rid of your hangover and back to class on Monday at eight o'clock sharp, now off to bed and Miss Ellery, this is not your fault, you did well. Collette puts her arm around Miss Ellery and as they stroll away Madam Rousseau says, "You forget yourself Patricia, you were their age once, they will be fine. All is well."

102

Things go nicely at the school, by the week of Thanksgiving, the Sunday before the holiday they perform their short version of 'Little Women.' Only the parents that lived locally attended. Annie really worked hard on her part because she so wanted Madam Rousseau to take her seriously and to guide her to Paris. Collette could see she was serious and this would be a worthwhile effort. Shannon likewise tried harder and was always impressed how knowledgeable Annie was.

Tuesday Annie would board a train back to Sailor Park for the holiday. Shannon acted depressed and wanted Annie to come to her house for the holiday, "Annie that would be a good time to talk to my father about going to Paris with you." "No, I have to break-in the idea to my mother and father first. They are going to want to know what you are going to do there; so, the reason you are going is…" Annie leads Shannon to say her line, "I'm going there to learn French well and study art and culture." Annie adds, "And to find a Frenchman to renew your faith in love and romance." Shannon hugs Annie and kisses her on the cheek, I have already found love and it does not put any danger between my legs. Annie returns the kiss on the cheek, "I will tell you what everyone keeps saying to me. You will change."

Shannon sees Annie to the taxi that will take her to the train. Madam Rousseau sees her off also, "say hello to your mother dear. Tell her I have letters from Paris we can discuss in the spring, we will find you the best acting school there, and give your father a hug for me and remind him of Collette. Your mother won't be jealous, she won him not me." Shannon

103

tearfully waved as Annie rode away. Collette could see Shannon's extraordinary emotion, "Shannon your father will be here soon to get you, are you ready?" Shannon replies, "Always Madam, always, you don't keep my father waiting." Shannon was her father's pride; the spoiling was endless. He arrived in a luxurious carriage for the half day ride to the eastern hills of Cincinnati. It was on this ride that she would allude to her want to accompany Annie to Paris for more studies. Shannon knew she would get her way, and she still played her father like a violin. It would not be completely easy since Sean Arthur Brennan was Irish Catholic to the core and James Marcus Dupree was French and English blended, as a completely Protestant devotee but never frequented any church. Sean knew the reputation of James but paid no mind. That was about to change.

Her 'will' be done

It is less than two hours from taxi to train to arrival in Sailor Park. Captain Dupree was home and would only make another run of the Louie Queen if he felt the weather would hold out. James rode to the station in a surrey though the weather was now turning cold. He was at the station long before the train arrived and he chatted with the station master about the Farmer's Almanac, particularly about the weather. James greets Pete the station master, "Hey there Pete, good to see you; trains going to be runnin' all winter aye?" Pete grins, "Yep, even if the Ohio freezes like it did in 1856, the trains still run, not like them paddle boats aye Captain Dupree?" James laughs and asks, "Is the 'four-fifteen' on time today, Pete?" That's the train Annie should be on. Pete replies, "Knowin' Smokie the engineer it will be about five minutes early. He always runs full steam from Cincinnati to here." Captain Dupree asks to see the Almanac Pete kept on hand. He looks up snow and cold predictions for November to December. He tells Pete, "I think I'll make another run to Pittsburg and then over to St. Louis; it's just on that return from St. Louis it could get mighty cold and I probably won't have many passengers. I may just dock the Louie Queen in St Louis for the winter and come home by train." Captain Dupree has arrangements to winter and repair the Louie Queen either in St. Louis or Louisville Kentucky. Of course Louisville is preferred because he has a brother there who can oversee repairs.

Like Pete had said, the whistle of the 'four-fifteen' was early by five minutes. Annie literally jumps of the last step of the front passenger car into her father's arms. She was feather light to him and he swings her around like on a carrousel. The porter handed James her one travel case and off they go to home. The ride was chilly and Annie retrieves a wool scarf from her case. Annie with rosy cheeks smiles, "We will have snow for Christmas and we can get out the sleigh, hey papa?" Annie clings to her father's arm as he handles the reigns of the surrey. They have just the one horse, a young gelded thoroughbred James bought from a gambler that frequented his Louis Queen. His name was Fancy Dancer but they just called him Dancer. He was a high steppin' horse. James had said the reason he bought him was because of the spring in his step. He was rarely ridden as a saddle horse and was mostly accustomed to pulling. James would let his sons ride Dancer but felt his heavy weight would take away his prance and lightness of foot. Annie use to attend to Dancer in the evenings when she was in high school. She would retrieve him from a small glen next to the house and walk him to the stable for his evening grain. She would brush his coat and talked to him about things. She would always greet him on any ride before she would get in the carriage and you could tell he knew Annie was in his carriage.

James remarked, "Old Dancer knows you're here. On the way into the station he just walked lazy like. Now you are here he is prancing. You lifted his spirit." Annie says, "He's not that old daddy, what is he, about eight or so? James thinks, "Yep and in people years that's about forty-eight ain't it?" Annie teases, "He's just board, and besides geldings are confused." James laughs, "How's that?" Annie explains, "They still want to be male, they just forgot how." James laughs deeply, "Girl you got a way of seein' things." Annie likes to make her father laugh but then she expounds, "Isn't it odd how things work between the male and female species?" James says, "Are we talkin' about some stuff from your school or are we talkin' about how barn yard animals act?" Annie returns, "Well both, I suppose. Remember the opera we saw this last summer?" "How could I forget?" Annie continues, "Rigoletto hides his daughter from the monstrous duke, then lust and jealousy and deception twists it all around in such a mess that Rigoletto stabs his own daughter." She adds, "Take away the lust and jealousy and there is no confusion; like Dancer, he forgot how to lust." James is astounded. "My word missy you have a busy mind. You look at things awful deep. Is everything as complicated as you think? He continues, "Sometimes it is just as simple as this old saying, - a man chases a woman till she catches him." James chuckles, "Don't you know it's a woman who runs things anyway. A man just tries to make her happy, that is all."

Annie is all too serious when she says, "What if a woman does not want to catch a man? What if she does not want to have babies? I'll tell you what papa, if that kind of woman isn't real smart, she will have to work some pretty bad jobs and not have much in life because of the way our society is." James sighs, "Annie, I feel we are headed for a dismal Thanksgiving if I can't get your spirits up. Your mama has the house all decorated and is looking for a happy time; please make it good for her."

Annie realizes she was pressing him to see things the way she sees things and she smiles, squeezes his arm and says, "Sorry papa, I'm happy, really, I just have some decisions to make about my future." James smiles and winks at Annie, "One day at a time, we'll get there aye?"

It's about five-thirty when they pull up to the house. Leah Anna is lighting candles in the front window and screeches, "Annie's home!" It was so loud the boys around back heard. Mary, Helen and Leah Anna run to the front porch as the boys come around the side. They all converge and swamp Annie in Hugs. They will have the long weekend, from Wednesday till Sunday afternoon when Annie will take the train back to Cincinnati. This would be a good long time for Annie to tell her mother about the plan for Shannon Brennan to go to Paris with her. She knows that her parents will have no reservations except they also know of Sean Brennan. They have never met but Annie fears her parents see them as highbrow judgmental people. They will just think this never knowing the folks, just because that is how people carry their judgments written on their sleeve so they can say 'see, I told you so.' The fact was Captain Dupree had investments and savings far to exceed Sean Brennans' estate but they lived on the upper east side of Cincinnati and with all the 'money-folks' just comparing each other all the time it was enough to make one ill. In fact sending Shannon to Paris would be a stretch for Sean but he will not be out done by a steamboat captain as we will see.

Thanksgiving was wonderful; so completely festive. Leah Anna played the piano and amazed Annie with how much she had improved. Leah Anna would be fifteen years old December the 7th. She was

108

gaining height fast and was almost as tall as Annie and her mother. Mary had remarked that Leah Anna may take after your father and be a tall one. Leah Anna starts in, "Oh mama, I don't want to be tall; it just makes it harder to find a man, besides men don't like tall women." Annie can't resist, "What is all this about finding a man, what about yourself, what do you want to be when you grow up, just a wife?" Leah Anna responds, "Not everyone is smart like you Annie and I wish you would stop thinking that being married and a mother is so bad; maybe that is right for me and you make it sound so demeaning." Annie is set aback and realized how she was being domineering over her little sister. She flashes back to the play 'Little Women' and realizes in an instant how different everyone is and just because she has issues with society's norms, not everyone does. She apologizes, "So sorry my sweet Leah Anna, I stepped on your toes. We all need to be reminded about grace once and a while and I just had my lesson."

Leah Anna turns while seated at the piano bench and leans into whisper in Annie's ear, "That beautiful Ben Hamilton came by and wondered when you might be home again. I don't mind telling you; if I were a little older, he wouldn't be asking for you anymore, I'd steal him from you. You don't want him anyway." Lean Anna laughs, "But, to him I'm just a little girl." Annie puts her hand on Lean Anna's, "It is not that I don't want him, it is not that I don't like him and it is not that he is not beautiful, there is no man in the county as handsome as him and don't you know he knows it. I heard all the girls talk and they said because of me they didn't have a chance. I was flattered but don't you see Leah Anna, Ben will have his way and that is it. Don't you see Leah Anna; don't you see?

Leah Anna sees alright, "I see that a man has to be a man, that is what make them strong and a woman who is a woman needs to let him be strong and adore him for it, and be his support and strength by loving him." Annie winces, "Argh," gurgles out of Annie's throat, "You have no idea what I feel, and I won't say to you what everyone says to me, 'you will change' because you may not and I am sure I won't. We are so different and that is something I can accept and I hope you will accept me as I am Leah Anna." They hug and Annie says, "Of course you told him I would be home for Thanksgiving." Leah Anna acknowledges, "Yes, but he won't come by, he just said that his father is involved with a man to make parts for this newfangled carriage supposed to run without a horse." Annie says, "Yeah, we saw one at Eden Park, it made a lot of noise and smoke, I don't like it much, it scared all the horses." Leah Anna continues, "He just told me that he would be leaving to go to Detroit for a long while and didn't know when he would be back and that if for some reason you might want to see him before he leaves, send a message and he would come." Annie just gazes out the window at the gray sky of November as the wind blows the last of the leaves to the ground. Captain Dupree is out back making a big fire with James Jr and Marcus. Winter is coming and the best way to face it is with celebration.

It is now the Friday after Thanksgiving and Mary and Helen are turning the leftovers of the turkey into lunch. There was stuffing and potatoes and corn and beans abounding for another feast, though

110

everyone is still full from the day before. Annie with her hair up in combs joins them to help and the girl chatter ensues.

Mary reaches for a cutting board, "Donnez-moi cela cher (Hand me that dear)" as she points to the cutting board, "I overheard Leah Anna tell you about Ben, don't you think it would be at least respectful to his parents if you would just acknowledge his presence. After all he has always been a perfect gentleman." Annie rolls her eyes, "Eavesdropping mama? Well mother, the last time he was here we said all we had to say, anything else will just open a can of worms that I don't want. I feel like no one can hear me. I keep talking but no one is listening. The women carrying sighs at Eden Park understood me; they said I made perfect sense." Mary says, "Ce que las femmes? (What women?)" Annie responds in French, "elles sont appelées (they are called)" she hesitates because she cannot find the French term and continues in English, "they are called 'Lucy Stoners', they are protesting for a woman's right to vote like Lucy who kept her maiden name with the approval of her husband and hell mother, whether he approved or not she would have kept her maiden name, like I am going to always be known as Antoinette Marie Dupree till the day I die. So there! Is everyone listening or must I continue to repeat myself till I scream."

Mary quietly responds, "ce n'est pas la révolution chère (this is not the revolution dear) just conversation." Annie quiets a bit, "Mother this is probably a good time for us to talk, Madam Rousseau said to say hello and that she had letters from Paris that you should discuss with her in the spring, she said

111

she would find the best acting school for me. I could tell that she was concerned and I could sense it was about the cost of the schools." Mary puts her arm around Annie, "So this is decided, you want to go to Paris?" Annie with calm confidence, "Yes mama, I have thought of nothing else, that is what I want to do." Mary turns in front of Annie and places a hand on each shoulder and looks her straight in the eye, "It is a good thing your father is a rich man, God help him; you are a lucky girl." A short lecture ensues, "I had no such hope or aspirations when I was a young girl in Paris, my parents struggled to just send me and my brother to school." Annie continues for her, "And you worked cleaning rooms for rich people and sneaking into the theater and…" Mary interrupts, "It is not the responsibility of children to pay for parents, just give thanks to your papa and don't punish him for being a man; he loves you so much and yes you will go to Paris when you graduate." Annie screeches and hugs her mother.

They continue to prepare lunch. Annie sits on a stool next to the sink as Mary deals with the carcass of the turkey. Annie then divulges the plan of Shannon joining her as companion and school mate. Mary begins with many questions about Shannon's family, about an Irish Catholic girl in Paris with a non-declared protestant as a confidant. Annie says, "I don't think Shannon will have any difficulty with her father, it is more her mother who will question the idea; Shannon is a bit wild and her mother keeps her on a short leash. In Paris she won't have the control she has here." Mary questions, "I will bet they think we are nothing but," Mary pauses, "rien que des joueurs (nothing but gamblers.)" Annie defends,

112

"Well they are nothing but a bunch of loan shark bankers; they're not so great." Mary returns, "We should have been more established in the Methodist church, perhaps we would look better." Annie sits up straight, "We are just fine and I don't care what people think. If Shannon can go is that acceptable to you?" Mary says, "bien sûr ma chère (of course my dear.)" Annie holds her mother's hands, "And if Shannon's mother won't let her go I know Shannon will throw a fit till she does. Shannon is unstoppable."

Mary has not a clue of the intimacy that Annie has with Shannon and actually it never crosses her mind. As the day progresses to evening James and the boys stoke up the wood burning boiler in the basement. It is not cold yet but the house will be chilly by morning. Night comes and Leah Anna plays again on the piano as everyone lounges. Helen says good night to all and retires. Helen is almost like an aunt to the children, always there always watching out for everyone. One by one they say good night and Captain Dupree and his lovely Mary retire to their privacy on the third floor. James starts a fire in the bedroom fireplace. The upper floor is the last to receive the heat from the boiler. It eventually warms the night but will be cold come morning.

James and Mary share some brandy and Mary tells her husband their daughter's plan of Paris and Shannon joining them. James retorts, "That Irishman will grind his teeth that his daughter is going to Paris instead of Ireland for more school. I don't think it is a good idea, Shannon will only get in the way of what Annie wants to do, besides what does Shannon Brennan want to learn in Paris?" "Annie says she wants to polish her French and study art." James

113

laughs, "That's going to boil his Irish beer. We will wait and see but I think this is nothing but trouble for our Annie." Mary injects, "Don't you think it will be good for Annie to have a friend with her instead of being all alone in Paris?" James thinks, "Not if Madam Collette Rousseau is directing us to a school with a dorm and attendants." Mary goads, "Oh you trust Collette do you." James laughs, "Yes and you do too." Mary continues, "Besides your daughter is not a little girl and though there are dormitories, she is still a woman alone in Paris, I would feel better if it was her and Shannon." James says as he is falling to sleep, "Shannon is on fire as much as her red hair, if anything it is good that Annie will be with her instead of vice versa." Mary squeezes her man and they fall to sleep.

It is cold in the morning Captain Dupree hollers down the stairway, "James and Marcus go down to the cellar and fire up the boiler before your sisters get out of bed." Helen has the stove in the kitchen heating well and the aroma of coffee wafts up and out of the kitchen through the whole house. James and Marcus hustle on their pants and shirt and scramble to see who can get to the cellar first.

Annie rolls over for another snooze; she loves her home and wonders if she could do what her father has done. She ponders men and power and falls into a dream. In this dream she is married to Ben and sees him sitting across a table smiling at her and she is in a rocking chair with a child. She lurches awake and snaps her torso up. God, she thinks as she shakes off the dream. She is mad that all this Ben stuff is even in her dreams. Cold or not, she is up, splashing cold water in her face form the basin in her room. She throws on slippers and a robe and flies down to the kitchen where it is warm. Helen hears her coming and has hot coffee in the cup ready for her. Annie swings open the door of the kitchen and plops down at the table, knowing that the coffee was for her. Coffee with cream and sugar tasted so good and helped brush away that dream. She ponders, '*Men don't know. They don't have women hemming them in to a point where they feel trapped and want to run. They are the hunter and we are the prey. Maybe I should see him like mother says and tell him to stop, just stop and let me go. It is my own fault, as a young girl I didn't know better and I encouraged his pursuit and now it won't stop. No, I won't see him or it will just start up again. I must leave it alone.*'

You can hear the boys in the cellar pitching wood and you can hear the boiler heating up. Captain Dupree comes into the kitchen in his pajamas and robe, "Helen that coffee smells fabulous, have you got some for me?" Helen says, "All you want Capin', all you want," as she pours him a cup and he sits next to Annie, "Sleep well my girl?" He inquires. Annie nodes yes. James is always direct and doesn't mince words, "If you want Shannon to go with you to Paris its fine with your mother and me. We will probably have to meet with the Brennans and you know that will be tough. I just hope that Irishman minds himself if you know what I mean. I won't take any down talking from the likes of him." Annie says, "Just give Shannon the benefit of the doubt papa, she will reassure her parents, I think everything will be fine."

Captain Dupree adds in, "And as far as Ben Hamilton is concerned, he needs to leave well enough

115

alone and that means to leave you alone as well." Captain Dupree takes a tray Helen had prepared for Mary with coffee and toast and proceeds to carry it to her in bed. Annie says as he leaves, "I love you papa, at least you understand me." The boys come up from the cellar to the kitchen and Helen gives them hot cereal. Annie refills her cup and heads back to her room. In a short while the house will be warm and she and Leah Anna will take turns in the second-floor bath with hot water. This nineteenth century luxury is well respected.

The autumn day was spectacular, the sun shone through the remainder of the colored leaves. The boys raked and burned the last of what had fallen. It was quite a chore because the yards and trees were large. Annie visited Dancer in his stall and Leah Anna was by her side everywhere. Annie strokes Dancers muzzle and kisses him, "It will snow by Christmas and you can pull the sleigh old boy. We'll put bells on you and dash through the hills boy." Dancer loves her presence; you can tell by how calm he becomes; so she will pet him more. She always has a carrot or apple for him. No one else gives him this much care.

Leah Anna had heard her mother and Helen talking in the kitchen about the demonstrators in Eden Park that Annie had been talking about and she begins to quiz her sister, "So what is this about those women carrying sighs in the park, mama and Helen were saying you were talking to them; what about?" Annie begins by giving her some history, "These are things you will probably not learn about in school because it is not in history books and much of this is happening right now, so you can only read about it in newspapers in the city." Annie explains about what is now being called the women's movement and how women cannot vote and have no say about the law. How women are completely subordinate to their husbands and if a woman is not married and has a man to speak for her, she is muted. She explains all about Lucy Stone and the maiden name issue. She tells her of how Florence Nightingale says that men are better suited to law making and how that riles most women who are seeking the vote. Nightingale says that most women prefer sympathy and were not as capable as men. Leah Anna asks Annie, "What does mama think about all of this?" Annie responds, "She listens but I don't think she knows what I feel. I don't want to be a married woman so what are my choices? To live at the grace of my father all my life or find a career for myself, and God help me, I don't want to be a nurse." Leah Anna winces, "Me either, I couldn't be around sick people all the time." Annie takes Leah Anna by the hands, "You are going to be fifteen and have years to think about what you want to do, but I will be twenty-two in April and I've decided I want to be a famous actress on the stage; first in Paris and then in New York." Lean Anna giggles, "Wow, can I come see you in New York?" Annie swings her sister's arms back and forth and they do an over under turn around like dancing, Annie grabs her sweet sister around the waste and lifts her off the ground, "Of course you will, when I am a star performer."

Annie and Leah Anna leave Dancer's stall and head for the house, they are giggling and laughing all the way. Mary sees the two and is tickled to the heart. She shouts out, "qu'est-ce que tu es fille (what are you girls up to.)" In unison they respond, "rien mere (nothing mother.)"

117

Captain Dupree had gone into town to the telegraph office to express a message to a dock foreman in St Louis, it read, 'May dock Louis Queen there for repairs this winter, stop, depends on weather, stop, must know space available, stop, RSVP, stop.' If there was no space available, he would have to steam the Louisville Queen back to Louisville, a very hard run in the cold and snow. Visibility is low and he may have to make anchor stops at night. That's always risky because of debris floating down river. It can hit the hull and damage her severely. Even standing watch with lanterns does not give you enough time to push off a heavy log if it comes to strike. If the weather is warm, he will come back upriver to Louisville. Several of his family still lives there. The Dupree's of Louisville were tradesman and businessmen. It was a large family. Annie barely remembers the one reunion she attended when she was twelve years old.

James returns to the house with news Mary does not want to hear. Captain Dupree comes in the backdoor in the kitchen where Mary is having afternoon tea with Helen. He pulls off his wool cap and retrieves his pipe from his coat pocket and lights it, "Going to make one last run; Pittsburg to St Louie, my love." James crosses his arms and waits for Mary's response." Mary sets down her tea and crosses the kitchen; she takes his pipe and she takes a puff of smoke. She lays the pipe on the sink and takes his arms and places them around her waist. She looks him in the eye, "Must be worth your time, because I know you don't want to go." James sighs, "It will make for a good end to this year." He laughs, "Besides we have a duckling that wants to go see her mother's Paris. I'm

118

glad they did not all come at once, we would be in the poor house." Mary places her head on James chest, "Not with a man like you, you would find a way." Mary believes and is amazed at her husband's ability and she is very good at stoking his fire.

Annie comes in to find her mother in the arms of James, "vous deux encore? (you two again?)" James this time in French, "toujours ma chère; toujours. (Always my dear; always.)" They all sit down at the kitchen table; Leah Anna comes in and joins them. Helen can tell this is family time and leaves for her room. Captain Dupree takes charge, "So Annie when you get back to school tomorrow you can talk to Collette and tell her we will come in the spring to make arrangements. You and Shannon have to arrange for us to meet her parents if they even approve. They may have told her no." Annie injects, "If they say no, I don't know what Shannon will do. Let us hope they say yes." James and Mary do not realize Shannon's attachment to Annie and Annie will not allude to it. Then she says something that sets her parents back a bit. Annie says, "If they say no Shannon will probably run away, she is old enough and I know her, she will be mad as hell."

James and Mary look at each other with question and Annie says, "If they say no, is there some way she can go anyway?" Mary jumps in, "No your father will not pay her way too. Annie, if her parents say no, that is it, final." In French and English it is the same "final" Annie knows her mother does not repeat or change when she says final. James comes in with, "The last thing you want to do is get in the middle of that Irish families decisions about their children. You need to accept whatever they say."

119

Leah Anna is silent and amazed at the interplay and wonders how she fits into all this. She thinks Annie is melodramatic and does not see what all the to-do about Shannon is about. She thinks, '*But, what do I know, I'm only fourteen.*' Mary comforts Annie, "Let's hope they say yes, it would be fun for you both in Paris, and I think it would be safer for you."

Annie puts her hand on her fathers, "I will tell Madam Rousseau all you said; will you be home for Christmas papa?" James pats Annie's hand, "Hell or high water and as long as that creek don't freeze; I will be here." He winks at Mary and Leah Anna laughs.

The day dims early in November; James Jr and Marcus return before dark. The fish had been jumpin' out of the lake onto their hook. Helen took their catch and they all had a fine fish dinner of Bass and Catfish with potato salad and green beans left over from Thanksgiving. The turkey was all gone. Tomorrow there was only one train into Cincinnati: the twelve-O-five. Annie would arrive in the city by three in the afternoon. James and Mary accompanied her to the station. It was not a tearful goodbye. She would be back for Christmas. Annie hugs her mother, "Don't let Leah Anna have her birthday present till her birthday." Annie had gotten her a locket but there were no pictures to place in it. She would leave that to Leah Anna. Annie hugs her father and he says, "You got your way sweetie, you always do because you are as beautiful as your mother. Remember your looks don't put good money in your pocket and there are all kinds of bad money out there; know the difference." That made so much sense to Annie and my how she respected her father's wisdom.

120

The Storms of Winter

All the girls are getting back from Thanksgiving and chatting about their holiday in the kitchen of the dormitory. The kitchen was always a warm place and everyone gathered. Miss Ellery was cheerful and excited about the next few weeks leading up to Christmas. It was always festive with decorations going up all over the city. Christmas music could be heard by little bands at the larger stores around the city. The Salvation Army soldiers were on every corner playing the trumpet and ring a bell for donations for the poor. Annie took notice of her wealth and was troubled about how if her family ever lost their father, they would be poor.

Annie looked for Shannon but she was nowhere to be found when Madam Rousseau came into the kitchen. She beckoned Annie from the door to come join her in her office. Annie speedily goes to the office. Madam Rousseau sits at her desk and Annie sits in the chair placed directly in front. All the girls call this the hot seat because it usually meant a reprimand. Madam Rousseau wastes no time, "Shannon's father brought her back to school from east hills and her mother came also. They asked me for a private meeting and sent Shannon off to her room. They were stern with me and I don't like to be instructed about how I run my school!" Madam Rousseau's voice was elevated. You could tell she was upset. She continues, "They told me in no uncertain terms that I was to follow the curriculum and not to be instructing their daughter about where she will go from here." Then Madam Rousseau in a mocking tone repeats their words, "And furthermore you should pay attention to the other girls and assure they are not a bad influence on Shannon."

Collette Rousseau was not one to be push around. She quickly had confronted Sean Brennan and got to the bottom of what was their concern and what was troubling them so, and she elaborated it all to Annie. "Annie, I had no idea you and Shannon were collaborating on a scheme to go to Paris together." Annie fires back, "It was not my idea, it was Shannon's and who am I to tell her what to do with her life. Why is this so bad?" Madam Rousseau comes out from behind her desk, "Sean Brennan is a strict Irish Catholic and for his daughter Shannon to go to the Cancan capitol of the world would stop the earth from turning. Young lady, do you not see the difference between your parents and hers?" Annie stands up and almost starts crying, "So my parents are bad and hers are good. You are right, I see the difference but I do not understand. They should know we are good girls not bad. They should trust us because we deserve it." Annie starts to cry and

Madam Rousseau puts her arms around her, "That is the difference between your parents and hers."

Annie pulls herself together, "Where is Shannon?" Madam Rousseau shrugs her shoulders, "She was in her room after her parents left. I don't know where she is now. You girls are adults now; you make your own way. She may have gone to that Pub you girls go to, what's the name, Malone's. Annie says, "I'll bet you are right; I'll find her." Annie bundles up and goes out front to find a taxi. Madam Rousseau has Miss Ellery go with her. She requests the driver take them to Malone's. Annie asks Miss Ellery if she had ever been there before. Miss Ellery responds, "No my friend does not like bars." Annie smiles, "Malone's is not a bar it's a Deli and Pub; that is different than a bar." Miss Ellery a bit somber, "Well she doesn't go places where they sell beer." It's about a twenty-minute ride to the Deli, Annie quizzes Miss Ellery, "You have never told me of your friend. I have seen you with her but you never say anything about her."

Miss Ellery delays, "Well, it is not allowed for us to discuss our personal lives with you girls at school, so we just avoid talking about ourselves. That is Madam Rousseau's orders." Annie says, "Oh I see. Well what Madam Rousseau does not know will not hurt you." Miss Ellery laughs, "Not exactly, if something gets back to her that I said, it could mean my job." Annie presses, "Your friend looks like a nice woman from a distance." You can tell Miss Ellery is dying to talk, "Yes, she is, very nice. We are probably both going to be old maids." Annie winces, "God I hate that term. Perhaps you should just drop the old part and just be maidens forever young and who refused to change their name." Miss Ellery knew Annie was in tune with the politics of the women of the day. Miss Ellery agreed but then again, she was not to influence the girls at the school. Half biting her tongue, "Her name is Christina Chambers and we have joined the Lucy Stoners." Miss Ellery snickers, "Do not you dare to tell Madam Rousseau that I told you, she will fire me and I need my job."

Annie laughs, "I knew it. Your secret is safe with me." Annie slides over on the seat to hold Miss Ellery's arm, "I'm worried about Shannon." Miss Ellery cautions, "Shannon's father thinks all the world wants to take his daughter away from him and if he keeps choking that girl, he will make it happen." Annie is intrigued; Miss Ellery knows more than she let on. Annie presses for more, "Does he not know that Shannon is a grown woman and can legally do as she pleases?" Miss Ellery says with a hump, "Not unless she wants to be poor and abandon. That man is vindictive, you do what he wants or else you pay the consequences." Annie begins to believe she does not know her friend Shannon at all. That she is more troubled than she lets on.

They arrive at Malone's and walk in arm in arm because Miss Ellery does not go into Pubs. There are a group of men at the end of the bar singing some Irish limerick and they sound drunk. There in the middle of the group as drunk as they are, is Shannon. Annie has Miss Ellery sit in the booth near to the door and tells her to wait. Miss Ellery gazes down because this scene is exactly what her friend Christina Chambers had expressed, 'bars are nothing but a bunch of drunken men.' Annie walks up to the group and just looks Shannon in the eye. Shannon stumbles and the men prop her up. Annie with her hands on her hips and in a stout voice says, "Is this the way you are going to be in Paris? I knew I could not trust the likes of you." Annie had used her Irish accent which was improving. Shannon leaps forward to throws her arms around Annie and literally puts all of her little weight into Annie's trust. Annie struggles to keep standing and says, "Come on girl, we are going home." Miss Ellery runs up to help. Annie turns to the men and says, "You have a good night gents." Miss Ellery and Annie stumble with Shannon out to the taxi that was waiting to take them back to the dormitory. Before they get into the taxi Shannon throws-up. The driver says, "Good thing she did it here. If she does it again, put her head out the door, will ya'?"

Shannon lays her head in Annie's lap and literally falls to sleep instantly and slept all the way back to the dormitory. They all, including Madam Rousseau help Shannon to bed. Annie sits with Madam Rousseau in the kitchen till late talking out this situation. Annie tells Collette all that her father and mother had said about plans in the spring to go to Paris. Madam Rousseau went on and on about the schools in Paris and who would be there to greet her and what to expect from headmasters depending which school her parents decide on. Of course it is all about the cost of the school and the accommodations.

Madam Rousseau explains, "Annie, you must know how extraordinary it is for a young lady such as yourself to go to Paris at the grace of her parents. In no uncertain terms it is because of your father Dupree and your mother Buffet who want you to know your heritage in France. I suppose that will extend to your brothers and sisters as they grow up." Annie grins,

"Perhaps not with my brothers but I'm sure Leah Anna will go to Paris someday. Father talks about us all going someday as a family trip but I do not think that will happen because of the Louisville Queen." Collette gets prophetic, "Your father will sell that boat someday." Annie says, "Humph, not till he is in the grave and even then, he won't sell." Collette lets out a belly laugh, "You are probably right. Go now, off to bed with you. I don't expect to see Shannon till late in the morning. Look in on her in the morning, will you? Annie rises and kisses Madam Rousseau on the cheek and retires.

The night passes without event, come morning Annie peeks into Shannon's room to see. Shannon is sound asleep; Annie moves in close to make sure she is breathing and can smell beer and whisky sweating from her hot body. It is chilly in the room but Shannon is sweating. Annie thinks, *'God knows how much that girl had to drink, she is lucky to be alive.'* Annie just slips away and joins the other girls in the kitchen. It is about six o'clock and the smells of bacon and eggs and coffee are wonderful. Annie tells Miss Ellery Shannon's condition and that she will not be down for breakfast, that she will wait an hour and take her some coffee. Annie enjoys her breakfast and conversation with all the girls telling of their families and Thanksgiving. The hour passes: class is not till eight so Annie prepares a cup of coffee for Shannon. Madam Rousseau comes in just as Annie is about to go to Shannon's room and says, "Here dear use this." Using an eye dropper she puts several drops of laudanum in the coffee; she continues, "tell Shannon she is not expected in class

126

at all today. The laudanum will make her sleep some more." Annie holding the coffee and with a shallow curtsy says, "Yes mum."

Annie lightly taps on Shannon's door and enters. Shannon is half sitting up gazing at the dim gray light coming through the curtains of the window. Annie does not open the curtains but sets the coffee on the nightstand and lights the kerosene lamp on Shannon's dressing table. Shannon says nothing. Annie then sits on the side of her bed and hands her the coffee. Shannon moans, "No, my stomach won't have coffee right now." Annie pushes the cup a little closer to her nose, "It has laudanum in it, it will make you rest." Shannon takes the cup which is slightly warm now and swallows it down in just a few gulps. Annie takes the cup, "My word, will you have another?" Shannon moans, "With laudanum?" Annie warns, "No, that is enough, it will just make you sick." Shannon rolls to one side toward Annie and mashes her face in her pillow, "Who cares, I want to die anyway."

Annie knows it is her hangover talking. She gets up from the bed, "You go back to sleep; Madam Rousseau says you need not come to class today." Shannon rolls to the other side and mashes her face into her pillow and moans, "Please don't leave; talk to me a while." Annie sits back down on the bed. Shannon has her back to her. Annie rubs Shannon's back lightly to which Shannon coos; Annie says, "I know what your father said to Madam Rousseau; I'm so sorry about all of this and feel it is somehow my fault. You would not have wanted to go to Paris if it had not been for me." Shannon turns to sit up like suddenly she was wide awake. As she does her brain

127

spins. She puts both hands on either side of her head to stop the spinning. Shannon blurts out, "It is not my father; it is my mother. She won't let me be. She is always correcting me like she is training a dog. At first daddy said he would think about it and had to talk to mama. Mother never said anything to me and then daddy came to me and said we could not afford Paris right now with the boys in Xavier and all." Shannon starts to cry, "The boys, the boys, the boys' they always get whatever they want, but me, me, no, not for Shannon. Besides Annie, it is not the money; it - is - my - mother!" Shannon drew out the statement 'it is my mother' with strong emphasis as she slinks back to a lying position, "They are not going to let me go; I even begged papa. I felt so stupid like a little girl saying oh daddy please, please."

Annie wasn't going to interrupt Shannon's catharsis but could not help herself, "Do you think it is because of my family Dupree and the steamboat and the reputation." Shannon as she lays there limp touches Annie's hand, "Do you know about Irish hypocrisy?" Shannon laughs as she cries, "We're fightin' in the pub on Saturday night; see you in church on Sunday and screw the bastards on Monday. I think it's the eleventh Irish commandment." Annie is tickled to the heart at Shannon forthrightness. Shannon says, "No Annie, I think my father is impressed with your fathers' success. He had said he would like to take a trip on the Louie Queen once and mother just scowled at him. Mothers a prude and thinks all men are dogs; my father is the exception as long as she keeps him in line. I know her; and poor daddy has a ring in his nose, at least that is what mama thinks. I know better. Sometimes I think papa has a mistress and my mother is blind. I've seen things."

Annie is shocked. Shannon had never revealed that she was so troubled at home. In contrast Annie has such an open relationship with her parents. Annie has questioned her mother about her father's fidelity but never has she ever seen anything but complete love from her father to her mother and her mother's response is always, 'he treats me like a queen." It would be completely odd if her mother was possessive and controlling like Shannon's mother is. Annie says, "Shannon I never knew; your family always seemed just fine." Shannon pats Annie's hand as the laudanum starts to put her back to sleep, "The men are on one side of this family and the women are on the other and never the twain shall meet." Annie realizes Shannon is falling off. She puts out the lamp and starts to close the door behind her when Shannon almost asleep says, "I'm old enough; I don't have to live with them anymore and if I want to go to Paris I will."

Annie thinks as she closes the door, '*and what will you live on, your looks.*' Then she thinks, '*with your beauty Shannon, that maybe possible.*' Annie does not know that Shannon's grandfather died and left each of his grandchildren a large trust that they inherit at the age of twenty-one. Shannon was of age. Shannon's mother knew this. Shannon no longer needed her mother's approval, it just hurt that she has never felt her mother's trust.

After the Thanksgiving holiday there would only be three weeks when everyone concentrated on their studies. Annie worked especially hard on her

129

French vocabulary; it would be so important at the acting academy. If she did not have to spend a lot of time memorizing scripts to plays with French words she did not know, it would help. Shannon was studying French also and they worked together. The other girls were not jealous of Annie and Shannon always being together; they were all spoiled in their own right; they were debutants protected from the vicious wolves of poverty by well-to-do families. The other young ladies did notice the apparent physical affection the two expressed openly and some of the girls emulated it. Like holding hands or sitting close; sharing a book instead of using two. Laying a head on a shoulder while reciting passages of rehearsed lines for plays and so forth. Actually in this era women never walked the street alone they were always arm in arm.

Annie and Shannon were often reading late into the evening in one or the others room and would fall to sleep together and when the other girls saw them in the morning coming out of one room, they assumed more was going on; and there was talk. One of the girls Marissa Brook whose family lived in the upper north side of Cincinnati said to Shannon, "This is Madam Rousseau's school for young women not lesbians." Shannon fired back, "You should know Marissa; tomboys are always shy when touched." Shannon put her arm around Marissa and kissed her on the cheek. Marissa blushed, stomped her foot and pulled away. Shannon had touched a nerve.

The truth was Annie and Shannon talked about each other's sexuality and even about orgasms and the mystery of them. They talked about men a lot and most of all about pregnancy and the raising of

130

children and how far away the idea of it all was to them. Yes, they were affectionate and they themselves question each other about lesbian identity but they did not have sex with each other. They felt they were heterosexual and in a very confusing place. Sex with a man was for marriage in a Christian family and that was that. Since marriage for Annie was not going to happen the orgasms, she knew privately were just that. Shannon on the other hand was not sure she was not going to be a mother someday. She openly told Annie that when she has an orgasm she is thinking about men. She says it is so wonderful that she can understand why it is so special and to be shared with a husband. She told how she caught her brother masturbating and the difference between nude male statues and a man with an erection was no mystery to her. She said her poor brother was so embarrassed but admitted days later she masturbated. Annie said she had never seen a man with an erection but new her brothers were masturbating. So the affection that people see between Antoinette and Shannon is completely feminine adoration in spirit and not lust. Well not completely. Shannon remembers Annie's kiss when she grabbed her breast. Perhaps things are not all on the surface.

As the time nears Christmas week, they are all planning for the two weeks at home. Shannon got a letter from her mother which only bolstered her mother's position and made Shannon mad. Madam Rousseau had information that trains were coming in from Chicago covered in snow and that the bad weather was headed to Cincinnati. She decided to cut school short by two days so the girls could all get home before it turned bad.

131

Annie is packing her travel case and Shannon comes in, "I don't want to go home for Christmas. I'm just going to be miserable and my mother, I know will not leave me alone. Can I come home with you?" and before Annie could say anything, "Oh please, please, please!" Shannon is like a little girl. Annie closes her case and has to push hard because it is overstuffed. Shannon helps and Annie gets it latched, "If you come home with me your mother will be livid. Your father will probably drive a carriage all the way from East Hills to Sailor Park with a sheriff to retrieve you." Shannon knows better, "I'm a legal adult they can say nothing. A sheriff has no authority. Besides, she needs to be taught a lesson; I'm not a little girl." Annie laughs, "I think it will be fireworks before the New Year." Shannon says, "So it is, yes? I can come?" Annie quizzes, "How are you going to tell your parents; we have to be on the train at Cincinnati Station at ten-fifteen tomorrow morning." Shannon spins around and dashes to the door of Annie's Room, "I'll telegraph papa. He won't be here till Friday. He will get it tomorrow morning and we will be on the train." Annie warns, "I sure hope he gets it in the morning. If he comes all the way in from East Hills and you were not here, he will explode." Shannon dashes out, "He will get it; I will send it now."

What Madam Rousseau had heard about the weather came true; it started snowing Thursday morning. She knew about the telegram to Shannon's Father and says to her, "I cannot tell you what to do but I sure hope your father gets the telegram in time because I will be the one to have to deal with him if he shows up here unaware." Shannon reassures her, "The telegraph operator said it would be there by ten

132

o'clock and that I should not be concerned; it will get there. Papa won't leave East Hills to fetch me till noon Friday. That's plenty of time."

Arm in arm Annie and Shannon travel by taxi to Cincinnati Station and make the train on time. A short two hours and they would be in Sailor Park. The snow was coming down heavy but for a train this was nothing. The ladies were snug and warm in the passenger car which had a stove and was burning warm. They had hot coco and pastries on the way. Annie did not know who would meet her at the station. She had not heard if her father made the run from St. Louis to Louisville. Considering the early snow she supposes he will have probably left the Louis Queen in St Louis and is on a train himself coming home.

They arrive in Sailor Park a little late at twelve-thirty in the afternoon. They depart the train and there is no one waiting for them. Annie reassures Shannon it is just the snow; that someone would be there soon. No sooner did the porter set their luggage on the platform when James Jr flies into the station with Dancer running and then stopping with a slide-in because the snow was slippery. Annie waves to James and he sees Shannon. He had heard of her but this was the first time he would see her and what a surprise because he only expected Annie. He jumps down from the surrey to introduce himself. You can tell he is beside himself. He had never seen red hair so vibrant and her blue almost green eyes are piercing him through. This eighteen-year-old young man stood tall and was suddenly no longer eighteen but much older. He said nothing just stood there hoping Annie would say something. Annie doesn't miss a thing, "Hi

133

James," She hugs him, "this is Shannon, you remember my friend in school? She will be here with us for Christmas." James puts his heels together places his hat on his chest and says, "Pleased to meet you, Miss Shannon." Shannon reaches out her down turned hand and James touches it with a light grasp and nodes." He jumps to take her case from her hand and Annie's likewise and puts them in the back of the carriage. Annie immediately says, "Where is papa?"

James helps them get into the carriage and of course he pays extra attention to Shannon. James hops into the carriage and Dancer is ready to go. Annie did not forget to say hello to Dancer before she got in the carriage. Dancer comes alive in the snow and prances like gravity is his toy, his Annie is home. James clicks the reigns, "Father sent a telegram from St. Louis; he is leaving the Louis Queen there and coming home by train. St Louis is already packed in snow. He should be here in two days."

Mary hears the carriage coming up the driveway and she goes to the veranda to greet her daughter home. They pull up in front and James jumps to the aid of Shannon of course, Annie can wait. Annie laughs, "James, Shannon won't break she knows all about how to get down from a carriage." She just embarrassed her brother. James does not ruffle he continues to help Shannon. Shannon says, "Don't you mind her James, I love a gentleman." James returns, "See Annie, some ladies still like men." Annie ruffles, "I like men, mind you brother."

Mary has never met Shannon but caught on immediately, none the less she had no idea she was coming to the house. Her mind flashes to the earlier discussion with Annie about the trip to Paris and the reservations she and her husband had. Seeing a young woman named Shannon suddenly appear as a guest caught her unprepared. She comes to help her up the snowy steps, "You must be Miss Shannon Brennan Annie's schoolmate." Shannon is stepping carefully up the snowy steps while Mary holds her hand, "Yes Misses Dupree, I am she, or is it I am her; I can never remember." Mary says, "With my English, both will do." Shannon was delighted to hear Annie's mother with a French accent of which Annie has none." Shannon says in French, "si heureux de vous rencontrer (so pleased to meet you.)" Mary returns, "ton français est très bien (your French is very good.)" Annie is now getting help from her brother; the steps were very slippery. Annie holding on to James tightly, "nous avons travaillé dur sur notre français (we have been working hard on our French)" Mary does not know that what she is about to say will cause a deafening silence, "I suppose since you are here Shannon, that your parents have agreed to let you go to Paris in spring." You could hear the snowflakes hit the ground. There was not a sound.

James Jr has not a clue, he looks at everyone in silence and says, "Mom, I'm going to put Dancer up and give him some extra grain." Mary nods approval, "Fine dear, and make sure he has water. Put a stick in it to help it from freezing till morning. It's not that cold, he will not need a blanket."

Annie finally broke the silence, "Mama, we will talk." Shannon says not a word. Mary gets it right away. Things are not so smooth about Paris. Mary takes Shannon's coat as they enter the foyer, "Annie, Shannon should be comfortable in the guest room next to Leah Anna, I'll have James bring your case's

135

up, let's go to the kitchen, Helen has made up lunch, I'm sure you are hungry." Annie leads Shannon to the kitchen behind her mother, "We had coco and a pastry on the train but I don't know about Shannon but I'm starving." Shannon trailing behind and again with the French, "je suis affamé (I am famished.) The kitchen is warm, almost steamy with the windows fogged with condensation. Mary introduces Helen to Shannon and they sit at the large kitchen table on one end. Mary is on the end and Annie is next to her mother on the corner with Shannon at her side.

Mary wastes no time, "So what is the matter, I can tell something is wrong." Shannon wants to start right in but Annie puts her hand on Shannon's signaling her to wait while Annie explains, "Shannon's parents will not let her go to Paris." Shannon again starts to speak up and Annie again squeezes her hand, "It is not her father as much as her mother and they say they cannot afford it with two boys already in college." Annie is trying to prevent Shannon from going into a tirade about her mother but it did not work. Shannon pulls her hand back from Annie, "Let's be honest Annie, my mother is the entire problem, daddy would let me go, it is her and her alone that has caused all of this." Mary understands Shannon's tone and comes to an understanding very quickly. Mary now puts her hand on her daughters, "Let me see, Mister and Misses Brennan are not aware and probably would not approve of Shannon being here right now?" Shannon now puts her hand on Annie's, "I sent my father the telegram. They know I am here and I'm old enough to make my own decisions Misses Dupree. Mary smiles, "oh ma douce fille (oh my sweet girl,) I have no doubt you are and I know my daughter Antoinette, you would not be here frivolously. I am sure this is very important to you but I must prepare to tell my husband when he arrives in another day."

Annie can tell her mother is about to take charge of this very difficult situation. Mary stands and helps Helen, who is all ears, put plates in front of the girls. Helen puts sliced ham and cheese with bread and fresh French mayonnaise on the table. She also places a platter of pickles and olives in reach of them both. Annie and Shannon show their hunger and jump right into the wonderful food. Shannon mumbles with her mouth full, "Why does she have to be so difficult?" Mary sits again at the head of table with a cup of tea, "Some mothers cannot let go of their daughters; boys are always left to their fathers and daughters to their mothers to direct into adulthood. Your mother is afraid for you." Helen asked if they would like milk or tea and they both ask for milk, it goes good with a sandwich especially when you are hungry. Shannon has a milk mustache, "My mother should trust the good sense she beat into me my whole life." Annie laughs as she uses a napkin to wipe Shannon's mustache. Mary watching Annie dote over Shannon in that way is telling; Annie is close to Shannon. Shannon acts so matter of fact as Annie wipes the mustache from her lips that Shannon responds to Annie's touch. Mary has never seen the two together; this is all new to her.

Mary continues, "So your father gets this telegram from his daughter that she is going to the Dupree's home, and I assume you will be staying through Christmas. He is going to be furious." Shannon interrupts, "Not daddy, but mother will be livid." Mary says, "Yes, of course, I do not think they will be so concerned as to come after you through all this weather, but they will be worried sick. So you need to send them another telegram as soon as possible. Tell them you are safe in Sailor Park with the Dupree family and will be home after Christmas. At least do that Shannon, it will stop a fire storm and perhaps put their hearts to rest." Shannon said, "Yes Misses Dupree, I will do that." Mary responds, "Good, and please call me Mary."

Annie is delightedly full, "Mama that was wonderful." She looks at Shannon and says, "I told you my mother would understand." To this Mary walked behind both as they sat at the table and put a hand on each of their shoulders, "I understand that this could be trouble. Shannon, I hope your parents will be patient to find a good end here for both of you." Mary then stands right behind Annie and squeezes both of her shoulders, "Annie, you let me talk to your father before you say anything." Mary kisses her on the top of the head and then looks out the kitchen window, "My, my, it is really coming down out there; we will probably have to use the sleigh to pick up your father at the train station tomorrow night."

Marcus comes through the kitchen door shaking off the snow. He has a large limp turkey held upside down by the feet, "Got em' with one shot Mom. He's a big one; must be twelve pounds. Marcus looks straight at Shannon and smiles. Shannon turns men's heads with her stunning red hair which Marcus has never seen before. Mary moves rapidly toward Marcus, "Take it out and remove the head and gut it. Hurry it is dripping on the floor. Pluck it as best you can and let it freeze. We will cook it on Christmas eve." Marcus is slow to move and just stares at Shannon. Mary sees the problem, "Marcus, this is Miss Shannon Brennan; she is staying with us for Christmas. "Maintenant va avec toi, va! (Now go with you, go!)" Marcus with turkey in hand turns, "Pleased to meet Miss Shannon." Shannon and Annie both laugh and Shannon says, "Pleased to meet you, Marcus."

Mary asks Shannon, "Would you like some hot tea?" Shannon says yes and Mary pours her some in one of her favorite China cups. Shannon goes to the window and sees Marcus chop the head off the turkey and then gut it. She winces. Shannon is a city girl. Their turkeys come from the butcher rapped in brown paper. She has never seen something so brutal. When the guts fall out she turns away from the window and sloshes her tea into the saucer, "Oh my, I know that is how it is done; I've just never seen it before." With her eyes closed she tries to forget the image in her mind. Annie who is a little closer to the natural world of hunters, and especially her brothers who were always killing some animal says, "finish your tea and I'll take you to your room. You can rest a bit if you wish."

Shannon hears banging coming from the cellar. Annie says, "That is James in the cellar adding wood for the boiler." Shannon remarks, "Wood, our house has a coal furnace, I cannot imagine there would be enough wood in all the world to heat all the houses in the city. It sure smells nicer than that smelly old coal. Annie says, "Even the trains are using coal now but Papa refuses to use it on the Louis Queen. He says it rots the boiler and he can only get it in the

139

cities, whereas with wood he can get it anywhere. Shannon says, "I cannot wait to meet your father, do you think he will like me?" Annie wraps her arm around Shannon's as they head to her room, "Everyone likes you, Shannon."

They get to the guest room and it is cold. Annie turns the valve on the radiator and the steam hisses as the radiator fills with hot water. Annie tells Shannon, "No sense staying here till it warms up, come to my room; do you want to take a nap?" Shannon follows Annie, "Lord no, I'm not even tired." Annie shows Shannon her room and Shannon remarks, "My, it is so big, mine at home is half this size." Annie laughs, "Papa says, 'you can never make them bigger after the fact.'" Annie has all of her childhood memorabilia displayed about. Everything from dolls to drawings she made as a schoolgirl and lots and lots of books. Shannon remarks, "Have you read all of these?" Annie replies, "Well when you are bored in the country what else is there to do? Not like you city girls with hundreds of friends to fill your time. Your family probably has all kinds of social clubs and things to do right?" Shannon plops down on Annie's bed with a book of Annie's titled 'Women of Prominence'. Annie remarks, "Mama gave that one to me. It is mostly about the many Queens throughout Europe and their influence in politics." Shannon holding the book in her lap, not opening it, "How boring, I could not be bothered but you read it all." Annie returns, "Like I said, when you are alone with nothing to do and your mother says, 'read this' what else is there to do. You see Shannon, when you are exposed to different environments you become different people. Now imagine girls who are poor;

140

what do they get to do." Shannon puts the book back, "Let's not be sad, it's Christmas and I'm here with you instead of with my family, I'm so excited to be here."

Annie pulls Shannon up by her hands, "Let's go see Dancer in the Stable." Shannon swings to her feet, "Is that your horse?" Annie says, "Well, he is everyone's but he likes me best because I bring him treats and brush him most when I'm here." Annie opens a drawer and pulls out some coveralls and long underwear, "Here take off your dress and corset and put these on." Annie and Shannon were the same size. Annie disrobes and puts on long johns and pants and a plaid flannel shirt. She tosses Shannon some boots from her closet, "These will probably fit you." She digs into a trunk and retrieves a short, wasted coat for Shannon and one for her from the closet along with some knit scarves. They were all set for the cold. They go bouncing down the steps and out the kitchen door to the back yard. Mary shouts as they head out, "Watch for your sister, Leah Anna should be home from school soon. This would be Leah Anna's last day of school before Christmas.

There is already four inches of snow on the ground and snowballs begin to fly with screams of joy coming from both the girls as they play like children. James Jr and Marcus just sit on the fence and watch until a snowball comes their way. Needless to say they return fire but they keep it easy. Neither one of the boys throw at Shannon they only throw at Annie who fires back with all her might. Shannon and Annie duck into Dancers stall and the fight is over. Annie pulls a carrot from her pocket. It is a large one and she breaks it into smaller pieces and feeds them to him

141

slowly. With a kiss on the nose, Dancer neighs in acknowledgement. Shannon touches his cheek lightly; she has never been around a horse and does not have a clue how to touch him. Annie says, "Here feel his muzzle. Shannon touches it like Annie did with a soft stroke. Shannon says, "Oh, it is so soft, will he let me kiss it like you did." Annie says, "Sure." Shannon leans forward to kiss his nose and Dancer licks her face. Annie laughs, "You just got a kiss." Shannon winces and wipes her face with her scarf, "Not what I expected." Annie hands Shannon a piece of carrot, "Here, feed him this and you will be cemented in his memory forever." Shannon feeds Dancer and Annie gets the curry brush and brushes him while Shannon watches.

Annie muses with Shannon, "Yes, Dancer is my kind of man aren't you boy? That is because your balls have been cut off." Shannon is not agreeing, "Come on Annie don't be a man hater." Annie laughs, "I'm not. I am just kidding, but it sure makes them calm if you know what I mean; not like my feisty brothers." Shannon adds in, "I like men that are feisty. I can always handle them. You just smack their hand if they touch you. They mind just like a horse. You say down boy and they get down; you say come here and they come here. For the most part they are like puppy dogs." Annie laughs, "Those puppy dogs sniff out the bitches in heat." Shannon replies, "Shame on you, where is your refinement." Annie laughs, "I left it on the train. Come on lets surprise Leah Anna, we will hide and hit her with snowballs."

It is time for Leah Anna to come home and Annie and Shannon hide behind the shed which is next to the path that Leah Anna will use on her way

142

to the house from school. Sure enough it is only a few minutes and Leah Anna comes around the corner of the shed. Annie and Shannon let loose with a barrage of snowballs. Leah Anna is confused, who is the other girl with Annie. Leah Anna is a good shot and fires back quickly but it was two against one and she cries, "foul play, stop it." Annie runs up and hugs Leah Anna, "This is my friend Shannon from school. She is here for Christmas." Leah Anna is delighted, "So pleased to meet you." Leah Anna curtsies. Shannon laughs and curtsies too, "Your sister talks about you all the time." Leah Anna smiles, "good things I hope." They all head for the house to get warm. Leah Anna leads, "Papa will be home tomorrow, I cannot wait to see him; Mama says he will come with lots of presents from St. Louis." Annie laughs, "Shannon, you see the only reason she is happy to see Papa is for the presents." Leah Anna punches Annie in the arm, "That's not true."

It is nearing five-thirty and on this December twenty-first it was already getting dark. Everyone gathered in the kitchen. They would not use the dining room till Christmas day. Helen had made a big pot of beef stew and fresh biscuits and everyone sat down for dinner. Mary said to James Jr, "Do you want to say grace in place of your father?" James took charge, "Heavenly father thank-you for our many blessings. Thank-you for keeping our family safe and bringing us our new guest Shannon. Please bring our father home safely and thank you for Helens stew, amen." Mary raises her head, "Well that will do." Helen serves Shannon first, guests are always first, and then she rounds the table to Mary and then Annie while the boys are just patiently waiting their turn. Helen knows

143

the boys appetite and gives them a double portion and three biscuits. Then Helen serves herself and sits at the other end of the table opposite Mary.

Mary starts the conversation, "Shannon you have two brothers also, don't you?" Shannon finishes her bite, covers her mouth a bit, "Yes Misses Dupree, two brothers both in Xavier University in Cincinnati." Mary insists, "Please call me Mary. Do you get along well?" Shannon speaks adoringly, "They have always looked out after me. They are very protective. Anytime I would talk to a boy they would warn them." Shannon put on a deep voice, "They would say to them that is my sister and if you know what is good for you, be a gentleman or else. Boys would not talk to me because of them." She laughed, "I didn't mind, most of the boys at the catholic school were creeps anyway."

James Jr says, "Yeah, boys can be creeps." He was just trying to get into the conversation because Shannon was there. Annie defends her brother, "You are not a creep James your just like Papa, a fine gentleman." James blushes though he did not want his sister's help. He can only dream about being with a woman as beautiful as Shannon and he thinks to himself, 'one day I will be old enough for a woman like that.' Shannon goes on about her brothers; "Fredrick will be a banker like my father and Robert the next in line is studying law. They are chips off the old block as everyone says. Robert and I get along very well because we are close in age. He is always coming to my defense. Like when I wanted to go to the school dance, even though no one had asked me. Mama said I could not go alone, but then Robert said he would be my date. Then she let me go. When we

144

got to the dance Robert left me alone so I could visit with all the girls." Shannon laughed, "Robert had said that I probably did not get asked to the dance because all the boys were afraid of him and Fredrick, and you know I think he was right."

Marcus had his fill and asked to be excused. Mary grabbed his shirt sleeve and said, "Not so fast, Helen made vanilla snow ice cream, don't you want some?" Marcus said, "Wow sure, can we put chocolate on it too?" Mary points to the canister with the chocolate, "Bring that down and I will shave it on top." Helen cleared the table and everyone helped. She went to the back porch and retrieved the mixing bowl full with this delicious slurry of snow and milk with vanilla and sugar. She scooped it into dishes and Mary shaved chocolate on top. Everyone was cooing at the flavor, Mary lamented, "I wish your father were here. Tomorrow we must make more for him."

Night came and lamps were lit. James Jr attended the wood boiler in the cellar and they all retired for the night. Shannon's room was warm now. Annie, by candlelight, escorts her to her room. Shannon kisses Annie on the cheek, "I'd rather sleep with you." Annie kisses her cheek also, "Mama would not understand. She would get the wrong idea. Sleep well my dear." Annie leaves and goes to her room. Shannon pauses for a moment and then just accepts she must sleep alone in a strange house. She is so lost being at odds with her parents and has trouble falling to sleep.

Annie waits till late and all in the house is silent. She can just feel Shannon's loneliness and tiptoes to her room. She can see because the white snow is reflecting the moon light so bright that even

145

with the curtains drawn it is light. She goes around the bed and slips in next to her from behind and puts her arm around her. Shannon comes out of her light sleep and feels Annie's arm around her and her warm body against hers. She just cries and says nothing and Annie just holds her.

Morning comes and Annie slips back to her room early. Nobody would know.

Like clockwork Helen starts the morning kitchen activity; James Jr and Marcus go to the cellar to stoke the boiler. Leah Anna calls firsts on the tub for a bath and Annie shouts, "Guests first!" Shannon feeling right at home shouts, "I'm not ready Leah Anna you go ahead!" Leah Anna heads for the bathroom to heat the water. Mary comes down from the third floor, "We're you ladies warm enough last night? You know all the heat seems to end up on the third floor." Annie puts her head out of her door, "We were just fine mama." Mary heads to the kitchen and Annie peaks her head into Shannon's door without knocking. Shannon is naked coming out of her nightgown. Annie quickly comes in and closes the door, "Sorry, I should have knocked." Shannon pretends modesty and covers with one arm over her breasts and her hand over her groin, sarcastically she says, "Oh, I'm so embarrassed. You know everything about me; nothing to hide." Annie just stands there and looks Shannon over, "My you are a redhead from stem to stern; you are." Shannon puts on her robe, "Well of course, just like my mother." Shannon sits on the bed, "I feel like such a baby, crying last night." Annie sits on the bed, "With all that is going on with your parents and being in a strange place, I knew you needed some reassurance. I can tell you that my

146

mother is feeling like she is caught between you and your parents and that we just thrust this upon her. Somehow, we have to make your parents understand so they don't see mother as an accomplice."

Shannon inquires, "Can we get to the telegraph office with all this snow. I will send daddy another telegram like your mother said. I will say, 'Dear father, safe at Dupree home -stop- my idea -stop- not their fault -stop- see you on New Year's Day -stop-. Annie says, "Please add I love you to it." Shannon quirks, "No, let them wonder."

The morning continues with each getting a bath in turn. Annie informs her mother that they need to go to the telegraph office. Mary has James Jr rig up Dancer to the sleigh. Since they are going into the small town of Sailor Park the girls dressed like they were going to the city; they always dress in their best form. James was looking forward to escorting them to the telegraph office and off they went. Dancer had bells on and was prancing high, Annie was in the Sleigh and of course she had kissed him on the nose.

The Sleigh was sliding easy and it was no effort for Dancer. James was showing off by sliding around corners which made Dancer side slip and prance sideways. Annie chastised James, "Don't do that to him he could slip and fall and break a leg." James obliged and slowed the pace. They get to the telegraph office and James jumps down an immediately reaches out for Shannon's Hand. Annie laughs, "If it was just me Shannon, he would not be helping at all. Brothers and sisters don't you know?" It is nice and warm in the office and James takes off his gloves to warm his hands by the iron stove. Shannon writes her message on the paper pad and hands it to the operator. He looks it over. Shannon says, "This needs to go to East Hills Green Ridge office." The operator says, "It will go to the Cincinnati main office and they will relay it to Green Ridge. Do you want to wait for conformation from Green Ridge, it may take 15 minutes for them to confirm." Shannon says they would wait. The operator starts tapping away. Shannon remarks, "These modern times, you can get a message all the way to Green Ridge and back in 15 minutes. Of course then they have to deliver it. Papa should get it yet this morning." They were amazed; they got confirmation in only 10 minutes. The operator said, "That will be twenty-five cents for the message but another seventy-five cents for the delivery, one dollar please." Shannon gives the man one dollar and a ten-cent tip. The chore was done. Somehow it made Shannon feel lighter. Annie and James watched as she pranced with a skip as they returned to the sleigh. She holds out her hand to James and says, "retourne-moi au château mon bon monsieur (return me to the castle good sir.)" James is not sure, "My French is not as good as my sisters." Shannon repeats it in English. Annie gets in the other side of the sleigh with no help from James. She takes Shannon's arm, "Are you feeling better now." Shannon simply says, "Beaucoup mon cher (much, my dear.)"

They are quite cold by the time they get back to the house. Annie helps James put Dancer back in his stall. She tells Shannon to run a head and get warm in the kitchen, which she does obligingly. James and Annie join her there in short order. Mary has hot coco ready for all of them. Annie remarks, "It is so cold, it feels like the temperature is dropping. I hope papa

148

will be home on time." Mary agrees, "Yes, it is getting colder; your father should be on the eight-fifteen coming in from Chicago." James and I will meet the train. If nothing went wrong he will be on it."

They spend the afternoon watching the clock and waiting. Annie would go up to her room to retrieve some other book or piece of memorabilia to show Shannon. She did this twice or more. James Jr would let the boiler slow down during the day to save on wood. The house would get a bit cold, so the kitchen was the most comfortable place to be. Helen had baked two pies, one pumpkin and one apple. She made a cinnamon roll out of pie crust and sugar which they all shared. The pies were for Christmas on Sunday. Mary remarked, "James and Marcus have picked out a nice pine tree for our Christmas. They will cut it Christmas Eve and we will decorate it. You know how much your father likes to decorate the tree or rather how much he likes watching us decorate the tree." Annie reminisces, "Mama, remember when the ladder broke while daddy was trying to put the star on the top? He almost fell through the window." Mary gasps, "oh, il m'a fait mal au dos (oh my he hurt his back.)" Marcus who was sitting by himself in the corner of the room next to the kitchen stove remarks, "English mom, what did you say?" Mary laughing, "I said, your father hurt his back." Marcus with an unsure grin; "Why is that funny?" Annie sides with her laughing, "Because Marcus, Papa is perfect in everything and I don't know, but when the king falls it's funny." You will have to read the fable about the 'King who had on clothes.'" Mary adds insight, "Your father laughed too, no harm done."

149

Shannon was amused at it all and was introspective in her thoughts, '*I wish my family was more like this. Just relaxed and having fun. I cannot remember my mother ever having fun. We decorate the tree and my brothers talk about school and mother knits, year after year. We get gifts and give hugs and thanks but no laughter.*' Annie can tell Shannon is withdrawn. She smacks Shannon on the knee, "Come with me miss." She takes Shannon by the hand and pulls her away from the kitchen and leads her down the hall to her father's den. There she takes two brandy snifters and puts them on her father's desk and pours them full with brandy. Shannon grins as Annie hands her a glass and Shannon says, "You know me too well."

It is chilly in the den but the brandy was worth the chill. Annie sat in her father's enormous chair and Shannon gazed at the extensive bookshelves, "Your father has been all over the world. Daddy says he got investors from France and England to build the Louisville Queen." Annie swings back and forth in her father's chair, "Yes, mama tells me that in five more years he will buy them all out and he will own the Louis Queen all himself. Your father knows all about my father's work?" Shannon sits in a chair that is in front of the desk, "My father knows everything about anyone who has money. It is like the gossip world of men. They spend all their time talking about who has what. Daddy says money is made by interest on loans but that your father made money through investment partners and that is something his bank thinks would be another way to do business. They all talk about this New York place called the stock exchange where all these bankers like my father sell

150

shares in each other's companies. It is all so boring to me but in my house that's all I hear, my brothers too. I feel so much outside every time they start talking money and law. But, with your family, they talk about theater and music and fun times you have had. You got to go to Pittsburg and see an opera. You are going to Paris to study theater and I am going nowhere."

Annie tries to intercept where Shannon is going with the conversation, "Shannon, don't get sad now, its Christmas." Annie comes out from behind the desk and puts her arms around Shannon's waist, "We will figure something out. Maybe my father can talk to your father. Papa has a way with people. Maybe mama can talk to your mother. Something will happen trust me. Now be happy." Shannon is inspired by Annie's optimism, "Very well not another word." She swills down the brandy and clinks her glass against Annie's and Annie downs hers also.

The time comes and James Jr and Mary depart in the sleigh to retrieve Captain Dupree at the train station. All good fortunes be known, Captain Dupree is there with a giant smile and with wrapped Christmas presents in his arms. He tells James Jr, "Son help the porter, he is coming with a cart." And, sure enough there is a cart with more packages all adorned with fancy paper and ribbons. Mary says, "My word James, did you spend all our savings." Captain Dupree laughs, "Not at all dear, it was a good trip to St. Louis and I had time to spare while I got the workmen started on the maintenance of the Queen." What he meant by it being a good trip to St. Louis is the gambling was substantial and the house did very well." Captain Dupree was on schedule to own the Louis Queen out right and to be free from his partners.

151

They loaded everything in the sleigh. James Jr drove and his father and mother were seated and holding onto all the boxes mounding over them. The snow was coming down hard again. At the house everyone could hear the bells on Dancer's harness jingling as they came up the driveway. Everyone dashed to the front veranda to greet them. They could hear their father laughing from the distance and they knew all was well. Upon arriving at the steps leading to the veranda Captain Dupree could see there was one extra silhouette than expected. Mary had waited till then to announce, "The young lady there next to your Annie is Miss Shannon Brennan. She is here to join us for Christmas." Captain Dupree is first and foremost a generous man, "Oh my Mary, if I had known I could have gotten her something for Christmas." Mary whispers in his ear because they were close enough for the others to hear, "There was no time to telegram, Shannon and Annie got here day before yesterday." James schemes, "I'll think of something."

They all surround the sleigh and Captain Dupree takes charge, "Marcus you take that sack there; James you grab this bunch here. Hello Miss Brennan, you can carry this one and Annie you can carry this one and Leah Anna take this one. Take them all to the front room where we will put the tree." They dust off the snow and head for the front room. Shannon puts down her package and turns to greet Captain Dupree, "Hello Captain Dupree, I am Shannon Brennan, I am sorry to drop in on your Christmas celebration, it was a last-minute decision. I asked Annie if I could join all of you, I hope I am not imposing." Captain Dupree removes his hat and gloves and extends his hand to take hers. Her hand is only half the size of his; she lays her fingers into his hand. James places his other hand on top of hers in a gentle caress, "My dear Shannon it is no imposition and on the contrary, it is delightful that you will join us on this merry occasion." Shannon is so impressed with this towering man. He has such a kindly face and a smile that can melt away fear. Shannon now felt so at home with the Dupree's. He did not ask a word about why she was there. He did not question about her parents, which she expected. He just melted the ice of winter.

Mary takes his coat and hat and gloves and James with his booming voice, "Who wants brandy? Marcus open that crate there and bring a bottle to the kitchen." Helen helps Marcus open the wooden case and they retrieve one of the six bottles; then they all go to the warm kitchen. Captain Dupree puts his arm around James Jr, "James best go stoke up the boiler early, it is going to be very cold tonight." James turns and goes through the door which is just off the kitchen to go down to the cellar. Everyone surrounds the table and Helen puts out eight crystal glasses. Captain Dupree uncorks the brandy and pours. He hands Marcus his glass first, "Don't make this a habit but it is good for celebration." He turns to Leah Anna, "The same goes for you missy." To which Leah Anna says, "Oh Papa please I'm not a little girl." James Jr makes it back quickly and retrieve's his glass. Captain Dupree raises his glass to toast, "Here's to all my loved ones and the devil can have the rest; Merry Christmas!" Shannon laughs loudly, "Sounds like my father. I feel right at home." Mary dose not laugh, "vous donnerez l'impression erronée (you will give

153

the wrong impression)." James Dupree returns, "je plaisante mon amour (just kidding my love.)" Mary adds, "Shannon speaks French dear." Shannon is amused, "J'espère en apprendre davantage à Paris (I hope to learn more in Paris.)"

Everyone downed their brandy and Captain Dupree pours more, "So are you going to Paris with our Annie?" Annie is worried about what Shannon will say next. Shannon is no stranger to brandy and is feeling the warm glow. She also feels the warmth of this family, "In spite of my parents, one way or another I am going to Paris." Captain Dupree is an intuitive man. He has an understanding right away and he says, "Is there rough water ahead? That is what we say on the Louis Queen and that does not always pertain to the river." He was relating to the dealings with people. Shannon got it. Annie is just enjoying the brandy and listening to her father. Captain Dupree continues, "I can understand your parents not wanting to let their most precious daughter go to a place like Paris because Paris has two faces and I know them both. One is the beauty of all the most famous art and culture and the other is debauchery and I am sure you parents are afraid of the second."

Mary has always been amazed at her husband. He can get to the bottom of things quickly, she just listens. She has told him nothing about the situation and he is reading it like a soothsayer. He continues, "So I can tell that you are at odds with your parents, they do not want you to go. You got mad at them and abandon them at Christmas." Shannon is dumbfounded, "you can read me like a book." Annie stands and gets behind Shannon and puts a hand on each shoulder. Her father reads this also; his daughter

154

is right behind Shannon regardless of the situation. Captain Dupree laughs, "Well I can tell just by the look in my dear wife's face that you young ladies are in charge no matter who says what. There is perhaps something I can do since I did not have the opportunity to get you a Christmas gift Miss Brennan, I can write your parents a letter and try to waylay their fears about Paris. Perhaps they do not know that I am well connected there and can assure your safety. I would not send my dear Antoinette into harm's way."

Shannon again is astonished. Annie gives her father a big hug. He has to bend down to get her and lifts her off her feet. Annie says, "Oh thank you papa." Shannon is smiling ear to ear, "I hope it will help. My mother is awful stubborn; Thank-you sir." He responds, "Please call me James dear, our home is your home and our family is yours." Shannon takes her turn and hugs this giant man but he does not lift her off her feet; that would be untoward for this moral man.

Helen was busy putting together ham finger sandwiches and put out a plate of cookies and everyone dined and talked. James Jr and Marcus had to ask about all the presents and Captain Dupree had fun teasing them about what was there for everyone. Leah Anna was all ears but she knew she would be pleased because her father always spoiled her; she could wait. It was just so good to have him home and he would be there all winter. Perhaps in February he would take a train to St. Louis to check on the Louis Queen since it was not in Louisville with his brother.

The evening was winding down, James Jr went again to the cellar to stoke and load the boiler with wood. The boiler had a spring wound auger that would slowly turn the ash out of the bottom of the burner and there was an automatic damper to control the burn. His father said it was truly the modern age with a self-controlling boiler you could forget during the night. He said it allows a man to sleep at night with no worries.

They all said good night and went to their rooms. Shannon sat in Annie's room. They had too much to talk about to sleep but as the wee hours came Shannon returned to the guest room alone.

Morning broke early because the snowstorm had passed and the sun was shining. It was terribly cold outside and there was Jack Frost painting on all the windows for the house was warm. The boiler was cooling and of course the first order of things was James Jr running down the steps to the cellar to stoke it up. Helen had coffee brewing; it was Captain Dupree's favorite. Mary preferred tea. It was Christmas Eve. Helen had started a batch of cinnamon rolls and the sweet smell was rising through the whole house.

Leah Anna was quick to light the kerosene water heater and to be first in the bath. Mary and Captain Dupree bathed together in their large private bathroom. Water was refiled each day by James Jr and Marcus to water heaters built into each bathroom. It would be their chore again this afternoon to refill them. Papa had promised that next spring he would buy a pump that he saw demonstrated in Pittsburgh that allowed for a tank on the roof to supply water to the bathrooms and kitchen. Hotels had them and more people were putting them in their homes. He remarked about how wonderful the modern age was.

Each one, as time allowed, meandered to the kitchen. They had coffee and tea and cinnamon rolls. Captain Dupree engaged the boys about the tree they would cut down together and drag to the house for decorating. Shannon, Annie and Leah Anna wanted to come along and they were off. They arrive down the road a piece off in a field. Captain Dupree identified the area as being free from anyone's ownership, "That's a fine tree boys, this is an easement by the railroad line, no one owns this land; we can cut the tree. Marcus, you head back and get Dancer in his harness so we don't have to drag this tree ourselves." Marcus heads off in a flat out run as James Jr lets loose with a double-bladed ax. They had estimated the tree to be about nine feet tall; just one foot under the ceiling in the front room. It would be spectacular.

Mary and Helen at the house were retrieving the ornaments from the storeroom on the third floor. It was a collection of items from the many places James and Mary had been. There were even some ornaments from Paris. There were ribbons made into a long garland that would drape the tree and always a large silver star for the top of the tree. They had heard horror stories about trees catching on fire so all the little candle holders were left behind. Mary and Helen reminisced about previous Christmas' when the children still believed in Kris Kringle. Helen had lost her only brother in the Civil War in 1864 and her mother had passed away from consumption in 1875. Her father died in 1880 in a fall from a ladder. Helen said she could not remember ever having a Christmas until she met the Dupree's in 1881 and every

Christmas from then on are her memories. The Dupree's were her family now and she adores them.

Marcus jogs alongside Dancer and arrives with harness and rope. They lash the tree by the base and off they go in a gentle walk back to the house. Annie, Shannon and Leah Anna stomp through the deep show remarking how they should have put on coveralls because the snow was so deep. They would be dry though because it was so cold. They arrive at the house, shake off the snow and open the door in front for the entry of this big tree. Captain Dupree and James Jr carried it in and placed it in front of the bay window in the same spot it goes to each year. Captain Dupree held it upright as James Jr puts the wooden support in place and nails it to the tree. With a push and a pull and a step back to see, and then with another nail it was secured and straight.

Mary and Helen came in with boxes of decorations. Helen said, "I'll make hot coco, who wants some?" Everyone said yes; they were so cold and shivering. Shannon was so right at home. Annie could tell that she was comfortable. They all shared putting ornaments on the tree and Mary and James told stories of memories about each ornament. Upon completion all the presents that Captain Dupree had brought were placed around the tree and the boys and Annie revealed the presents they were hiding for their father and placed them also under the tree.

All the girls help Mary and Helen put up more decorations over the fireplace while the boys start the fire. Captain Dupree announces, "Well, there is one gift that I brought for you Annie that I can't wait till tomorrow to give you." Annie is surprised, "Why is that papa?" James says, "You will see. Leah Anna, do you see that red package just at the left of the tree? Hand that to Annie." Leah Anna retrieves it and carries it over to Annie." Everyone comes over close to her. Captain Dupree says, "Go ahead and open it and I will explain why I couldn't wait." Annie opens the package carefully and the box that was under the paper. Inside is another thing that looks like a box but has brass corners and a leather cover. She has no idea what it is. Her father explains, "That my dear family is a Kodak." The mumbling goes around the room person to person, "Kodak, what is a Kodak?" James continues, "Do you all remember when we had our picture taken in Pittsburg at the Opera?" All the children acknowledge the memory. James says. "Well this is what they call a box camera and anyone can use it to take a picture. I learned all about it in St. Louis. I had heard about it before, but here it is. Now the reason I could not wait is because it only works in bright sunshine. Today is perfect and tomorrow the sun may not shine."

The boys ogle this amazing thing and quiz their father how it works but Annie does not quite understand, "Papa, why is this a gift for me?" James puts his arm around his daughter, "Because you can take it to Paris with you and send your mother and me pictures of your adventure." Annie smiles, "Do you think I can learn how it works?" James explains, "It uses a thing called film. You just have to be in bright sunshine and push this button. You then wind the crank for the next picture. It will take six. You then put the film in a box and mail it to me." There is a place in St. Louis and Cincinnati where they convert the film to a permanent picture. Isn't that amazing?" Annie is cautious, "It sounds complicated."

Captain Dupree instructs, "Everyone put on your coat and come out front we will try it out." They all oblige and go out front. Everyone at some time or another had their picture taken so they knew what to do. Captain Dupree lined everyone up and said, "I will take the first one and then James you can take my place to take the next." It all went quite well but to everyone's dismay, they now had to wait a long time to see the results. Annie again says, "I hope I can do it. Do they have this in Paris?" Captain Dupree did not know, he said, "After you head back to school, I will get this film converted in Cincinnati and if it works, wouldn't it be wonderful if you can send us pictures from Paris?" Annie agrees but feels now responsible for this thing called a Kodak camera.

As the sun sets on this Christmas Eve, Leah Anna plays the piano and they all join in Christmas carols. Dinner was a beef roast with carrots and potatoes. Tomorrow would be the big turkey Marcus had shot and prepared. It was now thawing in the kitchen. Helen would put it in the oven in the morning for their Christmas feast.

After dinner in the kitchen they returned to the front room where Captain Dupree opened another bottle of brandy. The boys were all looking at the names on the packages and organizing them while their father laughed at them. Lean Anna and Annie took turns reading from Charles Dickens 'A Christmas Carol' which was their father's favorite. Shannon read some of the parts about Tiny Tim. As they reached the ending Captain Dupree sitting with his arm around his love Mary who was curled up by his side says, "Fine story, damn fine story. It should make a fine play someday if they should make it.

160

Boys stoke the boiler one more time and off to bed."
It is late. It has been a fine Christmas Eve and as
tradition would have it they would open all the
presents in the morning. Everyone warmed with the
brandy retire. No one would notice that Shannon slept
in Annie's room and truly it was just to keep warm
for even with the boiler running full steam it was cold
in the house.

Morning again is sunny. Helen's room is on
the first floor and just adjacent to the location of the
boiler in the cellar. Her room was often so warm she
had to open a window. The second floor was the
coldest while the third floor would catch all the heat
rising. Captain Dupree was frustrated and would say,
"Better if we lived in a one room house than trying to
keep this place warm. First it is cold; then it is hot. I
just can't seem to keep it regulated."

Helen started the coffee and you could smell
bacon. She stuffed the turkey and put it in the oven.
She was always the morning's inspiration with such
good smells throughout the house. No one would
bathe this morning. The boys descended to the
kitchen ravenous. Helen made a big batch of
scrambled eggs with biscuits, sausage and bacon. She
stuffed them full. Annie, Shannon and Leah Anna
were next. They stood by the stove shivering. Helen
hands Annie her favorite which was coffee. She says
as she grasps it with her cold hands, "All the world
will freeze except this kitchen." Helen laughs, "I was
actually too warm last night. Here sit and put this over
your legs." She hands her a quilt. Shannon, Leah
Anna and Annie all sit together and put the quilt over
their legs.

161

Captain Dupree comes stomping through the kitchen grumbling and heads to the cellar, "Hot on the third floor freezing on the first." He's going to check the boiler himself. He is a steam Captain trying to solve the problem. He knows there is not much he can do. Drafts up the chimneys and the nature of heat rising and the sheer size of this house were beyond control.

As the sun rose in the sky the radiant energy warmed the house. They made a big fire in the front room and began opening presents. James Jr and Marcus each received a Colt forty-five caliber pistol. It was known as the peacemaker. Mary was not pleased. Leah Anna got a jewelry box with a music box built in and two gold necklaces. Annie in addition to the Kodak camera received a printed collection of Shakespeare and a Mink Hat and muffler. For his wife Mary he has twelve small packages one for each of the next twelve days. She opens the first. The aroma is unmistakable, French perfume. The rest would be opened privately on the next eleven days and no one said a word. For Helen he purchased her a beautiful bath robe and she was delighted. All was well with the world of Captain Dupree except this damn cold house.

Shannon is enjoying everyone's delight and Captain Dupree calls her aside and whispers, "I will write that letter to your mother and father tomorrow. You can help me on what to say. Madam Rousseau is a very trustworthy friend of my wife and if she recommends an Academy in Paris, it will be the best. I hope I can convince them it will be safe." That was the best present Shannon could receive she beams with a smile, "Thank-you Captain Dupree." The captain says, "Please call me James dear."

The boys start up another fire in the big dining room fireplace to get ready for the Christmas feast. All the ladies help Helen. There were sweet potatoes and white mashed potatoes. There was a large pot of green beans and onions. Helen had made candied carrots and cornbread and with the big turkey and stuffing, it was all ready. Marcus went around the big table and filled everyone's glass with warm cinnamon apple cider and the feast began. Captain Dupree said grace and they all stood holding hands. The boys said with a loud Amen, "Let's eat." They all laughed and did just that.

Shannon felt like one of the family. Annie could see the families lightness of spirit which made Annie light in her spirit. The meal was filled with the noise of clanking plates and forks and the mumble of chatter and laughter. Captain Dupree and Mary could not have been happier or more pleased with their children. As the meal comes to its completion Captain Dupree is patting his stomach, "I'm stuffed to the gills, boys what say we go try out those Colts you have and break some bottles?" Mary interrupts as the boys are scrambling away from the table, "bon seigneur soyez prudent (good lord be careful.)" Captain Dupree laughs, "ne crains pas mon amour (fear not my love.)" Shannon looks at Captain Dupree and this time she uses his name, "James may I come and watch?" Annie looks at Shannon with a quizzical look, "Do you like guns?" Shannon turns to her, "Don't you remember the nickel novel about Wyatt Earp and his gal Mattie who carried a derringer?" Shannon points her finger and says, "Bang, bang, I

163

think every woman should have one." Annie laughs, "I never knew you were that dangerous." Shannon says, "Come on, lets watch the boys shoot." Captain Dupree invites them, "You can shoot too Shannon, come my sweet Annie you can shoot too." Annie is not sure, "No, I will stay here and help mother and Helen clean up." Mary who is already picking up dishes says, "Don't you worry Annie, Helen and I will get this go with Shannon and make sure no one gets a bullet in the butt."

Annie really does not care for guns but she goes along anyway. They bundle up; the day is cold but sunny. Out far in the backyard the boys set up a row of bottles on the fence rail for targets. The Colt forty-five came with a leather holster and belt which James Jr and Marcus put on. Captain Dupree had prepared and had his very own nickel-plated Colt under his coat in an under arm holster. The boys knew he had it but he never wore it at home. He pulled it out from under his coat, took aim and blasted the first bottle. Shannon screamed and covered her ears. James Jr drew and shot the second bottle and Marcus drew and missed the third. Captain Dupree said, "Draw a slow bead on it and at this distance raise an inch for drop." Marcus does just that and smashes the third bottle.

Captain Dupree motions to Shannon to come take his pistol and take a shot. Shannon wastes no time. Captain Dupree tells her, "It is heavy, not like a derringer so hold it with your right hand and support you hand with your left. It is fine for a lady to use both hands." Shannon is an ample student and does just that. She takes aim at the fourth bottle and just an inch high, she fires. The bottle disintegrates. She laughs

164

and turns quickly delighted that she got it and was waving the gun around wildly. Captain Dupree grabs her and swings her arm upward to secure the situation and the gun goes off again shooting straight up in the air, Captain Dupree takes the gun, "Perhaps a derringer is best, it is easier to control. Shannon is embarrassed and blushes. James shouts to Annie who is standing a ways off, "Annie come and try it, just once." Annie, not to be out done by her brave friend takes her father's pistol. She was not a stranger to her father's firearm. She had held it once when she was young. She had found it lying on his desk in the den and knew how heavy it was. She takes it in her hand, supports it with the other and aims at the fifth bottle. She squeezes the trigger ever so gently. The fifth bottle disintegrates. Annie looks at Shannon, "got you covered missy, no bad guy is going ta' bother ya'." Annie hands the pistol back to her father, "Papa there are not any bad guys in Sailor Park so I don't think I need a gun." Captain Dupree laughs, "True girl but that's not so down on the Ohio."

James Jr and Marcus knock off a few more bottles while Shannon, Annie and Captain Dupree return to the house. Captain Dupree tells Shannon, "If you like we can write that letter to your parents now." Shannon agrees and they, including Annie go to the den.

Captain Dupree sits at the big desk and Shannon sits in the chair in front. Annie wanders about the den looking at her father's many collected articles. He retrieves some stationary from the first drawer and opens the ink well and dips his pen. He begins, 'Dear Mister and Misses Brennan.' He talks each word as he writes. After the salutation he pauses;

puts the end of the pen in his mouth to think then continues, 'It has come to my attention of a plan for my daughter Antoinette and your daughter Shannon to go to Paris for continued studies.' He pauses again to think and continues, 'I can understand the many concerns that I share with you as to these young ladies in Paris alone.' Shannon sits like a child before this big man's desk and is amazed. Captain Dupree continues, 'It is only with the great confidence in my associates in Paris that I would consider letting my daughter attend an academy there.' Annie comes and sits on the arm of the chair that Shannon is sitting in, to listen closer. Captain Dupree continues, 'Of great consideration are the accommodations of which I am prepared to pay for the duration. Please understand the cost for two is amenable to the cost of one considering the companionship of my daughter and Shannon.' Captain Dupree looks up momentarily while he thinks of a closure, 'I would be pleased to visit to discuss other concerns.' He then boldly sighs 'Sincerely, Captain James Dupree.'

Shannon jumps up and Annie likewise and Shannon says, "That is the most eloquent letter I have ever heard." Annie touches Shannon on the back as she leans over the desk. Captain Dupree folds the letter and puts it in an envelope. As is customary he drips sealing wax on the flap and addresses the envelope to Mr. & Mrs. Brennan and hands it to Shannon. He says, "Merry Christmas, I hope this works." Shannon with letter in hand runs around the desk to hug Captain Dupree. This time he plucks her off her feet. Shannon is like a feather in his arms. Annie says, "Thank-you Papa, I to hope it works."

For the remainder of the day everyone relaxes in the front room. The fireplace was roaring and it was cozy warm. Lean Anna plays the piano and Annie sits next to her on the bench and admires how good she has become. Captain Dupree falls to sleep on the big sofa and Mary is by his side curled up watching her lovely children. Shannon is waiting now with the hope of the letter to return to her family and make amends.

They stoke the boiler and remark about how cold the night will be. Mary instructs her flock to use extra blankets and everyone is off to bed. Annie and Shannon wait till last to go to their rooms. Annie closes her door with a bump from the outside and tiptoes to Shannon's room. They would not be cold.

The first out of bed in the morning was Captain Dupree who was grumbling as he came down from the third floor and knocked on the boys' doors, "The damn boiler went out boys, come on I'll need your help to stokc it up." James Jr and Marcus scrambled. Annie and Shannon heard the commotion and realized someone would know they were together in the guest room. Annie tells Shannon to just be quiet while she listens to footsteps trying to discern who was where. She noticed ice sickles hanging on the windowsill on the inside, it was cold. As she listens, she can hear James Jr and Marcus go down the steps. That would mean Leah Anna and her mother were the only sounds unaccounted for. She just had to dash to her room unseen and all would be well, so she makes the dash. No sooner does she move into the hallway when her mother is coming down from the third floor and Leah Anna came out of her room. Thinking quickly she swings around and knocks on Shannon's door like she is just approaching. The only problem was her mother and Leah Anna had seen her come out. None the less she continues with the charade she says, "Knock, knock, Shannon are you awake?" Annie does not wait but goes right in and closes the door behind her. Annie starts laughing and covering her mouth to muffle the sound. She runs and jumps on Shannon's bed, "I think they saw me coming out." Shannon joins in with a snickering giggle, "Oh well, que sera, sera (what will be, will be.)" Annie jumps under the covers, "It is freezing." She suggests the best thing would be to quickly dress and run for the kitchen. They could smell the coffee. They both jump-up, Annie runs to her room past Leah Anna's door. As she does she knocks and says, "See you in the kitchen." Leah Anna shouts, "I'm freezing."

Shannon makes short work of getting dressed and flies down to the kitchen with Leah Anna right on her heels. Both were laughing as they run. Annie was just a minute behind them and met her mother who had gone back up just so she could come back down as her daughter was coming down. Mary remarks as she slowly walks, "It is always warm on the third floor; all the heat rises." Annie holds tight to her mother as they descend the steps. Mary remarks, "It is always warmer when two sleep together." Annie looks at her mother knowing what she meant and smiles, "Not to worry mama, Shannon and I are just good friends." Annie feels compelled to assuage her mother's concern that her daughter may be a lesbian. Truly Annie does not understand because her mother had no such concern other than if she was lesbian, it was of no concern. Mary responds, "la féminité est seulement comprise par une femme (femininity is only understood by a woman.)"

In the kitchen you could hear the men in the cellar working to get the boiler back up to temperature. Helen was making a big batch of pancakes, bacon and ham. The kitchen was warm and the coffee and tea was steaming. Shannon expresses to all the ladies how she feels that she needs to return to Cincinnati soon. You could tell she felt a sense of urgency. Captain Dupree emerges from the cellar mumbling, "A damn log got stuck in the auger and the fire went out." He laughs, "Well its back on now. Helen that smells wonderful, may I have some coffee?" Helen had his cup ready and fills it up. Captain Dupree sits down with his hands still dirty from the boiler and sips his coffee. Mary informs James, "Shannon wants to get back to Cincinnati soon, when is the next train?" Captain Dupree estimates the time, "Well, I'm sure it is too late for the nine-fifteen," he ponders, "probably the next through will be one o'clock and the last will be at four-thirty. Unless there are weather delays they will be on time. Shannon you probably do not want to take the four-thirty because that will put you into Cincinnati after dark. Will you take a taxi from Cincinnati station back to the dorm?" Shannon replies, "Yes, it is probably best if I'm on the one o'clock. Captain Dupree suggests, "Plenty of time for breakfast and a hot bath before you go."

They all enjoy Helens breakfast and Shannon is off for that bath and to pack for her journey. Annie assists in every way. Annie would not return to school in Cincinnati till after the New Year. Captain Dupree instructs on a schedule of chores for the boys which

169

is about wood hauling, putting water back into the kerosene water heaters in the bathrooms and general cleaning instructions. Laundry in the winter was a big chore. They would open the doors on the solarium attached to the kitchen, heat pots of water and wash everything in washtubs. After multiple rinses to get the soap out of the clothes, the garments were hung on lines in the solarium. The doors would be left open for the two days that it took for all the clothes to dry. This involved all of Helens day and Mary helped in between the other things she was doing.

At eleven-thirty James Jr hooks Dancer up to the sleigh. Miss Shannon Brennan was dressed impeccably and came down the stairs. Marcus carried her travel case and Annie came after. Captain Dupree would take Shannon to the train station. Annie said her good-bye on the front veranda. Annie could see Shannon's flaming red hair beneath her feathered hat shining in the sun as they rode out of sight.

The Spring is for Adventure

The New Year celebration was pleasant at the Dupree Home. The entire family road the sleigh into Sailor Park on New Year's Day to visit with the merchants and friends there to wish all a Happy New Year. James Jr and Marcus rode into town standing on the back runners of the sleigh. That was so as if the pull became too hard for Dancer going up a grade, they could jump off and run behind to lighten his load. In town they enjoyed hot apple cider and cinnamon, cornbread and Jam at the Hardware and General Store; that is where everyone went each year.

Shannon had returned to Madam Antoinette's school where her father had prearranged for a carriage to take her all the way from the city to East Hills, over fourteen miles. She, upon arriving gave her father the letter from Captain Dupree. They gave her a chilly reception but after the four days leading up to the New Year the tension had lessened and she and her mother were back on hugging terms. Sean Brennan read the letter and through several bedtime discussions with his wife Aileen decided they would relent and allow Shannon to go to Paris. The stipulation had a condition; it was that Sean and Aileen would take the time and escort them to New York to board the steam ship they would take to Europe. They would not have them navigate New York City on their own. Sean had been there many times and wanted to assure their safe passage from Cincinnati Station to the waterfront docks. Beyond that, once in Europe Mr. and Mrs. Brennan could only worry till they heard of their safe arrival in Paris.

Needless to say Shannon was ecstatic about the decision and could not wait to see Annie back at school. Part of her elation was the end to her inner turmoil. She was going to Paris regardless of her parents' decision but now it was with their blessing and she did not have to spend her endowment from her grandfather. She was to arrange a meeting between the Dupree's and The Brennan's sometime in the spring so they could plan. For her it was a good New Year, a good New Year indeed.

All the young ladies returned the first weekend in January to settle in before class on Monday. Annie arrives in the middle of the afternoon on Saturday. As she came in she passed by Madam Antoinette's office and Colette called her in, "Hello Annie, glad to see you, will you please go straight to Shannon's room, she has been here in my office every thirty minutes asking if you were here yet, elle me rend fou (she is making me crazy.)" Annie laughs, "Oui madame (yes madam.)"

Annie lugging her heavy case heads up the stairs to the dorm, as she is lugging the heavy luggage, about midway up Shannon appears at the top of the stairs, she screams, "I'm going to Paris!" Annie stops, sets down the case on the steps to catch her breath, "That's good." She leans against the wall, "With your parents blessing I suppose." Shannon dashes down to the middle of the steps and grabs the case like it was nothing and takes it the rest of the way up while Annie follows. "So I guess the letter from my father worked?" Shannon sits on the luggage at the top of the steps and Annie slowly climbs up. Shannon still sitting on the case puts her elbow on her knee and her

172

chin in her hand and giggles, "Come on Annie climb those steps." Annie smirks at her, "I just carried that case a mile, you mind yourself you Irish twig." That's referring to how thin Shannon was. She finally arrives at the top of the steps and they both start jumping up and down laughing and screaming and hugging. Victory was theirs; all was right with the world.

They would have all day Sunday to lounge and gab before class on Monday. They schemed and questioned everything. What Steam Ship would they go on, do they go to London first and then France? How much luggage should they take? They did not even know what academy they would be going to. They could not help bothering Madam Rousseau with so many questions that she finally told them, "Girls, it is months away with many things not yet known, pay attention to your classes, you must pass here before anything else. We will focus on your French and European history. They have come though many wars and you must know all of it." Madam Rousseau's seriousness pulled them back to reality a bit and they settled down. At least till they got back to their rooms, then their gab and scheming continued. All the other girls could not help but be jealous as they overheard their conversation. Who would not be jealous it is a true debutants dream to go to Paris.

January through to the warmth of April was busy. On the dreary winter days they would get pushed to exercise in the dance hall. Madam Rousseau wanted them tired at the end of the day. She felt that too much sitting and studying without stimulating the circulation system lead to laziness and

173

sadness; she would say, "Shake off a cloudy day and get busy girls." She would play minuets on the piano and Miss Ellery would instruct on different dance forms from antiquity. They did this every afternoon from three to five in the evening. This made everyone hungry for dinner and by nine o'clock they were so exhausted sleep was easy.

The first week of March Madam Rousseau had received correspondence from Paris and was ready to present the opportunities at the two possible academies to the girl's parents. She had them both send telegrams to their home to arrange for a meeting in April. After several back-and-forth exchanges of telegrams they would all meet at the school the last week of April; specifically Saturday the twenty ninth. This was also selected since that was Annie's birthday.

Time for Annie and Shannon went slowly. They were already in Paris in heart and only the days and hours were in the way. The warmth of April finally came and they were able to enjoy getting out. The trees were budding and that smell of the last snow melting away in the April showers was refreshing. They were calculating from information Madam Rousseau could give them that they would be in Paris by the end of May when everything would be in bloom. Their excitement was building each day.

The day came for the meeting of everyone. It was cordial and Captain Dupree in his comfortable style and knowledge of Paris made the Brennan's feel at ease. Sean Brennan and Captain Dupree discussed business and how he financed the Louisville Queen; a topic in which Sean was very interested. Mary Dupree and Aileen Brennan were instant friends; of course Mary Dupree was able to assuage Aileen's fears. Madam Rousseau was also instrumental in helping Aileen. They all decided on the Renault Academy for performing arts. Though Shannon was not interested in acting, the Academy also had courses in French, Art History and Sociology which were Shannon's choices. They would be traveling on the 'SS La Bourgogne' a French ocean-going steam ship. They would travel first to London then cross the English Channel to Le Havre, France where they would be met by an academy concierge who would take them by train to Paris. The Dupree's were pleased that the Brennan's would be accompanying them to New York City and the docks. James remarked, I had more scuffles in New York than Paris and down by the docks can be a rough place." Sean adds, "It will be broad daylight, I've been there, it's not a problem till after dark. They will be safe with me." Sean Brennan is a six foot rock of a man.

Madam Rousseau would continue the arrangements with the academy. Captain Dupree would book the passage on the 'SS La Bourgogne' and Sean would take care of their passage by train to New York. Annie and Shannon just watched as all these preparations were being made. Captain Dupree had crossed the Atlantic four times in his life. He knew the calmest seas would be in May and reassured everyone about the crossing. In those days there were many stories of sunken steam ships but the 'SS La Bourgogne' had been in service since 1889 and she was a big ship with both steam and sails. Captain Dupree was a master boat builder and he went on and on about how the 'SS La Bourgogne' was built. Mary had to finally interrupt her husband, "Dear, I am sure

175

the ship is safe since you have given it your own approval. Aileen, he is just jealous, he would have a ship like that for himself if he could." Everyone laughed and James took the hint that he was going on too much.

James leaves Madam Rousseau's office but not before he whispered in Collette's ear and winks at his wife. He is gone for a moment or two and returns. He pokes his head in the room then back and whistles. With that he steps back and a porter with a birthday cake and twenty-two candles lit, rolls into the room. Everyone knew except Annie. They all shout Happy Birthday! Annie blushes in complete surprise and looks a Shannon, "You tart; you knew this." Annie in her best Irish accent, "Yar a good liar yar miss. I'll not be trustin' the likes of you." Mary and James each give her a wrapped gift. They cut the cake. James opens a bottle of brandy and Annie opens the presents. It was a broach from James and blouse from her mother. They all had cake and brandy and teased Annie about the surprise.

Everyone said their salutations with hugs and kisses and they departed. Annie and Shannon returned to their rooms dancing and giggling like little girls all the way. They were planning on their calendars. They would miss the schools graduation ceremony which was the last week in May. Madam Rousseau was letting them graduate two weeks early in order to meet their travel schedule. They would each return home, prepare their travel trunks and be back in Cincinnati for the train to New York. If all the reservations could be made they would be leaving Cincinnati on the fifteenth and be in New York for boarding the 'SS La Bourgogne' on the nineteenth.

176

Annie's father said depending on weather the crossing would be six to seven days that would put them in England by the twenty-sixth or twenty-seventh. At worst case they would land in France one day later. Annie is counting, "twenty-sixth, twenty-seventh, twenty-eighth, we should be in Paris May the twenty-ninth. Can you believe it Shannon; we will be in Paris in less than a month?" They both let out a yell that all the girls in the dorm could hear and they knew it was them, them again just rubbing it in about how much fun they were having. Shannon starts running down a list in her mind of all things she wants to take. Annie suggests they write it all down lest they should forget anything. They went on and on so late they just fell to sleep in Shannon's room. In the morning the other girls saw Annie come out of Shannon's room. This started more gossip about them being lesbian.

Shannon was coming out of the bathroom at the end of the hall when she overheard two of the girls saying, "They sleep together, they must be lesbians." Shannon turned into their room; the door was open. In a very loud voice and in a contrived Irish accent she says, "You banshee witches are goin' ta end up boiled in oil if you dun stop yar gossip." Annie heard the commotion and came out of her room. She holds back a laugh and covers her mouth. She liked to see Shannon on fire. Annie still in her robe now laughing, "French, Shannon use your French." Shannon stomps the floor, "sorcières méchantes (wicked witches.) She did not know the word for banshee. Annie laughs, "Close enough."

Everyone in the dorm heard everything and that put an end to the gossip.

177

The next two weeks went by slowly for the two. They got to take their final tests early which again caused friction among the other girls. Madam Rousseau told each one privately that if she had the money, she would send them all to Paris and how much she loved each and every one of them. All of these ladies at her school were pampered and well off from wealthy families but jealousy knows no boundaries when you are counting other people's blessings.

Finally the day came Miss Ellery and Madam Rousseau helped them pack and clear out their dorm room. There were lots of tears and hugs as they stood at the front door to the school waiting for transportation. Some of the other girls came to wish them well but not all. Shannon's father arrived in his carriage with both of Shannon's brothers along for the ride. Annie waited to call for a taxi so she could say hello to Mr. Brennan. Sean told Annie that her father sent him a telegram and the passage on the 'SS La Bourgogne' was set for the nineteenth. Annie was delighted because she had not heard. This was Friday the twelfth. She had to be home and pack and be back in Cincinnati the morning of the fifteenth. Captain Dupree and Mary would come on the train with her; that is if Captain Dupree can manage to be in port with the Louis Queen. The Louisville Queen had been back on schedule sailing the Ohio since the first week of April. Captain Dupree would make that happen, come hell or high water in order to see his daughter one more time. She could be in Paris for years and he would miss her dearly. The plan was that they would all meet at Cincinnati Station and Sean, Aileen,

Shannon and Annie would board another train for Philadelphia and then on to New York City.

Annie took a taxi to Cincinnati Station to catch a train to Sailor Park. She would not arrive there till five-fifteen that afternoon. She had missed the earlier train that everyone at home expected her to be on. Surely, they will be waiting when she arrives; she is concerned that her mother will worry because she was not on the expected train. It was a lonely two hours on the ride home and she was feeling melancholy about school being over and how much she would miss Madam Rousseau and especially Miss Ellery.

James Jr and Mary were at the station anxiously waiting when the train pulled in. Mary could see Annie through the passenger window, "Dieu merci, elle est ici (thank God she is here.)" Annie smiles and waves as the train cars come to a complete stop. James Jr sees that the porter is retrieving her travel case and goes to receive it while Mary waits for Annie at the cars entrance. As Annie is coming down the steps Mary entreats, "j'étais inquiet (I was worried.)" Annie hugs her mother, "Tu dois me croire (you must trust me.)" It is not you I do not trust Annie, it is everyone else," Mary kisses her cheek. "If you are never a mother, you will never know what it is to worry over your child." Annie is quick to respond with a laugh, "Well, I guess I will never know." James Jr carrying the heavy case heaves it into the carriage then jumps into the drivers' seat. Dancer prances away after his kiss from Annie.

Annie sits close to her mother and inquires, "Did papa make it home?" Mary explains, "He telegrammed he would dock the Louis Queen in

179

Cincinnati and be home tomorrow, everything is on schedule." Annie squeezes her mother's arm, "Mama, it is so wonderful; I'm so excited." Her mother pats her hand, "I don't know what I will do without you; I will miss you so much. You must write me at least once a week if you can. I won't worry as much if I get letters from you. I know it is a chore but it is something you need to do for me." Annie is very reassuring, "I will mama, I promise. I will set aside time each week. And likewise it would be good to hear from you and papa so I don't feel so alone and far away." Mary laughs, "You will have Shannon; you won't feel alone, that girl adores you." Annie sighs, "Me likewise mama, she inspires me." "She brings out the rebel in you, which may not be a good thing. The two of you together is a force no man can compete with." Annie recoils, "Et que voulez-vous dire par là (And, what do you mean by that?)" "I mean by <u>that</u>, that a man can never hope to be as good a friend to you as Shannon, and any man would give up and never even try to be your lover." Annie leans back with her mouth open and eyes wide in a bit of shock and amazement, "vous sondez (you are probing.) Mother, I'm not looking for a lover. At this time in my life, I just want to be an actress on the stage. There is plenty of time for other things when I am older. Besides what man would consent to a marriage without children. Shannon and I are not lesbian, we are just friends. Putain mere, assez de ceci (Damn mother, enough of this.)" Mary again pats Annie's hand, "I'm not probing dear, just observing. Ce qui sera sera (What will be, will be.)" James Jr was listening closely and absorbing like a sponge this women's chatter.

The next two days were daunting, washing and ironing and packing. There was one large split case trunk that was Mary's travel trunk she had brought from Paris when she married Captain Dupree. She remarked, "It is fun to think that this old trunk is finally going back to where it came from. It is yours now dear, it should serve you well. Now, you don't need to take too much because when you get to Paris you can shop. You will probably look out of place in your clothes. Stiles are new each year in Paris; we are always a year behind the new trends." Annie beams, "Oh mama can you imagine, I will be in Paris in two weeks?"

Captain Dupree arrives as planned. He tries to stay out of the way with all the buzzing around that is going on. On Sunday he calls Annie into the den, "Annie, here let me see how this fits." He places a money belt around Annie's tiny waste, "What is this papa?" "It is called a money belt." James adjusts it snug, "There, do you see these two pockets?" He slides the belt around back to front to expose the pockets; this is where I want you to keep your money at all times while you are traveling. It is to remain hidden under your dress and your suit coat will hide the bulge. You don't take it off until you are in your cabin on the ship. Never leave it in your cabin unattended. If you leave the cabin the belt goes with you; it should be always on and hidden. I'm going to give you a bank check for the Bank of Paris but you will have a thousand dollars for your travel money. Understand me girl there are thieves everywhere. Some of them are even well dress shysters. Don't trust anyone. Knowing Sean Brennan, Shannon will have one too. You young ladies stay together and avoid conversations with strange men and women too. Some of the best pickpockets are women. Carry only small amounts of money in your purse. The ships purser will give you change. There are twenty fifty-dollar bills, ten in each pocket. Only open the belt in the privacy of your cabin. Does that all make sense my sweet girl?"

Annie throws her arms around her father's neck and kisses his cheek, "Thank you Papa, I will do exactly as you say. We only have to buy meals for two weeks; that is an awful lot of money." "You can use the rest to help you get set up in Paris. You will then take the check to the Bank of Paris and open an account and deposit the money. It is five thousand dollars, with your tuition and board that should get you through the first year. I will wire more money as your need it throughout the year. Remember, if you come up short it takes three days to get a telegram to me from Paris. Be frugal and not foolish with your spending." Annie adjusts the belt back around with the pockets in the back, "I will papa, only necessary spending." James laughs, "Sure enough, that is till you see the dress shops in Paris. Try to keep it down to one new outfit a month; I have to provide for your brothers and sister too." Annie screeches, "I can't believe it papa, I'm going to Paris." She hugs him again.

Monday morning came too quickly. At sunrise everything was loaded in the carriage. Leah Anna was crying as she hugged Annie good-bye, "I won't see you Annie for two years," Annie is crying too, "You will be all grown up when I get back, stay away from those boys will you?" James Jr and

182

Marcus each give her a big hug and Marcus reminds her, "Be sure to use that Kodak and send us some pictures of you in Paris." Annie assures him that she would. Helen is crying too, "I'm going to miss you sweetie, you enjoy that French cooking; they tell me it is mighty good." Helen hugs her good-bye. The sun is just peeking through the trees and they are off. James Jr was driving the carriage to take the three to the station and he would return alone.

The seven-fifteen was on time. In an hour and thirty minutes they would be in Cincinnati. They had coffee and tea and sweet bread. The Brennan's met them at the Cincinnati station. Captain Dupree and Sean Brennan see to the travel trunks of both the girls as they would be loaded on the train going first to Philadelphia and then on to New York. Aileen Brennan and Mary are discussing the trip and their experiences in New York City. Shannon and Annie are both fussing and laughing about their money belts. Annie tugs at hers, "Even with my suit jacket over it, it makes me look fat." She laughs, "All the better to keep men from gawking at us." Captain Dupree sees them making to do over the belts, "You two have just shown everyone on the landing here that you are wearing money belts; So much for keeping them secret. Good thing Sean is traveling with you." Annie and Shannon sheepishly adjust their jackets and turn away a little embarrassed that they were acting childishly. The fathers direct the porters securing the travel trunks and everyone heads for the landing where the train to Philadelphia is steaming up readying for departure. The conductor is calling all aboard and the time has come. Hugs and tears pour from Annie and her mother while Captain Dupree holds them both, "It's not the end of the world girls; it's the beginning. Now, now, the train is ready, wipe your nose and telegraph us when you get to Paris and don't cavort with strangers." Annie hugs her father, grabs Shannon's arm. Shannon was standing close and leans in to kiss Mary on the cheek and the girls board the train. Sean and Aileen board behind them. Sean, after assisting Aileen turns on the steps of the train car and waves, "No worries, folks, I'll wire you from New York."

Philadelphia took a day and a night of travel. They changed trains at eight in the morning on the sixteenth. They traveled all that day, and then that night; then another day which was the seventeenth and another night. They arrived in New York City at nine o'clock in the morning on the eighteenth. Since they could not board the 'SS La Bourgogne' till the morning of the nineteenth, Sean had a surprise for them all. They would stay at the renowned Grand Hotel in Manhattan. Shannon and Annie were astonished at the size of the buildings in New York. Sean arranged for their travel trunks to go directly to the docks. They rode on a city train from Grand Central Station to the hotel. The girls were amazed when the train first went underground and then up on an elevated track over the streets. Annie was all questions, "Was that Broadway Street?" Sean was proud, "Yes Annie, but it is just called Broadway; that is where the playhouses are; after dinner we will go to see them." Shannon is just awe struck, "Papa, where is Macy's department store?" "It is over on sixth Avenue around fourteenth Street. I guess after we get checked in we can go see that too." Aileen smiles, "Don't you girls buy anything more; your

184

trunks are full." Shannon grabs Annie's arm, "We will just look and save our money for Paris." It is like Christmas in May, delight is everywhere. Where the train stops is still a block from the hotel so Sean hails a taxi. They each have a suitcase and it would be too difficult to walk even a block. They arrive at the Hotel and porters run up to the carriage and take all their cases. The girls remark how even the porters are dressed impeccably in their smart uniforms. It is now ten-thirty and Aileen suggests that after four days on a train it is time for a bath. The girls share a room and remark how wonderful it is that the Grand Hotel has running hot water and a bath in every room instead of a common bath; and the wonder of wonders, something they had heard about but not seen, is a flush toilet. They had to be instructed on how to use it.

By noon they all went to the dining hall for lunch. They were greeted by a maître d' in a tuxedo and white gloves. Annie had not seen such elegance even in Pittsburg at the opera. They were escorted to a finely set table. Aileen was seated first of honor, then Annie and then Shannon. Sean sat and addressed the maître d' for a wine list. Aileen remarks, "Girls have you ever seen such fine China as this, even with gold leaf around the edges?" Annie picks up one of two forks, "Mama showed me in a catalog silverware placements like this; one knife, two forks, a spoon and a soup spoon; two glasses, one for water and the other for wine. Though we talked about it at Madam Rousseau's we never really had it. She showed us how to sit, elegantly place our napkin and to never, never put our elbows on the table." Shannon laughs, "Like this?" She puts her elbows on the table and

185

plops her chin in her hands. Everyone laughs. Aileen puts her hand on her daughters' shoulder, "We spent all that money for school so you could to act like a lady and what we got was a comedian." Sean injects, "You knew that by the time she was two." He leans toward Annie, "She would put her oatmeal on her nose and grin at her mother." Shannon turns red in the face to match her hair, "Oh papa."

Lunch was wonderful they followed Sean's lead. He ordered a glass of sweet Bordeaux wine for the ladies while he had a glass of dry Cabernet. They had French Onion soup, lamb cold cuts with Swiss cheese on Italian bread and for desert a chocolate mousse and coffee. Annie remarked how much her mother and father would have loved it all. Time was pressing, the girls were to go to Macy's department store, so off they went. Sean hired a taxi for the afternoon. After an hour at Macy's they toured the streets to see the sights and Broadway too. Sean had the driver take them for a ride through Central Park and up to the Metropolitan Museum of Art to see the amazing building. They would not have time to go in because it was getting dark and tomorrows boarding was early, but he remarked, "Annie, when you come back as a famous actress to perform on Broadway, be sure you see the entire museum, it is a sight to behold." Annie laughed, "I don't know about the famous actress part, but I will definitely see the museum." Shannon pulls Annie close by her arm, "You will be famous miss, I will see to that." Aileen looks on curiously about her daughter's relationship to Annie. She had never seen the girls interact till this trip. She notices an affection that she senses is uncommon. She keeps it to herself, whatever it was, this was not the time.

On the steps of the museum was a group of women carrying signs that said, "Women Unite to Vote" Annie remarks, "See Shannon, like the women in Cincinnati, we have to stand together." Aileen is caught completely unaware, "Annie do you think men prevent women from their opinion?" "No, but I think it is only through the approval of their husband and if a woman has no husband to speak in her stead, she is mute." Aileen is set aback. She had not expected such a terse position from this young lady. Aileen directs to Shannon, "Shannon do you think the same?" Shannon looks at her mother and turns a little away, "I'm not as course as Annie mama but does not everyone; including women have an opinion?" This is a rude awakening for Aileen. She had no idea that her daughter was this opinionated. As a matter-of-fact Shannon had never expressed any political opinion whatsoever. She makes an immediate connection that this idea resides in the relationship of Annie and her daughter; that these ideas are inspired by Annie and are not original in her daughter independently.

Gas lights were being lit and Sean had the driver make a return back down Broadway to see the new electric lights come on. He mentioned, "That is the wave of the future girls, you don't have to have someone light the lamps, you just flip a switch at the dynamo and they all come on at once." Annie told him how she saw them at the opera in Pittsburg and how they were in colors. Sean said as they rounded the corner to Broadway, "Like these?" To their wonder, colored lights shone on the marquees of the theaters. They looked in awe.

Back now at the hotel the girls joined Sean and Aileen in their room. Porters brought them dinner à la carte. Sean had ordered duck with sweet potatoes, sweet peas and croissant's. They had cold English tea and afterward they all enjoyed a brandy before turning in. They had to be at the dock to board the ship by ten in the morning. The 'SS La Bourgogne' would sail at noon.

Annie and Shannon were exhausted and surprised when Aileen knocked on their door at six o'clock. Shannon opens the door and Aileen peeks in with her head just inside the door, "Need to get a quick wash-up and dress and be down in the dining room in about an hour. We will be waiting for you." Shannon yawns and stretches, "Okay mama, see you soon." Aileen withdraws; she had seen that only one bed had been used. She thinks perhaps she knew very little about her daughter."

The girls join Sean and Aileen in the dining room. Cinnamon sweet rolls and a platter of ham and bacon were ready on the table. A waiter took their order for coffee and milk. Sean looked up from the newspaper he was reading, "Sleep well girls?" He looks quizzically at the two. Aileen had told him what she had seen about only one bed being used. Annie and Shannon had not a clue. They responded in unison, "We slept wonderfully." Annie sips her coffee, "The beds here are lovely." Sean returns to his paper and mumbles, "Yes, they have two in every room." Annie did not know Aileen had peered into the room but Shannon did. Shannon caught on to her father's mumbling but was not going to respond. She would just let them wonder because nothing happened. She and Annie were just lying together

188

gabbing about Paris and they fell to sleep in the same bed. Again Annie did not have a clue and Shannon would let the sleeping dog lie. With breakfast over they departed. Shannon walked ahead and arm-in-arm with her mother she whispered in her ear, "Mama, Annie and I were just talking till late in her bed and we fell to sleep. We are just good friends, alright?" Aileen pats Shannon's arm, "I hope for grandchildren someday." Shannon laughs, "Not to worry mama." Annie looks on and just thinks how wonderful to see Shannon and her mother laughing together.

The porters carry their suitcases to the curb and there is a taxi waiting. Sean and Aileen would be returning and spend one more night in the hotel before their return trip to Cincinnati. The taxi takes them to Park Avenue to catch the train that runs down Bowery Street then Pearl Avenue and then finally to Water Street. Then they will take another taxi to the dock. This is why Sean needed to escort them to New York. He knew the way; had they gone by themselves, the likelihood of them getting lost in the Bowery or the infamous Five Points area was of concern. Robbers and pickpockets were everywhere in New York. Sean's coat concealed his revolver but his tall stature was sufficient warning for any would-be villain. Aileen feared nothing next to her big man.

They arrive at the dock. Annie and Shannon see the enormous ship with both smokestacks and masts for sails. Their excitement is great. Their hearts are beating. Annie and Shannon hold tight to each other as Sean locates a porter. He returns, "This man will take your suitcases, let us go now on board and locate the purser and find your travel trunks. They should be on board." They begin the long walk up the big gangway entry to the ship. It is steep. Sean holds on to Aileen to assist her but Annie and Shannon find no trouble and make short work getting to the top. Aileen is out of breath, "I would just a soon go with you to Paris as to have to go climb back down that plank." Sean is not out of breath at all, "I will carry you down dear, not to worry." Shannon takes her mother's left arm and Annie takes her right. Sean presents the passage tickets for the girls to the Master at Arms who is standing at his podium. Sean is given directions to the purser's office which is conveniently located. All the ladies sit on deck chairs and await his return. Aileen resting well now, "I'm going to miss you my sweet Shannon, you stay close to our Annie and write to me and if you find a man in Paris let him know full well, he must meet the approval of you father." Shannon laughs, "That would be enough to scare any man away if he could see my father. But I get the idea mama. Everything will be fine; I'm not looking for a Parisian man; who knows I could run into an Irishman in Paris, and that would please papa."

Sean returns, "The trunks are already in your cabins, they have done a fine job; this way ladies, we are going forward and up one deck." They head off toward the cabin the girls will be sharing for the cruse. Annie and Shannon are absorbing everything, this amazing ship, the smell of the salt air, the hustle of all the ships personnel getting everything prepared for the ships departure. The cabin for their journey is wonderful. It is like a hotel room with a lavatory for washing and a vanity with mirror. Annie peers out the porthole and on to the water below and remarks, "Not much of a view; I would not want to go out this way."

190

Sean opens the porthole, "That's so you can get a breath of air." As he opens the porthole the ships horn sounds and the salt air rushes in. "That will be the call for us to disembark since we are not passengers; time for us to go ladies." Aileen now tears-up, "Shannon my love, guard yourself with the care of my heart. Annie, watch out for her and yourself miss." Aileen hugs them both and likewise Sean. The girls walk them back to the gangway and watch and wave as they disembark.

The Brennan's are fearful for the girls being alone on this awesome journey. Annie and Shannon are elated that they are finally alone and free from parental over lording. They are as impetuous as two young women could be. They watch as the ship unties from the dock and the tugboats push the enormous ship to sea. They wave to their parents from the upper deck on this warm spring day as they sail down the Hudson River and out to the Atlantic Ocean as all the adventure unwinds before them. Paris awaits the arrival of two American debutants as if all of life is at a pause while they drift along on this dream cruise.

Shannon wastes no time in describing their liberty, "One would think that I am incapable of thinking as my mother would have you believe. I am a tart and as dumb as my brothers when it comes to the wiles of men. So many times she chastises me with her warning. To the point Annie, I would do it with a man just to spite her." Annie retorts, "We are not one whistle blow away from the dock and you are growing the horns of Lucifer. Be kind Miss Shannon for parents fear for their children. The sad part is that the likes of you, you Irish tart, cannot be protected, because you are bad, right down to your crotch."

191

Annie looks to see no one is near and then pokes
Shannon right where she described. Shannon stunned
just laughs and shouts, "I'm so damn happy to be free
I could scream!" And that they did on the second deck
of the ship. They screamed.

Their cabins were comfortable and the entire
journey was prepared, from morning to evening with
meals and entertainment. There was Badminton on
the upper deck and a parlor show each evening,
including singers and magicians. They walked the
upper deck each sunset. The seven days of the
crossing seemed like forever and this was only the
second evening. Their conversation over their
mothers concerns of them being lesbian was mostly
disdain and fearless in their discussion.

As they lounge on the upper deck Shannon
sits on a lounge chair in her light cotton dress and
white feathered hat, "I know mother thinks you and I
are femelle sur femelle (female on female) but they
don't know. They don't understand. I want to be a
mother someday, but not now. I like men. I dream of
him inside me. I love the idea of being a mother. I can
feel the sweet child wanting to live inside my body as
much as my mother giving birth to me. I can feel it
Annie, I can feel it."

Annie beside her holds her arm, "I could feel
it too; when my sister Leah Anna was born, mama
screamed in pain so much that I felt her pain. I felt her
pain! Is that the price that women must suffer? And if
woman were asked before this world started and she
said no, would God change the plan of life. Let men
have their guts ripped out in birth. I have a choice, and
it can remain a secret as far as I am concerned. I say

192

no. I would sooner have them call me a foolish lonely old maid or a bitch on Whore Street than be a man's fertile ground for his prowess.

Shannon is not as callous as Annie, "You need to be a little kinder; men are not so nonintellectual and abound in brutality as you would assume. They are just looking for a nest and you are the warm spot they find, and for the most part they ask rather than take and in my experience, they are lovely and kind and take no for an answer without recourse." Annie is set aback and leans in to kiss Shannon on the cheek, "I meant no offence dear, and I don't hate men. I just hate that I am predestined with no other consideration. You don't understand me Shannon. Why should I take a man's name? Am I not worthy of my father's name? Am I not a person unto myself?" Annie leans in close and stares into Shannon's eyes, "Am I not?"

Shannon throws her arms around Annie's neck and squeezes her tight, "I love you, no matter what; I love you. I will be with you forever."

As the sun sets, they see the captain of the ship approach, "Good evening ladies, I hope you are enjoying your cruise." They node and in unison, "Yes sir, very much." He continues, "Are you on your way to England or France?" Annie rises from her chair and extends her hand, "we are on our way to Paris to attend school." He remarks, "My, that is wonderful. Which school will you attend?" Shannon now stands and also extends her hand to the captain, "The Renault Academy for the performing arts." The captain again remarks, "My, that is wonderful." He seems to be at a loss for words when in fact he is just a little set aback by the beauty of these two women. He stutters a bit,

"I'm ah, Captain DuPont my ladies and what might your names be?" He directs first to Shannon. She responds, "Why my name is Shannon Brennan from Cincinnati." Captain DuPont smiles and then looks at Annie and she replies, "I'm Antoinette Dupree of Cincinnati also."

Captain DuPont now is holding each of the ladies hands at once bows slightly in formality and releases their hands. He raises his burly brow quizzically looking at Annie, he ponders "Hum, Dupree. Could you be related to James Dupree over in Louisville Kentucky?" Annie assures him, "No, but my father is James Dupree but he lives in Cincinnati." Captain DuPont puts his finger over his mouth thinking, "Well perhaps, it could be, maybe. The last I heard was James Dupree who I knew years ago was from Louisville Kentucky and getting a group of investors from Paris to build a steamboat." Annie gasps, "My, that is my father, James Marcus Dupree the captain of the Louis Queen." Captain DuPont laughs, "My God how is that old braggart." He catches himself, "Forgive me that was not appropriate. I knew your father as an American Frenchman in Paris trying to organize the financing for what you now tell me is the Louis Queen. That is wonderful. He actually built her, that son of a gun. Your father and I had some times together in Paris. I am from New York and spent years in the American Merchant Marine. When in France we always went to Paris. When I met you father, he was only twenty-five. I could tell you some stories but perhaps I should not."

Annie leans in, "No, you tell me all you want, I would love to know." He laughs, "Perhaps, but I

194

won't tell you everything. Ladies I have a wonderful idea, would you like to join me for evening supper at the captain's table tomorrow." Annie and Shannon are delighted and respond in unison, "Oh Yes." He says, "Delightful, I'm entertaining Doctor Howe and his wife Ellen also. He is a most prominent Doctor in disease studies on his way to Oxford to deliver his recent paper and his wife Ellen is some sort of activist with that women's movement or something. I don't know, she can tell you all about it. Anyway, I will see you tomorrow at five o'clock at my table; I look forward to seeing you there. Good evening, ladies." He tips his hat and backs up formally and departs.

Annie and Shannon look at each other and Annie laughs, "With that women's movement or something. You could tell he could care less." Shannon rolls her eyes, "He's pretty old Annie, but he is nice." Annie tugs Shannon's sleeve, "Old dogs are harder to teach but they still need to learn."

The next day they visited the ships library for some reading material and they also attended an afternoon musical presentation of a string quartet playing selections from Frederic Chopin and Claude Debussy. Annie and Shannon both knew each piece thanks to Madam Rousseau's school. It was a bit warm on this May afternoon and they felt sorry for the instrumentalists dressed in tuxedos sweating while the played. All the ladies were using fans and the gentlemen were removing their jackets. Considering the conditions they played wonderfully and were very glad when it was over.

The dinner hour was about to sound with five bells and the ladies entered the dining hall and were

195

directed to the captain's table. Already seated were the Doctor and his wife. The maître d' introduced everyone. Annie and Shannon were amazed that he already knew their first and last names like he was family. Doctor Howe and his wife Ellen stood to greet them. The maître d' explained that the captain would be there shortly and everyone sat down.

Doctor Howe remarks, "You young ladies look well on this rather unseasonably warm afternoon." The ladies agree it is a bit warmer than expected. Ellen remarks, "We ladies should not be so encumbered with too much clothing on days like today. Ladies of the 1890's still dress like it's the 1850's but times will change." Immediately Annie likes this lady. First of all she is stunning with lovely bright eyes. She is slender and dressed expensively in what looked to Annie as the latest fashions from Paris and she exudes confidence that is overwhelmingly obvious. Shannon addresses Ellen, "Misses Howe, your English is so refined are you from London?" Ellen corrects her, "My name is Eleanor Leah Brooks my dear and I am from London. Now don't you worry, you could not have known; call me Ellen. I'm one of those 'New Women' everyone loves to scoff at. I kept my maiden name when I married my wonderful husband, Franklin."

Doctor Howe leans over and kisses Ellen on the cheek, "And I love you too my dear." He turns to look at Annie and Shannon in a fatherly manner, "As my lovely wife will attest, it is high time that women play a more important role in all manner of government. My wife was instrumental in me be being heard at Oxford with my new publication." Annie returns, "Yes, Captain DuPont had said you were headed to Oxford, how fascinating can you tell us about your publication?" Doctor Howe is delighted, "Well it is not a good conversation of the dinner table but in a nutshell, it is about the scourge of Syphilis. We know it has to be a microbe as yet unidentified and seeing that there is no effective cure insight, the only plausible remedy is education and isolation. We must first quarantine the disease and then educate people how to avoid it. This is very complicated from a political standpoint." Ellen interrupts, "It is political my dears because they blame the women of ill repute and not the men that partake in their services. They license prostitutes in Paris; force them to have physical exams of the most demeaning nature and then lock them in a sanatorium if they are found infected, while men come and go without a care."

Doctor Howe agrees, "Yes dear, that is true and since we cannot seem to legislate morality all we can do is educate people as to the dangers of promiscuity." Ellen pats her husbands' hand, "My husband provides, in his publication, some very interesting ways we might isolate and identify this so-called microbe. This may lead to a cure but it will not cure the abuse of women in prostitution." "Do not the women do it by choice my dear?" Doctor Howe quizzes his wife. Ellen ruffles, "Women have the opportunity, if well bred, to marry. The rest of their opportunity is hard factory work, God awful nursing home and hospital work or as a nursemaid. Universities need to recognize that women are capable and teach young ladies such as these they are welcome."

Doctor Howe laughs, "I love you Ellen, and with your help we can solve all the world's problems.

Annie is elated, "Miss Brooks, I am so delighted to hear your point of view. In Cincinnati we talked to some of the group called the 'Lucy Stoners.' They were calling for the women's right to vote. Do you think it will happen?" Ellen feels instrumental in guiding young Annie, "I do. It will happen in England and Europe sooner than in America. The thing I am most concerned with is my husband's work right now, because also in this publication is the call to allow women who have been given Syphilis by their husband to be granted a divorce which currently they cannot." Doctor Howe interjects, "Not only has the wife been infected but her child too if she is pregnant. What most can be done to stop this damn disease right now is education."

Captain DuPont arrives, "I can tell by the looks of your faces that you are in deep conversation about the troubles of the world. My good Doctor friend will do that." Ellen adds, "My fault too Captain DuPont,". Captain DuPont is cheerful and a waiter arrives, "Please my friends give the waiter an order or perhaps some wine would be best first." Everyone agrees on the wine and a bottle is uncorked and poured. Captain DuPont hosts a toast, "Here are to my lovely guests and thank-you for joining me this evening." He continues, "Doctor Howe this young lady is Antoinette Dupree daughter of James my friend I was telling you about. She is headed to Paris to the Renault Academy for the performing arts and Miss Shannon Brennan also." Ellen is delighted, "Annie, I know of that school, I think you and Shannon will be delighted. Many students have gone on to great success." Annie agrees, "My mother has told me the same, but I am most interested in your position on women in politics, perhaps someday I could be more instrumental in political change. Perhaps I won't be an actress." She holds up her fist in jest, "I want to server at the front." Shannon laughs, "You are serious are you not?" "Yes, I am serious." Ellen likes these two, "You girls are two peas in a pod are you not?" Shannon laughs, "I'm trouble and she is more trouble." Everyone laughs and especially Caption DuPont, "I can see your father in you Annie, James always had such a good sense of humor and could drink any man under the table." To which Annie responds, "He does not drink much anymore."

The captain hosts a most wonderful dinner with hors d'oeuvre followed by soup and salad. The main course was prime rib of beef followed by liquor and coffee. The elegance was not wasted on Shannon and Annie, they felt quite honored.

Ellen had invited the girls to join her on the upper deck and for every other day of the cruse they met. Shannon and Annie absorbed everything Ellen had to say. She would be a lasting memory for them both. When they tied up at the dock at Brighton just south of London they visited with Doctor Howe and Ellen Brooks as they departed the ship. They had become great friends. Annie hope to continue with correspondence with Ellen and Ellen likewise made arrangements by giving Annie her address in London.

The ship would depart early in the morning to cross the English Channel to Le Havre France. Everything was on schedule and they would arrive in Paris on the twenty-ninth of May 1892 and Paris would be all the better for Antoinette Marie Dupree and Shannon Aileen Brennan were there.

Who is Acting ?

It was at fifteen 'Rue de Lamar' on the second floor where Annie and Shannon would reside for the next two years. It was owned by a real-estate investor Annie's father knew. It was comfortable and well furnished with a private bath and running water. There was a common water closet or rather in French, a 'toilet' just down the hall. They had two separate bedrooms, a kitchen with an attached solarium and a common room for entertaining. It was on the out skirts on the north of the city. It was only three blocks to the Academy and they had access to bicycles for daily use. They would not be taxied about as they were accustomed. They would blend in and be just like every young French lady attending school. They had to be frugal and prepare all their own meals. This was not a vacation it was work. They no longer had a Madam Rousseau or Miss Ellery to look after them. Not being in class on time was shamed quickly, do your work and don't embarrass you parents by being expelled.

Not only was the language of French but also Italian added to their required language studies because of the proliferation of Italian arts, operas and plays. Refinement of their English was a surprise to them. They were being taught proper English by a Frenchman. They laughed that they were being taught how to talk like Miss Eleanor Brooks of London.

They did have a liaison provided by the academy to guide them around Paris at times to aid in them not getting into areas that would be dangerous for single young women alone. They were instructed to stay away from areas where bordellos were. They

201

were also required to carry an academy identity card at all times. It also provided a guarantee of payment for transportation in case they were ever lost.

It was at the end of the first two weeks of classes and on this Saturday, they were free to roam. Shannon being the instigator suggested they try to find a cabaret that had the Cancan. Annie is just as much curious but felt they needed to disguise themselves. They came up with the idea to dress like men. What better way to get into a men's club than to be a man. This took some doing but they had access to make-up and props at the theater in the academy. They could get all the costumes they needed. Pants and suit jackets, shirts and top hats were all available; they just had to sneak it out. They would glue on very realistic looking mustaches; tuck their hair up under their hats and practice male like movements in the mirror. They had to alter the trousers to fit their derriere for the trousers were all too slim to fit.

Shannon pats Annie's butt, "You look like the real thing kiss me you hunk of a man." Annie does just that, "Do you like the whiskers. Don't they feel real?" "Yes and one got in my mouth," Shannon spits.

They wait till the gas lights are being lit on the street to exit their flat. Annie acting quite manly hails a taxi. It is a wonderfully warm June evening. Annie had a paper with the address of the cabaret written down. She, in as low a voice as she can muster says, "mon bon homme (my good man)" and hands him the paper. The driver responds, "Oui monsieur, (yes sir.)" The driver cracks the whip before Annie was seated which throws her back into the seat and with that, she yelps with a chirp that could only be produced by a woman. The driver is no fool but keeps his manner

202

and does not laugh. Upon seeing the address and these two and that yelp he knew it was two women dressed as men trying to see the Cancan. Now women go to the Cancan all the time but they are usually escorted by a man and many times the women are courtesans. So Shannon and Annie knew that as themselves attempting to attend the cabaret alone they would be mistaken for prostitutes. So they had to go in disguise.

They arrive at the cabaret. Annie jumps down trying to act like her brother James Jr. She does not turn to help Shannon because that would not be manly. Shannon steps out on the taxi's step and attempts to hop like Annie did but she stumbles. The driver laughs. Annie does not help Shannon again to look like a man. She hands the driver his money and just tips her hat not saying a word. The driver says, "Merci mademoiselle, (thank-you miss.)" Shannon gets to her feet and straightens her hat and with a manly voice says to Annie, "allez mon pote ne t'occupe pas de lui (come on buddy, don't mind him)". The driver drove off laughing.

They could hear the noise of the cabaret. The music and laughter was enticing. They stayed very close together but did not hold each other's arm which was their custom. They meandered through the crowd and discovered some tables up and in the back that were perfect. They would be out of the way and in the back where no one was looking. Everyone faced forward to the main dance floor where the dancers would perform. A waitress sees them sit down and approaches to take their order. Shannon booms low, "deux whiskies manquent (Two whiskeys miss.)"

Annie looks at Shannon and tries to boom in a deep voice, "Je ne veux pas de whisky (I don't want

203

whiskey,) donne moi du cognac (give me cognac)."
The waitress says, "Ce sera un demi-franc manquer.
(That will be one half franc miss.)" Shannon looks at
her in amazement and hands her one franc instead and
says, "fais que deux (make that two.)" The barmaid
leaves and Annie laughs, "I don't think our disguises
are working." The waitress returns with two whiskies
and two brandies just as the gas lights are being
dimmed. A gas-powered spotlight comes on and the
master of ceremonies takes the center of the dance
floor. He says, "Mesdames et Messieurs le cancan
(ladies and gentlemen the cancan.)" The spotlight
goes out and the gas lights are turned back up and out
come twelve ladies dressed in colorful dresses that are
full of petticoats and ruffles. The music starts and the
dance begins. The ladies are circling, laughing and
shouting as they hike their legs and kick and swirl and
spin. It all looks like great fun and the men are
cheering and shouting.

Shannon grabs Annie's arm and shouts in her
ear because the noise is deafening, "You can see their
crotch. They're naked!" Annie gasps, "My God
you're right. No one ever told me that, not even my
mother." Shannon shoots down her whisky, "I want
to leave." "Me too," Annie agrees. They get up to go
and a man next to them not realizing they are women
says, "Comment aimez-vous ces pussys? (How do
you like those pussys?) Annie gasps and they move
as quickly to the door as they can without making a
scene. Shannon's mustache comes loose and a group
of men at the front door see them and realize they are
women and laugh. One taps Annie on the shoulder,
"Pas ce que tu espérais? (Not what you expected?)"
The girls now run to the curb laughing and mocking

themselves. Annie tears off her mustache, removes her hat and shakes out her hair, "My God, mother never told me they were naked under the dress. It is as bad as striptease." Shannon shakes out her long red hair and there you have two women in men's suits hailing a taxi. Perhaps this is not an odd scene, it is Paris after all.

They return to their flat and decide to not waste this beautiful evening; they would dress and walk to a restaurant for some wine. Paris in the evening is beautiful. The Eifel tower was all lit and the streets were full of wondering lovers and the forlorn as well. Accordions' could be heard on every corner as musicians played for coins. Artists lined the streets with paintings for sale. Paris was everything Annie's mother had said it was; she was in love with just the very idea of being there and Shannon likewise awed at every scene as they walked arm in arm. They could not help laughing at themselves dressed as men and seeing such debauchery as women displaying themselves beneath their dresses so men could gawk. Annie is trying to find some logic in it all, "Do you think they get paid well; is that why they do it. Rather than work in a factory you can just show your body for money." Shannon shakes her head, "It would have to pay the rent but then think, would you do that day after day, year after year. And what man would want to marry a woman who every man knew the sight of."

Annie leads Shannon in the door of the café, "There you see, you again resort to the only thing for a woman is to marry. No, I rather think you would save the money and open a chocolate shop or bakery or even a dress shop or something to make a good honest living." Shannon sits at a window table and

Annie beside her. Shannon whispers, "Mother would tease and say, 'if your father ever leaves, I will just become a wealthy courtesan.' I asked her, 'does it pay well?' She said, 'my yes, you are the kept woman and secrets aren't cheap.' God knows my father is wealthy enough to have one, and maybe he does, I don't know." Annie grimaces, "Men are such liars, but I really think my father is true to my mother. Papa is happy, at least he seems so and Mama trusts him like he is fine gold." Shannon agrees, "If I could find a man like your father, I would fall completely." They order wine and some finger sandwiches and enjoy their leisure time.

Tomorrow was Sunday, they would attend different churches mostly out of curiosity; Shannon was only Catholic in that her family attended a Catholic church in Cincinnati. She had been christened in the church and went to Catholic school but she professed she did not like the churches fighting over Christ. Annie on the other hand was very outspoken mostly about the hypocrisy of church people. So one week they would go to a Catholic church and the next week they would go to a Protestant church. Mostly they love the beautiful architecture and art that were the beautiful churches of France.

They are walking back to their flat on this Sunday at about noon. Annie explains, "We are starting rehearsal on a play by Victorien Sardou. His production of 'Madame Sans-Gêne' is being played at the 'Théâtre du Vaudeville,' right now as we speak. If I could only meet him; his plays are the most exquisite. At least that is what the reviews say." Shannon follows Annie's every word, "I know some of his plays; mother liked 'Fedora.' The princess poisons herself in fear of her husband. It is such a dark tragedy." Annie agrees, "Then there is 'La Tosca,' in the end she throws herself off a balcony" "Isn't Monsieur Sardou a pretty old man by now?" Shannon inquires. "I know for fact he is sixty-two years old, we have already learned that in class. Our proctor said there was a chance he would come see our work, perhaps when we get nearer to the dress rehearsal in six weeks. I sure hope so, to meet a great playwright like him would be amazing," Annie exudes enthusiasm. Shannon notices, "Well, there is a man you respect besides your father." Annie smacks Shannon's hand, "Mind yourself."

Shannon announces, "As part of my Art history class we are going to Rome. Our proctor has arranged travel by train. Miss Beaumont our liaison is going with us. There are six of us going. We will leave Tuesday and will be back next Friday. Do you think you can make it without me for a week?" Annie laughs, "I am jealous, I have to work on this play and you get to go on a Roman vacation." Shannon defends her studies, "Shame on you, we have a curriculum and we will be tested on what we know when we get back." Shannon laughs, "But, yes it will be fun. Rome Annie, I'm going to Rome." Annie tries to hold her down as she jumps up and down, "Bring me a souvenir."

They arrive at their flat and spend the rest of the day cooking and cleaning, this next week would be all work for Annie and 'out-of-town' fun for Shannon.

'The Black Pearl' was the play written by Victorien Sardou that the class would be working on. It was one of his earlier works first produced in 1861 some ten years before Annie was born. She knows it as her mother had said, it was a classic comedy. Annie would play the part of Christiane the heroine accused of the robbery of Messieurs Balthazar's room. Cornelius her fiancé, by scientific deduction, proves that a bizarre act of lightning was responsible for the missing locket. The lines of the play give into many funny situations and the lighthearted presentation makes work on this play fun. Annie is surrounded with acting professionals and she is complimented by her instructors on her delivery. She is becoming comfortable performing and she is a natural on the stage.

Shannon has now returned from Rome. She stops by the academy theater to see Annie perform in an afternoon rehearsal. The director calls for a break. Annie sees Shannon in the seats and joins her, "Well what do you think, am I going to be a star?" "You are, and I wish I had your ability to get up on stage but I'm too self-conscious, I would get nervous and forget my lines." Annie stretches and yawns, "I'm tired. We have one more run-through of the second act and we will be done. Do you want to get some dinner when we finish?" "Sure, we can go to our favorite café if you like, my treat, I've got a little left over from Rome." Shannon pats her purse that was resting securely over her should. She watches the practice of the second act and then Annie joins her and they head to dinner.

About two blocks on their way they see a group of women carrying signs. The signs read 'les

femmes dans la chambre' (Women in the Chamber.)'
Annie approaches a woman handing out pamphlets.
"Nous voulons des femmes à la chambre des deputes
(We want women in the Chamber of Deputies,)" she
said as she handed Annie a pamphlet. Shannon is
knowledgeable of France's government, "That is like
the congress in the United States." Annie nods to the
woman who continues her calling, Annie says, "Je
vais lire ceci (I will read this.)" They walk on to the
café.

They order some wine and Annie reads the
pamphlet out loud to Shannon who follows along. It
is a call to elect women to the Chamber of Deputies
as well as a call for women at large to vote in the
election of these deputies. Shannon points out that
they are guests in France and any involvement in
France's politics would be in violation of their visa
and could get them deported. Annie laughs, "That is
all I need to embarrass my parents would be to get
deported from France. The same thing is happening
in America, I will wait till I return but I will work
toward the same goal as these women here." Shannon
laughs, "I'm sure you will."

They enjoy Cornish Hen and asparagus for
dinner and head home before dark. They again pass
the women who were carrying signs and shouting,
"Nous voulons des femmes à la chambre des deputes,
(We want women in the Chamber of Deputies.)"
Shannon tugs Annie's arm, "Let's go talk to them
again." Annie walks up to the very tall stately woman
who looks like she is the leader of the group; she
introduces herself, "Je suis Antionette Dupree
d'Amérique. (I am Antoinette Dupree from
America.)" The stately lady extends her hand, "Je suis

Marguerite Durand, (I am Marguerite Durand.) Mon anglais est bon, ton français sonne américain, (My English is good, your French sounds American.)" Annie laughs "My mother is French but I never accomplished her accent; it perhaps may be a problem when I'm on stage." "Oh you are an actress?" Marguerite inquires. "Well, I'm a student at the Renault Academy." Marguerite laments, "I so wanted to write for the theater." "You are a writer?" "Yes, I write for 'La Figaro' the newspaper. They don't like my protests but my controversial columns in the paper bring readers and sells papers especially to women and I must say not all women especially in the Bordellos." Annie inquires, "Why is that?" "It is because we want them shut down. The stupid courtesans and out right whores hate us, even though it is us, our group that get them out of jail." Annie is confused, "Why are they in jail?" Marguerite places her motherly hand on Annie's shoulder, "You are naïve my dear, when a woman in that profession is found to have Syphilis, they are put in jail to prevent them from infecting the holy righteous men who use her. The men don't go to jail because they can't find them and don't know if they are infected or not. So the women sit in jail without aid. We bail them out and help them in an infirmary until they get over the disease or die." Annie is getting an education, she had not heard of this, "Can they get over the disease?" "In some cases yes, it just goes away but not till after she is disfigured. Most die a horrible death. Oh I hear all about how it may be cured one day but people are dying now; we just have to stop the scourge. The Bordellos must go."

210

Shannon was listening on intently when she turns suddenly having heard shouting a ways off over her shoulder. Suddenly bottles and rocks fly at them from a group of women across the street. Annie ducks and Shannon gets hit on her forehead by a glass bottle. Marguerite catches her as she falls. She grabs the bottle while she holds Shannon with one arm and flings the bottle back across the street, "putain de pute stupide (god damn stupid whore," Marguerite shouts. The bottle breaks at the feet of the perpetrators. Marguerite pulls out a handkerchief to put on Shannon's bloody bruise as she passes out. Annie cries, "My God why, we didn't do anything!" Marguerite tries to comfort her, "It is just because you were here with us; you got caught up in it. I'm so sorry girls. I will help you get her home." Shannon is slowly waking but she is very dizzy. Annie inquires, "Shannon, can you get to your feet?" She stumbles a bit but stands up. Annie explains it is only two blocks to their flat. Marguerite and the other ladies in the group all walk with them home. Shannon now coming clear starts to cry, "I have never hurt anyone in my life, why me?"

They go into the apartment along with all the ladies. They lay Shannon on the couch in the main room. Marguerite inquires of Shannon, "Do you want to see a doctor? I know one in this area." Annie puts a damp cloth on the bruised bump on her forehead. Shannon whimpers, "Ouch, no, this is no worse than when my brother threw a baseball and hit me in the head, I am alright." Annie proceeds to make tea for everyone and they spend the next hour sharing stories of the sad cases of women in the Bordellos. The ladies depart but not without exchanging addresses, they had all become friends. Annie and Shannon were invited by Marguerite to visit her at the paper. She was going to do an article about the incident. 'American woman Injured at protest,' would be the title. She promised not to use their names. She did not want them to have undue attention. After they leave Annie laughs, "First month here and you are already in a fight." Shannon smirks, "I did nothing."

The remainder of the month Annie was dedicated to the play. There were more rumors of Victorien Sardou visiting them. They get to the dress rehearsal and everything goes splendidly; they are ready for opening night. The theater at the Academy is not large. It will only hold about two hundred people. The seats fill quickly, mostly with students and their friends and family. It comes off as they say, 'without a hitch.' The audience laughs at all the right places and the acting company is thrilled. They get two curtain calls. Shannon had arranged to give Annie flowers at the curtain call. Shannon goes with Annie behind the curtain back to the dressing rooms when the plays director pulls them aside, "Annie, I would like you to meet Monsieur Victorien Sardou." Monsieur Sardou removes his hat eloquently and bows as he extends his hand, "You were most delightful as Christiane; I cannot remember anyone ever playing her better." Annie is in shock, "Monsieur, je ne sais pas quoi dire, (Monsieur, I don't know what to say.) Merci beaucoup. (Thank you very much.) Annie goes on about how she had only hoped that someday she would meet him and asked about how his current play was doing at the 'Théâtre du Vaudeville.' He indulged all of her questions. Truth to be known he was taken by Annie's beauty. He invited Annie and Shannon to be his guest at the theater in his private box on the next weekend. It was a dream come true. Shannon whispers in Annie's ear, "He is married but you know Frenchmen, be careful." The date was set; they would be going to the theater as the guest of Monsieur Victorien Sardou, what could be more perfect.

Annie would perform only two more times once on Saturday and a Matinee on Sunday. Since it is a school production that is all that was required; three showings only and the class would move on to the next production. Sets were broken down; props were stored and new canvas was stretched on the back drops awaiting paint artists to paint new wonders on the stage. Shannon was as eager as Annie to go to the theater in the private box of Monsieur Sardou. They would spend all Saturday bathing and preparing and dressing in their finest; they would share from each other's closet since they were both the same size and between the two of them they had a considerable wardrobe to choose from. Their concierge was all excited for them and she knew what a big deal this was. She had arranged for a carriage to take them to and from the theater. It was a night to behold. It was clear and just mildly warm. They would carry shawls in case it was cool after the play let out and they took fans in case it was warm in the theater. Monsieur Sardou had told a theater usher to watch for their arrival and to greet them and usher them to his box.

When they arrive at the box they are pleased and surprised to meet Mlle, Monsieur Sardou's wife, "Mon mari a dit que tu étais adorable. (My husband said you were lovely.) mon cher, tes beaux cheveux roux. (My dear, your lovely red hair)" Shannon blushes, "c'est la faute de ma mere. (That is my mother's fault.)" "c'est adorable. (It is lovely.)" Monsieur Sardou arranges the chairs so they can all talk while they await the curtain on Act one. "This play, my young students of the theater, is my next attempt at comedy with a little flair of melodrama to keep it interesting. I won't tell you, I don't want to spoil the story, but I would like your opinion when it is over."

With that the master of ceremonies performs the play's introduction. As the story goes, Cathérine Hübscher is known as 'Madame Sans-Gêne' which is translated to 'Madame Without-Embarrassment' basically she speaks her mind. Through twists and turns Cathérine rescues an Austrian nobleman against her fiancés will and they help him escape. Time passes and she is now married to Sergeant Lefebvre who through good fortune in the army finds himself as 'Marshal of the Empire' for Napoleon. Cathérine with her plain speaking offends Napoleon's sisters and the ladies of the court. Napoleon demands that Lefebvre divorce Cathérine. Lefebvre refuses. Napoleon calls for Cathérine at which time she confronts him about her support for his revolution and produces a laundry bill that she never collected from him when he was a penniless young soldier. This amuses Napoleon to no end and he dismisses the request for her divorce from Lefebvre.

The Austrian nobleman returns to the scene and is accused of an affair with Marie Louis Duchess of Parma the wife of a French diplomat. Napoleon orders him executed. Cathérine exposes René Savary a duke who plotted to have her and her husband

214

shamed before the court. The nobleman is exonerated and Savary is dismissed from court.

The play is complete and the audience having been thoroughly entertained erupts in applause and call for the author. Monsieur Sardou stands in the box and bows. Annie and Shannon are applauding and smiling ear to ear. It is so wonderful that they could be there to see a truly professional playwright and to share this moment. Mlle inquires if Annie and Shannon would join them for evening liquor at their hotel, "If you will join us you can give my husband that critique, he inquired of you, will you join us?" Before Annie could speak Shannon blurts out, "Ma parole oui. (My word, yes.)" Mlle laughs, "J'aime ton enthousiasme. (I love your enthusiasm.)" Monsieur Sardou, "Merveilleux, je vais demander à votre chauffeur de nous suivre. (Wonderful, I will instruct your driver to follow us.)"

They arrive at the Hôtel Continental which is elegant and posh. They are escorted to the lounge which is open late for entertaining. There is a violinist and cellist playing softly. The tables decorated with flowers and candles are a lovely scene. Monsieur Sardou orders a bottle of Courvoisier Cognac, "Have you ladies heard of Courvoisier, it was introduced in 1889 at the opening of the Eifel Tower." "Oui monsieur, mon père en a acheté par New York. (Yes sir, my father bought some by way of New York,)" Annie explains. They enjoy the Cognac and chocolate treats. The conversation is illuminating for all. Monsieur Sardou and Mlle learn all about the Dupree's of America, the steamboat and how her father and mother met. They learn all about the association of Shannon's family and the Dupree's and

215

how they came to be studying in Paris and of course Monsieur Sardou got the glowing critique of his play by the girls. They departed that evening as adopted daughters by the Sardou's. Even with the promise that Monsieur Sardou would keep track of Annie's progress and perhaps when she finishes school, she might join his company to travel and act.

Shannon has to listen to Annie all the way home in the taxi overwhelmed as she is with this amazing man. Of course it is because he enamored her with attention almost to the point of jealousy by his wife Mlle who said, "Mind your heart Annie, he loves to dazzle pretty girls." Annie did not care she was drifting in the clouds and it felt wonderful.

The rest of the summer was all study. They would practice their Italian together as Shannon would remember all she had seen in Rome. In September Shannon hurt Annie's ears, "I have met this young Frenchman in my art history class, Max Freneau and he has asked me to go to Switzerland for the weekend. His parents own a chalet at the foot of the Alps." Annie is just silent. She does not know what to say. Shannon to fill the silence yammers on, "He is really nice and we get along and laugh a lot. We are just friends but he is really cute and a perfect gentleman. It is a chance to see Switzerland and..." Annie interrupts, "You can't see Switzerland in one weekend, hell its one day to get there and one day back." Shannon can see Annie's irritation, "Alright we are going to take two extra days." "You're going to cut class too?" "No, I already cleared it with my proctor and she said I could see some paintings by Giovanni Giacometti for credits and write a report."

216

"So you have this all planned. You are going to spend nights with this Frenchman in a Swiss chalet alone." "You sound like my mother Antoinette Marie Dupree. I'm a grown woman and quite capable to make my own decisions. I just wanted you to know. I'm going and that is that."

It was a bit of a wake-up call for Annie. In the back of her mind was always that Shannon would someday find a man and that would be the end of their very long relationship. She was just not ready. She did not want to admit her attachment to Shannon as with her mother's question about her being lesbian. Maybe she was. She and Shannon had never approached the topic. She knew Shannon wanted a man and short of a hug and a kiss and some jesting physical grabs and walking arm in arm that was it. But, with this venture of Shannon's it was a break in the relationship and Annie did not react well. She only said, "Well I hope he does not hurt you." "He's a perfect gentleman; we are just friends having fun." Now that statement meant to Annie more that Shannon knew for Shannon was Annie's fun.

The weekend came and Annie helped Shannon pack. Shannon had to listen to Annie's foreboding warnings of does and don'ts with men and what to watch out for. Shannon laughed, "You would think this guy was a murder and going to send my body back in a trunk. Damn Annie it is just a weekend and some days, I will see you on Thursday and I promise you I won't be pregnant." Shannon finally gets a laugh out of Annie. She sees Shannon to the taxi; gives her a hug and puts two hundred francs in her hand, "If you have any trouble you get on a train

217

back here quick, I'll be here." "I'm sure you will mother, ah, I mean Annie." Shannon is off and Annie is lost.

The days are slow, Annie had never been alone in the flat; it was eerie, she could not sleep. She would startle at every little noise the old building made. She kept lamps burning all night and was up and down, tossing and turning. She thought that perhaps her mother was the same way and decided to write her an extra letter to tell her about her worry over Shannon. She then tore it up thinking that she would appear overly attached to Shannon making her mother think even more that she was lesbian. '*I'm not lesbian; Shannon is just a dear friend.*' To prove it to herself she decides to have an orgasm and monitor in herself, in her thoughts that it is the prowess of man that entertains her. She conjures up images of erotic scenes she has remembered in art studies over the years and works herself into a fervor. As she physically heightens, she has flashes of images of Shannon being made love to by this Frenchman she had never met. She sees Shannon writhing in ecstasy from front and behind and with this she climaxes.

Her confusion is manifest. The image of the man and his penetration was paramount but it was Shannon's ecstasy that caused her climax. Annie would hide this away; she did not know what to do with these thoughts.

Thursday came and Shannon had not returned home. Annie goes to the proctor to inquire as to what she knew about the arranged trip; its schedule and anything else she might know. The proctor was no help and was equally concerned, but what could they

218

do but just wait. The young man she was with came from a prominent family. The proctor was going to try to find out from the family if they knew anything. This day was nothing but worry for Annie and as the evening comes, she lights the lamps in the apartment and sits in anguish. Near midnight the door opens and in walks Shannon. "Where on earth have you been, all of us and your proctor were worried sick." Shannon looking disheveled sits on the couch next to Annie and starts to cry, "I had to take a late train because I was hiding from him." "What do you mean you were hiding form him." Shannon is sobbing, "He raped me and I ran out with just my clothes and hid. Thank God, you gave me the two hundred Francs. It was in my pocket. I hid till I could get a late train." "My God Shannon, he raped you." She gathers herself; Annie wipes her nose and cheeks. "It was on the second night; we were getting along just fine; we had some wine and he kissed me. I was good with that but then he started to take off my blouse and I said no. I explained we were to new and things take time. He got mad and called me a tease and one of those girls that like to get men all excited and then makes them feel stupid. I said that was not so. He pushed me over the arm of the couch, held me down and violated me from behind. He said he would teach me a lesson about teasing men."

Annie is incensed, "I'm going to go to the police first thing. His family is going to know about this. They put rapists in jail." "No Annie, he said if I did that, he would claim extortion, that I faked it to get money out of his family and that I was a charlatan, and then he laughed at me saying 'that will teach you bitch.'" Shannon sobs some more and Annie hugs her.

Annie then stands up and starts pacing the floor, "There has to be some way to get that bastard." She pours Shannon some brandy and she gulps it down. Annie likewise swallows the brandy like a needed medication. Between them they finish the bottle and fall to sleep together on the couch. Annie's Shannon was home, she was bruised but she was home. Tomorrow would be war and hell as far as Annie was concerned.

As the sun came up Shannon went to bed. Annie bathed and dressed, downed some coffee and headed straight to the proctors office. Her mind was reeling, *'what if Shannon did get pregnant?'* her whole life could be ruined. She would leave Paris in shame, her father would vow to come kill this man, and she knew he would. The Irish are good for vengeance, hell he might come to kill him even if she is not pregnant. Annie flies into the proctors' office expediently. Miss Beaumont is at her desk. "Well, our Shannon is home. She got to the flat at midnight looking like hell. She had been on the train late and by herself. She hid herself from that bastard because he raped her." The proctor gets up and closes the door to her office, "My God Annie is she alright?" "No she is devastated and what is more he told her he would blame her for extortion and faking it to get money out of his family."

Miss Beaumont takes charge, "First thing we must do is see that no one else knows. So you keep your mouth shut." Annie does not understand, "No we should go to the police and tell them everything." "Annie, I know you are mad as hell but to catch this guy we need to make him sweat through silence. The

220

silence will drive him mad. I want him to think there is a secret plot going on and that is exactly it, there is a secret plot. He will hang himself with his own actions. You must trust me and let me handle this. There have been other complaints against this young man and his family just makes excuses for him. Now, you go home and tell Shannon what I just said. Have her get herself together and have her act like nothing happened. Have her come see me as soon as she is well." Annie did not know what Miss Beaumont had planned but she seemed so confident she trusted her.

   Annie returns to the flat; makes breakfast; puts it on a tray and carries it to Shannon's bed. She had made Ham and eggs, toast and coffee. Shannon comes slowly awake. Annie sits in a chair next to the bed munching on an apple as Shannon eats. "Well, I talked to Miss Beaumont and she has a plan." Shannon interrupts with toast in her mouth. "I'm not going to do anything. This will outrage my parents and ruin any chance of me continuing here in Paris. My parents are never to know Annie; you have to promise me now, that you will never say anything." Annie raises her voice to get Shannon's attention, "That is exactly what Miss Beaumont said you Irish tart." That got Shannon's attention. Annie continues, "she said that the first thing to do was to make sure no one else knows. Somehow, she says he will hang himself and she knows how to do it." Shannon comes back with her logic, "Even with that if she gets him convicted my parents will find out and make me go home and I don't want to go home." "Your parents are all the way, far away in America. They will never know anything if you don't tell them. Shannon agrees with the plan as long as it never reaches her parents.

She laughs, "Even if they find out years from now, my father will come to France just to beat this guy to death, I know my father." Annie laughs, "And my father would be with him." Shannon laughs herself to tears, "I didn't tease him Annie, I was just being nice to him; I liked him, why did he do this to me?"

This would take a toll on Shannon. It is like any innocence she had known was gone and she was angry. She was bruised and the confusion of her emotions caused her to justify her understanding. Her father would never rape a woman. Her loving brothers would never rape a woman. Annie's father and brothers would never rape a woman. She rationalizes there must be some good men. She knows now that she cannot trust her own judgment. This young Frenchman seemed nice and they had a wonderful time and then he turned on her. This scar will be with her for years. Annie sensed the change and could only walk beside her friend and be her rock to lean on.

Early the next day Annie and Shannon head to Miss Beaumont's office. On the way, walking arm-in-arm Shannon teases Annie, "You would never get raped; you would never get close enough to a man for him to grab you." Annie laughs, "I don't hate men Shannon. I think they are beguiling; it is just they can get me pregnant, so they can keep a proper distance." Now Shannon laughs loud, "My idea of a husband just got pushed back a bit. It is going to have to be a really special man, but isn't that the idea, someone special?" Annie is gaining wisdom with leaps and bounds and expounds, "There is Monsieur Sardou's play with 'Madame Sans-Gêne' who is so outspoken that she offends Napoleon's sisters and ladies of court. Being outspoken gets you in trouble but papa

222

says, 'you need to show people who you are up front so you attract people of your own sort.' So here I am knowing that I do not want to bear children but I may someday want to adopt. If, when I am ready there is a man that is kind enough to understand that, I would consider marriage, but then there is the issue of sex and that I have not figured out yet. As you should remember Marguerite Durand that lady who writes for La Figaro," Shannon nods remembering her, "Well, she says the prostitutes say men have needs and she says, 'do you remember?' those men can put there needs in their hand and put their money back in their pocket and go home to their wife." Annie goes on with her catharsis, "The world is mad Shannon, with so many people trying to live good lives and so many other people doing just the opposite. They will have sex even if it means they will get sick with Syphilis.

With that Shannon gasps, "My God Annie what if he has Syphilis, maybe he goes with whores." Shannon stops and turns, "My God Annie, how will I know." Annie takes her hand and pulls her on, "Let's go ask Miss Beaumont to see a doctor."

They arrive at Miss Beaumont's office; enter and close the door. Miss Beaumont hugs Shannon. Shannon tears up and sits in the chair directly in front of Miss Beaumont's desk. Annie stands behind Shannon with her hands on her shoulders. Shannon wipes her nose, "Annie says you have a plan Miss Beaumont and you must know that my parents must not know about this or all hell will break out." Miss Beaumont again takes charge, "Please call me Susan. You must know that I know this boy and his family. I also know the magistrate. I want you to ignore Max

223

Freneau entirely. We will act like nothing happened. It will only take a day or two and he will be mad with curiosity. The Dean has engaged a young professional detective to come in as a student transferring into class midterm. He will befriend all the young men that are in that click. Are you getting the idea? Bullies like to brag. Curiosity kills the cat; Right Shannon?" Susan comes around from behind her desk. Shannon stands up and Susan gives her a big hug. "Once he confesses the magistrate will lock him up and his parents can pay for his defense because he will be prosecuted. It will all be done quietly and no one needs to know. So if you don't want to tell your parents that is up to you."

Shannon is very thankful, "You seem so sure." Susan walks her to the door, "This is not the first time I've been through this. The hard part is going to be for you to act nonchalant and turn away from him; we will be watching everything." Shannon and Annie head off for their days activities at the academy. Shannon is imagining this man's arrest and savoring the mind sight of the event over and over again. She wants to see him in handcuffs.

Days go by and nothing happens but of course Shannon and Annie do not see what goes on in the men's dressing room or in storerooms or even the local pub that most of the male students frequent. The student insurgent spy William Lorain has to slowly become befriended by this click. About the third day he was in. They were all going to the corner pub for beer. They were having a great time drinking and throwing darts. William intentionally works his way to familiar ground with Max. He would boast of some of his wild days getting in trouble with his brothers

224

and getting whippings by his father. Max offered up his stories in kind and they all laughed. Then William asks if he had seen the beautiful Irish red head in the art class. Max said he knows her and yes she is beautiful and then he mumbles, "I had her." William says, "What, really?" Max grins, "Yeah, she is something." William says, "Wow, I think if I were with that beauty and she said no, I would just take it anyway." Max laughed and boasted, "That's what I did, she said no and I taught her a lesson, the tease."

With that William turns to the other young man who was listening, "Did you hear that, he taught her a lesson." This other young man said yes. William pulls out a badge and shows it to Max, "I am deputy constable William Lorain." He turns to his witness and says, "I'm sending you a subpoena to testify what you just heard. If you lie it will be contempt of court." He turns to Max and says, "Max Freneau, you are under arrest for the rape of Miss Shannon Brennan." Max turns to run and William shouts, "Just walk Max there is a cop just outside the front door who will tackle you, just stop." Max gives up. He spends the night in jail and is brought before the Magistrate early in the morning.

Max is released on bail to his parents and ordered to appear for a hearing in one week. Shannon and Annie are having breakfast when a knock comes at the door. Annie answers it in her robe and slippers. It is Susan Beaumont with the news that Max Freneau was arrested and bailed out by his parents. Susan joins them for coffee at the kitchen table. Shannon breaks into tears, "I did not want to be part of a scandal." Susan wants Shannon to toughen up a bit, "Welcome to the real-world Shannon, bad things happen to good

225

people all the time, you need to toughen up a bit. The next time a man invites you to a Swiss Chalet for a week you should probably know a little more about him before you run off." Shannon stops sobbing, "What will happen next?"

Susan elaborates, "I talked to the Magistrate and here are the complications; the alleged rape has been confessed to by Max and William Lorain has a witness to the confession, however the alleged crime happened in Switzerland. In order to prosecute, the crime has to be filed in Switzerland. The Switzerland authorities will accept the testimony of William and his witness as lawful evidence even though they are the French authority, but Max will have to be extradited to Switzerland. You will have to go to Switzerland and the local province to file." Shannon is weak right down to her spine, "How am I supposed to do that. I don't have enough money which means I will have to tell my parents and I just cannot do that." Susan already knew how Shannon would react, "I know dear, so here is what I think you should do; once again say nothing. Your silence will have all of them stewing, both Max and his family. They won't know that you are not going to go to Switzerland to file. They will retain an attorney and he will recommend they try to settle with you." Shannon pulls back in her chair, "What with money? Is money supposed to fix this?"

Susan consoles her, "The Dean has already said that Max is expelled; he will no longer be at this school. They will probably offer you a large sum of money in exchange for you to drop what will be a formal complaint since they cannot file a crime in France. They will file a restraining order against Max

226

that if he ever comes near you he could be arrested. That will be the end of it unless you file in Switzerland. That would be lengthy and cost a lot of your money, but by Switzerland law he would go to jail for at least a year and you would get nothing. Shannon took it all in, "So take the money?"

Susan responds, "I would." Annie is incensed, "A God damn man with a dick did all this."

The next week passes and Shannon keeps to herself at school. There are rumors circulating because Max is suddenly missing from class as well as William Lorain. Annie is looking for Shannon and asking everyone her whereabouts when a friend said she was on the roof of the east wing. Annie finds Shannon feeding pigeons on the roof. Annie approaches her, "I just heard from Susan Beaumont, the Freneau family has responded through their attorney to the Magistrate and you have to be in court at nine o'clock." Shannon throws the last of the breadcrumbs to the pigeons, "Well fine, let's get this over."

Susan goes with Shannon and Annie. They enter the small court room. To their surprise it is only the judge, a court reporter, a bailiff and the Freneau's attorney and no one else. The ladies are invited to sit and the Magistrate begins, "In the case of Shannon Aileen Brennan verses Maximilian Franz Freneau of the alleged rape by Maximilian Franz Freneau of Shannon Aileen Brennan I Magistrate 'Marcus Lemont' declare this hearing open." He strikes his gavel and the court reporter declares his acknowledgement that the case was open. The bailiff has Shannon and the Freneau's attorney swear to honesty on the bible and the Magistrate continues,

227

"Susan Beaumont has told me that you are aware that since the alleged crime happened in Switzerland, we in this court entered a formal complaint on your behalf until you decide whether you want to prosecute in Switzerland. This complaint will be judged in this court regardless of whether you file in Switzerland. As a result the Perpetrator is required to answer to this court as to the complaint. It was the decision of the defendant and his family to plead 'nolo contendere.' These means they plead to the mercy of the court and they will accept the court's decision without contest but do not admit guilt. Do you understand this so far Miss Brennan?" Shannon nods yes. The Magistrate instructs, "You must say yes miss, the reporter is not allowed to affirm your nod." Shannon says, "Yes, I understand."

The Magistrate continues, "The court will find for you the plaintiff in this decision but the defendant is allowed to apply stipulations to his plea. The defendant's attorney filed an affidavit and as such it reads. 'Maximilian Franz Freneau does not wish to dispute the complaint by Shannon Aileen Brennan by a plea of nolo contendere. Maximilian Franz Freneau agrees to pay Shannon Aileen Brennan ten thousand franc's for uncontested damages in this complaint. Furthermore in exchange for no further indictment in any other jurisdiction this settlement of ten thousand franc's is paid." The Magistrate explains to Shannon, "Miss Brennan, what this means is you will be paid ten thousand franc's to drop the charges and not seek prosecution in Switzerland. Do you understand?" Shannon again nods to which the judge looks at her in earnest, she quickly says, "Yes, your honor I understand."

228

The Magistrate explains, "You do not have to except." Shannon erupts and stands up, "That is it, ten thousand franc's, how about twenty thousand franc's or maybe one hundred thousand franc's, how much am I worth judge." Susan puts Shannon back in her seat and puts her arm around her. The Magistrate tells the court reporter to stop recording and he says, "Miss Brennan it is your right to refuse but it is at the discretion of this court to rule on the amount of this settlement and it is the opinion of this court that upon reviewing the defendants family worth, this substantial sum is near to the breaking of their estate. I would not entertain an increase in the amount; your position is to either except or refuse the offer; that is all."

Susan whispers in Shannon's ear, "Take the money and let's be done with this." Shannon tears up, "I accept."

The judge instructs the court reporter to enter the acceptance of the now contract not to prosecute or sue the defendant Maximilian Franz Freneau. The judge strikes the gavel, "Case dismissed." Shannon jumps up, "What about Syphilis, what if he gave me Syphilis? Or what if I'm pregnant what then?" The Magistrate considers and pauses a moment and then addresses the court reporter, "Duly noted, it shall be stipulated that Maximilian Franz Freneau shall report to the court in three months to this date to be inspected to be disease free. If that is so, then no other action is in due course, if found to be infected the court will site extenuating circumstances and file another complaint on behalf of Shannon Aileen Brennan." He turns to Shannon, "That is all I can do. Let us pray he is clear of disease for your sake and if you are pregnant, you come see me; that would be a more complex situation."

The attorney approaches Shannon and hands her a check for ten thousand francs and he leaves. The Judge comes out from behind the bench and removes his robe, "Miss Brennan, for your information, I know Maximilian's family and they are devastated, embarrassed and ashamed. Max's father is forcing him to enlist in the army so you will not see him again. You are also protected by a restraining order; if he ever comes near you he will be arrested. Anyway he will be in the south of France in the Army; I doubt you will ever see him again. Shannon reaches for the judges hand, "Your honor, I would rather this have never happened. The ten thousand francs make me feel like a courtesan. Thank-you I know you did all you could."

Susan, Annie and Shannon depart for the café on the corner and proceed to drink. Shannon orders Irish whiskey while Annie and Susan have some wine. Annie whispers in Susan's ear, "I need to watch her, she will drink the entire bottle." Susan whispers in Annie's ear, "We'll carry her home if need be." Shannon says, "I heard that," and they all laugh.

Winter in Paris is like winter everywhere; difficult to say the least. Christmas is lonely for the ladies, not being at home and only letters from family to cheer them up. Shannon did not come up pregnant and this is a good reason for celebration. New Year's Eve in Paris is quite an event. The celebration is fabulous. The fireworks at the Eifel Tower is a sight to see. Annie and Shannon return home from the gala a little after one in the morning. They are drunk on

Champaign and they open another bottle. They sit on the couch in the main room and have another glass of Champaign again toasting the New Year 1893. Shannon rests her glass on the end table and leans back against Annie's breast, "I could not have gone through all that with the court and all if it had not been for you." Annie brushes Shannon's hair away from her forehead and kisses her on the temple. Shannon rolls around to face her and kisses her passionately as she would a man. She drops back down to rest her head again on Annie's breast and says, "Screw men." Annie pulls her back up and returns the kiss. She runs her hand down Shannon's back and Shannon coos. Annie pushes Shannon up and leads her to her bed. They disrobe and climb into bed. Again Shannon says, "Screw men." The night was discovery for them both.

January and February were very cold and complaining to the landlord was of no avail because there was nothing he could do; the building steam heat was running at maximum. Annie and Shannon slept together to keep warm and for other reasons too. The report came from the Magistrate that the Adjutant General at the Army base Max Freneau was serving at has reported that he had no apparent infectious disease. This was welcome information but just a reminder to Shannon of the horrible ordeal.

Spring was a welcome joy. Paris was in bloom again. The ladies were advancing well with the academy. Annie had now completed another play; it was an adaptation of Shakespeare's 'A Midsummer Night's Dream.' It was the most difficult play to learn and perform. It went well and Annie was ready for the

231

spring break they would get. Shannon had a surprise she had kept quiet about. School was out at ten o'clock and the ladies were going to meet at the café for brunch. Shannon sees Annie is already there and joins her, "Well, Miss Antoinette Dupree I have a surprise for you." She reaches in her purse and retrieves two train tickets to Rome, "We will celebrate your birthday in Rome. We have passage to Rome and all expenses paid for a week at 'Villa Roma Cortina' courtesy of that bastard Max Freneau." Shannon laughs, "I sure hope you want to go with me; Happy Birthday." Annie screeches, "Yes, yes, a whole week in Rome, yes!" Shannon pushes back in her chair; humor has left her; she remembers Max and is sullen. Annie notices, "Shannon stop thinking about that horrible memory and that horrible man." Shannon smiles, "Never, he can rot in hell."

So they make wonderful plans for departure, they would leave at noon tomorrow which was Saturday. They would arrive in Rome on Sunday evening. Shannon having been there before became Annie's guide. It was a wonderful week that the two would remember forever. On Monday they went to Rome's theater district and discovered that Monsieur Victorien Sardou had a play being presented at the Teatro Quirino. It was 'Theodora' and the famous Sarah Bernhardt was playing the lead. Annie could not resist and inquired if Monsieur Sardou was there. He was astonished to discover the two young women in Rome and he took them to dinner. His wife was not in Rome with him. This kind old gentleman lamented that she was not there and how she was usually his travel companion, "She loves Rome in the spring when things are fresh. So you are on break from the

232

academy ladies?" Annie is delighted to be having dinner with him, "Yes Monsieur, we are free for a week and then back to work." Monsieur Sardou insists, "Please call me Victor, short for Victorien." Annie tells him of her last play by Shakespeare and Victor agrees it is the most difficult to play, "It is difficult but fun with all the craziness." Shannon remarks, "It was strange with everyone running around half naked in their night clothes." Victor says, "oui, mais un amusement romantique, (Yes, but romantic and fun.)"

They enjoy a wonderful Italian dinner of Gazpacho, followed by Lasagna and fresh Italian bread along with a wonderful Chianti wine. Victor laid out his plans for a production in New York City, "I'm in the midst of writing a new play called 'Gismonda.' It takes place in ancient Athens. I will try it out in Paris and then if it goes well, I want to take it to New York. Will you finish the Academy by next year?" Annie's heart is beating fast, "Yes, in the spring." Victor puts his hand on hers, "would you consider acting in my play? We will start casting and auditions in May of next year in Paris. I would want you to be Sarah Bernhardt's understudy. She has expressed that she would probably not want to go to New York and at that point you would have the lead." Annie could not have hoped for a better start, right out of school than to get a part in Victorien Sardou's play, "My dear Victor, yes, I would be honored. Monsieur Sardou, yes, my mother would be so proud of me, Thank-you." Shannon is delighted for her, "Annie you could not have a better Birthday Present than that." Victor smiles, "c'est ton anniversaire? (Is it your Birthday?)" "oui monsieur, avril vingt neuf et j'ai

233

vingt trois ans (Yes sir, April twenty-nine and I am twenty-three years old.)" Victor kisses Annie's hand, "vingt trois ans jeune, tu es adorable. (Twenty-three years young, you are lovely.)"

Victor brings her down a notch from her cloud, "Now bear in mind it pays standard rates for actresses, but it can lead to other more lucrative parts in your future." Annie smiles ear to ear, "It is a delightful start." Shannon is taking it all in while in the back of her mind she is thinking, *'I suppose after the academy, I will be just going home while she will be staying here.'* She puts it out of her mind; that is a year away.

Victor invites them to a matinee of 'Theodora' on Wednesday afternoon; he would however not be there till the last curtain and he promised to introduce the ladies to Sarah Bernhardt. For Annie this was a real treat; to meet a real actress of her reputation was something she could talk about with pride her entire life. Shannon was entertained but was not as enamored with the idea of show business and could take it or leave it. Upon meeting Miss Bernhardt they discovered she was a very kind and pleasant person. She showed the ladies around the stage and talked openly about her acting and how much she enjoyed working with Monsieur Sardou. She explained how they do the play in French and how most of the Italian population can follow most of the play but she knows they don't quite get it all. Annie mentioned that Victor had offered for her to join the company in a year. Sarah told her how wonderful that was to be invited; that she must have impressed him with her ability, and that he does not give compliments lightly, let alone offering parts

234

without audition. Annie explains that he had seen her in the academy's production of 'The Black Pearl.' Sarah explains, "How fortunate that he got to see you perform, especially in 'The Black Pearl,' that play is fun and funny, I did it years ago."

With that said, Victor comes in behind the curtain, "Well ladies, has Miss Bernhardt made you afraid of me, remember I'm just the writer, it is the director you have to be afraid of and that is because he is afraid of me." Victor laughs, he is such a gentle personage, no one could ever be afraid of him. Annie smiles, "Miss Bernhardt has made us feel right at home." Sarah responds, "Please call me Sarah and an early welcome to the company in a year from now when you finish school. I hope to see you then."

Victor escorts them to the front of the theater and sees them into a taxi to return to 'Villa Roma Cortina.' He instructs Annie to contact him by April next year and he gave her a mailing address and said he would expect her to contact him lest he forget. On the ride Annie is thinking out loud, "It would be a nightmare that he would forget who I am in a year." Shannon laughs, "Could you imagine if he had a memory laps, he is old you know." The rest of their time in Rome was visiting all the sights and art their hearts could absorb. Annie remarked that one week was not enough to see Rome, that you must live there for a year if you are to really see Rome.

When they return to Paris it is right back to work. Shannon was now engaged in the history of art in Greece and she is totally involved and loves Greek Mythology. Annie began work on their next very large project, Shakespeare's 'Hamlet.' She was of course cast as Ophelia. She laments to Shannon that plays are mostly written for men in leading rolls' although she points out that the Monsieur Sardou's play 'Theodora' was written expressly for Susan Bernhardt. Annie jests, "Perhaps one day he will write a play for me."

Annie, in memorizing her lines was aided by Shannon who by the time it came for dress rehearsal could have played the part as a stand in, although she knows she does not have Annie's performing ability or the nerve to be on stage. Because they would be performing on the next weekend the school allowed the performers to take off mid-week.

With the time off Annie found her way to the publishing office of 'La Figaro' the newspaper that Marguerite Durand wrote for. After meeting the women protesters, Annie had been reading her column and was curious if she knows of any women's movements in the United States similar to what she was doing in France. At the front desk of the paper Annie inquires as to her whereabouts, "cher monsieur, je cherche madame Marguerite Durand. (Dear Sir, I am looking for Marguerite Durand.)" The clerk sends her to the second floor and a few doors down the first hallway she sees Madam Durand's name in bold black letters on the glass of the door. Annie knocks softly and peeks in the door. She can hear a typewriter hammering away and she sees a women with her hair pinned up and two pencils protruding out that were poked in her hair like ornaments. The woman stops typing and looks up. Annie inquires, "Je cherche Marguerite Durand. (I am looking for Marguerite Durand.)" The woman responds, "Je cherche. (Yes she is here.)" Then she

236

shouts, "Marguerite, quelqu'un est là pour te voir. (Marguerite, someone is here to see you.)" Annie hears Marguerite say, "envoie-la. (Send her in)" The woman with the pencils in her hair stands up and extends her hand, "bonjour je suis Helen, s'il vous plaît aller dans. (Good morning, I am Helen, please go in.)" Annie shakes her hand and proceeds to Madam Durand's office. Marguerite stands up from her desk upon which she had mounds of newspapers, "Why hello there, Miss Antoinette Dupree, please do not mind this mess, I have to read a lot of newspapers from around Europe so I can quote other writers. How are you? I'm so pleased that you stopped by, and how is Shannon? No more bumps on the head I hope."

Annie is delighted that Marguerite remembered her, "I am fine; getting along quite well, and thank-you for asking. As for Shannon, no more bottles in the head but something worse." Marguerite comes around the desk and reaches out with both hands in a warm grasp, "My word Annie, what happened?" Annie tells her the whole story with all the details of the rape and the hearing and the judgment and the payout and the remaining fears Shannon has, "Thank God she did not get pregnant" Marguerite takes her back out to where Helen was working, where there is a table and where they could all sit. Helen makes tea and they talk about women's issues. Marguerite talks about Christabel Pankhurst in London who was struggling to get her law degree even though she cannot practice law; so she councils women and then has a male attorney file if need be, in court. Marguerite expounds, "How outrageous it is that women are muffled always having to have a man speak in their stead. What if a woman has no one, like

237

so many of those girls in the brothels? They have no father or husband. They are left without defense unless the can afford an attorney.

So that is what we do here besides write articles, we organize a league of women and take donations to help women in need. I have fought to keep the grubby hands of the taxation authority out of our business and because we are not a church or religion, I had to fight for tax free status. They audit us to make sure we are not skimming money, but we are usually broke because of paying bail to get women out of jail.   We have a home we support to help women get back on their feet after they have gotten in trouble with the law. We try to educate them to find work or go to school, but many of them end up right back on the streets. You are a fortunate young lady Annie to have your education supported by your parents."

Annie agrees, "In no small way I am so appreciative. Do you know of any women in America that are doing what you are? We need to do more. When I return home, I want to get involved." Marguerite is not sure, "I will inquire. We are so involved here in France but it would be good to know. I will send a letter to our United States Ambassador and see what I can find out for you. It is young women like you that will be the future. I am glad to call you 'A New Woman,' spread the word."

Annie departs but with arrangements to meet again in a month to see what Marguerite could find out from the Ambassador about the women's movement in America.

It is Thursday and they begin the dress rehearsal at one in the afternoon. It is the second week of June and the little theater at the academy is a bit warm. They begin the rehearsal and stop to open every door they could to try to get a breeze through the theater. The director tells them to just muddle through, that tomorrow night; the opening night would be cooler and not to worry and just to concentrate on their lines. Annie in full costume and make-up was sweating. At the end of the rehearsal she shouts, "Ophelia needs a bath!" The director laughs, "Hamlet is dead Ophelia. I don't think he will care." That gets a laugh from the entire cast. The director calls out, "The curtain is at seven o'clock; be dressed and made-up by six-thirty. See you tomorrow."

Annie removes her dripping make-up and heads home. Shannon was making dinner as Annie walks in, "You would think we were just like an old married couple with me coming home from work and my lovely Shannon making dinner or that could be turned around and you were coming home to your lovely Annie and I was making dinner." Annie does a bow with a sweeping arm like a gentleman greeting a damsel. Shannon laughs, "neither of us is masculine enough to play the male role best we just not attempt to be a husband and or wife. I still want to have children someday and you cannot do that my dear." Annie says, "Truly it takes a man to make your belly swell. What's for dinner?" Shannon presents, "Cold sliced lamb sandwich on French bread with watercress salad and tomatoes. It is too hot to cook. Help me carry everything to the solarium, it is in the shade now and there is a breeze."

They relax and eat slowly. Shannon was right, there was a delightful cool breeze coming through the solarium windows that faced the courtyard and there are large trees blocking any view into the room. Annie opens her blouse completely and fans her breasts, "These things sweat underneath. She uses her napkin to wipe under her breasts. Shannon comments, "They are beautiful, mine are too small." Annie replies, "and as a result you don't sweat beneath, consider yourself lucky, besides you are lovely you Irish twig." Shannon laughs, "I can't seem to gain weight no matter how much I eat." Annie laments, "You are lucky; I have to watch my figure and starve sometimes to fit into my clothes."

Shannon pours more tea, "I think it is natural for women to like breasts, it is not just a man's adoration. Women are nursed on the breast just like a man; it makes sense that women should like them too." Annie agrees, "But I think men have an inordinate lust for them because after they are weaned, they cannot see them again till they are married or otherwise go with a whore. As a result it is a hidden fascination for them." Shannon snickers, "Pour babies just need a tit to solve all their problems." "You are bitter Shannon, because of what happened to you." "You are damn right I am, he just took me and put his sperm in me and it makes me sick to think of it." Annie puts her hand on Shannon's, "Women are not innocent; they have lusts too. It is a compulsion that wells up in you to have an orgasm. It is somehow a strange joke. That is, I mean, well, some women squirt just like a man, it is just that a man can get you pregnant, and they can just walk away." Shannon touches Annie's exposed breast, "You know

240

I do." "Do what?" "Squirt silly." Annie leans over and kisses Shannon, "I know; me too."

Shannon elaborates, "I have thought how I could help a man, or perhaps my future husband when he wants me, but when we don't want to get me pregnant. Now I mean us, we, my husband and me, because after you already have a family, you may not want any more children and him likewise." Annie interrupts, "Oh I see, men have needs right?" Shannon defends, "Women too, not as much as men but women like an orgasm too. The church wants to call women evil for their sex and a woman is only supposed to be chaste and not have desire. I think it is stupid to say only men have desire. Women are equally guilty. We are just better equipped to say no because our sex comes at a price." Annie laughs, "And whores know how to charge for it." "Come on Annie you know what I mean, it comes at a price because it is our body that suffers." "I'm not making light of this Shannon but I still think that illiterate women go into prostitution because they lack opportunities at a decent occupation and opportunities for education. Marguerite Durand told me of a woman, Christabel Pankhurst in London who was trying to get a law degree to practice law and all she can do is council women about the law."

"When we are on the way home, I want to stop in London and look that woman up. Did I tell you Marguerite Durand is trying to find out more about the 'New Women's' movement in America for me?"

Shannon teases Annie, "That's it; I can see you as a protester carrying a sign; your next profession." Annie returns to what Shannon had mentioned, "So what is it that you can do to help your

241

husband with his urges after you no longer want children?" "Annie, you act so naïve sometimes. Remember how we use to tease wondering where Miss Ellery hid her rough candle. Women fantasize about being penetrated. Only they are not going to admit it. They know a lot more about a penis than they will admit; it is this dark fantasy and physical adulation that causes the orgasm. So I will help my future husband have his orgasm without penetration and not blame him for having desire to which I have also and not make him feel guilty." Annie is astonished, "Not bad for a woman who has been raped." "I don't hate men Annie; I hate that man."

Annie was off all the next day because the opening was that evening. As the time for Act I curtain approached the theater was still warm. Even with the doors open it was warm and there was no breeze. Faithful patrons and other students file into the theater and take a seat. The ladies are all fanning themselves and most of the men are meandering outside till curtain time. On schedule the curtain goes up. Actually the curtain goes up on a disaster. Hamlet was dropping lines and had to be prompted, all female actresses were sweating and their make-up was running. At the intermission, everyone including the cast and director went outside. Everyone was trying to maintain their composure and tried to find solace in humor.

They resumed the play. It was a bit cooler and the cast worked hard to just finish. Hamlet dies, everyone applauds mostly because they are happy it is over. All the cast takes a bow and the young man playing Hamlet steps forward to thank the audience,

242

"Thank-you and truly the question is, 'to play or not to play, that is the question." This erupts into wonderful laughter form the audience and a standing ovation.

They had to suffer through a Saturday evening performance and a Sunday matinee and they were done. There would not be another play put into production until September. In July and August the theater was closed. Classes were only a half day. They would study topics about theater support. This would be script writing, lighting, stage and scene construction and manipulation and props. Also they would study various theatrical styles, one man plays and small ensembles.

Shannon had added to her curriculum 'Theater Support and Business.' A class she had known of but never considered. This idea came to her and Annie had not a clue. Let us say she did not make any connection as to why Shannon decided to take extra classes when in fact there was a specific reason, she did this. Shannon knew that in the spring Annie was going to stay in Paris. Annie had already written to her mother and told her about Monsieur Sardou's offer to join his theater company. Her mother was familiar with Sardou's reputation in theater and gave her enthusiastic approval. Shannon would be finished with school and she would be returning home. This left her empty. The thought of going home after this amazing time in Paris sadden her deeply but she kept it to herself. Even though she got hit in the head with a bottle and raped, all else was delightful and she did not want this exciting life to end. Thus her scheming plot was to approach Monsieur Sardou to become a theater assistant in whatever capacity and join the company too. She felt it was a slim possibility but possible. She kept this all secret because she did not want to put a burden on Annie if it did not come true.

September brought the next production, 'Axël.' Annie would play the lead female role 'Sara de Maupers.' She was so looking forward to this play. This was a play produced in France in 1890 to acclaim. It was written by Auguste Villers de l'Isle-Adam. The authors life was a tragedy and he never saw his play performed because he died one year before. The play is intriguing; it has suspense around a hidden fortune, romance and mystery and both the protagonist and the heroine die in the end by suicide. It comes off as a mystery drama with the mystique around a secret religious society. Since everyone knows the story to be pure fiction the drama is not traumatizing but oddly compelling.

Shannon's new studies would have her in the theater more often as she learned about theater accouterments and logistics. She basically was learning how to run a theater and enjoying it immensely, plus it gave her more to talk about that was in common with Annie.

In mid-September on the fourteenth a Saturday, Shannon was at home in the apartment when a knock came at the front door. It was a fellow student who told her she was needed by the director to help find some missing props. Shannon jumps on her bicycle and hurries to get to the theater. The director is waiting by the front door, "We are missing the alter pieces, the chalice and incense fob, have you seen them?" Shannon goes with the director and they look everywhere. It takes about half an hour and they

244

give up. The director says he will just have to buy new props and not to worry, so Shannon returns home. She parks the bicycle and climbs the steps to the flat. She swings open the front door expecting to see Annie but no one is there. The shades are drawn which was odd and it was dark in the apartment. Shannon proceeds to open the drapes.

"Surprise! Surprise! Surprise! ... as people come out from everywhere. Annie comes from the kitchen with a cake and candles lit. "Bon anniversaire! (Happy Birthday!)" And there on table were the missing alter pieces. Shannon is laughing large, "You fooled me and you made me go all the way to the theater on my bicycle." Annie places the cake on the table, "Come and blow out your twenty-three candles and make a wish." Shannon does just that; squinting her eyes and saying, "I wish, I wish, I wish, and blowing really hard; all the candles go out." Annie asks her, "What did you wish for?" Shannon knows full well her wish and in an Irish accent, "I'll not tell the likes of you, it won't come true." Her secret wish was to stay in Paris with Annie after the academy. She would never tell.

All their friends had contributed and brought enough Champaign to drown in. She received gifts of perfume, fragrant soap and night cream. Annie gave her a locket. It contained no photos as yet and Annie had a remedy. She brought out the box camera her father had given her for this trip. Everyone went outside in the sun and took turns doing group pictures. Annie took a single picture of Shannon and Shannon took a single picture of Annie. Annie explains, "I found a local artist who can develop the film. He is a professional that does portraits. So you can put your picture in the locket and when you find that husband you are looking for you can put his picture in the other side." Shannon laughs, "Well until I find him, I will put your picture on the other side." Annie chides her, "Shush, someone will think I'm your lesbian lover." "Shush yourself, I'm not lesbian but I love you just the same." "Are you sure," Annie is laughing and pinches her cheek, "I will never tell."

The next weeks are beautiful. The air is beginning to chill. The rehearsals in the little theater are comfortable and the warm days are gone. In one week, on Friday, October 14 was opening night. Everyone was ready. Shannon had proved herself to be most adept at coordinating and supporting the theaters effort. On several occasions she put in place important changes that were instrumental to the plays success. She was getting accolades from her proctor who said she would not only receive the best grade for the class but she would write a letter of recommendation she could use if she ever seeks employment in theater arts. She had applied herself. She had reason and Annie noticed.

"Do you think you might consider asking Monsieur Sardou about staying here in Paris and working in his theater company?" It was as if Annie just woke-up. Shannon was thinking, 'It is about time.' "Who me, stay in Paris with you; my I never considered it." Annie cannot believe she had been so blind, "Oh Shannon, I am so stupid and self-absorbed. Here I am just working on this play in my own little world paying attention to no one but myself." Shannon sits up on the stage next to the kerosene foot lights and Annie stands in front of her and takes her hands, "So many times I heard you say, 'I guess after the academy, I will go home and I never thought…" Shannon gazes off, "You never thought that I would want to stay in Paris too?" Shannon tears up, "maybe you are stupid." Annie grabs her with a big hug, "yes, I am. I will figure this out. Monsieur Sardou said he would be back in Paris this winter. We will present him with the idea of you joining the company. God knows you have a lot to offer. Why didn't you say something?" Shannon puts both hands upon Annie's shoulders and looks her in the eye, "because that would have put a burden on you and I would feel like a poor relative just tagging along." "Never. I would never think of you like that." They both were tearing and laughing and hugging.

Opening night was a sensation. The entire cast was perfect in their delivery. Not a dropped line and the director did not have to prompt a cast member once. It was a well-deserved standing ovation and double curtain call. There was a surprise guest, Marguerite Durand from the newspaper 'La Figaro.' Annie was delighted. Madam Durand would write an article about the American 'New Woman" Miss Antoinette Dupree and the success of the academy's play. She also included quotes of how Miss Dupree was seeking out women in America and the women's movement. This would label Annie as an activist for the 'New Women' and her name found its way into newsprint in the United States because reporters are always looking for something to write about and a woman activist in Europe was news. It was three weeks later but Annie received her weekly letter from her mother. Mary told her she was reading in the local

247

paper the 'Cincinnati Enquirer' about a young woman activist, Antoinette Dupree from Cincinnati, Ohio. Mary said she did not know her daughter was an activist and that this perhaps was not how she would want her name to appear in the news.

Annie let Shannon read the letter. Actually Annie let Shannon read all her letters and Shannon likewise. Shannon teases Annie, "I think perhaps your mother does not know the half of you." Annie laughs, "Nor your mother either."

Winter was on its way. There would be one more play to finish out the year. They would work all November and the play would be performed the weekend before Christmas. It was Charles Dickens 'A Christmas Carol.' Annie's small part as 'tiny Tim's mother would take very little of her time. She mostly watched from the wings and assisted others of the cast. Shannon and Annie both were homesick. Christmas was their favorite time of year and to not be with family seemed just wrong.

Christmas came and went and another New Year celebration found them inebriated and melancholy. The first week in January, Annie received a letter from Monsieur Sardou. Things were on schedule and he would be in Paris in March to discuss plans for his new production. Shannon could only hope that on that meeting she could entice Monsieur Sardou in her talents as an assistant. Annie reassured her that she would be invited and not to worry but worry she would. She was haunted by the idea of returning to America alone.

Shannon
Before the Magistrate

The Real-Life Theater

At the end of March snow was still on the ground but the trees were budding; it would not be long and springs warmth would remove the chill from their bones. The damn apartment kept them mostly in the kitchen where they would keep the gas stove burning most of the time they were home. The landlord complained about the bill and they would complain right back about freezing and if he hoped to rent this icebox when they left, he best revamp the boiler heating system.

Monsieur Sardou was due on Saturday. They would meet at the corner café at noon.

Annie and Shannon were at the café waiting when Monsieur Sardou arrives by private carriage. To the ladies delight Mlle his wife was with him. He escorts her into the café. Annie and Shannon greet

249

her, "Je suis tellement ravi que tu sois venu aujourd'hui, (I'm so delighted that you came today,)" Annie extends her hand. Shannon curtsies. Mlle laughs, "Oui je ne pouvais pas laisser mon mari seul avec de si belles jeunes filles. (Yes, I could not let my husband alone with such beautiful young ladies.)" Annie unnecessarily reassures her, "Monsieur Sardou has always been a perfect gentleman." Again Mlle laughs, "My dear, my husband travels all over the world, if he were anything but a gentleman, I would hear about it." Victor is amused, "My wife is the spine by which I am able to stand and my greatest fortune." Shannon extends her hand to Mlle, "I only hope that someday I am fortunate enough to meet a man like your husband." "Flattery makes him feel young, doesn't it Victor?" Mlle teases him. "I'm too old and gray to blush ladies but thank you anyway," he muses.

They all sit and order some hot tea and sweet breads as Victor tells them about the preparations for 'Gismonda,' "I hope you are still planning to join the company. We have the 'Théâtre de la Renaissance,' and we will begin set construction the first week in May at which time we will do readings and rehearsal. Annie is ecstatic, "yes I'm still interested, I have thought of nothing else, but the 'Renaissance' is so far away from our flat." "Now don't you worry; I have arranged for apartments for the entire cast. It is just down the 'Boulevard de Saint-Martin.' You will find the accommodations fitting for you and Miss Shannon." Shannon's eyes get twice their size and she chokes on her sweet bread.

Monsieur Sardou smiles, "I have little birds everywhere and I know the Dean at the academy and yes I most definitely could use your assistance Miss

250

Brennan, if you would consider joining the company." Shannon tries to regain her composure still choking, "Oh, my, my word yes, how did you know." Dean Bellerose and I go way back, I helped him start this academy. I think it was your proctor Miss Beaumont who told the Dean about your excellent work in theater management. Besides I can tell you and Annie are the best of friends. Les amis ne devraient jamais faire partie, (friends should never part,) ce n'est pas bon pour le Coeur, (it is not good for the heart.)" Shannon jumps up and rounds the table and kisses Monsieur Sardou on the cheek, "You have made me so happy." Mlle injects, "peut-être que tu devrais m'embrasser ma chère, (perhaps you should kiss me my dear,) Victor told me of his conversation with the Dean and I suggested it may be a bad idea to separate you two." Shannon does just that and kisses Mlle on the cheek.

Annie is delighted; she did not have to try to sell the idea of Shannon joining the company and she did not have to reveal to anyone that if Shannon did not stay, she would not allow her to go home alone and that she would turn down his offer to join the company.

Victor then elaborates on the play 'Gismonda' and the ladies are so attentive and absorb every word. It is truly a love story and Gismonda the protagonist is presented as a strong woman befitting the times when women are fighting to be heard. Victor admits that the current movements by women were inspiration to write about a woman deceived by men and her victory over the villains and how his wife assisted in his ideas for the story. Mlle points out that in the end a man is still Gismonda's hero. Victor laughs, "Yes but remember he is a good man who saved her child."

They enjoy a light lunch and then arrange to meet next at the apartment that Victor was arranging for them. They would graduate from the academy the first week of May and move immediately. Shannon had not yet mentioned to her parents her plans to stay in Paris. It would probably not please her mother but Shannon had employment with the theater and even if they disapproved, she no longer needed them to support her financially. She also had her grandfather's trust which she was overdue in claiming. She knew that after two years in Paris, her mother just wanted her home.

The graduation from Renault Academy for the Performing Arts was not a cap and gown graduation, it was more of a celebration and party where everyone said their good-byes with tears and hugs. Yes, they got a nice framed diploma but the academy was more of a way to make connections in the performing world. Most of the students found employment right after school. There were scores of theaters throughout France in need of talent whether in performing or support. Annie and Shannon were the only Americans the school had seen in years and all the staff would miss them dearly and since they were staying in Paris, they would come by to see their dear friends. Miss Beaumont made Shannon promise to come to see her; they had a special bond.

Monsieur Sardou sent a private carriage to chauffer them to their new apartment. It was quite a ride all the way across Paris. Annie had seen

252

Marguerite Durand and gave her the new address so they could stay in touch. It was like a new Paris on this side, like a whole new adventurous world. Annie had gotten a letter from her father wishing her luck and showing his disappointment that she would not be home this year. He was very excited about the idea of the play coming to New York and said that when that happened, they would come to New York to see her.

They got busy right away. Shannon was introduced to the set foreman and the director. She would aid the director primarily in procurement. Annie sat beside Sarah Bernhardt on every move in rehearsal. She memorized every line just as if it were her playing the part because if anything would happen, even simple things over the one month run of the play she would have to stand in as the lead. It was already decided Sarah did not want to do the play again in New York. So this was Annie's big break. She would be the lead in 'Gismonda' in the biggest city in the world, New York. The idea of this made her weak to think about. It seemed like a dream. Sarah was aware she was scared and would guide her through. Annie had been adopted by the most famous actress in Europe, Sarah Bernhardt so what was to fear.

The play would open the first week of June and unlike the little theater at the academy the 'Théâtre de la Renaissance' was huge. The enormous building would stay cool all day and by evening when they opened the doors the temperature was comfortable. There was still three weeks before opening and Annie and Shannon come home together to make dinner. They are going to make spaghetti. Shannon is chopping up some vegetables for a salad

253

and Annie puts water on to boil the noodles. Shannon goes into the toilet room of necessity and is gone for quite a while when Annie shouts, "It is almost ready, are you?" Shannon cries out, "No. Oh no!" Annie runs to see what the matter was. Shannon is sitting on the toilet weeping. She is bleeding and it was not her time of the month. Annie could tell that this was not a normal thing because of the obvious odor of infection; "Oh my God Shannon!" Annie lights the gas heater on the bathroom boiler to run hot water into the bath. Moments later she helps Shannon get down in the warm water. "I'm going to find a doctor."

She runs two blocks to the theater where there are still men working. She is screaming that she needs help. The set foreman ascertains from her even through her-out-of-breath words that Shannon was in trouble and needed a doctor. The foreman new better and he ran to the fire station a block away to send an ambulance while Annie ran back home.

The ambulance came. Annie directed them to Shannon in the bath. Annie covered her with her robe as the men lifted her out of the bath and on to a gurney. Annie rode with her to the hospital where doctors and nurses came running to meet them. She was rushed into the emergency room and Annie followed. The doctors asked question after question as the nurses cleaned Shannon. The bleeding had stopped. The doctors were evasive and said they would not diagnose this case until they made some tests. They said it could be many things such as premature menopause but they did not want to scare her about more serious possibilities before the tests. They took Shannon to a hospital room to stay for observation and to be near the medical staff. The nurses were very kind; they said they would get a second bed so Annie could stay with her. They also gave Shannon some morphine to make her sleep. They probably should have given Annie some morphine because she did not sleep at all.

The light of morning was coming through the window as Shannon awoke. A nurse asked them if they would like tea or coffee. Annie had coffee but Shannon wanted nothing. Shortly thereafter a doctor came into the room, "bien manqué Brennan comment allez-vous ce matin. (Well, Miss Brennan how are you this morning.)" "I'm weak and sick to my stomach." "Yes, you lost a lot of blood. We looked at some specimens under the microscope and your blood looks normal. We know so much more these days. We checked symptoms against the new discovery of diabetes which causes this type of episode of bleeding because of high blood sugar but found you blood again to be normal. We did however find high amounts of dead white blood cells and serum.

Shannon is hearing nothing she can relate to, "what does all this mean?" "Shannon, I have to give you an examination for me to know for sure." "What do you mean examination?" "I have to look inside your vagina."

"My what?" Annie jumps in, "He needs to look up inside you sweetheart. He's not a bad man Shannon he's a doctor." Shannon rolls her eyes back in her head and falls into her pillow, "My God what is next."

The doctor is intentionally not being easy in his speech, "I will prepare the examination room and we will get this over quickly. It will not hurt."

A nurse and an orderly come in with a wheelchair. The orderly picks her up and puts her in the chair and the nurse wheels her away. Annie holds the door, "I'll be here waiting."

It was only fifteen minutes and Shannon was back in her bed. This time the doctor came in with another doctor and after just a minute another doctor came in. Shannon does not know what to make of all the fuss. The examining doctor starts, "Miss Shannon I had all of my fellow doctors concur on this diagnosis because it would be horrible to tell you this if we have any doubt." Now Shannon is scared. The doctor just blurts it out, "You have Syphilis."

The world just stopped. Annie's heart sinks. Shannon screams and bursts into tears, "God damn-it." She screams, "God damn-it. That son-of-a-bitch has killed me. No, oh Annie, no! Annie jumps on top of her. The doctors say they will come back in a while. Shannon pushes Annie off, "No, don't leave, what can I do now; what must I do."

The doctors pull back and mumble to themselves and again the examiner speaks, "We think you should go home to your family. There are some treatments but you need to be in bed and resting. There is tincture of mercury which is known to relieve some of the symptoms but we think you have had this infection for over a year and it is very advanced. There are cases where people just get well but you need to go home to your family." Shannon is indignant, "You already said that I need to go home. There are a lot of cases where people die a horrible death too doctor." Now she is completely indignant, "God damn bastard. They said Max was clean that he had no disease, Annie; did they lie to me?" The doctor inquires, "Do you know how you got infected."

Shannon is sarcastic, "Yes, there is only one man and he raped me." The doctor wants to go on about how there could be reciprocity but Annie stops him, "Doctor it is more complicated than that, they paid her off and made her sign an affidavit for no further prosecution.

The doctor does the best he can and offers to contact the magistrate with extenuating circumstances. Shannon again indignant, "That's not going to make me well, please just leave me alone." The doctor departs, "We will help you anyway we can, just let us know." Annie thanks him. The nurse comes in and asks Shannon if she would like another morphine pill to sleep. Shannon says yes and give one to Annie, she hasn't slept either. The nurse accommodates the request and Annie and Shannon fall to sleep together.

Shannon is able to walk out of the hospital. Monsieur Sardou and Mlle were waiting outside with a carriage to take them home to their apartment. Annie helps Shannon walk up the steps to the flat. Mlle assists, "Nous allons prendre soin de vous. (We will take care of you.)" Annie thanks Mlle but the cloud of sadness surrounding these young ladies is inconsolable." Victor and Mlle know that Shannon will be going home to America. They also know that Annie will not let her go alone. The next few days would be tears and argument. Shannon wants Annie to stay in Paris and continue with the play. "You will be ruining everything you worked for if you don't stay and do this play." "I'm just an understudy; I can take you home and ask Victor if I can join them when they go to New York." Shannon disagrees, "He wants

257

someone who can practice here and then take the stage in New York. You can only do that if you stay here. Otherwise he will find someone else." Annie refuses, "I'm not letting you go home alone on that long voyage." Shannon is adamant, "You can't make me well Annie, and if you don't do the understudy I will hate you, I will hate myself even more. Don't you see? You must make me proud of you. If you do not make me proud of you I won't love you anymore and you cannot make me proud if you go home now."

Days went by. Shannon bled more but it stopped. Annie is grief stricken and she takes ill. Mlle stop by to check on the ladies and saw that Annie was ill and insisted she go with her to see her own doctor. He found she had a flu and was feverish. He prescribed aspirin, lots of fluids and bed rest. Mlle took her home and ordered her to bed. Mlle reports back to Victor and they send their maid to stay with Annie and Shannon to cook and clean. Days pass and Annie recovers from her illness. Shannon finally gets Annie to agree to stay in Paris and study while she returns home. They work together to write a letter to both of the families to explain what has happened and what they have decided to do. It was painful and would send Sean Brennan, into a frenzy of rage. Aileen, Brennan collapses in grief. She wants to reach across the ocean and have her daughter home now and her helplessness is overwhelming.

Annie meets with Victor and Mlle and explains that she wanted to continue. The Sardou's know how difficult a decision this was but Annie explained Shannon's adamant instance that she continue on. Mlle was concerned that Annie would not be herself as she worried about Shannon over the next year. Victor interrupted, "It will not be a year my dear, we will be in New York in November. We start rehearsal at the 'Fifth Avenue Theater' for presentation in early December. Annie is inspired by that news; she would be back in America in six months. It does not make it any easier for her knowing Shannon would be sailing home alone but in a short while she would follow.

The arrangements are made. Annie would ride on the train from Paris to Le Havre, France where Shannon would board the 'SS La Bourgogne' for the long journey home. Shannon's father had made special arrangements for her to be attended by the ships doctor on the voyage home. Annie goes on board to help get Shannon settled in her cabin. Shannon laughed at how she came to Paris with one trunk but was going home with two. Shannon had to push Annie with tough talk, "You are going to work your ass off and come home a star, or I will kick that ass of yours right out of my house. Now I'm not going to sit here and cry over spilt milk. Go do your work. I will come to New York as soon as you land in November. I'm going to be one of the ones that this damn disease just goes away, I promise you. Now go." Annie kisses her on the cheek, "I will miss you, you Irish twig." Shannon laughs to tears, "Go, go, go now." Annie pulls herself loose and walks away. The hardest thing she has ever had to do.

The ride on the train from La Havre back to Paris was surreal. The two years in Paris with Shannon was reeling through Annie's mind. So many wonderful times and memories were now only painful remembrances. Annie would lock her emotions away.

259

Victor took on the role of father and mentor and steered her to put passion back into her acting. He instructed her that she would have to be the hero and at all cost do the job at hand, which was the play.

The play opened and Sarah Bernhardt was receiving wonderful reviews. This was something to which she was accustom. At the end of the second week Sarah fell ill with a sore throat from speaking too much. This was an opportunity that Victor took advantage of. Annie would have to step in and play Sarah's part. Annie was unafraid and well prepared. In the back of her mind she thought that if they hated her performance she could just quit and go home and she would not care one wit. Victor was in the wings along with the director just in case she needed to be prompted. Victor worried over Annie. All his worry was unnecessary. She performed flawlessly and received a standing ovation at the curtain call. The critics in the paper gave her accolades as the best up and coming star of the stage.

At the same time Shannon arrived in New York being met by her mother and father. As she was coming down the gangway her father runs up and scoops her up off her feet and carries her down, "Oh papa, I'm not that bad, let me down I can walk." Her mother grabs her in her arms and weeps. They take a taxi to the Grand Hotel which is where they stayed during that happy time when they were first leaving for Paris two years ago. Shannon remarked that is seemed like just yesterday when they were here before.

They would be on a train to Philadelphia and then on to Cincinnati in the morning but when morning came Sean informed Shannon he was staying on in New York on business and that she would be going home with her mother. Shannon made nothing of it. He mother goes on to explain, "Your father has business with another bank here in New York; he may be here for a while. We have your room ready at home and your father has retained Doctor Hughes of Christ Hospital in Cincinnati. You will get the best care." Sean goes with them to board the train and see them off and he returns to his business.

Sarah Bernhardt healed in a couple of days and again took the stage. She remarked that she needed to go back before Annie stole her place permanently. Sarah was delighted for Annie because it cemented the part for her in New York. Victor was proud like a father of his little Annie.

The play was held over and ran all the way through to the end of July' Annie would take Sarah's place the second week of July for one week while Sarah had a rest. You could see Annie's acting gaining polish. Victor knew she was going to be a hit in New York and because of the hold over and extension of this run in Paris, the financial profit for it was substantial. Annie received a hansom bonus and her compensation as the lead in the presentation in New York would be a percentage above her salary. Sarah Bernhardt became director of Monsieur Sardou's European productions while Victor was away in America. After the close of the play and the making of all the arrangements Annie was headed home in a few days.

Resting alone with worried thoughts about Shannon, there is a knock at her door. She was not expecting anyone and shouted through the door,

261

"Who is there?" "It is Sean Brennan Annie." Annie is shocked and quickly opens the door. Sean is standing with his hat in his hand and a suitcase, "How are you Annie?" "Mister Brennan, what in heaven's name are you doing here?" "Invite me in Annie and I will tell you." "Oh, my of course, please come in."

Sean places his hat on the hat rack and suitcase below. Annie shows him to the living room, "Would you like some tea sir." "Please call me Sean Annie and yes that would be lovely." Annie excuses herself to make tea but they continue talking through the door of the kitchen. "Is Shannon doing well," Annie inquires. "She is as good as can be expected, for a girl who has been raped and infected by a horrible disease." Sean does not wait in the living room but joins Annie in the kitchen. The tea pot comes to a boil and she pours, "You know she would not let me come home with her short of her hating me." "I know Annie, and she was right, there is nothing you could do for her, she has the best doctor and we have hope. You must know why I am here?" Annie is not sure, "I cannot imagine, unless…" She pauses, "Oh my." Sean knows Annie perceives, "Now you must understand that man, Max Freneau is not going to get away with what he did to my daughter and I don't care about a stupid affidavit she signed or how much he paid her, he is going to see justice."

Annie puts her hand on Sean's, "Max is somewhere in the Army." "Sean holds Annie's hand, "Is that all you know?" "Yes, that is all I know; he is somewhere in the south of France." Sean presses, "Is there any way to find the information without letting the authorities know?" Annie leans in and looks Sean in the eye, "Sean, if you take the law into your own hands…," she pauses. Sean is locked eye to eye with Annie, "I'm not going to hurt him. He just needs to know what he did and his family too."

Annie explains how they could talk to Susan Beaumont at the academy to see what she can find out without going to the magistrate. Sean relaxes for a moment, "Do you think we can go tomorrow?" "Yes, first thing in the morning." They talk more about the incident of Shannon's rape. The more Sean listens the more it wears on him and he breaks down. Annie can see a father's love so deep that any ideas she had of her hatred of men were erased. One can never generalize in that because one person is bad not all people are bad and because one man is bad not all men are bad and because one woman is bad not all women are bad. She does the best she can to comfort Sean but she knew nothing would ease his pain.

Annie reaches up on a kitchen shelf and retrieves a bottle of Irish whiskey that was left behind by Shannon. Sean agreed and they both got drunk. Sean slept on the couch in the living room. He awoke to Annie making coffee and after a quick cup they were off to cross the city and find Susan Beaumont.

When they reached the academy, they inquired within and found Susan in her office. She was delighted and surprised to see Annie. She had heard of the success of the play and how it was held over. She apologized that she had not been able to come see it herself. Annie introduces Sean and upon learning who he was the joyfulness of the meeting turned somber. Susan was consoling to Mister Brennan and she explained and defended her position and the action she took in advising Shannon to agree and sign the affidavit. Sean held no grudge against her and understood her position. Susan was then informed that Shannon had contracted Syphilis. Susan falls back in her chair and drops her head, "Oh my God no; Not Shannon; Oh my God no." Sean explains he needs to know about the where-a-bouts of Max Freneau. Susan like Annie felt that Sean would do something violent. Sean assured her that he just wants him to know what he did and that he would not harm him. Susan gives in reluctantly, "I know exactly where he is, he is at the army post in Montpellier in the south of France. It is two days by train." Sean seems disappointed, "Oh well, that is perhaps too far. Perhaps I will just send him and his family a strict letter explaining my disgust at this whole situation." Susan agrees perhaps that would be enough shame for Max Freneau. Annie gives Susan a hug and a good-bye, it would perhaps be the last time they would see each other. Sean and Annie returned to her apartment as the sun was setting in Paris.

Sean would spend another night on the couch at Annie's. He bought them another bottle of Irish whiskey but Annie only had a sip while Sean again got drunk.

Annie would be leaving in three more days for the journey home. In the morning Sean raises with a hangover and Annie guides him to the bathroom to bathe. He dresses and comes into the kitchen where Annie had coffee and sweet bread ready for him. They sat in the kitchen. "Annie, I am going to go home on the same voyage you are in four days. I'm going to Montpellier. Miss Beaumont was wrong; it is only one day and a half there and with a quick turn-around on a late train I can be back in another day and a half and continue on to Le Havre. I can meet you at the

264

boarding pier on time." Annie is silent and Sean continues, "I can't let this go with just a nasty letter. Max is going to look me in the eye." Annie realizes that she is helpless. Sean Brennan was going to do whatever it was he was going to do and Annie could not stop him. She just stands up next to his chair. Sean is almost as tall as Annie when he is sitting down. She just gives him a hug, "Be sure you make the pier in time, I don't want to sail without you, it would be a lonely trip home." Sean assures her that he will make it on time. Sean was gone before noon and Annie was alone.

On schedule Victor and Mlle escort Annie to the train station to leave for Le Havre. It was not a tearful departure but a joyous one Annie would see Victor and Mlle in November in New York. Annie was excited but her happiness was always subdued with Shannon always on her mind.

It was only a day by train to Le Havre she would have to spend the night somewhere before boarding the 'SS La Bourgogne' in the morning. Victor told her of the Inn Verlaine that was in Harfleur that was just outside of Le Havre. That is where she would spend the night. Annie never felt so alone. She did not sleep well in this strange place and was awake most of the night to every sound that occurred. As the morning light came up, she wasted no time in leaving the Inn. She found a carriage to take her to La Havre and had to argue with the driver over her two large trunks and one suitcase that he did not want to lift. Finally after the promise of an extra tip the driver put her trunks in the carriage. She quickly discovered that the only way to get anyone to do anything was to hand them money. It was of little concern. She was going home with a bank check for ten thousand American dollars and she had another two thousand in the money belt her father had given her. She was a wise traveler.

She arrives at the pier and passengers are already boarding. She hires a porter to transport her trunks on board. She hands her passage ticket to the Master at arms and he directs her to her cabin. The Master at arms shouts down to the porter who is waiting with the trunks below, "Take them to the second deck cabin twelve" The porter nods and proceeds to hoist the trunks up by block and tackle. Annie climbs up to the second deck with her suitcase and finds her cabin. She waits for the porter with her trunks. Once they arrive, she tips the porter and goes out on deck to have tea and to watch for Sean Brennan. She is afraid he won't make it in time.

Just two days before while Annie was still packing for her journey Sean had made it to Montpellier on the last train of the night at eleven o'clock. He had been questioning as best he could in English to passengers that spoke little English as to where he might find the army base. He managed to get enough information and found his way to the army post. He slept a little in the train station till early light and then went to the post. He just walked right into the main office and asked where he might find Max Freneau. They did not even ask him why and they did not suspect anything. The administrator looked through his roster and says that Max was in the infirmary and that he was sick. Sean as best he could said, "malade de quoi? (Sick from what?)" The administrator became agitated. He said he did not know and that he should just go to the infirmary and see for himself." Sean gets directions and goes.

At the infirmary he inquires at the desk and they confirm that Max is there. Sean asks to see him. They ask if he was family and he lied and said he was his uncle. They thought nothing of it and allowed Sean to go in. He is escorted down the hall where there are rows and rows of beds and they take him to Max's bed. There in bandages and looking very poorly is Max. He is disfigured with part of his nose missing and part of one ear. He has blisters everywhere on his face. Sean stands in front of the bed and Max says, "Who are you?" Sean grabs onto the foot of the bed and winces and growls as he stars at Max, "My name is Sean Brennan. I am the father of Shannon Brennan the girl you raped." Max could understand only a little. He heard 'father' and he heard 'Shannon Brennan.' Along with the shaking of the bed and the anger in Sean's eyes Max makes the connection and is afraid. Max yells, "aide, infirmière, aide, cet homme n'est pas ma famille, aide! (Help, nurse help, this man is not my family, help!" Sean shakes his bed, "Go ahead and yell you sick bastard, you've killed my daughter with the same God damn disease you have. You are going to rot in hell." Max yells again, "Aide, aide! (Help! help!)" With that the doctors, nurses and orderlies surround Sean and drag him out as he yells, "Rot in hell you bastard!" The doctors take Sean to the front door and shove him out. One doctor says, "Il est déjà en enfer monsieur! (He is already in hell sir.)" If Sean had the opportunity, he would have killed Max but as he made his way out of Montpellier he realized that he was already dead. The ride back on the train to Paris and then on to Le Havre was long, he was tired and broken in his heart. He reached the pier to board the steam ship just in time. He looked disheveled and dirty but he did not care. Annie saw him from the upper deck as he boarded and she shouted down to him. He looked up and waved. She was afraid something horrible had happened because he looked awful.

Annie ran down as fast as she could to meet him. He was about to climb to the second deck when she came flying down and threw her arms around his waste, her head only came up to his chest, "I was so worried, Sean. I was so worried you would not make it or something bad would happen." Sean picked Annie off her feet and then set her down, "I am fine; I am just dirty and tired." Annie follows him up to the second deck. His cabin is several doors down from hers. She escorts him to his cabin door. "Annie, I am going to sleep now, everything is fine and I will tell you all about it but I need to sleep. So you will know, I did not hurt Max. He is dying. It is what he deserves. I will see you tomorrow." With that Sean closes the door and Annie leaves him alone.

The ship crosses the English Channel and ties up at London. The layover would only be for the night. Annie thought about Christabel Pankhurst the 'New Woman' activist she wanted to meet here. There would be no time for such an excursion but she in her heart vowed to one day return to London as she gazed at the skyline of the busy city. Sean did not come out of his cabin until the next day and the 'SS La Bourgogne' was underway. He knocks on Annie's cabin door to no answer so he heads to the dining room and finds her there, "Good morning, Annie." "It is past noon Sean; come, sit would you like to eat?"

"Yes, I am starved." He looks much better. He is rested and has had a clean shave. Annie remarks, "You look so much better today, did you sleep well." "Yes, I blacked out." Annie smiles, "It has been almost two days. We are out of London by almost six hours and headed home Sean. I'm so glad you are here with me. It would be such a lonely trip without you." Sean places his very large hand on Annie's "Likewise for me Annie, I don't like Europe very much. It will be good to get home." Annie is waiting for him to talk about his encounter with Max but she will not ask."

A waiter comes to take his order and he asks if it is too late for breakfast. The waiter said he could have anything he wants, so he orders breakfast. Annie has more coffee. Sean knows Annie is waiting to hear about his trip to Montpellier and he does not keep her in suspense. What Annie hears makes her ill. Sean apologizes, "Annie I am sorry, it is a sick world we live in but Max got what he deserves and my Shannon is innocent and punished for no crime." Annie is overwhelmed and excuses herself from the table. Sean understands. She leaves the dining room quickly and runs to the guardrail and throws-up. A passenger comes to her aid and she gives the excuse of seasickness but truly she is sick to the heart over Shannon.

The seven-day journey lingered on and on. Sean and Annie sat together on the upper deck every day. Annie would read newspapers and novels from the ships library. She would tell Sean excerpts of what she was reading and he would comment. He explained that normally he read everything he could get his hands on but now he was not in the mood. "I'm going to read everything I can find about this damn

Syphilis when I get back. We have to find a cure. I know we can find a cure. For Shannon's sake we have to find a cure. This giant man weeps and pounds the arm of the chair. Annie just listens. She cannot help him; she is trying so hard to be strong.

Finally they reach New York. Sean takes charge and guides Annie all the way. They do not stay at a hotel but go directly to the train station. Sean helps Annie send a telegram informing the Dupree family they would be in Cincinnati in three days; they then board the train for Philadelphia. Annie was glad to be on American soil, "As much as I enjoyed Paris it is good to be in America again." Sean laughs, "Exactly, my great grandpa, god rest his soul, came from Ireland in eighteen-fifty during the potato famine. My father said he would joke about how good it was to be back in America. Papa would say, 'when were you here before?' He said grandpa would say, 'always in my heart I was here.' there is no place like the United States of America." Annie added, "And we will make it better when women have the vote." Sean laughs, "And you will make that happen, I am sure." Annie grins, "Yes I will."

They arrive late; it was eight o'clock when the train pulled into Cincinnati. Captain Dupree upon knowing their arrival was late in the evening has arranged lodging in Cincinnati for everyone. It was a home coming. His Annie was home after almost two and a half years. The entire Dupree family was at the platform when they arrive. Aileen Brennan was there alone to meet her husband. When Annie comes down from the train Leah Anna was the first to run, she could not wait. She leaps into Annie's arms. Annie

laughs and grabs her, "My God you have gotten tall."
"I'm taller than you; mama says I take after father."
Mary can see the change that two years had made in
Annie. She looked like a mature woman. All the
girlish lightness was gone. Mary was aware of
everything that had happened and knew it had taken a
toll. Mary was hugged next and Annie squeezed her
and held long. Next was James and he laughed and
picked her off the ground, "So your going to New
York to be in Sardou's play are you girl. Well that's
amazing." Annie feels like a little girl in his arms and
she does not care, she knows she will always be her
father's little girl. James Jr and Marcus were patiently
waiting for their hug. James Jr was as tall as his father
and Marcus was only a short way behind. Annie
remarks how handsome they had become.

Sean Brennan hugs and kisses Aileen and he
greets the Dupree's. Captain Dupree announces the
plan for them all to stay at the Lodge he had retained
and they would all go together to the Brennan home
to see Shannon and her brothers in the morning.
Aileen explains to Sean that his sons stayed with
Shannon because she did not want to come into the
city. Annie had arranged for her trunks to be off
loaded in Sailor Park at the freight office. Marcus
carries Annie's suitcase and in two carriages they
head for the lodge.

Privately at the lodge that evening Sean told
James and Mary about the rapist Max in the infirmary
in Montpellier. "If that had been me and my Annie
had been raped, I don't know if I could have
controlled myself. I would have gone to jail because I
would have killed him." "I know, I was about to
strangle him but the orderly grabbed me and threw me

271

out. I decided he will suffer more alive, my killing him would get him off easy." Mary asks about Shannon and Aileen explains how they are giving her mercury tablets that she throws-up. How she is weak but thinks it is because of the mercury. "I don't know, she has stopped bleeding, maybe the mercury is working. I can only hope. Her eyes have dark circles and she is pale. That's my baby Mary and I was right when I did not want her to go to Paris. This would have never happened." Mary can only hold Aileen's hand; this could have as well happened to Annie. Mary turns and sees Annie standing in the doorway and Annie responds, "I do blame myself Miss Brennan and I think over and over if I had not encouraged Shannon to go to Paris this would have never happened but you know what? This happens everywhere not just in Paris; women get raped." Annie starts to cry, "I did not want Shannon to go to Switzerland with that man Max but Shannon has a mind of her own and when she decides to do something you cannot stop her." Aileen realizes she had put an unfair burden on Annie and runs up to hug her, "You are right my dear. This is not your fault and I am an overprotective mother." Mary sees her daughter as brilliant and wise and though her heart is breaking, she is proud.

By ten in the morning the entourage in the two carriages Captain Dupree had hired take the four hour ride out to east hills where the Brennan's estate is located. It is a large stately home on a beautifully landscaped ten acres. Sean's two sons Fredrick and Robert were waiting in the carriage breezeway to tend to the horses and the carriages. Mary remarked how

272

lovely Aileen's home was. Aileen laments that it is almost too much to care for but it was Sean's dream home.

Everyone joins up in Sean's large library and den. Fredrick had gone to help Shannon come down from her room. She comes in the den on Fredrick's arm and smiles when she sees Annie. Annie runs up to hug her. Shannon is gaunt and frail. Annie flashes on remembrance of calling Shannon an Irish twig because she was thin and how she would never say that again. As coincidence would have it Shannon laughs, "Now I really am an Irish twig." Everyone greets Shannon and Aileen asks who would like tea. Everyone says yes to tea and they all go about visiting and allow Shannon and Annie to sit alone and talk.

Shannon goes on about her disgust with the doctors and how she thinks the mercury and other medicines they are giving her are making her sick. That the blisters and bleeding only hurt a bit but the medicine makes her sick. Shannon knows nothing about her father's trip to France. She thinks her father was in New York on business. Annie has no intention of saying anything. Shannon is optimistic, "I'm going to get well I know it. I'm going to be one of the ones were the disease just goes away. And then I'm going to go back to France and shoot Max Freneau." "I will go with you and we will both shoot him with two guns." Shannon laughs and coughs, "He should live that long so I can give him just reward." Annie holds Shannon's hand till she stops coughing and cannot bear it, she has to tell her, "Shannon, Max is dying in a hospital in Montpellier, France." "What, how do you know?" Annie realizes she has made a mistake. Shannon raises her voice, "How do you know that?"

273

Shannon was obviously upset and everyone turns to see. Sean knew what the matter was and came up to Shannon, "Now don't you be upset with Annie, it is not her doing, I was in France and saw him, I almost killed him but he is dying on his own." Shannon feels as though secrets are being kept, "Was anyone going to tell me or were you all hiding this." Sean reacts, "Calm down now lass, I just got home and I was waiting for the right time to tell you in private. Well so much for that. Now you know and that is that. The bastard is dying or from the looks of him he is probably already dead."

Shannon cries out, "And, that's what is going to happen to me papa." Annie can't bear it. She takes Shannon by the hand and leads her away. She takes Shannon to her bedroom and puts her in bed. The rest of the family go about visiting as house maid Lilly, Aileen and Mary prepare dinner for all.

Shannon and Annie move on to lighter conversation. Shannon wants to hear all about the play 'Gismonda.' Annie gives her all the details and how they were held over. She brags about the bonus she received and how she feels like a professional actress. They talk all about the upcoming play in New York. Shannon tells Annie regardless of her condition she is coming to New York to see her in that play. Annie also affirms that she wants to whole heartedly work in the 'New Women's' movement and when she gets to New York she is going to visit an organization that Marguerite Durand had found called the 'National American Women's suffrage Association,' they call it the 'NAWSA' for short." Shannon instructs Annie, "When you find out write me so I can join too. After being hit by a bottle I feel like a true soldier." Annie laughs, "Oh my Shannon, you always find trouble; even in Madam Rousseau's school with the other girls, you would get into a fight." "It's not me Annie. It is just if someone is being unfair it makes me mad. I don't go lookin' for trouble lass." Shannon's Irish bluster was Annie's favorite. "That's my Shannon." Annie laughs.

The family sits down for dinner and they take the meal up to Shannon and Annie. They obligingly leave them alone. As night approaches Aileen shows everyone to the guest rooms of which there were plenty. Annie curls up with a blanket on the lounge that was in Shannon's room. It was the first week in September and the evening was cool.

In the morning they had a large breakfast and decided on future arrangements. Annie had until the last week in October when she would board a train for New York. She would go home to Sailor Park for a week and then come back to stay with the Brennan's and Shannon for three weeks. She would then return again to Sailor Park until her departure for New York. They departed the Brennan's home for the train in Cincinnati at noon. They would be home in Sailor Park by sundown.

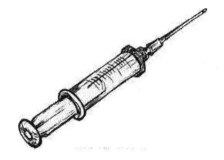

Home for a Time

September was still warm in the day but cool at night. It was good to be home. Mary and Annie talked at length about Paris while sitting in the swing on the front veranda. Leah Anna sits on the railing listening. Leah Anna was now seventeen and would be starting at Madam Rousseau's school soon. Annie was telling her how much fun it was and how not to let the other girls intimidate her. Leah Anna was outspoken and not shy at all, "I won't be intimidated by anyone especially having been raised next to my brothers. If you can survive them, you will have no problem." Annie laughs, "They are a hand full." Mary leaves her daughters to talk and goes into the house.

Leah Anna sits next to Annie on the swing and prods her, "Guess what?" Annie pokes Leah Anna in the ribs, "What?" "I saw Ben Hamilton in town and he is looking as handsome as ever. I'm getting almost old enough for him don't you think?" Annie is quick to respond, "No, he is my age, twenty-four, you are only seventeen. He is way too old for you." "Well anyway, he has not married anyone. He manages his father's company up in Dayton now making stuff for those automobiles. He is really rich you know, like papa says, wealthy." "Oh is he now and what is that supposed to mean to me." "Well if you were to marry him you would be rich forever." "Is that what it is all about Leah Anna, being rich, or rather wealthy?" Leah Anna inquires, "Isn't it. Isn't it the most important thing? Papa is rich isn't he?" Annie laughs, "Yes, well he is rich enough to send you to school anyway."

Lean Anna finally gets it out, "Well, Ben Hamilton said if you were ever to come home again that he would like to see you. He was so apologetic and sad like a poor minion asking to see the great queen. I felt sorry for him." Annie surprisingly is not annoyed at his persistence, "I'm not as course as I was or maybe I'm not as angry at men as I use to be. I think I was afraid and it made me hold men in general at a distance." Leah Anna is surprised, "So will you see him while you are home; he is visiting his family. I think he said he would be here for another week." "Perhaps, why are you so pushing me toward Ben Hamilton, are you trying to play match maker? Well, let's see how I feel tomorrow. I like to sleep on things and see if I feel the same in the morning." Leah Anna is delighted; she always felt such a separation between herself and Annie because she wants to marry someday and could not see why Annie hated the idea of it so much, "To answer your question, I'm not playing match maker, I just don't like it that you hate marriage so much and to me it seems natural, I guess I just want us to agree, your opinion means so much to me."

Mary overheard their conversation from the living room and thinks, '*I knew she would change. Maturity comes to us all.*' "And if you are listening mother, I'm still not going to have children with this body." Annie knew her mother was eavesdropping. "oui chéri je sais. (Yes, dear I know.) Mary consoles herself, '*time is long. We will see.*'

Captain Dupree was again gone on the Ohio on the Louis Queen. He would be in Cincinnati for Annie's departure to New York by the last week in October. He had promised to be in New York for the

278

opening of the play in December. Thus was the life of a steamboat captain making sacrifice for his family by working eight or nine months out of the year.

They all join Helen in the kitchen to help with the preparation for dinner. Annie was so delighted to be home. It was almost like she never wanted to leave except for her will to not be another home bound wife. That is what compels her. She was opening with the lead role in a play by Monsieur Sardou, 'Gismonda.' How fitting the roll was. She is a woman who has to fend of wicked men trying to see her demise. As she tells everyone the story she laughs, "Perhaps I play the part well because I can feel her angst." Mary agrees the part fits Annie well. Helen pats Annie on the shoulder, "Hell hath no fury like an Annie scorned." They all laugh, Annie most of all.

The following day was rainy and there was a chill in the air. Mary remarks that she thinks winter will be early this year and if so her husband will be home by mid-November. Annie knows how much her mother loves having her husband home. It would only be a few years and all her children would be gone from the house. Annie wonders, "Mama what will you do with this big old house after your last child leaves?" Mary is quick to respond, "I envision a house full of grandchildren no thanks to you my dear Annie." Annie took that as an affront, "Just because I don't want to bear children does no mean I won't have children someday. I can adopt. There are so many needy children and it would be a good cause. Damn mother, it is just the idea of bearing children. Having your body ripped apart by a cute little bundle of fat." "Annie you are so crass. I should have sent you away when your sister Leah Anna was born. You were too

279

young to have been exposed to childbirth. Besides look at your beautiful sister, isn't she worth it." Leah Anna smiles, "Thank-you mother." Leah Anna comes over to the table and kisses her mother, "It is a good thing you were not my mother Annie; I would not be here."

Annie surrenders, "That is enough. You are right. I will have nine children and raise them all in this house so you and papa can have all the grandchildren you want. Leah Anna, go tell Ben Hamilton that I want to marry him and he will need to be rich because I want nine children." Mary laughs, "No Annie that would be a curse to those nine children." Leah Anna chimes in, "So do you want me to tell Ben you want to see him?" "Oh God Leah Anna; I have slept on it and decided it would be rude of me to not say hello since I am here only for a few more days." Leah Anna is delighted, "I don't want to act pretentious; James is going to town, I will tell him to look out for Ben and if he sees him to mention that Annie asked about him so it won't look like an unscrupulous plan." Annie turns down the idea, "No, there is no need for that; I have more pride than to have someone behind the scenes do my bidding. I will send Ben a note directly, telling him I would like to see him. I am an adult woman not a little child." Mary says nothing. She just smiles, she is so proud.

Annie goes to her father's den and writes a note. She then goes out to find James Jr and finds him at the stable with Dancer. James was about to saddle Dancer to go to town and Annie asks him if he would deliver her note to Ben. "tell him I will only be here three more days. Tell him to read the letter and wait for his response." James laughs, "A note to Ben

Hamilton. Are you going to break his heart again?" Annie does not want any chiding, "James just deliver the note, please." He mounts Dancer, "As you wish miss, your wish is my command." Annie kisses Dancer on the nose. Dancer answers with a gentle nay. James turns him and they trot off. Dancer was stepping high with that kiss from Annie.

James is back by dinner and joins everyone in the kitchen. He comes in and sits at the table and says nothing. There is a long pause. Helen and Mary are silent. Leah Anna looks at Annie to see who would speak first. Annie is just gazing out the window; she knows that James knows that everyone is waiting to hear Bens answer and that he is trying to goad Annie. James also stares out the window and starts to whistle when Annie smacks him on his hand, and hard. James withdrawals his hand fast, "Ouch, damn, ouch" Mary says, "James, regarde tes mots! (James, watch your words!)" "Désolé mere. (Sorry mother.) James gives in while he rubs his hand. Leah Anna laughs, "See what I have to put up with all the time?" James blurts out, "Ben said he would love to see you at the time you suggested at noon at Stallman's café." Annie pats his bruised hand, "Poor dear, hope it doesn't hurt too much, and remember I am your older sister. Do you remember when you were ten and you snuck-up on me in the swing and pulled my hair so hard it almost bled; do you, do you remember?" "Yes I do. You would not have caught me if I had not tripped on that old tree root." "If I remember correctly, I bloodied your nose boy." "Yeah, but I didn't cry." Annie laughs, "Yeah, but you wanted too and you never pulled my hair again. If you pick on Leah Anna, it will come back to haunt you." James looks down, "A little

281

fun doesn't hurt, I love you sis." "I love you to James."

Annie knows that being raised alongside her brothers gave her a perspective on the male world that she would not have had otherwise. She sees how differently men are raised compared to women. She can see how boys early on are denied hiding behind their mother's skirt. How fathers require their sons to toughen-up as it were, brush-it-off so to speak and stop whimpering. While fathers' daughters are scooped up if they fall and daddy wipes their tears away. The perspective she gained from her brothers is that brothers do not care about hurting their sisters' feelings and in fact boys are jealous that little girls are coddled and subconsciously and intentionally goad their sisters.

Marcus comes home and they have dinner. Afterward, James Jr and Marcus head out back to do their chores. Helen and Leah Anna do the dishes while Annie and Mary go to sit in the swing on the front porch to watch the sun set. Mary sits with her arm around her dear daughter, "c'est tellement bon de t'avoir à la maison. (It is so good to have you home.) You have matured so much." Annie had written every week that she was gone. Mary knew about the sneaking into the Cancan and Annie's and Shannon's embarrassment over the nudity. Mary found it all so funny. Annie derided her mother, "tu aurais pu me le dire. (You could have told me.)" "Non, je t'ai juste dit de rester loin. (No, I just told you to stay away.) I did not think you would go because I told you to stay away from the bordello district, so it is not my fault." Mary laughs, "Oh, quand j'étais une fille... (Oh, when I was a girl...) we lived just two blocks from the

282

bordellos. My mother your grandma, God rest her soul, walked me to school every day and took me to the theater and all she said was don't be like those whores. Your grandmother was, how do you say, 'dur comme fer' (hard as iron.)" "Just like you mama, hard as iron or don't they say tough-as-nails?" Mary laughs, "I'm not as tough as your grandmother."

Annie goes on about being tough and how it is men that make it so hard. Mary defends men, "Survival in the wilderness is hard and men did not cause that. She defends that it is mostly men who have invented all these wonderful things like boiler heat for our home and the new electric lights and now the motor car. It is because of the steam engine that your father has a steamboat that has paid for your extravagant trip to Paris." Annie looks away in a gaze, "I know mother and I am so appreciative; papa is an amazing man. Why can't they all be like him? I have learned not to generalize and lump people together, but what makes men like that Max Freneau who raped Shannon. Where do evil men like that come from?" Mary consoles her, "They have prisons for men like that but it is sad that they have already hurt someone before they are caught." Annie pounds the arm of the swing, "Shannon may die mother; she may die because of him. He had to put his sperm in her. Why? Is it just because of the compulsion of the orgasm? With no concern for her he just had to do it?"

Mary expounds with some of her wisdom, "Women in France are more open about sex than women in America. Here in America it is something you don't talk about. Women are closed up even amongst themselves. If they have an orgasm with their husband, it is something of shame. Even their

283

husbands think that if a woman enjoys sex and has an orgasm, she is a loose woman and he fears she will be unfaithful. Women are to be chaste, prim, and proper. They are to have babies and nothing else. Times are changing, even with you and your 'New Women's' movement. You are not afraid to talk about such things as an orgasm; most women cannot."

"Mother, I am talking about the male compulsion to have an orgasm. I do not think women have a compulsion. If we have an orgasm fine but we will not brutalize someone for it; men will; at least some men." Mary tries to give balance, "les femmes ne sont pas toujours innocents Annie. (Women are not always innocent Annie.) If they dress provocatively and entice men, they are asking for trouble. Shannon should not have gone to Switzerland alone with this Max Freneau." Annie ruffles a bit, "Shannon never dressed provocatively. Others tried to blame her for teasing and try to put blame on her and that makes me so mad. She knew Max as a student at the academy. He was from a good family. She went with him as a friend and it was a chance to see Switzerland. Shannon did not tease him. She liked him and he turned it into something it was not and he just took her. Anyway, I believe men have a compulsion and I am sick of hearing that men have needs. Mary breaks the seriousness, "Men are like puppies you just pet them once and a while and they are happy." This made Annie laugh. Her mother just took life so casually, an attribute she most admired. She hopes someday she would feel as natural and relaxed as her mother. It is soon to be dark and the house is quiet and they all retire for the night.

James Jr hooked Dance to the surrey and would take Annie in to meet Ben at Stallman's café. James was going to the hardware store and would just mosey about for half an hour. He had strict instructions to be back to get her at the café on time so she would not be alone with Ben too long. Annie gives Dancer his expected kiss. God knows how Dancer would react if she ever forgot his kiss. He probably would refuse to move. High stepping and proud Dancer trots them to town.

They arrive right at noon and Ben is standing in front of the café. He is dressed in a fine well pressed suit with a straight brim western style hat and a string tie. He adopted the western style of the wealthy oil men he was involved with in his business. James remarked, "He looks like those Texas fellows we see here more and more." Annie reminds James about the time as Ben comes up to the surrey to help Annie down. "Good-day Miss Dupree; my, it has been a long time, I am so happy to see you." James clears his throat as he goes unnoticed, "Nice to see you, Ben." Ben laughs, "But James, I see you all the time. I have not seen Annie for years so please forgive me." Annie steps down from the surrey. Her long dress snags on the step of the surrey and she falls right into Ben's arms. Her wide brim feathered hat gets pushed back and the feather hits Ben in the face. He is delighted to feel her frail slim body in his arms and he more than slowly lowers her to the ground. Annie laughs, "So much for being graceful." Ben remarks, "You are always graceful Annie even when you fall down." "See you two later," James departs knowing he was no longer wanted.

285

Ben escorts Annie into the café, "I hope you will have lunch with me." "Perhaps there will not be enough time, James will be back in half an hour." "Oh, well, let us have tea and some hors d'oeuvres." Ben is trying to impress her with his worldliness by using the term hors d'oeuvres. Annie responds, "Oui ce serait bien. (Yes, that would be nice.)" Ben did not understand a word, "I'm sorry what?" Annie laughs and repeats in English, "Yes that would be nice." A waitress comes to take their order and Ben relinquishes control to Annie, "Please Annie will you order for us?" Annie looks at the menu, "We will have English tea and perhaps the cheese plate with crackers." She looks at Ben, "Will that be good with you Ben." Ben nods yes. She could have ordered day-old biscuits for all he cared; all Ben could see was this beautiful woman sitting in front of him.

"I have been keeping up with all your travel and I must say it sounds so exciting, the acting and all." "Keeping up? How do you keep-up?" "Well, Leah Anna is in town almost every week and talks to my brother. I am here in Sailor Park about once a month and he tells me all the stuff that Leah Anna tells him. I know it is like playing post office, I get the information second hand." Annie is amazed, "So they tell you what?" "Well I hope you will forgive me but Leah Anna reads your weekly letter to your mother and I pay my brother a dollar to tell me everything Leah Anna says." "My little sister has a big mouth and those letters were to my mother and some of them really personal." Ben turns red but Annie puts him at ease, "Not to worry, I'm not ashamed of anything. I should be flattered that you were interested enough to even pay your brother for the information," Annie laughs and Ben relaxes. "I heard about Shannon getting hit in the head with a bottle and ..." Annie interrupts "Don't tell me you heard about our excursion to see the Cancan?" Ben laughs loud, "Yes; that was hilarious. Do they really have no underwear on?" Annie gasps, "Oh my God yes. We were so embarrassed that we ran out." She looks around to see who was listening for fear they would be overheard.

"I've missed you Annie and I miss your sense of humor and yes I know you don't want to be married and I know you don't want children and I know you are going to be a successful actress but that won't stop me from missing you and your wonderful spirit. So there I said it." Annie gives him a kind smile and thinks, *'My, he is a good-looking man and he has the kindest eyes.'* She knows any woman would be delighted to catch him for a husband not to mention he is very successful.

Ben goes on, "I'm so sorry to hear what happened to Shannon, is she going to be alright?" "I, do not know Ben, she is very ill. They say some just get better from this damn disease, I don't know. They are giving her mercury which makes her sick even more." "I'm so sorry Annie, I wish there was something I could do." "There is nothing anyone can do, just pray." "I will definitely do that." Bens' family are Methodist and go to church regularly and Annie had been to church with Ben back when they were in high school together. Annie inquired about their pastor and he acknowledged that he was well. The fact that Ben was a churchgoer made her comfortable with Ben's moral character. He was a good man and that was never the issue.

"So if you know all these things about me Ben, like marriage and children, are those not things that you want?" Ben pauses, "Yes, I think everyman does but I think that even if that does not happen with me and you, I'm still not going to lie to myself and say I don't miss your sense of humor and joyful spirit because I do. So I want you to do whatever those things are that make you happy but I'm still going to love you anyway." "You are amazing Ben Hamilton. Everyone gets this wrong, I never said I did not want children, I said I do not want to bear children and the only thing about marriage is that women give up their career for marriage. I have since met some amazing women who are married and have their career too."

This is enlightening to Ben. He just loves Annie and if nothing else he does not want to lose touch because of any pressure he might have put on her. They talk about her upcoming play in New York. He asks if she would mind if he would come to see her in the play. She explains how Shannon wants to come and how perhaps he could come with her and her family and for that matter her parents were coming also, that they could all ride the train together. Ben is delighted.

James Jr returns at the appointed time. Annie is enjoying talking with Ben so much that she is sorry that James did what he was told. She asks him if he would mind coming back in another half hour. He gets the hint and agrees. James is delighted that they are getting along so he goes out to tend to Dancer and leave them alone. Ben tells Annie all about his father's business and how they are making seats and upholstery and other parts for the Ford Motor Company automobiles. Annie is impressed with his

288

success. He explains how he has not built a home and is not sure where he wants to settle. Annie inquires, "With all the young beautiful girls, why haven't you found one to marry and start a family?" "I'm only a year older than you and at twenty-five I've got plenty of time to let you figure out that I'm the one for you even if you don't want to bear children, that's fine with me besides if one comes along who is as beautiful as you I might consider it but till then I will be patient." Annie laughs, "So if you find one prettier you will be gone. Ben, I'm going to New York. Who knows what will happen after that. Monsieur Sardou has more plays and other cities and I'm not going to let you waste your life on this idea of marriage to me. You are a lovely and handsome man but I am not going to lead you on. You have your career well on track and I am just hoping for one through the theater. Who knows, I may fail in New York but I have to try, I am not a star like Sarah Bernhardt, I am a young hopeful and that is all and till I try I will never know. I want to be successful on my own. I want to be an independent woman and then if I marry it is not because I need a man's money, I will have my own means. Does that make sense to you?

"It makes perfect sense. I read about the woman's movement. I know what the Lucy Stoners are all about and I know about the 'New Women's' movement. I know Shannon got hit in the head with a bottle because of the group called 'Women for the Chamber' in France. I get it and I'm all for it. I believe that soon we will have women in congress and women will get to vote. It will happen and I am all for it. That is what I like about you; it is your independence. Annie is impressed, "Then you also must be aware that in France the women of the bordellos are blamed for Syphilis and arrested and put in jail if they become infected and the men go free with no incrimination." Ben reaches out for Annie's hand, "Yes Annie I know and it is especially heinous in that it is the men who are spreading the disease."

Annie takes this opportunity to discuss a deeply personal matter, "Ben, I have to speak frankly. You and I had a little romance when we were children. Kissing and hugging when you are children is so innocent but as adults it becomes much more. Well, what I am trying to say is, how can I make a man happy when I will not have sex. I mean even if you risk it and try the so-called methods approach, I could come up pregnant. And yes, I know that you know that my mother says I was traumatized by witnessing my sisters birth, but it is my choice and as of now I choose to abstain. I could never make you happy." Ben blushes a bit, "My you did mean to speak frankly didn't you. I will not lie to you Annie there are compulsions we men have." Annie laughs and says, "Uh huh! I knew it. I told my mother that men have compulsions and there you said it. That is amazing. Go on Ben, tell me more." Ben is confused because Annie has a sense of humor about this serious topic. "Well, I think we choose to control these, uh ... compulsions, besides marriage is more than sex it is companionship." Annie lets go of Ben's hands, "Ben, you said you would not lie and I don't think you are lying but you are not telling the whole truth. I have seen marriages where the woman won't have sex. The men end up going to the bordellos to satisfy their compulsion. In France men have wives and courtesans. Have you ever been to a prostitute?"

290

Ben is incensed, "Shame on you Annie. My family are dedicated Methodist. I'm an honorable man." "Forgive me Ben, in France it is common." "Well it is not here Miss Dupree." "Again, I am sorry." Annie takes his hand, "So there are ways I believe that a woman can satisfy her husband's so called needs and still not get her pregnant, besides women have needs too and it goes unknown because women will not talk about it. They do not have compulsion but they do have desire. They are often ridiculed about their sexuality so they hide it."

Ben is not accustomed to such frank talk. He wants to ask her about the ways a woman can satisfy her husband but he would not dare. In his imagination he flashes on dozens of ways that might be accomplished and he puts it out of his mind. "I must say Annie I am a little embarrassed about all of this but I want to grab you and kiss you and have you show me the ways." Annie pulls her hand back, "I am sorry Ben; perhaps it was inappropriate for me to talk this way. In France they might say, 'honte à vous teaser, (Shame on you teaser,)' that is a shameful thing to do even in France. "Well, I will keep that idea of the 'ways' tucked away for future use Annie. My you are something to reckon with, I will say that for you."

It had been over an hour that James Jr was waiting in the surrey and Annie suggests that it is time to go. Ben agrees with anything Annie says. They head out to the surrey and James was half reclined in the back seat with his hat over his face sleeping. Annie pinches his arm and he jumps up, "You two ready now?" He is still half asleep. Annie walks around the surrey to the other side and James gets in

291

the driver's front seat. Ben helps Annie step up in the surrey. When she is almost to sit down, he pulls her out into his arms and kisses her. Annie responds with an adoring kiss that lasted. She put her arms around his neck and for a moment they melted together. He then sweeps her up and her light frail frame rests in his arms and like she was weightless he places her oh so gently on the seat of the surrey. James laughs, "Good job Ben." Ben tips his hat, "I suppose the next time I see you Antoinette Dupree will be in New York. I will arrange with your father to join them on the train." "Thank-you Ben, see you." James nudges Dancer and they are off. Annie looks back at Ben as they ride away and waves. Ben is a happy man.

Annie admonishes James Jr that he is to say nothing to Mary about this encounter at the very cost of his life, "And if you tell, you will wake-up one day with spiders in your bed and you will know it was me." James assures her the secret was safe, of course he had his fingers crossed behind his back. It may be after she left but he knew he would tell his mother everything. Annie likewise knows he would tell but that it would be after she left. Annie is smart like a fox and honing her skills at manipulation. It is a nice ride home; she thinks *if only I could have manipulated Shannon away from that trip to Switzerland, she would not be sick.* She now feels a sense of urgency to get to Cincinnati to see Shannon.

Rather than stay for two more days she wants to leave tomorrow for the city. Mary is disappointed but understands. Mary adores Shannon and will come to Cincinnati in October when Annie is ready to leave for New York. It is now September the twenty-eighth that will give Annie and Shannon a whole month to share.

Shannon has good days and bad days. The mercury treatments are the worse part of it. It makes her mouth drool for days. They say that expectoration is the way to flush the disease. It is horribly uncomfortable. She becomes dehydrated and cold with shivering no matter how many blankets she has on. Annie has a pact with Shannon. Shannon has bound her with a chore. She must go to the store and sneak Irish whiskey into her without her mother knowing. She stays drunk most of the time in between salivating and spitting. Annie has a few shots now and again too.

They both laugh a lot and joke. Shannon refuses to be dismal even though she feels bad. "I'm going to get over this disease and be an alcoholic." Annie teases, "You were an alcoholic even before the disease." Shannon howls with laughter, "Well, it's an Irish trait, what can I say." Shannon reminded Annie about the time she found her in the pub singing Irish limericks with a bunch of men. Being now a little drunk and gay Shannon makes her sing a limerick with her. 'There once was a man from Nantucket, who kept all his cash in a bucket. His daughter, named Nan ran away with a man; and as for the bucket, Nantucket.' They both laughed till it hurt, then drank some more whiskey. Aileen heard the two always laughing and could tell they were drinking but said nothing. She was just glad to hear her daughter laugh.

The month went by all too fast. Annie was now feeling anxious about getting on to New York. It is all so overwhelming to now be going on the stage. When thinking about it she sometimes gets short of

293

breath because of her nerves. Before as an understudy she had no stage freight because all the attention was transferred to Sarah Bernhardt, now it was all on her. She confides in Shannon, "Sometimes I just think if I flop, I can just come home and be done with all the stress, but then I think if I'm good and I get a good review, it will be all so easy. Then I tell myself to just stop thinking. I'm over analyzing and making myself crazy." "When you get there and rehearse for a while you will relax. You have forgotten how good you are, and you are right, you need to get to work and stop thinking." Shannon's advice is taken to heart and it made her feel better.

It is October the twenty-fourth, the train leaves at noon. Sean Brennan will ride Annie and Shannon to the station to meet the Dupree's before she boards the train. Sean knew Shannon had been drinking because he could smell it on her. He does not care. Whatever will make her feel better is alright with him. On the long ride in he pulls a flask of whiskey from his jacket. He takes a swig and hands the flask to Shannon, "Thanks papa, you're a dear." Shannon hands the flask to Annie, "No thanks dear, I'm fine."

They arrive at the station. Captain Dupree had brought Annie's travel trunk and checked it in with the porter. This was the hardest good-bye. Granted it was hard on Shannon and hard on Mary and James but it was doubly hard on Annie. No one realized that even on the return trip from Paris she was traveling with someone. She was with Sean. This time she was traveling completely alone. Perhaps her father James has an inkling because he had an insistence and he pulls Annie aside. He pulls out from his coat a two-

294

shot derringer in the palm of his hand. "I'm not going to argue with you over this. Put this in your purse. You know how to use it. A woman traveling alone, especially in New York City needs protection." "I do not disagree, papa; I just would not have thought to carry one. Thank-you I will keep it handy." He gives her a box of cartridges, "Keep these with it and learn how to reload fast. See here, there is a push out rod here because the shells will stick. You push them out and pop in new ones, see." He demonstrates it for her. You practice it otherwise when the time comes you won't know how." Annie assures him that she will practice.

Everyone is curious about what was going on. Captain Dupree had his back to everyone and they could not see past his big frame. Shannon goes over. Annie reveals the derringer to her concealed in the palm of her hand and then she drops it into her purse. Shannon nods, "That is good, God, I pray you never have to use it but that is good you have it." Annie laughs, "Bang, bang bad guys. I will never have to use it but it makes papa feel better."

The hugs and tears were substantial. One would think it would never end but the train was departing. For Mary to see her dear, dear child enter the train alone and through the window as she takes her seat and the train pulling away was a tearing of her heart strings. She consoles herself that she would see her again in New York in December. Captain Dupree comforts Mary on their ride back to Sailor Park. Mary rests against him all the way home. He was her strength.

Fifth Avenue Theater

Monsieur Sardou and wife Mlle met Annie at the train station in New York. Any trepidation about being alone in this huge city was gone. She felt protected as she rode in the luxurious carriage that Victor had hired to escort her to the Grand Hotel. This would be her home for the duration of the run of the play. Victor and Mlle would also reside at the Grand. They were on the uppermost floor where dignitaries stay. Annie's apartment was luxurious. It was not like a hotel but a home with private bath and toilet. It was attended to by hotel servants and she would want for nothing. As she is shown about her new home she was astonished, "Mlle, this must cost a fortune." "Victor could not have his next star performer have anything less dear. You must understand that in New York it is all perception. This play comes preconceived as a success since it was a sensation in Paris and held over. Tickets are already being sold for the opening night to all the aristocrats in the city. Opening night will be something to behold. You are already receiving newspaper coverage as Sarah Bernhardt's endorsed successor. She is famous here. Victor knew that without her very public statement about you being her understudy and personal choice to play Gismonda that no one would accept anyone but her in the part. Victor is shrewd in this way.

"That is all the more pressure for me to perform flawlessly." Mlle assures her, "Annie, I have seen your performance and just between me and you, you are better in the part than Sarah and once people see you, they will know why you are here and not Sarah." That does a lot to bolster Annie's confidence.

297

November is all work during the day and promotion and entertaining in the evening. Annie is introduced to every aristocrat Victor could find. So much so that she begins a journal to write down the many names. She reviews her notes to memorize who is who. She finds it embarrassing to not know someone's name and she knows whoever it is whose name was forgotten will always remember that they were not important enough to be remembered. Victor and Mlle were masters at socializing and they were right beside Annie as much as possible to help her. Annie was as much their investment as the play and they would not let her fail.

There was a fascinating side benefit that Annie was taking advantage of; She was meeting the most prominent and powerful women that were the wives of bankers, lawyers and politicians. On every opportunity she would engage in conversations with these women about the 'New Woman's' movement. She learned all about Elisabeth Cady Stanton who was getting on in years and was instrumental in the foundation of National American Woman Suffrage Association. Also there was Susan Brownell Anthony of Rochester, New York who was involved in the formation. Annie was encouraged by the ladies to join and on one sunny afternoon she went with a city councilman's wife to the local office where she became a member. She received an official card that denoted that she was a member. This card she was told could be used to gain access to many private women's clubs around the city. Annie was a natural fit for this group and found great friendships wherever she went.

298

Most of her time was rehearsing on stage. She knew the part so well that her lines flowed with an ever-evolving transformation of her role. Victor could see her becoming Gismonda. She lived the part and the part was her. Everyone in the cast had the wonderful feeling of being ready. Opening night would be December the eleventh, just three days away; the cast would be off till the tenth which would be dress rehearsal. Annie received a telegram from her parents that they were on the way. Victor had reserved an entire box for the entourage. There would be Shannon, Sean, Aileen, Mary, James, Leah Anna and Ben Hamilton. They would arrive on the tenth and would stay also in the Grand Hotel. The dress rehearsal would be on that afternoon when everyone arrived. They would see Annie at the hotel for dinner after the rehearsal.

Annie, Mlle and Victor arrive at the hotel in Victor's private carriage. Annie leads the way into the dining room where everyone is waiting. Leah Anna is the first to see her coming and runs to meet her, "Oh Annie you look so lovely!" "And you too Leah Anna, mother bought you new clothes for New York didn't she?" "Oh yes and for herself too. Papa even bought a new suit." They laugh and hug.

Monsieur Sardou and Mlle see Shannon sitting and go directly to see her before ever greeting anyone. Mlle bends to hug her in her chair, "Oh my dear, we have been asking always after your wellbeing, how are you?" "The doctors keep telling me I am doing well but I have to take their word because I don't know. I do not feel all that good, but I'm here." Mlle sits beside her. Everyone comes over and Annie introduces Victor and Mlle.

The hotel staff was all very attentive and the Maître d brought out two bottles of wine complements of the hotel. Victor proposed a toast to the occasion and everyone saluted. Annie clinked her glass to Ben's and she gave him a kiss on the cheek. Ben relaxed, he was feeling a little on the outside looking in but Annie made him comfortable, "I'm so glad that you are here Ben; was it a good trip?" "Wonderful, your father and I got along quite well. He wanted to know all about this new automobile business. We talked quite a bit and your mother; well she always was kind to me." "I know that; sometimes I felt she like you more than me. She always took your side in defense."

Leah Anna comes up to Ben and takes his arm, "I always told Annie if she did not want you could I try." Ben blushes. Annie chides Leah Anna, "Hush, you. You will make Ben embarrassed." Ben says that was alright, "You flatter me miss and if Annie will not have me I will let you know." Annie slaps Ben's hand, "So you are just like all men after all." They all laugh knowing it was just silliness.

The evening was wonderful; after dining everyone went to the lounge where they spent the evening mingling and talking. Shannon would find any moment to laugh. She was delighted to see Ben there. This was a real milestone Shannon believed, that maybe her ideas about marriage were rubbing off on Annie and perhaps she was not as opposed to the idea after all. She found Ben delightful and told Annie so. For the most part Annie sat next to Shannon. She would go get some brandy, mingle a bit but would come right back to sit next to Shannon. Ben understood and left them alone for girl talk. He could

300

see that with all of her laughter Shannon was suffering and alcohol was masking the pain. She was obviously weak and she lacked color. Annie new Shannon was tired so she made the excuse that in order for her to be at her best on opening night that she must retire. Everyone could see that this was the best thing to do. Annie whispered in Shannon's ear that she would come see her in her room.

Annie kissed Ben on the cheek and whispered in his ear, "I'll knock on you door at eleven will you let me in." "Of course I will; I will have brandy waiting." Annie smiles, "See you then." Ben departs. Captain Dupree and Mary say their good-night and they escort Lean Anna to her room and then retire. Victor and Mlle tell Annie good-night and tell her that for whatever reason she might need, to knock upon their door.

Shortly thereafter Annie knocks on Shannon's door and she beckons her in. Shannon is sitting at the vanity looking at herself in the mirror. "Mirror, mirror on the wall, who is the fairest one of all?" Shannon responds, "You are, I look terrible." She pulls out a bottle of whiskey and a glass hidden in the drawer, "Want some?" "No dear, I have had enough. I can see the headlines, new actress found drunk and cannot perform." Shannon pours and drinks, "I am so glad to see you with Ben Hamilton. Now I think there is hope for you yet." "Please, Shannon, do not read too much into this, just because I am seeing him does not mean I will marry him and he knows that." Shannon laughs and pours another, "Please don't be mad at me for drinking, it is the only thing that takes away the pain." Annie hugs her where

301

she sits. Shannon hugs her back, "Poor Ben, make sure you do not just lead him on." "I'm not leading him on; he knows this is a let-us-see adventure into the unknown. I am not making any promises but I am open. There is so much to learn about someone, it does not happen overnight." Shannon again laughs, "God knows that is true with you, you think everything to death, no love at first sight for you. Can't you ever be whimsical, que sera, sera?" "No, of course not, you know me well Shannon, I was born conservative."

"I think I will tell Ben that you are going to break his heart and that he should run away. Then I could have him for myself. Shannon tears up and looks at herself in the mirror, "That will never happen for me now Annie." Annie grabs her and sits on the vanity seat beside her. "You probably should not touch me; I may be contagious." "Nonsense, I won't get sick and if I do we will go together." Annie helps Shannon to bed and lays her back with a kiss to her forehead. "You sleep now, tomorrow is a big day." "I'll be there Annie. I'll be there." Shannon closes her eyes; she is so tired.

Annie leaves her and goes to knock on Ben's door. He answers immediately. Annie goes in and sits in the first chair she sees. She is crying. Ben does not know what to do, "Annie, what is the matter?" "I just left Shannon Ben; she is so sick. She should be home in Cincinnati not here in New York. She is killing herself just to see me in this damn play. It just makes me think if it had not been for me going to Paris in the first place this would have never happened to her. It is my fault." Ben pulls another chair close and sits in front of Annie holding her hands, "You are blaming

302

yourself for something an evil man did Annie; it is not your fault. It could have happened here as well as there, there are evil men everywhere in the world not just Paris." "Why, why did this have to happen to her?" Ben stands her up and holds her while she cries. He had never seen her like this and it melts his heart. He is hopelessly in love with Annie Dupree.

Annie eventually rests from her tears and has a brandy with Ben. He convinces her that the most important thing right now is the play. He comforts her and explains he will stay close to Shannon and look after her. "It is late Annie you need to rest; tomorrow is the biggest day of your life. You have worked so hard for this." Annie agrees and stands to leave. She pulls this six-foot-tall man by his neck down to her five foot three inch height and kisses him. Ben melts. Annie releases him, "Now don't you take advantage of me Ben Hamilton, I am weak right know." Ben laughs, Annie smiles and departs.

She would be at the theater in the late afternoon to dress and prepare her make-up for the curtain call at seven that evening. Mlle was right by her side. Victor gave Annie a kiss on the cheek, "You will give the performance of your life, just relax and breathe slowly. Mlle will be in the wings. I will greet your family and show them to their box. Most of all have fun. You will be great." With that Victor left it all in Mlle's hands. Annie was ready.

Victor greeted the entourage and guided them to the box seats. Both he and Ben were on either side of Shannon as escorts. She looked stunning and most elegantly dressed. She would be seated in front for the best possible view. She remarked to Victor, "I have seen Annie in so many plays at the academy; such wonderful memories we have." "And there is more to come my dear, many more to come." Victor was suggesting that Shannon had yet a long life ahead.

The 'Fifth Avenue Theater' had electric lights. The Edison Electric Light Company turned on the power at six in the evening. The beautiful chandeliers sparkled and the stage lights were different colors depending on how the operator controlled them. This new innovation was dazzling. The marquee lit up at six. Victor inspected it well "Gismonda staring -Antoinette Dupree-" There were two color posters of Annie that Victor had made of her in costume hanging in frames on either side of the main entrance. They were lovely. Guests were arriving and the theater was filling to capacity. It was time. The house lights were dimed and then brightened to signal the curtain was about to go up and everyone quieted down. The director takes center stage to do the introduction and the play begins.

Shannon is gripping the railing in front of her in the box the whole-time during acts one and two. There is a short intermission before acts three and four. As the play resumed in act three the audience applauded at their joy that it was continuing and Annie again takes the stage they applaud. She takes a short bow and continues. Victor was often standing up in the back of the box. He was so involved he could not sit down. Line by line he watches the casts delivery. It was perfect. The audience would respond with oohs and aahs at the right moments which for an author are complements. This means the audience is responding emotionally at the proper points and this means that the cadence of the play is working.

As the last act unfolds the villain is revealed and Gismonda bloodily kills the perpetrator with an ax. In so doing she saved her lover Almeiro who is waking after having been knocked unconscious. Upon awaking he takes the blame for the killing to spare Gismonda shame and to hide their affair. The people of Athens call for Almeiro's death. Gismonda masterfully reveals the villain's plot that almost killed her son in act I and Gregorez the final villain is sent to prison. Almeiro and Gismonda wed. The theater organ plays 'Gloria' and the curtain falls.

The applause is thunderous. Victor knows he has a hit on his hands. A standing ovation is calling the cast to come out. They all file out from behind the curtain and Annie is the last to come out. They are calling for the author. Victor was already on his way with a huge bouquet of roses that Mlle had ready for him to present to Annie. Victor runs up and climbs onto the stage and presents the flowers to Annie and he takes his bow. The applause goes on, Annie extends her hand over the stage to the many who had pushed up close to touch her hand. Victor holds on to her so she won't fall. Finally Victor calls the director for a bow and the crowd begins to thin out. Mlle comes up to help Annie back to the dressing room where all the family was waiting.

Shannon wraps her arms around Annie, "I knew you were going to be a star. You were fabulous." Mary and then James got to hug her. Leah Anna was patient but got her turn and Ben just watched and waited. He was still savoring the kiss he had gotten the night before. This was a spectacular moment, so much joy.

Shortly they would all retire to the Grand Hotel for the opening night party Victor and Mlle were having. All the cast would be there. Since opening night was on Saturday there would be no production on this Sunday. The play would reopen on Friday, Saturday and Sunday the following week and continue to run as long as they could fill the seats, but tonight was the review party where everyone would wait all night to read the Newspaper reviews. They would be out by sunrise. This was a theater district custom and the Champaign would flow.

Everyone makes their way to the Grand Hotel ball room. Mlle was hosting and greeting everyone as they arrived. Victor and Annie delayed their arrival till last so they could make a grand entrance. They finally arrive at the ball room and everyone erupts in applause. Annie had changed into an elegant gown and Shannon rushes up to meet her. Shannon was dragging Ben by the arm. She gives Annie a hug and then she pushes Ben to Annie's side. Annie gives Ben a kiss on the cheek. Captain Dupree and Mary are quietly pleased about Annie and Ben. Especially Mary is delighted to see the two together.

The Hotel had setup a buffet and everyone dined and drank Champaign. Shannon would sneak whiskey and Annie would join her from time to time as they lounged and waited for the newspapers to hit the streets. Everyone was gay and joking and laughter was throughout the ballroom. Finally at four in the morning a porter came running in with an arm full of newspapers. He had the 'New York Times,' the 'New York Post,' and the 'Wall Street Journal,' the three most prominent newspapers. He handed them to Victor and Mlle. Victor thumbed through the 'Times'

306

and Mlle thumbed through the 'Post.' He reads, "Last night was just the beginning of Monsieur Sardou's most exquisite production of 'Gismonda.' Sure to delight audiences for weeks and weeks to come, this is a must-see play. The outstanding performance of newcomer Antoinette Dupree lit the stage such that Sarah Bernhardt would be proud. Her dazzling performance will astound you as this professional thespian graces the stage. She is a delight to see perform. Come one and come all to see 'Gismonda' as the New York Times solutes Monsieur Victorien Sardou;" everyone toasts and solutes with shouts.

Next Mlle reads from the 'Post, "'Gismonda' by Monsieur Victorien Sardou is his greatest play of all. From the first curtain to the last your breath is taken away by Miss Antoinette Dupree, whose performance is outstanding. You cannot take your eyes off of her as minute by minute the drama unfolds. Truly we have seen the beginning of a great career by this young star. Here at the 'Post' we all agree, everyone must see Miss Dupree. Congratulations Monsieur Sardou on your great success." Again everyone toasts and solutes with shouts.

And finally Victor reads form the 'Journal,' "'Gismonda' opened last night at the 'Fifth Avenue Theater' with the hit of the decade. Monsieur Victorien Sardou has outdone himself with this marvelous play. The new star, Miss Antoinette Dupree was superb and captured your heart at the outset. The drama is wonderfully done and holds you in anxious suspense from start to finish. Investors in this play will rejoice because it will have a long run." Everyone laughs and solutes because it was a typical

'Wall Street Journal' position of money and investment."

Captain Dupree scoops Annie off her feet and carries her around the ball room as Victor tosses flower peddles before her. Everyone is drunk and they don't care if they are making fools of themselves. They all join the drunken parade and march around the ball room in a line. The hotel staff, caught-up in the gaiety joins in. What a wonderful night.

The sun comes up and they all retire. They would sleep most of that Sunday. Since they had rooms on the same upper floor they ordered breakfast in their rooms and with their doors open they wandered from room to room socializing and relaxing rereading the critics' reviews again and again.

The hard part now was figuring how to get their heads out of the clouds and get back to work. All the family must return home and Annie had to now prepare for the long run. The anticipation is that this play would run for an entire year. It would play every Friday, Saturday and Sunday matinee over and over again.

Shannon would return home to her mercury treatments. Annie had a hard time letting her go. Annie explains, "I will write to you every week. I have Monday through Thursday with nothing to do, I will be so board." "What about Ben will you write to him too?" "Yes, I suppose I will." "Ben is in love with you Annie, are you reconsidering your stance on marriage?" "No, not exactly, I want to see how my acting goes and he knows that. We have talked a lot about things Shannon and he is willing to just live day by day with no plans." "You will break his heart and someday and he will give up." "Being married could ruin everything Shannon, because there is a certain mystique about a young single actress that even Victor agrees is a drawing card to be played in the press." "That mystique will vanish with your beauty as you get older." "True you are but not yet."

Annie goes to the train station to see everyone off. Annie had asked Ben to stay behind an extra day and agreed. Mary and James were delighted. Captain Dupree shook Bens hand, "Come by and see us at home Ben. I sure would like to come see that factory of yours in Dayton." They make plans upon his return to arrange a tour of the factory and James would get to meet Ben's father.

Shannon cannot help but cry and Annie likewise, "I will see you in the spring regardless of what the plays schedule is; I will come to Cincinnati." "Promise, I will be looking for your first letter. I will miss you dearly Annie." Watching Shannon board the train and leave was difficult, Shannon was so frail. Annie held on to Ben's arm and Shannon smiled as the train left the station.

Annie had one more day to relax before the presentation on Friday. She spent that day with Ben wandering about in New York. It was getting colder with a light snow falling. They both laughed because the few motor cars there were about were all stuck on slippery streets while the horse drawn carriages had no problem. Ben remarked that it will improve with better tires and such, seeing as how this was his business, he would be an innovator. They enjoyed dinner in the hotel and upon retiring for the evening went to Ben's room. Annie could no longer resist because Ben was so docile following Annie's lead wherever it would go. She had lured him with her affection and decided to demonstrate how a woman and a man could find pleasure without the penetration that would leave her pregnant. She did not know if that would be sufficient or if he would somehow feel as she called it 'compelled' for more than she was willing to provide. None the less she gave him all that she had to give in her own manner.

Ben was overwhelmed and even more in love with Annie than he had ever imagined. The difficult part now was leaving which he must. Annie likewise was sorry that they had to go separate ways but life has its demands and we do that which is commanded of us at all times and work. Annie promises to write and he does likewise. She sees him to the train with her own private chauffer and returns alone. Now she feels oh so alone. She immerses herself in her work and soon many other involvements.

The Fifth Avenue Theater

The New Woman

Marguerite Durand responded to a letter Annie had written, 'It is so wonderful to hear of your success in New York. It is good to hear you have joined the 'NAWSA' (National American Woman's Suffrage Association). I wrote to Christabel Pankhurst and told her about you. You will find on the back her address. She would be pleased to hear from you. I am sure that with your notoriety you will be an asset to the American movement. We are making headway here in France, we women just need to band together and make them listen. Please stay in touch as you travel. I hope someday to come to America and if you are ever again in France, we will have a celebration in your honor; Most Sincerely *Marguerite'*

After the Sunday matinee she would always have dinner with Victor and Mlle. The play was doing splendidly; people would come from as far as Chicago and Victor could see no end date for months. They were filling the seats months in advance. Annie was becoming a rich lady and Victor was talking to theaters in San Francisco and asked if Annie would consider going there for a time. Annie was thrilled at the prospect.

She was free to do whatever she pleased Monday through Thursday. Her favorite place was the Office of the 'NAWSA' where she found conversation and reading and involvement. She would help in finding donations and write letters to government dignitaries to show her solidarity with the movement and like Marguerite had said they were pleased to have her notoriety to aid the cause. She

311

would make signs and help print pamphlets or whatever needed to be done.

Late on a Wednesday evening in February she offered to go over to a Delicatessen to get some coffee and sandwiches. Everyone was preparing for a march through Central Park in the morning. Yes, it would be cold but there would be a thousand women there to show how strong the movement would be. They used the Postal Service code of honor, *'Neither snow nor rain nor heat nor gloom of night stays these couriers from the swift completion of their appointed rounds, and then added, 'Women will be heard'* Their sighs read, 'Women for Congress.'

Annie took everyone's order. It was large enough that her friend Carol would help her carry the food. Annie always paid for the snacks; she felt it was her obligation and not charity. It was a cold night and the ladies went as fast as they could walk to get to the Deli. After checking all the order they went quickly back. With their arms full of packages they pass beneath the gaslights and down an alleyway because it was closer. In a shocking instant a man jumps out from a pile of trash and knocks Carol on the ground. He pulls out a knife and puts it in Annie's face. Carol was hurt, he had pushed her hard. He waves the knife and grabs onto Annie's purse string and says, "Let go or I kill you!"

Annie says nothing. She pulls the trigger on the derringer that was in her pocket and shoots the man, point blank range in his gut. He gasps and falls back against the wall. Annie helps Carol to her feet and she spits in the man's face. It was only nine o'clock and everyone in the street heard the shot. It was not very long and the cops were there. The man

312

was not dead but bleeding badly. One of the officers recognizes Annie and sums up the situation quickly and knows they were being robbed and the robber met his match. He offers to escort the very scared young women to the office and helps with the packages. He says, "Don't worry about him Miss, he won't die." Annie does the unimaginable; she reaches in her purse and gives the man a one-hundred-dollar bill. She is crying, "maybe you are cold or maybe you are hungry, I don't know, you could have just asked, I would have given you money." The officer tugs at Annie's arm, "Miss you are too kind, he is a bum and a thief and he would not do the same for you." The officer takes them back to their warm office, "You will need to come to the precinct and sign a witness statement. You can press charges if you want but considering you gave the man money for robbing you I suppose you will not, good-night ladies."

The office was stirring now. Everyone heard the shot and now knows what had happened. The door swings open and in come two reporters one from the 'Times' and one from the 'Post.' They are firing questions at Annie and she is saying she does not want this in the paper. They explain that is a forgone fact. It will be in the paper because it happened, all we are asking, that is if you will, tell us what you say happened. If you don't, we will print what others say. It is always best to have a firsthand account. Carol jumps in, "I will tell you what happened, Annie saved our lives and shot him." One reporter asks, "What type of gun do you have Miss Dupree?" The other reporter not waiting asks, "Do you always carry a gun?" Annie relents and gives them a complete account as to what she thought happened.

313

The morning release of the 'Times' on a lower column on the front page reads, 'Actress Robbed – Attacker Shot … Antoinette Dupree of the Fifth Avenue Theater production by Monsieur Sardou was robbed in an alleyway last night as she and a friend were fetching snacks at Neumann's Deli on Park Avenue in the upper east side of Manhattan to return to the office of the 'NAWSA' (National American Woman's Suffrage Association). Unknown to the assailant, Miss Dupree carries a derringer given to her by her father for just such a situation. The perpetrator upon arrest pled guilty to the arresting officer. He survived the shot to his belly because the bullet passed through Miss Dupree's coat and through his thick clothing thus slowing the bullet down. The bullet was removed with no serious damage to the stomach of the robber. Of note was the comment by the arresting officer that Miss Dupree gave the man who robbed her one hundred dollars and said, 'I would have given you money if you had only asked.'

Upon reading the article all the ladies at the 'NAWSA' office were thanking Annie for the wonderful publicity they received on the front page. That day saw another two hundred women who joined and donated to the cause.

The rally and march around Central Park Thursday morning was huge. Thousands of women with banners sailing walked and chanted *'Neither snow nor rain nor heat nor gloom of night stays these couriers from the swift completion of their appointed rounds, and then added, 'Women will be heard.'* It was cold. They had resting points where there were steel barrels with wood burning in them and they would get warm. Vendors saw and opportunity and

314

were selling hot coffee and pastries. There were reporters in and amongst the crowd taking pictures and getting quotes. Annie was immediately recognized and some reporter told her that Annie Oakley the famous sharpshooter would be proud of her. Annie was not amused, "My name is Antoinette only my father is allowed to call me Annie." That shut him up. It was not true because everyone called her Annie. She just laughed and told Carol, "I had to shut him up somehow."

Annie wrote home to Shannon and told her all about the rally and the robbery but that she should please keep it to herself. She did not want her mother to worry. A lot of good that did because two weeks later in March Annie gets a letter from her mother. Mary lets her know in her expression how she felt. 'I know there are times when you think you should protect me by keeping me ill-informed but I assure this is not the best course. Your father is proud that you took his advice and carried the weapon and so is you mother. Next time keep me informed. P.S. do you need more bullets?'

Annie was just mad at Shannon and wondered how her mother found out so fast. As it were Mary made regular visits to see Shannon and to look after her. Shannon was now like an adopted daughter and she knows how she would probably still be at Annie's side if it were not for her illness. The treatments were taking a toll and no longer seemed to be relieving any of the symptoms. Shannon was getting worse. Sometimes she would get infectious boils under her chin. Doctors would lance and bandage her. She had very little disfigurement except that she was gaunt and lacked color. The mercury treatments always followed with days of nausea.

April saw no slowdown in box office sales. Annie tries to deliver a stunning performance for everyone who had waited months to see the play and sometimes she was tired and would spend days in her room just resting and sometimes dreaming of home. She would write Ben the most joyous letters and spoke of how good it will be when they see each other again while in the back of her mind she is melancholy for home.

On April the fourteenth Annie receives a letter from her mother. It is short and to the point. Annie's heart sinks. '*I know how engaged you are with the play and I do not know how you might find the time, but I am afraid that you need to come to Cincinnati for at least a week to see Shannon. She is not well. So my dear however I may help, Mother.*'

Annie shows the letter to Victor and he has a plan, "Annie, I will talk to the theater owner to quietly require the theater to close for needed repairs for two weeks. I will offer refunds or future stubs for any ticket holders so you can go home." Mlle has deep concern and wants to accompany Annie home. Victor agrees and with all expediency they pack to travel and on the next morning they are on the train.

Annie's mind is reeling and Mlle tries to comfort her to no avail. Annie is sleepless all the way to Philadelphia. They change trains and Mlle insists on taking a private cabin. She makes Annie lie down even though all she does is toss and turn. She finally falls to sleep in the last six hours into Cincinnati. Victor had telegrammed Mary Dupree as to the

316

schedule of travel; Mary was waiting at the train station. Sean Brennan was there with his son Fredrick to aid the ladies. They would all go together to the Brennan residence.

When they arrive at the estate Shannon is waiting on the porch of the breezeway. She is in a wheelchair. Fredrick helps Annie get down from the carriage and she runs up to greet Shannon and gives her a big hug. "Oh you look fine; everyone had me so scared saying that you were getting worse." Shannon laughs "They fooled you on my account because I wanted you to come home for a break; I knew they were working you too hard." Shannon yells, "Papa break-out the whiskey it is time for a party, Annie is here." Sean does not hesitate and he opens a fresh bottle of 'Jameson' which was Shannon's favorite. Mlle and Mary would have one and then have some tea. Aileen and Sean toasted the arrival of Annie. All seemed well but Annie knew her mother would not have hurried her home if that were the case.

Shannon would not let on that she was very ill. Her driving spirit would see past all negatives and she would find all reasons to be optimistic. The day was fun; Annie and Shannon were reminiscing and just happy to be in each other's company. As the day passed away and the sun went down, they enjoyed dinner with all the family. Aileen had rooms ready for Mlle and Mary. Annie and Shannon stayed in the library till late still drinking and talking. "I want to know more about Ben. Are you a little more intimate with him or is he still waiting on this prudish French maiden?" "Prudish, you Irish vixen, you would equate being chaste to being a prude. I'm just reserved and don't throw myself at every man like you do."

Annie realized she made a mistake as soon as she said that. "Shannon I'm sorry, I'm drunk and just playing with you." Shannon immediately responds, "I know it was my fault for going with him, but he seemed like a nice man and I did not throw myself at him."

Shannon reaches for the bottle and pours them both another whiskey. Annie sips, "To answer your question, I think Ben is a happy man and I think our naked bodies together pleased him." Shannon grunts a garbled laugh and snicker, "You didn't?" "No I didn't, of course, I don't want to get pregnant, you know that but I still made him happy." Shannon presses for more, "Well, how do you know." Annie smacks Shannon on her hand, "Well how to you think silly, a man cannot hide his orgasm." Shannon responds, "Oh, well, yes I see. Was he embarrassed?" "No, I made him feel welcome and I had an orgasm to." Shannon withdrawals, "Oh, that's good. Was it as good as when I gave you one?" "Why would you say that Shannon? You always wanted to find a man to marry. Are you jealous?" "Well, yes, I guess a little. Finding a man now for me won't happen."

Shannon starts to cry. Annie wraps her arms around her till she stops. She has another shot of whiskey but Annie has had enough. She rolls Shannon in her wheelchair to the guest room on the first floor. This was now Shannon's room because of the wheelchair. She was not crippled but climbing the stairs was a chore. Annie helps Shannon change into her nightgown and get into bed. It was late and all the house was silent. Annie gets into bed with Shannon and gives her an orgasm like she knew so well how to do. Annie was not concerned about getting the disease because it was well known that intercourse was how

318

the disease was transmitted from open soar to open skin. Annie so much wanted to pleasure her. As for the idea of being lesbian it was of no concern. They well understood procreation and the love of family and the desire they both had for a man in their life. Annie knew how much Shannon wanted to be a mother and since that was now questionable for her, a moment of pleasure was immensely important. Afterward Shannon slept and Annie went to her own room.

The next day it was decided that Mlle would go with Mary to her home in Sailor Park. They would stop and see the Louis Queen that was docked in Cincinnati and visit with Captain Dupree. Annie would stay with Shannon for the week.

In the afternoon when Shannon was napping, Aileen was having tea with Annie on the veranda, "Annie, you have to know that the doctors are very cautionary about Shannon's condition. They think that she is not one of those who develops an immunity to the disease. They are concerned because she has coughed-up blood from her lungs and at times on her period the bleeding does not want to stop. They are sure she will never be able to have children and the biggest concern is with each period the bleeding gets worse." Annie tears up, "This is so unfair. Through no fault of her own this has been thrust upon her. Oh my God Aileen. I got a letter from Susan Beaumont from Paris. Max Freneau died. May he rot in hell!"

Shannon comes rolling herself out on the veranda, "What is all this blubbering going on out here? I'll not have it, someone tell a joke. Did you hear the one about a Priest, a Rabbi and a Minister in a rowboat?" Aileen stops her, "Shannon, wash your mouth." Shannon is feeling chipper, "With whiskey mother, I certainly will." Aileen departs, "I'll leave you with my degenerate daughter Annie, see what you can do with her." They all laugh including Aileen.

"Do you still carry that derringer your father gave you?" "Yes, I keep it in my purse with extra bullets. If I go out I put it in the pocked of my coat, always ready, especially in New York." "I want to buy it from you and then you can buy another one." "What for, I cannot imagine you being alone, or …" Annie pauses, "Oh Shannon, you wouldn't" "You bet I would, if it gets bad enough, I'll just get drunk and bang!" "Well, not with my gun you won't." "Awe, Annie you are too serious, besides I would not want to leave my mother with a mess to clean up. I would just take a bunch of those morphine pills the doctor gives me anyway. Where is the whiskey? Let's get drunk again." "Not for me girl but I'll get you some.' "Would you dear, it makes me feel good."

Annie goes to get a bottle of whiskey. She passes Aileen who was in the kitchen, "More whiskey? It is in the library." No one cares that Shannon drinks because she makes jokes and laughs a lot. Somehow in all of this Shannon refuses to be dreary, she just wants merriment. Annie adores when Shannon is feisty and ready to pull someone's leg and tease. Fredrick and Robert did not stand a chance in the teasing, Shannon learned early on what boys were all about and she gave them every ounce they gave to her so-to-speak. Annie would remark that she was the same with James Jr and Marcus, *You can't give them an inch.*

320

During this week Annie learned so much about the Brennan family. It was obvious that they were close and the reason Shannon is so confident was the enduring love the family had for each other. Annie came even closer to Aileen and could feel the anguish she was feeling. Sean Brennan would withdraw at times and sit in his den and read the bible till early morning. He would from time to time read passages to Shannon. She would listen but Annie knew her thoughts. She was angry and found no comfort. She felt like a leper and wanted to be healed by Christ. Where was her miracle?

She told Annie, "I weep for Christ and curse Max Freneau. Perhaps that is my curse, I cannot forgive that bastard. God damn it Annie, I can still feel him pounding me from behind. He had me pinned and I am screaming for him to stop and hearing him say 'Je vais t'apprendre; vous taquinez! (I'll teach you; you tease.)' So no miracle for me, I hate the bastard and will never forgive him." Annie will not accept that as an explanation, "I do not think you're not forgiving that evil man has anything do with receiving a miracle or not. I think we are all fools and God uses us as examples and the punishment is harsh. The sexual compulsion that brings us all here in birth is to be used for that holy purpose and because the dumb animal only knows that it feels good abuses it in utter stupidity like a toy. It is a God-awful thing that men have such a compulsion that some evil men will do harm to have their pleasure. Then there are men like your father and my father who control their compulsion. Ben even said he thought the orgasm in men is a compulsion."

Shannon interrupts, "I think it is a compulsion in women too. Perhaps not as strong and it is ridiculous to think of a woman raping a man. It is the one-sided result of fornication, men just walk away and a woman gets the burden of pregnancy. The only saving grace is the child. I so much want to be a mother with a loving husband like my papa. I could see myself with a daughter and not so much a son; thanks to my brothers but what the hell I could see sons too." Shannon laughs, "I could use that one on my brothers, do you get it; I could tell them because of you I don't ever want sons." Annie laughs, "That's a good one; I will use it on my brothers too."

Shannon is having fun. Annie has a shot of whiskey, "What the hell, I don't have to work tomorrow. You are a bad influence on me Shannon; I will have to sober-up and get back to New York or die drunk in a gutter with the likes of you." Talking about the gutter brought to Annie's mind, "France is so different than the United States; we don't have legal bordellos." Shannon responds, "But we still have prostitutes and hidden whore houses. Papa knows the city commissioner and says the police are always busy trying to shut them down." Annie takes sides, "Do you think those poor women are doing that because they like it? I think they have no choice. They are poor and illiterate and unless they work in a dirty factory for slave wages, they have no opportunity. They have found an easy way to make money. And from what I understand if they are smart, they make a lot of money. Like the courtesans in Paris." Shannon quizzes Annie, "You sound like you are making excuses for them." "I am not; I think it needs to change that is why I joined 'NAWSA.' Shannon

322

laughs: she is a little drunk, "Antoinette Dupree for President!" Annie laughs along with her, "Why not!"

"Oh, Annie I will join right along with you when I get well." Annie likes her happy up-turn, "Here is to the 'New Woman!" She pours a whiskey and they toast.

It is Saturday and on Monday Annie would leave to return to New York. Annie had sent Ben Hamilton a telegram when she first arrived inviting him to come out to the Brennan estate for a visit. He would be there at noon. Annie and Shannon are sitting in the carriage breezeway watching for him. "Sometime this afternoon when mother is napping you and Ben can sneak into my room and ..." Annie breaks in, "We will do no such thing, we are not animals." Shannon teases, "I am! No really you will not see him again for a long time." "Shannon stop; the next time, if there is a next time, I will be married to him." "So you are considering marriage?" "Yes, but that would be way off and I still do not know if he will accept a marriage on my terms." "Oh, you mean no children." "No, why can't people get this, I want children but not to bear them. There are so many orphans that need mothers and fathers. Do you not think this noble of me?" Shannon injects a little reality, "Noble it maybe but men want their own blood carried on. You should hear my father go on about the Brennan honor and pride. So I think you are making a mistake to think Ben will not want sons and daughters of his own blood." Annie pauses, "I suppose you are right, maybe it will not work and I should break his heart now instead of later." Shannon is apologetic and sarcastic, "Oh Ben, I am so sorry, I

323

talked your Annie out of love with you and she will not be your wife now." Annie's had enough, "Just stop Shannon."

They see Ben coming up the drive. To everyone's surprise he is in a Ford automobile. He masterfully pulls right up, stops very smoothly and turns off the motor. Annie was surprised that it was not as loud as some of the ones she had seen. "You ladies want to go for a ride?" Aileen comes out because she heard the noise. "Oh how wonderful! You girls first then I want to go for a ride" Shannon and Annie jump in and off they go. Ben ends up giving everyone a ride. Sean says he wants to get one, that it was the wave of the future.

Ben finally gets to park the auto and have lunch with the family. He and Annie wander around the grounds after lunch and talk. Shannon watches them from the veranda and sips whiskey. Shannon so much wants Annie to change her mind; marry Ben and have their flesh and blood children. Shannon was just traditional and thought the pain of childbirth was worth the joy it brings with the new born.

As the sun set Ben kissed Annie good-bye. He would go again to New York in summer. He drove away in the dark with the head lights shining. Annie feared for him driving in the dark. Ben was fearless.

Sunday passed all too quickly and Mlle returns from her visit to the Dupree home. Mary came along because this is the last time, she would see Annie till the play was over. They had to be to the train station by eleven in the morning. Sean brought around the carriage to take Annie, Mary and Mlle to the station. Shannon gave Annie one last hug and

324

stood in the breezeway still in her night clothes as they got in the carriage. She has tears in her eyes, "Remember the one about the Priest, the Rabbi and the Minister. Tell it to Victor, he will laugh." Annie laughs while Mary and Mlle have not a clue.

Shannon has a sinking fear she will never see Annie again.

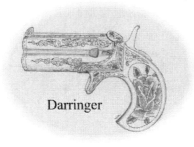

Darringer

Curtain Call

Mlle and Annie arrive in New York Wednesday evening. Victor meets them at the station and takes them back to the hotel. Annie had a day to rest before the play resumed production on Friday. She went over her lines several times because she had been away from it for two weeks. Refreshed and ready to go she gives a wonderful performance. She was back.

Victor had more information about opening the play in San Francisco. It looked like it was going to happen. He had investors there that saw the great success of the play in New York and they were ready to sign contracts. Victor explains to Annie because the production here in New York was entirely his production there were no contracts except between him and the 'Fifth Avenue Theater' but with the move to San Francisco the costs were such that he needed partners to finance the move. As a result they want you to sign a contract saying you will do the play for the duration of one year before they agree to invest. Annie was delighted and she was ready to go. It was no problem signing a contract. She had been paid over fifty thousand dollars so far in this New York production and would stand to make twice that in San Francisco.

Since Annie was in agreement Victor scheduled the final presentation of 'Gismonda' for June fifteenth. Annie would have the entire summer off and be able to go home. She would not be needed in San Francisco till the last week of September. Victor and Mlle would meet up with her the first week in September in Cincinnati where they will ride the train together for three whole weeks to get to San Francisco. Victor was excited about the adventure because he would be able to see the Great Rocky Mountains a mile stone in his travels.

Annie had sent a telegram to Ben because she knew his plans were to come to New York to see her. Her plan was for him to wait till the last performance in June to come. They could ride the train back to Cincinnati together. Ben telegrammed back that it was an excellent idea and he would see her then.

So Annie works on performance after performance trying to be perfect every night. As always on her days off she was at the 'NAWSA' office. She was introduced to Frances Clark who wrote under the pseudonym of Sarah Grand. The reason for her pen name was obvious; her writings were so controversial she would not be recognized when she traveled and thus avoided conflict. Frances had renamed herself when she wrote 'The Heavenly Twins' and this is when the term 'New Woman' was first conceived. Through Frances Annie learned of Josephine Butler who had fought against the 'Contagious Disease Act' that had been in force in the United Kingdom. Josephine Butler had formed the 'Ladies National Association for the Repeal of the Contagious Diseases Acts' and in 1886 the Act was repealed. The legislation allowed police officers to arrest women suspected of being a Prostitute in certain ports and army towns. The women were then subjected to compulsory checks for venereal disease. If a woman was declared to be infected, she would be confined in what was known as a lock hospital until she recovered or her sentence finished. The original act only applied to a few selected naval ports and army towns, but by 1869 the acts had been extended to cover eighteen subjected districts.

In one of Josephine's appeals she quoted a prostitute, *'It is men, only men, from the first to the last that we have to do with! To please a man I did wrong at first; then I was flung about from man to man. Men police lay hands on us. By men we are examined, handled, doctored. In the hospital it is a man again who makes prayer and reads the Bible for us. We are had up before magistrates who are men, and we never get out of the hands of men till we die!'*

In all of this women were seen as cause for the spread of the disease. Annie talked to Francis at length about her personal knowledge of the disease and how finally in this modern age of 1895 women have been released from the blame and how only education, changing of the laws and better work conditions and wages for women will stop prostitution. Annie knows this is her avocation and that over time she will dedicate all of her efforts to women being heard in congress.

It is only two weeks to the final presentation of 'Gismonda'. Annie is looking forward to seeing Ben and the prospect of going home for a rest and seeing Shannon. It is Wednesday morning about nine o'clock and there is a knock on her hotel room door. It is Ben.

"My, Ben, I did not expect you till next week. What a nice surprise. Did you get away early?" Ben smiles standing at the door with his hat in hand. Annie bids him, "Please come in." She wastes no time and presses her body against his and kisses him with

328

passion." He returns in kind and holds her close. After the kiss he hugs her and does not want to let her go. Annie remarks, "My you do miss me don't you." Ben says nothing but starts to cry. He finally releases Annie and she pushes back holding on to his arms and looking at the tears rolling from his cheeks. With deep concern, "What is the matter, Ben?" He is having difficulty and with all weakness in his arms he puts his hands on Annie's shoulders, "Shannon past away."

Ben moves fast to catch Annie as she collapses. He picks her up and carries her to the bed. The words Ben had said drained the blood from Annie's head. She awoke to Ben putting a cold damp cloth on her forehead. As she slowly awakes, she grabs Bens arm and pulls herself over and throws-up on the floor. She then falls back in the bed and is again unconscious. Ben leaves her for a moment and finds a bellhop in the hall and tells him that he needs a doctor quickly.

Annie awakes to smelling salts. The doctor had elevated her legs and continued with the cool compress to her forehead. Annie calls for Ben and he appears over her. She starts to cry. Ben sits and holds her hand. The doctor instructs, "It is shock. Keep her legs up and keep her covered. Annie, I gave you a sedative injection it will make you sleep. Ben, she will be alright just let her rest." Ben hands the doctor fifty dollars, "Thank-you doctor, I'm glad you were close by."

Annie is getting groggy but she has to know, "Ben, when did she die" "It was a week ago. Everyone decided that I should come. No one wanted you to receive a telegram or letter with this horrible

329

news." "What happened, she seemed fine when I left." "The doctor said she had an internal hemorrhage in the middle of the night. They say she died in her sleep and felt no pain." Annie just weeps as the sedative takes effect and she sleeps.

While she sleeps Ben gets in touch with Victor and Mlle to give them the bad news. Mlle breaks down "Oh my poor dear, I must go to her." Ben explains that she is under a sedative and will sleep till morning. Victor comforts Mlle, "We will close the play, Annie needs to nothing more. We can take her home to Cincinnati; she will need her family now."

Over the next few days Ben helps Annie collect her things and arranges for them to be shipped to Cincinnati. Annie just sits most of the time and gazes out the window of the Hotel. She is empty. She is so thankful that Ben was seeing to everything. Victor, Mlle, Ben and Annie take a final ride through New York City to the train station. Annie clings to Ben's arm, he has become her strength. The ride on the train seemed long. Annie just sat holding Bens arm and gazes out the window of the train as the landscape passes in a blur.

Upon arrival in Cincinnati, Captain Dupree and Mary are waiting. They will all go to the Brennan estate, not for a funeral because Shannon was buried a week earlier but they would go so Annie could see Aileen and Sean. At the Brennan home Sean lifted Annie down from the carriage and hugged her. Aileen came up and they wept. They went into the library one of Shannon's favorite places to sit and drink whiskey. Needless to say they all shared some whiskey in

330

Shannon's honor. Aileen handed Annie an envelope with a note Shannon had written. It follows …

'This is in case I don't see you again. You take care of Ben and I know someday you will have children. Don't be afraid it only hurts for a short while and the babies are worth it. You were the best part of my life and I have no regrets except going to Switzerland. I remember all the fun we had and how much we laughed. Truly I am an Irish twig and you are a French tart.
All my love,
Shannon
P.S. I would do it all again for the love of Annie Dupree.

Annie wept; Aileen gave Annie the locket she had given to Shannon, it had a photo of Annie on one side and Shannon on the other.
Annie would go on. Her cause became even more for the advancement of the 'New Woman' movement. They took the production of 'Gismonda' to San Francisco where it was a success. After a year in California she returned home. She married Ben and they had two children. She told Ben to thank Shannon for the children. She did it because Shannon told her to.

La Fin (The End)

Suffrage

I stood upon the precipice of tomorrow.
I only wish to erase the sorrow.
But there is a need to remember,
the generations' tales we borrow.

Never forget their suffrage and pain.
From their wisdom we all will gain.
They made ignorance a dying ember,
extinguished by a righteous rain.

Post Script

All the names of persons in the women's suffrage movement depicted in this novel are historical. Monsieur Victorien Sardou's plays are as near to factual as possible with the exception that the production of 'Gismonda' in New York was played by Fanny Davenport. It opened December 11 1894 and played through to February of 1895 at the Fifth Avenue Theater. The theater was located at Broadway and Fifth or actually at 1185 Broadway. It was demolished in 1939. To my knowledge 'Gismonda' by Victorien Sardou ended its production in New York and did not play again in the United States. Someone may know otherwise.

Some accountings place the number of prostitutes in The United Kingdom at over 25,000 in the year 1890. At the same time in the eastern United States the number is estimated to have been 65,000. The great scourge of syphilis had no true cure till the discovery of penicillin in 1928. In 1909 a German bacteriologist Paul Ehrlich found the arsenical compound 'Salvarsan' cured the disease though the treatment was difficult. Mercury slowed the advance of the disease while Salvarsan cured it over the course of a year; if not carefully administered the patient died from Arsenic poisoning. It however did nothing against the other venereal disease Gonorrhea.

In 1916 in the United Kingdom the Royal Commission recommended private clinics for free treatment and took the line that it was counterproductive to place blame and differentiate guilt or innocence between men and women. It held that any policy had to be even-handed, expert and free. (Reference – Reduce the Burden . Org – reducetheburden.org ('The Great Scourge')

Lest there be any confusion, the reason for this novel is for the adoration of women and to bring to light that we seem at times to be completely at the mercy of the compulsion of the orgasm with no more control or morality than dumb animals. Science attempts to heal from the outside after-the-fact diseases that with a little knowledge could be avoided. One's own moral discernment of the orgasm and its use is perhaps a horrible fact of freedom and free will; while the act of narcissistically pleasuring oneself is disguised and called an act of love when it involves two.

Perhaps an absent God designed the device of the orgasm because this God would not be around to say, 'Be fruitful and multiply.' 'Thus insuring the population of the world and survival of the species regardless of the pain and suffering ignorant copulation can produce. Heaven help a world that abandons the child without guidance as to its compulsion and the connection to procreation.

I define stupidity as one who could learn but refuses.

I define intelligence as one who can learn by seeing the frying pan is hot and not have to be burned to prove it.

Must we destroy this world to learn we should not? We will see.

Many Regards

TJ Ginn

PS A toast to Shannon but then again this is fiction. False emotions make you cry but it is history that inspires remembrance of the true tragedy. Never forget.